THE BRIEFING

"Gentlemen, this won't come as a shock to either Tyler or Barry, but Kirk's Armory was broken into by men who had trained here sometime in the past. By now you've been informed that the area surrounding Kirk's Armory is used as a weapon training center for men attached to the nation's crack military units. These are units, like the Green Berets and Navy Seals, who are not only devastatingly effective small fighting units, but highly trained and motivated covert units as well."

Brennan spoke when the general finished. "Mr. Holden, the general is correct. These men are very special. Naturally, the CIA uses them whenever they're available. They are highly trained and motivated. We're ecstatic whenever the military allows us access to them."

"I get the picture," Holden said. "But why the secrecy stamped down on this robbery?"

"We don't want this to leak to our enemies or even to our allies. We don't want the world to know that we have rogues out there. . . ."

Thomas L. Muldoon

An
Execution
of Honor

LEISURE BOOKS   NEW YORK CITY

For my wife, Kathy—
my best friend, lover, and life companion—
who makes every day better than the last.

A LEISURE BOOK®

January 2002

Published by

Dorchester Publishing Co., Inc.
276 Fifth Avenue
New York, NY 10001

ISBN 0-8439-4957-0

Visit us on the web at www.dorchesterpub.com.

An
Execution
of Honor

Book I
1986

Chapter One

The torrential rain pounded the jungle, mashing flat the two-foot-high grass in the clearing. Just inside the tree line on the clearing's south side, the thick undergrowth had been removed and a green canvas shelter erected. On all sides of the shelter stood armed guards, vigilant despite being thoroughly soaked; although the guards were shielded from the force of the downpour by the triple canopy jungle above them, a steady torrent of water fell on them from the trees.

Unconcerned by the condition of the guards, the three Cardona brothers sat in aluminum chairs and stared out at the wall of water falling in the clearing. Each brother was handsome, had brown eyes, wore an American baseball cap, and had on an immaculately tailored, camouflaged, jungle uniform.

Jorge, the middle brother, reached into the pocket of his camouflaged shirt and withdrew a pack of cigarettes. He offered one to Juan, who was the oldest and the leader. Juan waved it away without speaking. Jorge turned to Benito, the youngest.

"Sí, gracias." Benito withdrew a solid gold lighter from the pocket of his camouflaged trousers and lit Jorge's cigarette, then his own.

Juan became alert when the rain suddenly slackened to a light drizzle. Satisfied that the heavy rain had ended, he walked into the clearing. His two brothers quickly followed.

From under the brim of a Los Angeles Dodgers baseball cap, Juan stared upward, searching the leaden sky above the clearing.

Benito, who worshiped his older brother, also wore a Dodgers cap. He made his own study of the sky. "They aren't coming," he said, speaking in English rather than Spanish so that none of the soldiers in the jungle could understand.

"They're coming," Juan answered in English. "They need us."

"The Yanquis abandoned the Cubans at the Bay of Pigs," Jorge said casually. He was the rebel of the three: he wore a New York Yankees cap. "Why wouldn't they abandon us too? San Tomas is lost to the Communists."

Juan whirled on Jorge.

"Don't ever express that defeatist attitude again! If Father heard you say that, he'd rip your skin from your bones," Juan said savagely. "This is only a temporary setback. We'll be back in control of San Tomas within five years."

Jorge, who was almost as frightened of Juan as he was of their father, was instantly contrite. "It's just that it is humiliating to be driven out by these peasant dogs."

"It's the fault of the fucking American Congress," Benito spat. "If they had only given Father more guns and money, he would have destroyed the Communist rabble."

"Someday the Americans will pay for humiliating the Cardona family," Jorge swore.

"Oh, Father will make them pay," Benito joked. "He will make them pay through the nose."

All three laughed at Benito's jest. Juan abruptly stopped. "I hear choppers. Back into the jungle!"

They hurried into the cover of the trees. Five seconds later, two unmarked, camouflaged gunships streaked over the clearing, followed almost instantly by two more. The sound of their engines changed as the helicopter gunships circled the clearing, their occupants studying the impenetrable jungle below.

"Are they ours?" Jorge whispered.

"Hiding in the jungle isn't going to answer that question," Juan said, preparing to step into the open.

Jorge grabbed Juan's arm. "Don't!"

"They know we are here," Juan said, shaking off his brother's hand. "Most assuredly they are equipped with infrared detection devices."

Juan marched into the center of the clearing. A gunship dropped down to hover thirty feet above the ground. The door gunner aimed his weapon directly at Juan's chest.

Juan removed two bandannas from his trousers pocket. With his right hand, he waved the red one twice at the chopper; then, using his left hand, he waved the green bandanna three times. Without acknowledging the signal, the gunship pulled up, and out of sight.

Juan moved back from the clearing's center to the jungle's edge. Less than a minute later, a huge helicopter dropped into the clearing. Juan ducked in alarm as the rotating blades zipped above his head, barely missing the surrounding trees. The whirling blades didn't slow; the pilot remained alert, ready to ascend instantly. The chopper's rear ramp dropped; a crew chief, carrying an automatic rifle, jumped down.

"Let's go!" he said, waving anxiously at Cardona. *"Vamanos!"*

Juan looked back into the jungle's foliage at his two brothers.

"Benito, you ride this chopper," he said softly in Spanish. "Jorge will take the second. Divide the boxes between the two of you. Each of you will take ten soldiers as a guard detachment. The rest of our soldiers will control the LZ until I return with Father."

"We'll handle it," Jorge promised. Benito nodded in agreement.

"Will you motherfuckers speed it up!" the crew chief screamed over the clatter of the helicopter. "The goddamn Commies are closing in fast!"

"American asshole," Juan muttered before issuing an order in a loud voice. "Fall in."

The surrounding jungle sprouted fifty armed soldiers wearing the uniforms of the elite Presidential Guard of San Tomas.

"Pick up your load," Juan ordered. The soldiers bent down, each hoisting a footlocker wrapped tightly in green waterproof material.

Juan turned to Benito and warned, "The contents of those footlockers are our father's ticket back to San Tomas. Guard them with your life. Kill anyone who becomes too curious about their contents."

"I will, Brother." Benito smiled. "See you in sunny Florida!"

Benito headed toward the chopper, followed by the burdened troops.

"He's a tough one," Jorge said with pride.

Juan grunted, continuing to count the passing soldiers. He halted the twenty-sixth and turned back to Jorge. "All of Luis Cardona's sons are steel. If we weren't, El Presidente would have squashed us at birth."

"That could still happen," Jorge laughed. "Father is not a patient or forgiving man. And being driven from the country he has ruled for the last twenty years has not improved his temperament."

"I'd better go get him," Juan said. "The second chopper will be landing for your load. Father and his staff better be here when the third chopper arrives. I don't think the Americans want to hang around. If the weather clears any further, the traitors in our former Air Force might even find the balls to take their planes off the ground."

Two hundred regulars, the remnants of what once was the largest standing army in Central America, surrounded Luis Cardona's camp. Although all of them knew that they faced a sentence of death if captured by the advancing Communist rebels, they remained loyal to El Presidente, Luis Cardona. El Presidente had promised them that their loyalty would be rewarded, and that they would be transported safely from San Tomas.

Inside the camp, thirty members of the elite Presidential Guard stood sentinel. The people of

San Tomas had another name for Cardona's Presidential Guard: Los Carniceros, the Butchers. Every member of Los Carniceros was fanatically loyal to Cardona, and each was an experienced killer.

Camouflaged netting hung above the camp. To provide shelter from the rain, canvas awnings had been rigged at several points under the netting. Under one of the awnings were all that remained of the former government of San Tomas: five of El Presidente's personal staff and eight of his ministers. They were nervous, anxious to depart for Florida. The Communist rebels were closing fast, delayed only by the hit-and-run tactics of Special Forces units of the American military that had been assigned to the task by the CIA.

The group's morale had picked up at the distant sound of helicopters, which had drifted in through the constant drum of rain. The landing zone was only a quarter mile away, and it represented safety: a helicopter to fly them out of San Tomas, beginning the trip which would ultimately end in luxurious exile in the Florida sunshine.

Salvation wasn't guaranteed yet; any of their lives could be snuffed out instantly by the jungle's most dangerous denizen: Luis Cardona. To his face, Cardona was always addressed as El Presidente; behind his back, he was more commonly known as El Sepulturero: the Gravedigger. He had a vicious temper; he was quick to torture and kill anyone who displeased or disagreed with him.

Ignoring the drizzle, El Sepulturero was prowling the camp like an angry jaguar, his personal bodyguard and loyal dog, Ernesto Guavaro, at his heel.

The staff watched Cardona carefully whenever he approached their end of the camp, but averted their eyes when he returned to the camp's far end.

At that end, two bloody, mutilated human carcasses hung from ropes looped around their torsos and tied to a large tree branch. Standing by the swinging bodies was William Means, an operative of the American CIA. Means was the CIA's liaison with Cardona.

William Means was fighting an urge to vomit. In twenty years of active service in the Company, he had acquired the reputation of being a hard man who was willing to do his share of wetwork, the term used by the CIA to indicate murder and torture, but this was beyond anything he had ever seen or imagined.

The two pieces of human meat hanging in front of him had been brutally abused. Every limb had been amputated; their noses, ears, and genitals had been hacked off; their eyes had been gouged out; sharpened wood had been driven up their anuses; and what remained of their bodies had been abused with knives, cigarettes, and other instruments of torture. Only their tongues and lips were left intact so that Cardona could enjoy their screams of pain.

Insects crawled into the holes where their eyes, noses, ears, and genitals had been. Not one inch of skin remained on their bodies, they had been peeled like ripe fruit. Yet, incredibly, they were still alive.

A medical doctor was assigned to make sure they lived to suffer more pain. To prevent loss of blood, the doctor had sutured the worst punctures. The doctor had given them IV's to prevent shock and replace lost fluid. He used all his skill to keep them alive so that Luis Cardona could continue to inflict more pain on the two men.

Thomas L. Muldoon

Periodic moans came from them, sending shivers down Means's spine. He wanted to shoot the poor bastards to put them out of their misery, but he restrained himself: their suffering was irrelevant compared to the long-range plans of the CIA. Luis Cardona was extremely important to those plans; therefore, El Sepulturero could do whatever he desired as far as William Means was concerned.

Cardona approached the hanging torsos and administered each a vicious kick, eliciting a weak moan from the one on the left. The silence from the one on the right infuriated Cardona; he kicked the torso again without drawing any response.

Cardona stepped back and motioned to the doctor, who stilled the swinging body, checking it for vital signs.

"Es muerte," the doctor said with a shrug.

Cardona pulled the forty-five from the holster in his belt and fired the full clip into the torso's flesh.

"He's very dead now," Cardona said as he placed a fresh clip into his forty-five. "What about the other one?"

The doctor checked the torso on the left. "Still alive."

"Good," Cardona said. "He will provide a few minutes more of amusement."

Despite all his professionalism, a look of disgust crossed Means's face. Cardona noticed it.

"You don't approve, William?" he asked, his voice tinged with scorn. "You think I am inhuman?"

"It makes no difference to me, El Presidente," Means said hastily. "I'm just worried that it may cause problems in the future."

"Your agency promised to take care of any future

difficulties so that I could concentrate on restoring my country to democracy!"

"That's what will happen. It's just that these two were American Marines."

"They were shits," Cardona screamed. "They interfered with my plans from the moment their unit was assigned to me. They criticized the way I handled my enemies. They didn't approve of my finances and businesses. They even ordered me to leave all the cocaine behind!" Cardona stared malevolently at the two bloody hulks. "They ordered me! The Presidente of San Tomas!"

"They were wrong," Means said placatingly.

"And they deserved to die for their errors!"

"Yes," Means said reluctantly. "But the rest of their unit won't feel that way. They are out in the jungle right now holding back your enemies, but they will arrive here soon expecting to find these two alive and waiting for them. When they see the two bodies, they'll want revenge. The one thing we can't afford is to have an angry team of Force Recon Marines after us."

"I'm not worried," Cardona scoffed. "My Presidential Guard will protect me. Besides, we will leave clues to make your Marines think the rebels killed these two."

Juan rushed into camp at that moment. Seeing his father near the bodies, he ran over.

"Father, we must go!" he said. "The evacuation helicopters are waiting!"

"Yes, let's be on our way," El Presidente said. "Juan, tell our people to follow. William, you go with Juan."

"What about the one who is alive?" Means asked, pointing at the swinging body.

17

"Ernesto will kill him."

Means nodded his approval, and followed Juan Cardona.

Guavaro removed the pistol from his belt. He looked at Luis Cardona before shooting.

"Do not hit him! Fire into the jungle," El Presidente ordered. "Let the bastard suffer a little longer before he dies."

Dutifully, Guavaro pretended to aim at the suspended body, firing five shots harmlessly into the trees.

Book II

1988

Chapter Two

Fort Benning, Georgia

On all official maps, nine square miles in the north-west section of the sprawling Army base were labeled off-limits to all military and civilian personnel. Each map had a skull and crossbones printed over the area, warning that it was an environmental hazard; the United States's Chemical Warfare Program had tested chemical weapons there, and the soil remained highly toxic.

In case anyone ignored the maps, the area was enclosed by a twelve-foot-high chain-link fence topped with vicious razor wire. Hung every fifteen feet along the fence was a sign carrying the skull-and-crossbones logo and the warning that it was a hazardous area off-limits to all personnel.

The only apparent break in the fence was a slid-ing steel gate across a blacktop road that disappeared into the heart of the off-limits area. It branched off from a seldom-used base road that ended two hundred yards past the gate. Inside the gate was a stone guardhouse. From zero seven-thirty to nineteen-thirty hours every single day, the guardhouse was manned by two soldiers wearing camouflaged uniforms completely unadorned by any insignia that identified their unit or rank. The guards changed daily; the same two were never seen manning the gate again.

Between the hours of nineteen-thirty and zero seven-thirty, the task of guarding the area fell to Fort Benning's First Guard Company. Each evening, a truck belonging to the First Guard Company arrived promptly at the gate at nineteen-thirty hours. The gate was opened, and the truck, containing the night's duty complement of fourteen soldiers, a sergeant-of-the-guard, and an officer-in-charge, drove inside and stopped. Two soldiers jumped from the truck and relieved the two from the unknown unit who had guarded the gate during the day.

The soldiers who had been relieved of their duty didn't speak to anyone from the First Guard Company. They ran, not walked, down the road outside the fence toward the main base.

The soldiers of the First Guard Company were intensely curious about the silent guards, but all efforts to discover who they were or where they went failed. Several times, off-duty members of the First Guard Company had tried to follow the running soldiers; they failed every time.

Shortly before zero seven-thirty the next morning, two new guards would come running down the road. They would stand rigidly at attention outside the gate until the First Guard Company truck came out of the compound carrying the night guards. As soon as the gate was opened and the truck exited, they marched inside and closed the gate. They never uttered a word.

The blacktop road ran through thick timber for two miles inside the first gate until it came to a second gate set in a twelve-foot-high electrified fence equipped with the most advanced surveillance devices in the world. This gate was always shut and unmanned when the First Guard Company's truck arrived. The officer-in-charge and the sergeant-of-the-guard jumped down from the truck and marched to separate keyboards on opposite sides of the gate; they pressed in their combinations simultaneously and the gate slid open.

Inside the gate was a fortified guardhouse connected to a building containing a command post filled with monitors displaying the views from cameras set inside the woods surrounded by the electrical fence. One mile down the road, in the exact center of the area surrounded by the electrical fence, sat a concrete blockhouse.

The only time the soldiers on guard duty ever left the command post near the gate was to stand a four-hour watch at this blockhouse. The road ran up to the platform in front of the blockhouse's thick steel doors. On both sides of the road and platform grew a fifteen-foot path of grass, which ran around the blockhouse, separating it from the woods.

The First Guard Company were told the blockhouse was a storage facility for the contaminated remnants of the chemical warfare experiments. They had been assured that they were in no danger: the blockhouse was permanently sealed, and the wooded area inside the electrical fence had been totally decontaminated. Still, they took few chances; only the bravest strayed even a few feet off the grass strip into the woods, and none of them, including officers, would venture off the blacktop road in the two-mile section of woods between the electrified fence and the main gate.

The blockhouse's foot-thick steel doors were considered impenetrable; they were impervious to explosives and were electronically monitored from the command center. Human guards were unnecessary, but the U.S. Army never feels totally secure unless humans are posted to guard duty. Four soldiers of the First Guard Company walked patrol in the grass area around the blockhouse, and a fifth stood rigidly by the entrance. The blockhouse had human guards from twenty hundred hours until zero seven hundred hours. The first five stood a four-hour shift, slept at the command center for four hours while five new soldiers stood guard, then returned for one final three-hour shift.

It was boring duty. The guards were lulled by the soft sounds of nocturnal animals and insects; not even the occasional distant rumble of a moving vehicle could break the monotony of spending an autumn night guarding the blockhouse.

Private First Class Beauregard "Bo" Hewitt leaned his six-foot-four frame against a tree and stared angrily toward Private First Class Hank Mathis, who was standing ramrod straight in front of the steel doors. On this night, Hewitt, Mathis, and three others were standing the middle guard shift.

"What the fuck you doing, Bo?" asked one of the guards, Private Bernie Wannamaker. "Sleeping on your feet?"

"Just thinking how much fun it would be to kick

the living shit out of Mathis," Hewitt grunted. "That prick is always sucking the sergeant's hind teat."

"Yeah, Mathis is a lifer for sure." Wannamaker spat on the ground to indicate his distaste for lifers.

"Fuck all lifers," Hewitt said. "What time is it?"

"One-thirty. Two and a half more boring hours to guard this lousy building before we go back to the command center."

"We still have to stay awake in there until zero seven-thirty. And being cooped up with Master Sergeant Blackman and Lieutenant Billis is pure torture."

"It's not so bad. By eight, we'll be back at our barracks catching some Z's. And it's Friday. Our weekend passes start at noon. Are you going home to Coral Cove?" Wannamaker asked.

"Hell, yes! This is the big weekend. It'll be one hell of a party."

Tonight, most of the residents of Coral Cove, Florida, would travel forty miles to Sand Dune for the big football game. The animosity and hatred between the two towns was legendary in the Florida Panhandle; it was fueled by the heated rivalry of their high school football teams, which annually dueled for Florida's 2-A division championship. Hewitt had played four years of football at Coral Cove High School. His first two seasons had been spent playing on special teams as Sand Dune had narrowly defeated Coral Cove. In his final two years, he'd been the starting middle linebacker, leading his team to victory both years.

"There will be one shitload of drinking and fucking in Coral Cove before and after the football game," Hewitt bragged.

"And if your team loses?"

"Shut your fucking face! We won't lose," Hewitt

snarled, looking down at Wannamaker, who was six inches shorter. "But even if we did, it'll only dampen the enthusiasm some. It won't halt the party."

"Why won't you let me come home with you?" Wannamaker pleaded. "Haven't we had fun whenever we've gone down to visit Lisa?"

Hewitt's sister Lisa was a junior at Florida State University in Tallahassee, eighty miles east of Coral Cove. During the last four months, Wannamaker and Hewitt had been to Tallahassee six times together. The first time, Hewitt had been broke and invited Wannamaker only because Wannamaker had promised to bankroll the weekend. It had been a fantastic time, spent drinking and partying with Lisa and her boyfriend, Terry Malloy.

Malloy was in his late twenties, older than the normal college student, and so were his male friends. As a group, they were determined to squeeze every ounce of enjoyment out of each moment of college life; women swarmed around them and booze flowed freely.

Hewitt was flush with money the next time he had a pass, so he had gone down alone, but Malloy and his friends complained, saying they liked Wannamaker. They had insisted that Hewitt bring Wannamaker along on any future trips. Hewitt had agreed, not because he liked Wannamaker overly much, but because he wanted to continue spending weekends in Tallahassee.

Even though he had enjoyed himself, Hewitt had struggled to restrain his more aggressive tendencies around Malloy's group. Hewitt had an aborted career as a football player at the University of Florida, and remained a devoted fan. As a true Gator, he detested Florida State and the Seminoles; Malloy and his friends were a Gator's natural enemies. It was just a matter of time before he challenged one of them to a fight. Hewitt still thought of himself as a football player; he worked out with weights and exercised daily. He was cocky about his tremendous physical strength, and believed he was unbeatable.

"I'd take you, Bernie, if it was up to me," Hewitt lied. "But it isn't. It's my weekend with my dad and sister. We're not only going to the game tonight, but tomorrow we drive to Jacksonville to attend the biggest outdoor cocktail party in the world." Jacksonville, two hundred miles east of Coral Cove, was the site of the annual football game between the University of Florida Gators and the University of Georgia Bulldogs. "Both my dad and I played for the Gators, and we're huge Gator fans. My dad barely tolerates Lisa coming along because she's a Seminole. He wouldn't allow you to come."

Wannamaker looked disappointed.

"We'll go down to Tallahassee together in two weeks," Hewitt said. "How about that?"

Before Wannamaker could answer, the sergeant-of-the-guard stepped out of the darkness and barked, "What the fuck are you two doing? You're supposed to be on guard duty, not having an evening social."

Hewitt sputtered, but Wannamaker said quickly, "Sergeant Blackman! Private Hewitt thought he heard someone in the woods. He called me from my post to back him up."

"What did you hear?" Master Sergeant Lyle Blackman asked Hewitt.

Hewitt had recovered. "Just a possum, Sergeant."

"Possum, huh? Did it make your lips smack? A

big old country boy like you must eat plenty of possum."

"Never tasted it, Sergeant," Hewitt said through gritted teeth. Blackman was always baiting him; he was a Yankee from Rhode Island who believed Southerners were stupid. Hewitt swore that one day he would catch Blackman off the base and out of uniform; when he did, he'd put the Yankee in the hospital for a month.

"How about you, Wannamaker?" Blackman asked.

"Jesus, Sergeant. I'm from Cleveland." Wannamaker shuddered. "I wouldn't eat one of those fuckers if you paid me a million dollars."

Sergeant Blackman glared at the two soldiers. "Who do you two think you're fucking with?" he snarled. "I've been in this man's Army for twenty-nine years, and I'm an expert at recognizing gold-bricking soldiers." He shoved his face into Wannamaker's. "Get your ass back to your post!"

"Yes, Sergeant!" Wannamaker hurried away.

Blackman turned to Hewitt. "You better keep on your toes, Private Hewitt," he warned, "or you won't be going anywhere this weekend."

"Yes, Sergeant," Hewitt said automatically.

"You can be sure I'll be around again. You'd better be alert and at your post." Blackman stalked off to check the other guards.

"Bullshit," Hewitt muttered under his breath. He'd been standing guard duty under Blackman for the last six months and knew the old soldier wouldn't return until it was time to relieve the guard at 0400. Blackman was less than a year from retirement; he was just marking time until then.

"Bastard will keep his ass warm," Hewitt said to himself. It was November; the temperature was in the fifties. Blackman wouldn't venture out of his warm command center again tonight. He wouldn't even bother to call Hewitt on the radio, which all guards carried strapped to their belts. Blackman didn't believe in unnecessary radio chatter; he felt it was the guard's duty to report any trouble.

Hewitt moved methodically back and forth on his post for the next fifteen minutes until he was confident Blackman had returned to the warmth of the command center. Hewitt checked Mathis at the blockhouse's door; he was looking the other way.

Hewitt furtively walked a few steps into the woods. Leaning his M-16 against a tree, he slipped a marijuana joint out of his left sock. He struck a match and lit the joint, sucking the pungent smoke deep into his lungs.

As he held his breath, a blur whipped in front of his eyes and a padded garrote closed around his windpipe. His hands went frantically to his throat, clawing at the tightly drawn noose. Desperately, Hewitt tried to use his strength to reach the man behind him, but the attacker handled him like a baby. Hewitt sank to his knees, struggling to breathe. His last conscious sight was of the tree's bark as blackness closed over him.

The figure, who was dressed in a mottled camouflage uniform and a camouflaged hood, immediately released the pressure on Hewitt's throat. Stepping on the burning joint to snuff it out, he carefully surveyed the blockhouse for any sign of the other guards being alerted.

Satisfied, the figure quickly trussed up Hewitt, tying his hands and feet together behind his back. Hewitt's back was bowed, his bound hands and feet sticking straight up in the air. The attacker checked to see if Hewitt was still breathing before inserting a gag in Hewitt's mouth and thrusting Hewitt's head into a black, eyeless hood.

The figure's earphone clicked to indicate that the other three guards at the walking posts had been immobilized. He checked the area far more diligently and with greater skill than Hewitt had. Seeing no danger, he used his tongue to manipulate the wire that transmitted a series of coded clicks to his subordinates. Immediately, a figure wearing a similar camouflaged outfit dropped from the roof of the blockhouse and subdued Mathis at the front door.

When his confederate at the door signaled, the leader moved forward quickly to join him. Three other hooded men joined the pair at the steel door, while two more, both armed, stood watch nearby.

To avoid any possible voice-activated alarms, the leader used his hood clicker to issue the order to open the door. One hooded figure moved to the task. The others stood vigilantly while he worked. When the door opened, five of the men disappeared inside while the other two stood guard.

Chapter Three

Fort Benning, Georgia

Special Agent Patrick Holden of the Federal Bureau of Investigation arrived from Atlanta at 11:30 a.m. on Friday and was immediately ushered into Colonel Tyler Burns's office.

Both Holden and Burns were a shade under six feet tall, but that's where the resemblance ended. At fifty years old, Burns was a razor-sharp soldier, thin and wiry, with brush-cut graying hair and piercing brown eyes. Ten years his junior, the green-eyed Holden was a much sturdier man with a slight paunch; his brown hair was a bit too long and his gray suit was rumpled. Holden simply didn't fit the visual image the Bureau liked to foster, yet he had been one of its top agents for twelve years.

"Is it a bad one?" Holden asked.

"It's a bad one all right," Burns said. "Haven't you been told anything about what happened?"

"Only that a robbery occurred and that I was to rush here to hook up with you. I wasn't even told what your position is."

"I'll brief you during the drive." Burns placed his green beret squarely on his head and marched out of the office with Holden trailing. Outside, the two climbed into the backseat of a waiting staff car.

"Has an FBI forensic team arrived yet from Washington?" Holden inquired as the car pulled away from Burns's office.

"It's here. The Army's Criminal Investigations Division team is here. In addition, there are a couple of other investigative teams which haven't bothered to introduce themselves to me."

"Why's that?" Holden asked.

"Because this isn't merely a robbery, it's a fatal blow to the nation's security. You may have noticed that my office building had a sign on it reading that it was the headquarters for the Army Resource Evaluation Center and that I was the commanding officer."

"Who could miss it?" The sign was directly in front of the building and it was larger than the signs in front of neighboring buildings.

"It's a phoney. No such unit exists. I'm actually in charge of the Special Training Brigade. That's classified and not to be repeated."

"Okay, but what is it?"

"We train very specialized soldiers from all branches of the U.S. military. That's all I can tell you until I receive further authorization."

Holden gave Burns a hard look. "I'm an FBI agent."

"Sorry, not good enough."

Holden's red face indicated his rising anger.

"Just hold on," Burns said, trying to calm Holden. "You've been cleared to enter the area. I'm sure that by the time we get to the armory, your total security clearance will arrive."

The car pulled up to a closed gate in a chain-link fence. Behind the gate, four hard-faced soldiers, wearing uniforms bearing no rank or any other insignia, leveled automatic rifles at the car.

"I'll be right back," Burns said. He stepped out of the car and approached the gate, holding his identification card out in front of him. Two guards kept their weapons aimed at the car while the other two trained theirs on Burns. One of them stepped close to the gate and studied the card. He nodded at Burns, but didn't salute. The gate slid open wide enough for Burns to slip through; it was immediately closed behind him. Burns went into the guardhouse with the soldier who had checked his identification; the other three guards kept the car covered.

Five minutes later, Burns and the soldier stepped out of the guardhouse. The soldier said something to the other three. They lowered their weapons, and one of them opened the gate, allowing the car to enter. The gate was shut again after the car passed through it and drew to a halt. Two soldiers approached the car while the other two aimed their rifles at Holden and the driver.

One soldier opened the front door, the second watched Holden. "Identification!" the soldier ordered.

The driver handed his identification card to the soldier, who studied it closely before returning it. He closed the front door, stepped away from the car, and focused his attention on Holden.

The second soldier stepped forward and opened the rear door. "Identification!" he demanded.

Holden dug out his identification and handed it out. The soldier carefully studied it, and then stared at Holden's face. Abruptly, he handed it back and closed the door.

Some signal that Holden didn't see must have been given: Burns walked to the car and the four soldiers resumed their posts, paying no further attention to the car.

"Don't put your ID away," Burns said after he was back inside the car. "We have to go through this again in two miles. That's the bad news. The good news is that your security clearance has been approved. That's the only reason that the guards allowed you inside."

"What is this place?" Holden asked, staring out at the thick woods running alongside the blacktop road.

"It's a training ground used by the Special Training Brigade."

"I suppose you can tell me what that is now?"

"Yes. Its purpose is to teach the elite Special Forces soldiers from every branch of the U.S. military how to use the weapons contained in the armory that was robbed early this morning."

Before Holden could ask any further questions, the car pulled up to a second gate, which bore a sign stating that it, and the chain-link fence it was set in, were electrified. There were eight armed soldiers behind this gate, as well as five civilians who looked as if they would shoot first and ask questions later. Next to the gate was a fortified guardhouse connected to another building. Holden could see the snout of a machine gun sticking out of a hole in the wall of the guardhouse.

Once again, Burns left the car to present his identification. It wasn't as readily accepted at this gate; Burns was allowed inside, then frisked by a soldier. Another soldier ran an electronic device over Burns's body. After that, the car was allowed through the gate, where the driver and Holden were ordered out of the car and subjected to the same scrutiny. Then the three of them stood under the pointed weapons of three soldiers while their identification cards were taken inside the guardhouse. Four minutes later, their ID's were handed back to them, and they were told to proceed down the blacktop road.

"What's so unique about this armory that requires this kind of security?" Holden asked as soon as the car was moving.

"This is a special armory, storing highly classified secret weapons and equipment. It has an official name, but no one calls it anything but the Kirk Armory. That's for Captain Kirk of *Star Trek* fame. The weapons inside here are futuristic, to say the least. They aren't normal issue for the American fighting man."

"You mean they're nuclear? Nuclear weapons have been stolen?"

"Calm down, Holden. It's bad, but not that bad," Burns said as they pulled up to a concrete blockhouse where scores of men were combing the grounds. As they stepped out of the car, Burns said, "There are nuclear weapons stored inside, but none of them were touched."

Holden stopped and stared at Burns. "You mean terrorists managed to successfully penetrate a U.S. Army base, break into a futuristic armory, and failed to steal any nuclear weapons? They must have been stupid terrorists."

"Far from it," Burns answered. "They knew exactly what they wanted. They weren't interested in any of the nuclear weapons."

"I don't understand, Colonel. The armory was penetrated and it contains nuclear weapons. Why wouldn't terrorists want nuclear weapons?"

"This armory has overlapping security layers within it," Burns said. "The nuclear weapons are in the section with tightest security. However, I feel the thieves still could have penetrated that section and stolen a nuke if that was what they were after. But they didn't want any nukes."

"I'm confused," Holden said. "If nukes weren't stolen, then why is this robbery so bad?"

"I'm not being clear," Colonel Burns sighed. "Let me go through it once again. This is a unique armory, the only one of its kind in the world. It contains specialized weaponry and equipment, which are issued only on a mission-by-mission basis to members of the military's elite Special Forces who have been trained to use it. When not being used in a mission, the weapons and equipment are returned to this armory. Special Forces troopers use the weapons to train, but only within the sealed perimeter surrounding the armory. A normal soldier never sees any of the weapons or equipment within this armory. They don't even know these weapons or equipment exist.

"To keep this weaponry and equipment safe, the armory is guarded by the most advanced and sophisticated security system known to our military forces, which means it is the most advanced and sophisticated in the world.

"Inside the armory are additional advanced and sophisticated security systems which further protect the contents. Each of these systems is separate from the ones at the door, and each area of the armory has separate as well as overlapping security systems. The area containing the nuclear weapons has so many overlapping systems, we have theorized that it would take one hundred years for a thief to crack the security measure. That's if it was even possible."

"Did anyone think it was possible to break into the armory in the first place?" Holden asked.

"No," Burns admitted. "That, also, was considered impossible."

Burns stalked toward the open steel door. Holden followed.

"There were five soldiers posted outside the armory, but they were just symbolic, part of the Army's tradition of having men stand guard duty. The integrity of this armory was never meant to rely on them."

Burns reached the door and motioned for Holden to examine it.

"The steel door, which would baffle even the most expert burglar, isn't the primary security system," Burns said. "As you can see, the concrete blockhouse is unimpressive, but the genuine armory is underground protected by thick steel walls. What's really pertinent, however, is what's inside the armory itself. It's a maze of state-of-the-art electronic, laser, motion, sound, and other detection devices. It is also monitored by TV cameras."

"Sounds formidable."

"Try impregnable," Burns said. "At least, that's what we've always believed. Yet intruders broke in, took what they wanted, and got cleanly away without us knowing about it."

Burns looked at Holden.

"The thieves even locked up behind them."

"What!"

"That's correct," Burns said. "They relocked the whole complex. We've tested the security systems, and they're all working perfectly. The only thing the thieves didn't bother to put back in place were the sentries. They were left trussed up."

"They didn't kill the sentries?"

"They weren't harmed at all. A padded garrote was used to suffocate them into unconsciousness. The sentries were then tied, gagged, and hooded."

Holden surveyed the area. "They must have come down the blacktop. How did they get by the guards at the security gates?"

"They didn't come in that way. The guards at the security gates never knew the area had been penetrated. The command center at the gate monitors every square inch of the territory inside the electrified fence. There wasn't any hint of the area or the armory being penetrated."

"How did the thieves circumvent the electronic monitors?" Holden asked.

"We don't know," Burns responded.

"If they didn't come down the blacktop, which way did they come in?"

"Obviously through the woods, but we don't know how they avoided the electrical fence and the monitors set in the woods. We don't know which direction they came in from. We don't know anything at all! What we have here is a professional, experienced group which successfully infiltrated a military base, opened a top security armory, took what they wanted, locked up again, and didn't leave a goddamned clue!"

"That's imposs—" Holden started to say.

Burns interrupted. "I know it's impossible, but that's the way it is."

Frustrated, Holden took a deep breath. "Something just struck me, Colonel. You keep saying they took exactly what they wanted. Why do you say that?"

"It's obvious. It was a clean operation," Burns said. "They took a number of specific items, stored in different sections of the armory. The items are top secret, but I've been authorized to tell you about them. I'll give you a detailed inventory list later. Generally, the stolen items consisted of weapons, electronic gear, several types of gas, plus infiltration and surveillance equipment including underwater gear. Unless they had a huge force, the quantity taken would've required several trips from the armory to the exit point from this area."

"That means it took time," Holden said.

"One of the sentries told us that the attack must have taken place shortly after zero one-thirty hours," Burns said. "He remembers looking at his watch at that time. The relief guard came on at zero four hundred hours. They found the sentries tied up and the steel door closed. The thieves managed to break in, bypass the security measures, take everything they wanted, and lock up again in two and a half hours. A base alert was declared at zero four oh five hours and Fort Benning was sealed tight. It was too late; the thieves had already escaped."

"I hate to keep sounding stupid, Colonel, but just because they were fast doesn't automatically mean they took everything they wanted."

"You still don't get it, Holden. The Kirk Armory is only used by a specialized group of the American military. It stores equipment and weapons supplied to only the military's elite combat troops, who specialize in covert warfare behind enemy lines. The

Army's Green Berets and the Navy's Seals use this equipment."

Comprehension dawned on Holden. "Oh my God, it wasn't terrorists!"

"That's right. It was men who we trained. To steal from this armory would take the elite of the elite; only our finest soldiers would have any chance of avoiding all of the security measures. Even then, I couldn't tell you how they did it. But I can assure you of one fact."

"What's that, Colonel?"

"They are one dangerous group of motherfuckers."

Coral Cove, Florida

Coral Cove was located on a small bay in the Florida Panhandle; its population was a few people short of one thousand. It was the only town, and therefore the county seat, of Sycamore County, a large, heavily forested county on the Gulf of Mexico, which had a population of 21,000. There were several islands, all privately owned, along the shoreline.

The county had forty miles of white, sandy beaches, totally undiscovered by tourists. There were no hotels along those beaches, and that's the way the county's residents wanted it. Despite its diminutive population, Sycamore County was an atypical rural Florida county: it wasn't poor; an inordinate number of millionaires lived there. The county's wealthy insisted on retaining their privacy.

Not only was it a rich county, it had tremendous political power in the state capital of Tallahassee and throughout Florida. County Sheriff Ethan "Bull" Hewitt was the man who wielded that power.

On this sunny afternoon, the six-foot-six-inch, three-hundred-pound Bull was the king of all he surveyed as he drove his patrol car through the town's streets. He'd been the sheriff of Sycamore County for over twenty-five years.

Born fifty-three years ago in the town, Sheriff Hewitt had spent only eight years away from Coral Cove. Bull had earned his nickname on the football field at age fifteen, when he stole the ball from a rival Sand Dune player and, like a bull, carried most of the Sand Dune football team on his back into the end zone. His titanic effort had given Coral Cove an upset victory over its hated rival.

Bull had gone on to the University of Florida and played defensive tackle for the Gators. After college, he had spent four years playing professional football with the Green Bay Packers before returning to Coral Cove and joining the sheriff's office as a deputy. Two years later, he had been elected sheriff, never relinquishing the position. His political power was unrivaled, his temper was fearsome, and he never forgot anyone who crossed him. Unlike his son, Bo, who had inherited only his aggressiveness, Bull was an intelligent man.

Since his football days, Bull had given further credence to his nickname on the field of love: he had women stashed all over the county. His wife had died twelve years ago, making him the county's most eligible bachelor. Women loved him in spite of his massive size, completely bald head, and ugly face with its broken nose.

Bull had many women, but the only woman he truly loved was his daughter, Lisa. She had his brilliant mind, and beauty to top it off. The girl was the light of his life, and he was delighted that she had returned from Tallahassee to spend the weekend with him. Tonight they, along with his son, Bo, would attend the traditional football game against Sand Dune; tomorrow she would go to Jacksonville with him and Bo for the Gators game against Georgia.

To add to Bull's pleasure, Lisa had come home alone. He didn't like her new boyfriend. Terry Malloy was eight years older than Lisa, who was twenty-one, and there was something unsettling about him. Bull's dislike of Malloy was more than the normal father's dislike of his daughter's suitor; the professional policeman in Bull was uneasy when Malloy was around. Malloy was charming and handsome enough, and he certainly treated Lisa courteously, but there was an underlying core of danger surrounding the man. While Malloy was polite to Bull, the sheriff could sense that the young man didn't fear him. Bull had run a background check on Malloy; it revealed that the man had served nine years in the Marine Corps before resigning to attend Florida State University. Malloy had an exemplary military record and had served in several of the world's hot spots.

In the four months that they had been dating, Malloy had accompanied Lisa to Coral Cove many times. Bull had swallowed his objections toward Malloy; Lisa was head over heels in love with the former Marine, and Bull knew his daughter well enough to know that she would back the man she loved in any dispute. In that respect she was just like Bull, who had stood up to his own father when he had bad-mouthed the girl who was to become Bull's wife.

Bull also disliked Malloy's friends. On a number of occasions, Malloy had brought a few of them along. They had moved through Bull's town and county as if they owned it. Once, the town's toughest brawler had purposely picked a fight with Malloy's friend Gonzalez. Bull's deputies had to peel the town brawler off the ground and rush him to the hospital. Gonzalez hadn't even broken a sweat.

Bull drove into the driveway of his large wooden house. The sight of Lisa waiting for him on the porch brought a smile to his face. When she moved down the steps toward him, he marveled at her perfect blond beauty: her figure was classic, her skin clear, and her eyes blue. He heaved himself from his car and gathered her into his arms. Planting a kiss on her lips, he said, "I missed you, darling."

"I missed you, too, Daddy."

"I'm glad you're here."

"I wouldn't miss the game. You know that, Daddy."

"Where's Malloy?"

"He and his friends went up to South Carolina to watch the Noles play Clemson. He knows this football weekend is special to us and he didn't want to intrude. I'll see him on Monday in Tallahassee."

"Malloy has more sense than I gave him credit for," Bull said as they went in the front door.

"I wanted him to come, but he said I could be with him anytime and this weekend I should be with you and Bo."

Lisa's mention of her brother brought a frown to Bull's face. The boy had been a major screwup, getting in serious trouble in Gainesville while playing football at the University of Florida. Only Bull's political power, and some well-placed threats to a college professor, had saved Bo from jail. But it had cost Bo his career as a Gator football player; part of the deal Bull made to save Bo required his quick induction into the Army. He was doing penance there now. After his discharge, he would come back to Coral Cove and take his rightful place in

Sycamore County. Bo would become the Sycamore County Sheriff when Bull was ready to give up the position.

"Is Bo home yet?" Bull asked.

"No," Lisa said. "He hasn't called, either."

"Goddamn that boy. It's five p.m. We have to leave for Sand Dune in an hour."

"Don't worry, Bo wouldn't miss this game for anything. He'll be here before it's time to go."

Fort Benning, Georgia

Bo Hewitt was under barracks confinement. This wasn't the first time he'd been in trouble, but he had never been frightened of the possible consequences as he was this time.

It didn't seem possible that Bo would fear anything. He was a strapping man, six feet, four inches tall and 235 pounds of muscle kept taut by daily weight training. Bo had been an animal on the football field in high school, and in his first year in Gainesville he'd earned the starting middle linebacker position on the Gators football team.

Unfortunately, his aggressiveness wasn't tempered off the field; several times he had been arrested for brawling in local bars. Each time, the charges were quietly dismissed because he was a Gator football player.

Bo had thought of himself as above the law. But eventually he went too far. After the final game of his sophomore season, Hewitt and three teammates crashed a local high school party. Before finally passing out from liquor and drugs, the football players had beaten four teenage boys senseless and repeatedly raped their girlfriends.

Not even the Gainesville Police could ignore this transgression.

Hewitt and his teammates regained consciousness in jail, and remained there despite their coach's impassioned defense that boys will be boys, and these particular boys were indispensable to the Florida Gators' football program. Still, the police had enough sense to merely hold the players in custody without formally charging them.

Their coach diligently gathered enough money from the faithful Gators football boosters to bribe the teenagers and their parents into forgetting the whole affair. Eventually, the incident would've been glossed over, like most incidents involving football players in Gainesville, except that one of the victims was the son of a prominent professor at the university. The professor wasn't swayed by the coach's arguments about the future good of the Gators' football program. He refused the considerable bribe money offered to him and his son, demanding that the players be formally prosecuted as criminals and dismissed from the university.

Bo Hewitt wasn't sure what happened next, except that his father had taken charge. Two days later, all demands for formal charges were dropped by the professor, who left town with his family for a new position at the University of Tennessee. A bewildered Bo discovered he was no longer a student at the University of Florida; instead, he was a member of the United States Army, beginning a three-year tour of duty. Later, his father pulled more political strings: after Bo completed basic training he was assigned to Fort Benning, which was only about two hundred miles north of Coral Cove. His Army job wasn't too arduous: as a member of the First Guard Company, he stood permanent guard detail on the base.

But now he was in serious trouble. For the first time in his life, his father couldn't help him.

At his guard post last night he'd been subdued by an intruder and trussed like a chicken. He couldn't see a thing because of the hood over his head; the gag in his mouth prevented him from calling out. He lay awake on the cold ground for an eternity before the relief guard finally arrived and freed him.

Sergeant Blackman had been furious to find his guards trussed up. The sergeant's anger escalated when he was forced to call in the camp's MP's and admit that someone may have broken into the armory. The stubbed-out marijuana joint was discovered, and Blackman was threatening to court-martial Hewitt.

The day had worsened when he had been interrogated by an FBI agent.

"Why did you step into the woods?" Holden, the FBI agent, had asked. "Why did you place your rifle against a tree?"

"I had to take a leak," Bo had lied. "I put my rifle against the tree and was starting to unzip my fly when I was attacked from the rear."

"Where did the marijuana butt come from that was found next to you?"

"I don't know," Bo had sworn. "It must have already been there. It wasn't mine."

He didn't think the FBI agent believed him. Holden had questioned him for ten more minutes before moving to the next guard, Mathis. The FBI agent had assured Bo that he had more questions to answer.

After Holden had finished, the guards were marched to their barracks and placed under confinement. They had remained there the whole day except when they were marched under guard to the mess hall for chow. It was now five p.m., and his father would be furious with him for not being home. All of Bo's requests to use the telephone had been refused. Bo was terrified as he awaited his fate.

Fort Benning, Georgia

Forensic experts and investigators from several military and government units were assembled in Colonel Burns's office. As the highest-ranking FBI representative on the scene, Holden had been given the job of coordinating the investigation.

"This isn't going to look good to our superiors," Holden stated. The room filled with the quiet shuffle of people moving nervously.

"We are all highly trained experts and we haven't come up with a clue. We don't have one bit of physical evidence. Were these people ghosts?"

Two tall, well-built men entered the room. Colonel Burns jumped to attention. "Sorry, General. I didn't know you were on the base."

"It's okay, Tyler," the older of the two said. "Please clear everyone but Mr. Holden and the head of the CID team out of here."

"You heard the general. Clear out!" Colonel Burns bellowed. The room emptied quickly.

"I'm General George Downs," said the tall, white-haired man in civilian clothes. He introduced the equally tall, dark-haired man next to him. "This is Barry Brennan. He's CIA."

The CID man identified himself. "I'm Major John Harvey."

The general motioned for everyone to take their seats.

"To answer your question, Mr. Holden," the general said gruffly, "yes, these men are like ghosts. They could cross a field of fresh snow and you would never know it."

A skeptical look crossed Holden's face; the military men present remained impassive.

"I see you find that difficult to believe," the general continued. "Well, I'll explain in a minute. First, I have to inform all of you that the specifics of this investigation are top secret and must remain within this room. Of course, Mr. Holden, in your case, and Mr. Brennan's, your agencies' heads will also be privy to any information."

"Wait—" Holden interrupted, but Downs beat him down.

"Don't worry, Mr. Holden. You'll soon receive orders from the Director of the FBI stating exactly what I just told you."

Holden settled back.

"Major Harvey, what you hear will be treated with strictest confidentiality. It is under the highest security clearance."

"Yes, sir," Harvey said.

"Now, gentlemen, this won't come as a shock to either Tyler or Barry, but Kirk's Armory was broken into by men who had trained here sometime in the past. By now you've been informed that the area surrounding Kirk's Armory is used as a weapons training center for men attached to the nation's crack military units. These are units, like the Green Berets and Navy Seals, which are not only devastatingly effective small fighting units, but highly trained and motivated covert units as well."

"You mean spies, General?" Holden asked.

"Not spies as you probably would define them. These men work in military units. They will sit in a hole outside Peking or Moscow for weeks to supply us with military intelligence. They are top-notch fighters, trained in guerrilla warfare and clandestine infiltration. They will walk into the Kremlin, if ordered. In fact, some of them have done so. No, these men are much more than spies. These men are this country's ultimate warriors."

Brennan spoke when General Downs finished. "Mr. Holden, the general is correct. These men are very special. Naturally, the CIA uses them whenever they're available. They are highly trained and motivated. We're ecstatic whenever the military allows us access to them."

General Downs said, "We're speaking about the modern versions of these units. They are far better than the units in the seventies, sixties, or fifties. A few years ago, we realized that the press had romanticized the Green Berets and the Navy Seals to the point that they were more legend than actual fighting force. In Vietnam, the Special Forces, or Green Berets as they are popularly known, were so romanticized that the Army was pressured to allow nearly anyone in who wanted to join. Initiates didn't even have to conform with the standard guidelines, which had made the Green Berets special in the first place. That's not the case today. The Green Berets have returned to its original concept; the members speak several languages, each has several military specialties, and they work together in small, compact units. The same with the Seals."

"I get the picture, General," Holden said. "But why the secrecy clamped down on this robbery?"

"We don't want this to leak to our enemies or even to our allies. We don't want the world to know that we have rogues out there."

"I'm basically a cop," Holden said. "It's my concern that we catch the people who committed this crime. But I see your point. Okay, how do we handle it?"

Relief was evident on Brennan's and Downs's faces.

"Well, that's a problem," Downs said. "We're positive some of our people did it. In fact, they wanted us to know it. That's why they left an operational signature behind."

"Call me Pat," Holden said. "What is this operational signature?"

"It's the manner in which they trussed up the sentries," Downs explained. "Didn't you tell him, Tyler?"

"No, sir," Burns said. He looked at Holden. "Pat, the guards were tied in a manner our people are trained to use whenever we want the enemy to know that we were there. It's a psychological warfare tool. Sometimes it's better to show the enemy that their most secret and private places are vulnerable to us, so we have our people leave sentries alive and trussed like those at the armory. The enemies of the United States know that operational signature."

"Why would the perpetrators leave this operational signature?" Holden asked. "Wouldn't it have been better for them not to do it?"

"That's the puzzle," Downs said. "They left no other clues, yet they clearly told us who they were. For what reason, I can't fathom."

The room was quiet until Holden broke the silence. "General, how long has Kirk's Armory been here?"

Downs looked at Colonel Burns, who answered, "Twelve years."

"As I understand it," Holden said, "while the stolen equipment and weaponry may have been exotic, nothing out of line was taken?"

"That's right," Burns said. "It was equipment which would be issued to a unit undertaking a penetration mission. Of course, quite a bit of exotic weaponry was taken, but that's not abnormal if the unit expected heavy fighting."

Holden thought for a minute before continuing. "I imagine everyone who has ever been through this facility is on record in a computer somewhere?"

"A very secret, heavily protected computer," Burns admitted. "Even I can't access it without permission from higher authority."

"But you can get that permission?"

"Yes."

"As soon as you do, we can start looking for anyone who may have the capabilities of breaking in here."

"The computer won't tell you who did this," General Downs said. "I'm sure that Tyler told you this armory was considered impregnable. The videotapes from the TV monitors are normal; they don't indicate that anyone was inside."

"I think the computer will give us some clue to the identity of one of the invaders," Holden said. "One of them had to be an expert in electronics to beat the security system. The computer will give us a list of electronics experts who have trained here. We'll widen the search to pull in any other specialists skillful in infiltrating security systems. The list of those names will provide the basis of our initial investigation."

"If we are just looking for electronics and infiltration specialists, we'll get a shitload of candidates," Burns muttered.

"Some will stand out from the others," Holden said. "And I'm sure we'll have more to go on soon."

"What do you mean, Pat?" Downs asked.

"The perpetrators left their operational signature."

"So?"

"Well, whatever else they are, they're still loyal Americans," Holden said. "They left the sentries trussed as a sign for us not to worry about the security of other installations. They were assuring us there wouldn't be any more break-ins, and informing us that they weren't terrorists or enemies."

Relief washed across the faces of the men in the room.

"Of course, that's exactly what they wanted us to know," Downs exclaimed. "If they hadn't done it, we'd be anxious about every military security installation in the world, since they all are guarded by variations of this system."

"And, more importantly, you would have been frightened about the nukes," Holden said. He looked at Burns. "Despite your glibness, I understood that anyone who could beat the security on Kirk's Armory could have taken the nuclear weapons inside."

The military men and CIA agent glanced warily at each other.

"You don't have to confirm it," Holden said. "But I know it's true."

The CIA's Brennan quickly changed the subject. "Why do you think we'll have more to go on soon, Pat?"

"That's easy. They wanted the equipment for a specific reason," Holden said. "I have a gut feeling we're not going to have to wait very long to find out what it is."

Chapter Four

Coral Cove, Florida

Bull and Lisa finally gave up waiting for Bo. Lingering any longer would make them late for the eight p.m. kickoff at Sand Dune. At six-ten p.m., Coral Cove and Sycamore County were nearly deserted, their residents en route to the game. Traffic was moving slowly on the forty-mile, two-lane road between Coral Cove and Sand Dune; in Sand Dune, a massive traffic jam was already slowing progress toward the football stadium.

Bull made a final check with his headquarters over his car radio. "Ed, anything going on?"

"No, all's quiet," replied Deputy Ed Throne, who was stuck with radio dispatch duty for the night. On the off year when the game wasn't in Coral Cove, the police force was reduced to minimum manpower. Every policeman wanted to attend the game; the 125 members of Bull's department drew lots to determine who would be stuck on duty. Eight unlucky souls had drawn the X-marked slips.

Theoretically, the unlucky eight policemen were expected to ignore the radio broadcast of the football game and pay full attention to their duty. In reality, they would all be glued to a radio somewhere. Bull knew that; he'd done the same thing when he had unluckily drawn the duty while he was a deputy.

"I'll call you with the score as soon as the game ends," Bull said. It was traditional for the Sycamore County Sheriff to pretend he didn't know his men would be listening to the radio; it was the sheriff's duty to telephone the police dispatcher with the score as soon as the game ended, and the dispatcher was supposed to inform the other men on duty.

"You're in charge," Bull said into the microphone. "Take care of my county. Out."

This was an especially tricky night for Bull. Sycamore County's many wealthy families demanded police protection, and most of their homes would be totally vulnerable since they would be in Sand Dune watching the game. To further complicate matters, he had an overriding obligation to keep three squad cars stationed twenty-fours hours a day within two miles of the large secluded beach estate, which was ten miles out of town, of Luis Cardona, the former president of the Central American country of San Tomas. Six of the eight deputies currently on duty were in those three cars.

With Ed on the radio, only one deputy remained to actually patrol the town and the rest of the county. Since there was minimal crime, Bull wasn't concerned about any major problems. But Luis

Cardona would get very annoyed if he discovered that the majority of the police force was forty miles away rather than on call for his protection. Cardona secretly paid Bull a substantial amount of money to insure this protection; Bull kept the lion's share, but he did pass on some of Cardona's money to his deputies.

It wasn't as if Cardona relied solely on police protection. He had a private army of his own stationed inside the walled estate. Cardona also had reinforcements bivouacked on U.S. government land five miles away from his estate.

The residents of Sycamore County were supposed to believe that Luis Cardona was living a quiet life in exile, but no one was actually fooled by that charade; everyone was aware that Cardona's soldiers were bivouacked on government land and were being trained by U.S. military advisers. Fully trained soldiers left the area after six months. The whispers were that they were sent to bases established in San Tomas's neighboring countries to await invasion orders.

Bull had no interest in Cardona's politics, only his money. As long as he was paid, he'd provide Cardona with the protection the former dictator craved. That is, he would provide it every other night of the year except this one; football was more important tonight. Bull held Lisa's hand as his car pulled out of radio range of Coral Cove.

"Goddamn your brother," Bull muttered. "How could he miss this game?"

On the roof of the building directly across the street from the police and fire stations, a man wearing a black and gray mottled camouflaged hood and uniform listened intently to the sheriff's and dispatcher's conversation on a miniaturized radio the size of a deck of cards. As soon as Bull Hewitt signed off, the watcher sent a coded signal: "This is Five. The town is clear."

In sending this signal, the watcher, designated Five, never moved. He continued to hold the miniaturized radio near his ear, and his eyes continued to scan the street, police station, and fire station.

The watcher sent his signal through an apparatus weighing less than four ounces, which was held firmly in place by his skintight, slitted camouflaged hood. He used his tongue to vibrate a vulcanized rubber prong resting on his lower lip; it connected to a stud held against his right cheek, from which an insulated wire ran down to a button-sized transmitter under his chin. Inside the transmitter, a microminiature cell translated the vibrations into clicks, which were then transmitted in an ultra-quick burst over shifting radio frequencies. Only similar transmitter/receivers could pick up the ultra-quick burst communication, commonly called a UQBC, slow it down, and translate it back into intelligible clicks that were then delivered to the jack worn in the ear. It was virtually impossible for enemy surveillance to pick up a UQBC; even if a UQBC was intercepted and slowed down, it was untranslatable: the clicks were automatically coded by the apparatus's internal computer chip, and only receiver/transmitters whose computer chips were set on the same code sequence received an intelligible message.

The UQBC radio unit was designed for the use of covert military units in the field. The normal range was two miles, but a flick of the tongue on the control wire caused the UQBC signal to bounce off the nearest orbiting spy satellite, which extended the range to the coverage area of that satellite; in turn, the user could extend the range globally by sending a coded order to the satellite to transmit the signal to other satellites. In this case, the watcher, Five, needed to communicate with his team leader, Six, who was ten miles distant, so he had bounced his message off the satellite.

If it hadn't been necessary, a satellite wouldn't have been used. It was dangerous: UQBC transmissions off satellites registered on an electronic board in the CIA's satellite-monitoring station in West Virginia. Using a satellite for UQBC transmissions required authorization; the CIA would attempt to locate the origin of unauthorized UQBC transmissions. If successful, the CIA would order the nearest military Special Forces unit to the scene.

The team leader bounced another UQBC transmission off the satellite: "This is Six. Operation Retribution is a go."

West Virginia

At the top secret communications center inside a mountain near Wheeling, the CIA's radio officer, Bill Knack, registered a flash on his board at exactly 6:48 p.m. Eastern Daylight Time; a second flash followed immediately. Knack manipulated his keyboard to analyze the flashes before picking up his phone and calling the installation's duty officer, Harry Grimes.

"Harry, the board just registered two UQBC transmissions channeled through satellite B-21."

"Where's that satellite located?" Grimes asked.

Knack consulted his log. "Over the northern Gulf of Mexico off the coast of Florida."

"Did the equipment tape the transmissions?"

"Yes," Knack said. "I slowed them down. They were a series of clicks, the kind used by the military covert units to communicate. Without the code chips being used, they're untranslatable."

"Does that satellite pick up signals from Eglin Air Force Base?"

"Yes."

"Probably just a Green Beret or Seal unit training."

"I don't know," Knack said. "We haven't been notified that our satellite would be used for UQBC transmissions tonight."

"Who else could it be?" Grimes said. "No one else in the world uses that type of communication."

"Guess you're right."

"Are the UQBC transmissions still going on?"

"I don't know. The satellite isn't being used anymore," Knack said. "What do you want me to do?"

"Just log it in. Langley will look at it tomorrow and raise hell with the military for not notifying us of the satellite use."

"Will do," Knack said.

Coral Cove, Florida

"Is the estate secure?" Luis Cardona asked his son.

"Yes, Father," Juan answered. "Fifty armed members of your Presidential Guard are patrolling the grounds. Two hundred additional members of the Presidential Guard are on alert at the camp. If they are needed, they will be here in less than five minutes." A direct telephone line ran from the estate's command center to the camp.

"The electronic security is working perfectly," Juan said. "Additionally, your trained dog Hewitt has a number of police patrol cars constantly circling the perimeter of the estate. At the first sign of any trouble, Hewitt will push the panic button installed in his office by the CIA. It will bring additional support from various U.S. military facilities. You are well protected, Father."

Luis stared coldly at his oldest son. "Are you being sarcastic?"

"No." Juan shivered. "I didn't mean to sound sarcastic."

Luis changed the subject. "Where are your brothers?"

"Jorge and Benito are with the ministers and the generals in your study."

"Then let us begin."

With Juan at his heels, Luis marched out of the bedroom and down the staircase. As the former dictator of San Tomas angrily entered the study, ten men snapped to attention.

"Sit down!" Luis didn't waste time shaking hands but moved directly to the desk in front of the wall opposite the large glass doors facing a tiled patio looking out on the Gulf of Mexico. Juan stopped at the door next to Jorge and Benito. They impassively watched their father as he berated his government-in-exile. The four ministers and two generals were seated in cushioned chairs in front of Luis's desk; two other generals were standing stiffly by the bar, glasses of cognac in their hands.

"I want some answers," Cardona screamed in Spanish. "Why have sales fallen? Why are supplies lower than normal?"

Cardona's voice rang through the house, but he wasn't concerned about being overheard. The women and children had moved to the house in Miami where they would remain until next April, and his American advisers and liaisons had been banished from the estate for the night. He had even banned them from his Presidential Guard's camp on U.S. government land five miles away. During this crucial weekend series of meetings, he wanted complete isolation from the Americans.

"What is happening?" Cardona demanded of his underlings. "Why is the money pipeline slowing down?"

"It is an election year, and the Americans are anxious about drugs," General Antonio Morales, Cardona's military chief of staff, answered from the bar. "It is a political issue right now. Our friends in the CIA and American military are being very cautious. There could be a new president sitting in the White House next January. The repercussions could be disastrous if President Mason doesn't win a second term."

"I don't care about their problems," Cardona roared. "What do they think we will do, cut off our drug trade just because there is a new president? I have expenses. I need the money to pay for our lives in exile and to retake San Tomas!"

"We have explained that to our friends in the various U.S. government organizations," Morales said. "They are very worried about our cause being defeated by lack of funds. They have promised to pave the way so that we can increase our sales and obtain more supplies."

"How soon will this happen?" Cardona demanded. "I don't like it when our cash flow is slowed down!"

"It has already happened, El Presidente," Morales said. "Two days ago, our friends in the CIA diverted a ton of cocaine from the DEA's incinerators. It now rests in one of the estate's bunkers. The CIA also gave us twenty million dollars in cash for operating expenses. It resides in the armored bunker with the fifteen million dollars in cash from last month's drug sales."

"Good," Cardona exclaimed. "That will tide us over for the short run. What about the long run?"

"The CIA has provided maps outlining the unprotected routes into the United States," Maximillian Gomez, Cardona's Minister of Finance, said. "We will use these routes to smuggle in cocaine. Of course, we will continue to ship our product on military and CIA aircraft, but those shipments will be slowed down until after the election."

"Let's see the maps," Cardona ordered. "Move the large table over here."

The men in the room jumped to carry out his orders, then gathered around as Morales spread maps and papers over the table.

Three men, each hooded and clad in a dark-mottled uniform, watched from the woods surrounding the camp of the Presidential Guard. The three looked like space aliens: they had strange bulges on their bodies, their heads were covered by hoods, and their hands contained odd-looking shapes.

The moment the "go" signal clicked in their ears, they moved to their predetermined positions. They moved easily, with the assurance of men who knew that they were virtually invisible on this dark, moonless night.

They were practically invisible even in sunlight, since they had been thoroughly trained in the art of moving without being noticed. Since Friday noon, they and three others of their team had been quietly moving in and out of the Presidential Guard's camp, as well as Cardona's estate.

Five miles away, an electronics expert sat behind a miniature electronic control board in the woods ten meters from the perimeter wall of Cardona's estate. At twilight, the electronics expert, with the help of his comrade, the watcher at the sheriff's office, had evaded the numerous security devices located on the wall and successfully infiltrated the estate. The two intruders had surreptitiously approached a TV surveillance camera suspended on an eight-foot-high steel pole; this camera was in the only unkempt area of the otherwise immaculately groomed grounds, making it vulnerable to a stealthy approach.

The expert and his comrade had made that approach at twilight. His partner had crouched on hands and knees, and the expert had climbed on his back. Quickly and cautiously, the expert had opened the camera without impeding its surveillance routine. Specialized electronic components and a microcomputer had been attached inside, and the camera was closed again. The microcomputer and the electronic attachments were the invention of the electronics expert, and had been successfully used the previous night on the TV surveillance monitors in the Kirk Armory at Fort Benning. Essentially, the microcomputer forced a feedback loop that allowed the electronics expert to control the whole TV security system from his own miniaturized control board.

After he received the "go" signal, the crouching electronics expert had begun to systematically take control of the two hundred TV cameras on the estate, preparing them to broadcast scenes of the expert's choosing back to the command center in the blockhouse next to the main house.

"One ready," the electronics expert clicked.

When he was given the final command, he would allow the control center to see only scenes of his choosing: the guards walking the grounds as if nothing abnormal were happening.

At the camp five miles from the estate, three of the expert's comrades-in-arms had moved into their attack positions, silently waiting. All three were equipped with night vision glasses built into the gas masks covering their faces.

Many times over the last four months, the three had infiltrated the camp. They had spent hundreds of hours observing the daily routines. They knew there were two hundred troops stationed there, and that there was an unbreakable buried security telephone line direct from Cardona's estate; if the estate pushed an alarm, these troops would quickly scramble to Cardona's aid.

The three men were also aware that no Americans were on the camp's premises tonight. Without the authoritarian figures of their military advisers and instructors, the Presidential Guard of San Tomas were sloppy and lax about camp security. The vast majority of the Guard's soldiers were inside their wooden barracks, lolling in their bunks, playing cards, or watching TV. Forty men were otherwise occupied: five were on duty in the command center, twenty-five were eating in the mess hall, and ten were randomly moving around the camp.

"Two ready," one of the three men clicked. The electronics expert carried the designation One.

"Three ready," another clicked.

"This is Six. Prepare to suppress the camp on my signal."

Six took a final look at the camp. When he was positive that he had pinpointed every soldier outside the buildings, he clicked to his team, "This is Six. Go!"

Earlier in the day, Two, Three, and Six had snuck into the camp and attached small gas capsules in the air-conditioning ventilation ducts of all the buildings. These capsules were the size of an average man's thumb, and were divided into three sections; the first contained a potent lethal gas called Snuff, the second a small but powerful pressurized air capsule, and the third a miniaturized radio receiver. At Six's signal, all three men simultaneously pressed their hand-held electronic detonators, sending signals to the capsules' radio receivers, which burst the capsules at the same time that it detonated the pressurized air chamber, forcing Snuff through the buildings' ventilation systems.

Twenty seconds later, all 190 men inside the buildings were dead.

Only the ten men outside the buildings escaped the Snuff, but their lives were extended by mere seconds. Two, Three, and Six were armed with several different types of specialized weapons, including sniper rifles, which unassembled could pass through any airport security system in the world. Assembled, the sniper rifles were slightly over two feet long, completely silent, had a miniature night sniper scope, and used a magazine carrying twenty rounds of caseless ammunition that looked like thick, one-inch nails. This sniper rifle was called a Snick by the men who used it. Within its limited range of 100 meters, a Snick had the killing effect of a .44 magnum, lacking only the terrific wallop of the magnum bullet's impact.

A Snick was the perfect weapon for killing discreetly and furtively. An expert could snipe a whole line of men, shooting one after another without warning the next victim. Even the blood flow from a Snick wound was minimal since the fired slug was so small. But inside the human body, a Snick's slug did horrendous damage.

Naturally, neither the Snick nor its ammunition would have been approved by the Geneva Convention, but that was of little consequence to the elite soldiers who used Snicks. No member of the regular military forces of the United States, nor of any foreign military unit, knew it existed, and therefore no one objected about its use.

Two, Three, and Six were experts with a Snick, and nine of the soldiers below died quickly. Something alerted the tenth; he dove for cover, screaming for help at the top of his lungs. His cries were brief; Three quickly slipped down and silenced the screaming soldier by using a short-bladed knife to rip his throat open. On the off chance that someone might have heard the soldier's screams, Two climbed to the top of one of the barracks and scanned the approaches to the camp, while Three and Six methodically checked every building and counted the corpses. It was seven p.m. before they were convinced that everyone in the camp was dead.

"This is Six. Camp suppressed." He sent the message off the satellite so the watcher in town could hear. "Moving to next objective."

Two, Three, and Six slipped out of the camp.

West Virginia

The UQBC transmission alert lit up Bill Knack's board again. Once more, he called for Harry Grimes.

Coral Cove, Florida

Five received Six's message just as three patrol cars pulled in front of the sheriff's office; five policemen exited the cars and entered the building.

"This is five. Two patrol cars assigned to Cardona's estate and the car on town patrol have just returned to the station."

"This is Six. For what reason?"

"This is Five. Reason unknown."

"This is Six. Five, take police out now!"

Immediately, Five pressed his detonator, blowing the gas capsules he had earlier placed in the air-conditioning ducts of both the sheriff's headquarters and the fire station. The capsules had only one important difference from those used at the camp: the first of the three chambers contained a potent, nonlethal, knockout gas called Snooze, which immobilized human beings for six hours. Snooze caused no serious effects to the human body unless a victim had a respiratory problem. Unfortunately, Deputy Ed Throne was a chronic asthma sufferer whose lungs couldn't handle Snooze. He died choking in his seat in front of the radio.

"This is Five. Task completed. Checking results."

"This is Six. Be careful. You have no backup."

"This is Five. Will be careful. Remember, still one car on duty at estate."

"This is Six. Roger, one car. We will handle."

West Virginia

Harry Grimes arrived quickly.

"Harry, there are more UQBC transmissions on satellite B-21," said Bill Knack.

His board flashed. "They are continuing."

Coral Cove, Florida

Five lowered himself from the roof; swiftly crossing the street, he entered the firehouse. The only two firemen inside were sleeping soundly.

Five studied the street before moving next door to the police station. The main rooms were empty. As he approached the radio room, he could hear the radio broadcast of the Sand Dune–Coral Cove football pregame show blaring from a ghetto blaster. Around a table littered with coffee cups, five unconscious policemen were lying on the floor. They were breathing deeply.

"Shit!" Five muttered to himself when he saw Ed Throne slumped in the radio dispatcher's chair. Throne's face was blue from oxygen deprivation. Five quickly checked for a hint of a pulse, but there was none. He tried giving CPR to Throne; after six minutes, Five quit.

"Damn it to hell!" Five said aloud.

Five was a total professional, Throne's unexpected death stopped him for only a few seconds before he began to dismantle the emergency signal equipment designed for use in the event of an attack on Cardona's estate. Finally, Five ripped up the emergency contact list and stuffed the shreds in a pocket.

Outside once again, he sent his message: "This is Five. Mission completed."

"This is Six. Five, return to estate. Further use of satellite for transmission is forbidden."

West Virginia

Harry Grimes was speaking by phone with his superior in Langley.

"We have had several satellite uses, but we don't have any notice that it was supposed to occur," Grimes said. "Can you check it out?"

"You say it was satellite B-21?" his superior asked.

"Yes."

"I'll look into it."

Coral Cove, Florida

On a dirt road outside the Cardona estate, Deputies Charlie Pond and Ezra Blount sat in their patrol car, smoking cigarettes and listening to the pregame show on a transistor radio. Fifteen minutes remained before kickoff. Pond, sitting in the passenger seat, remarked, "I sure wish we were there instead of sitting out here playing with ourselves."

"Yeah, it sucks," Blount replied. "But the money that this spick dictator pays us sure goes a long way toward settling my family's bills."

"You mean the money he pays Bull and Bull passes on to us," Pond drawled. "How much do you think Bull keeps?"

"I don't know, and I ain't gonna ask Bull," Blount said, blowing smoke out of the car's open window. "Eating is a helluva lot easier with all my teeth still in my head."

"I guess you're right. Bull can keep his secrets," Pond said. "I'm gonna take a piss."

"Just don't piss on your shoes again," Blount laughed. "The inside of the cruiser still stinks from the last time you did it."

"Screw you," Pond said, stepping out of the car and walking toward the woods. He heard a soft thud. Quickly he spun around. Blount was slumped in the driver's seat; a hooded man was pointing a weird gun at Pond.

Three pulled the Darter's trigger, and Pond collapsed. Neither deputy was dead. A Darter fired capsules loaded with liquid; the liquid ammunition varied, but in this case Three had used a variant of Snooze gas. The two deputies would sleep for the next six hours.

After checking both bodies, Three easily lifted the two-hundred-pound Pond and carried him back to the car, placing him in the backseat. Three then pushed Blount over to the passenger's side, climbed behind the wheel, and drove the car into the woods, concealing it from the road and the estate.

"This is Three. Patrol car neutralized."

"This is Six. Three, move to station."

Three headed through the woods toward the estate.

"This is Six. Attack commences in exactly five minutes."

Chapter Five

Coral Cove, Florida

Once Luis Cardona was satisfied with his subordinates' promises to increase the cash flow by flooding the streets of the United States with more cocaine, he ordered the kitchen staff to bring canapes into the study. "Dinner will be served at nine p.m.," he told his followers.

The former dictator sat in an overstuffed chair, while his three sons and eight followers arranged their chairs in a semicircle in front of him. A discussion began on various military and political strategies, none of which had any relevance to an invasion of San Tomas.

"Do you think our political friends could lose the election?" Luis Cardona asked. "If those who are simpatico to us lose control, the top echelons of the CIA may be replaced with people who don't have our best interests at heart."

"I don't believe it is a serious problem," said Pablo Munazo, Cardona's political expert and former Minister of Foreign Affairs. "President Mason will surely win a second term. He will not relent until San Tomas is restored to democracy and you are back in the presidency."

"So, we can look forward to four more uninterrupted years of business." Cardona glowed. "By then, we will have so much money that it won't matter if we ever set foot in San Tomas again."

"With all the documentation you have accumulated of illegal activities of members of the American military, intelligence services, and government, you will control the United States in four years," Munazo laughed. "Why would you want San Tomas?"

"I'll drink to that," Juan Cardona said, standing to offer a toast. The other men jumped to their feet. "To my father controlling the U.S., and putting the gringos in their place!"

They raised their glasses to Luis Cardona.

"This is Six. One, seal estate."

Instantly, One took control of the estate's security system, ordering all cameras to continually replay an hour tape he had recorded off the surveillance cameras. He flicked a switch, locking this image into the estate's system. Inside the security command center, the monitors showed peaceful night scenes of guards walking their posts.

"This is One. Estate sealed."

"This is Six. All units attack!"

One left his board and swiftly moved to the estate's wall. In a tree behind him, Six sat with his Snick sniper rifle, alert for guards. Before One reached the wall, Six had efficiently used his Snick to eliminate two guards and their dogs.

At its base, One looked up at the ten-foot-high wall. With his specialized night goggles, he could clearly see the electronic beams and random laser shots guarding the top from intruders. One climbed like a monkey, using hand and foot holds that had been secretly dug out over the last month. The top of the wall at this point had been systematically cleared of all motion sensors, pressure plates, and embedded broken glass; the intertwined layer of electrified wire had been routed around this spot.

As he slid over the top of the wall, a random laser burst, invisible to the naked eye, hit him squarely without any effect; its destructive power was absorbed by the special cloth of his dark-mottled covering. The electronic beams intersecting at the top of the wall were useless against him; two playing-card-size electronic devices, one on each side of his weapons belt, absorbed the beams and passed them on without breaking their pattern. Another miniature electronic device attached to the rear of his belt provided an electronic blanket around his body, foiling any motion sensors. These devices had worked admirably the night before in the armory, and were worn by all of the attackers now.

One hit the ground on the other side, scaled the nearest tree, and unlimbered his own Snick; he might be an electronics expert, but he was also an expert marksman.

"One in position."

"Six is moving." The team leader slid down the tree and headed for the wall while One provided cover. As Six crossed the wall, One eliminated a lone guard plus another guard-dog team.

This same scenario was being played at a second spot, where Three and Five were also successfully infiltrating the estate.

Langley, Virginia

"Our center in West Virginia is reporting that satellite B-21 was used for unauthorized UQBC transmissions," night duty officer Steve Boswell said to Dino Manetti, night supervisor of satellite operations. "What area does that satellite cover?"

"Are the UQBC's being bounced off other satellites to B-21?" Manetti asked.

"Harry Grimes didn't say, so I presume not," Boswell said. "But I'll double check with him while you put together a computer scenario covering the area the UQBC's could be coming from if B-21 is the only satellite used."

Coral Cove, Florida

On the Gulf of Mexico side of Cardona's estate, three divers had gained their attack positions. During the last two hours, two of the divers, designated Four and Seven, had swum slowly in on their objective, avoiding all underwater traps and security systems designed to prevent an underwater invasion. Behind them, they had left a series of phosphorescent marks visible only to their specialized diving masks, marking the cleared trail through the underwater defenses.

This allowed a third diver, designated Two, to swim rapidly and catch up to the first two without fear of detection by Cardona's security. Two had participated in the attack on the Presidential Guards' camp; he was second-in-command to Six.

A normal scuba diver wouldn't have recognized any of the equipment that Two, Four, and Seven wore; no bulging tanks, only a mask and breathing assembly which had two flat rectangles fitting snugly against their cheeks. This system allowed the divers to breathe normally without leaving a visible bubble trail on the water's surface.

The divers' wetsuits absorbed sound, making sonar useless against them. Sleekly designed fins on the divers' feet allowed speed with a minimum of effort. Their goggle masks had special visual enhancers and miniature computerized detection systems built into them, allowing the divers to avoid underwater traps. This equipment had been stolen from Kirk's Armory.

On their backs, they had waterproof packs containing all equipment and weaponry they would need on dry land. They weren't helpless beneath the sea; each was armed with several types of exotic weapons designed specifically for undersea warfare.

Four and Seven waited thirty feet off the beach until Two appeared; then Four glided into the shallow water near the beach and set himself up in firing position. Water lapped over his back and legs; only his head and the waterproofed version of the Snick, which was called the Seasnick, were above water. The Seasnick didn't have the range of a Snick, the dry land version, but it was murderously effective up to fifty yards.

Seven glided under the huge yacht attached to the concrete wharf at the rear of Cardona's house, swam to its end, and crouched under it in the shallow water. Opening his waterproof pack, Seven removed a weapon that looked like a plastic staple gun but was actually a silenced machine pistol. Nicknamed a Spitter, it used a smaller version of the sniper rifle's ammunition in a fifty-round magazine. As its ammunition was expended, the magazine crumpled and could be discarded like an empty cigarette pack. The Spitter was so silent, even the triggerman couldn't hear it being fired; it was a devastating assault weapon.

Two closed on the yacht, climbing stealthily up a line dangling from the fantail. Two removed his Spitter from his pack before he slid over the rail onto the deck. From past observation, Two knew that at least five men were stationed on the yacht. He encountered the first sitting with his feet over the side, drinking from a bottle of rum and staring out to sea. The man never saw Two; he died silently from a three-round Spitter burst.

Moving carefully down the deck toward the main cabin, Two discovered the other four men eating in the galley. From a waterproof pouch on his belt, Two removed a lipstick-size gas grenade.

"This is Two. Using Snuff in five seconds."

Two pulled his diving mask over his mouth, counted to five, depressed the trigger on the lethal gas grenade, and flipped it into the galley. Three seconds later, the four bodies were lifeless lumps. Two looked into the galley without entering, confirming that all four men were down.

Two kept his breathing mask over his mouth and nose, taking no chances with the Snuff gas; it would take a couple of minutes for it to dissipate and lose its potency. Silently he moved to check the rest of the boat. His caution paid dividends; he found two additional guards sleeping in a stateroom. Two shot them with his Spitter.

"This is Two. Yacht clear. Seven eliminated."

While Two was occupied on the yacht, Four had picked off two guard-dog teams and a lone sentry with his Seasnick, allowing Seven to move from under the wharf into position on dry land. Seven provided cover while Two and Four slid out of the water and into cover of their own.

One at a time, while the other two provided cover, the three divers hit the plastic catches holding their dive suits together and pulled off the material. Underneath, they were clad in the same outfits as their comrades who had infiltrated from the land side of the estate.

"This is Two. Unit has feet dry."

"This is Six. Two, move unit to house."

Since the house was closer to the beach than to the walls, Two, Four, and Seven reached it first. Four and Seven set up in positions covering the seaside of the house, while Two moved in on the command blockhouse.

Meanwhile, One, Three, Five, and Six were methodically moving toward the house, eliminating anyone and anything that moved. So far, they remained undetected.

At the command blockhouse, Two moved to the ventilation system and attached two Snuff capsules.

"This is Two. Ready to use Snuff."

His six comrades donned their gas masks and one by one clicked their readiness. Six kept count; when he was sure that everyone had checked in, he clicked a message to Two.

"This is Six. Two, okay to use Snuff."

Two settled his gas mask on his face and pressed the Snuff detonator. Inside the blockhouse, all life ended.

One, Three, Five, and Six moved into position around the house as Two entered the command center and checked the bodies. Two made his report.

Meticulously, Six demanded the kill counts from the other members of the attack team. After totaling the kills, he clicked, "This is Six. Three enemy still loose. Forty-seven have been eliminated. One, Four, Five, and Seven. Hold positions. Acknowledge."

The four attackers each clicked their acknowledgment.

"This is Six. Two, recheck your area. Three, join with me to recheck our area of estate."

Moving swiftly, Two, Three, and Six crisscrossed the grounds. Three found one of the missing guards quietly snoozing against the back of a garden shed; the quick slice of a combat knife across the throat insured that he would never awaken. Another was inside the garden shed, smoking a cigarette; Three shot him.

Despite twice scouring the grounds, the fiftieth guard eluded them. The leader finally signaled: "This is Six. Return to house. Last guard must be inside."

Langley, Virginia

"West Virginia says only satellite B-21 has been used for the UQBC transmissions," Steve Boswell told Dino Manetti.

"I've brought up the area which that satellite covers," Manetti said, motioning to the computer screen in front of him.

Boswell looked at it. "It covers Georgia, Florida, Alabama, Mississippi, Louisiana, and a good portion of water in the northeast section of the Gulf of Mexico. That's prime territory for the military's Special Forces units to train in."

"So you think it's a Seal or Green Beret unit which has forgotten to inform us that it would be using UQBC off a satellite?"

"Probably," Boswell admitted. "But that's completely unauthorized. I have to determine who is doing it, and have their headquarters ream out a few asses. I want you to call Harry Grimes and set up a surveillance on the satellite. If there are any further UQBC transmissions, maybe you can focus in on the area they are being sent from."

"It won't work," Manetti said. "UQBC transmissions are designed to be untraceable and indecipherable."

"I know it, but I figure that your big brain combined with Grimes's might come up with an innovative way of doing it."

"Don't hold your breath," Manetti said.

"I won't, I'll be using it to telephone the military covert warfare people."

Coral Cove, Florida

The seven attackers were in position.

"This is Six! Three, Four, Five, move into house."

The three moved silently to the house. At the base of the house's stucco wall, they put on special gloves and shoe wrappings that they removed from their packs. The gloves and shoe wrappings were made of an adhesive material that allowed the users to walk up walls. The three attackers climbed the wall one after the other, and entered an open second-story window.

"This is Three. Upstairs empty."

The remaining attackers moved closer to the

house and checked the downstairs windows. Cardona and his associates were clearly visible through the closed study doors to the patio.

"This is Six. Two and Seven, clear the bottom floor except for Cardona's location. Three, Four, and Five, remain in position."

Two and Seven slipped knives between the eaves of the darkened windows of a front room, and sneaked into the house. They carefully checked each room, one providing cover for the other. Two entered the elaborate dining room, and froze. He clicked a message, "This is Two. Kitchen is occupied."

Seven slid into the dining room and moved across to the kitchen's entrance. Two moved to the other side of the door.

"This is Six. Two, Seven. Hold position." Two and Seven halted. "This is Six. Three, Four. Prepare to attack kitchen."

On the second floor, attackers Three and Four moved silently down the back stairs, which led to the kitchen. Five remained on guard upstairs.

"This is Four. We are in position." Four and Three were outside the stairway door.

"This is Six. Make ready," Six clicked. In the dining room, Seven reached for the doorknob as Two prepared to enter the kitchen: at the stairway door, Three held the doorknob, ready to open for Four.

"This is Six. Execute!"

Three and Seven opened their respective doors, and Two and Four rushed into the kitchen firing, taking care not to fire toward each other. The six servants dropped under the hail of gunfire.

"This is Two. House cleared."

"This is Six. Was the last guard in the kitchen?"

"This is Two. Negative."

Six considered the problem. All of his men deserved and wanted to be in on the finale. But one of the enemy was missing; prudence dictated that there should be a rear guard.

Six clicked the problem to his team. The answer was unanimous; they all wanted to be present at the finish.

"This is Six. We all attack. Just watch your rear."

He positioned his team to assault the occupied room.

"Where the hell are the servants?" Luis Cardona roared as he pressed the button next to his chair. A bell rang in the distant reaches of the house. "Why aren't they answering my summons?"

"I'll go see, Papa," volunteered Juan, who was anxious to go to the toilet.

Before Juan could reach the closed hall door, it suddenly shattered inward in a shower of wood splinters. At the same instant, the side door connecting the study with the library crashed open, and the patio's sliding glass door shattered.

Seven hooded, armed intruders rushed in from three directions. Juan was first to die, nearly cut in half by an eerie, silent burst from one of the intruder's weapons.

A shocked Luis watched as Juan's blood splattered over the floor. Before he could react to his son's death, his advisers were also dead: Munazo and Morales were shot as they attempted to rise from their chairs; the other six officials died in their seats.

"Don't shoot!" Benito Cardona begged. A white-faced Jorge stood beside his brother.

"We can give you money," Jorge said in a quivering voice.

"All we want from you is your lives," Six said in a clear voice.

Only Two and Seven fired into Jorge and Benito; the two dropped to the bloody floor. Ignoring the former dictator, Six openly addressed his team. "Be careful of the blood. Don't step in it."

"Who are you?" Luis Cardona asked plaintively. He stood alone in the blood of his associates and sons, staring wide-eyed at the terrifying men whose faces were concealed by hoods. He felt his bowels loosen. "What do you want from me?"

Cardona's fear rose as one attacker pointed an odd weapon at him while the other six, taking care to avoid the blood, methodically moved around the room, firing into the heads of his sons and friends. When this grisly act was completed, all seven faced him.

"What have I ever done to you?" Cardona pleaded.

Six spoke aloud, "Two years ago, you tortured two of our friends for more than a day, keeping them alive because you enjoyed their suffering. Finally, they died from the wounds you inflicted."

"It wasn't me," Cardona cried. "I never tortured anyone!"

"It was you!" Six said, his voice rising. "El Carnicero, the Butcher. The torturer and murderer."

"I'm not! Besides, why would I do any harm to your friends?"

"They discovered you were importing cocaine into the United States. You killed them for it."

"Why would I kill anyone over drugs?" Cardona said with false bravado. "I have permission to sell cocaine in the United States. Members of the CIA and U.S. military help me import it into this country. Even White House executives have approved its sale. They all believe that the sale of cocaine is the only way to finance any invasion of San Tomas and take back the country from the Communists."

"You're never going to invade San Tomas. You sell drugs to make yourself rich. You happily poison the citizens of the country which has extended you a helping hand! Our friends were going to blow your drug operation wide open. You killed them for it. Our honor demands that we execute you for their murders!"

Six stepped back, and the seven attackers fired in unison. Cardona screamed; his body danced from the impact of so many slugs. Even after his corpse crumpled to the floor, the seven kept firing until their weapons were empty.

Shaking off his savagery, Six said, "Let's get to work. We have to be far from here by the time everyone returns to town."

The group split up to do their prearranged jobs, but not before receiving one more order from Six. "Watch for the missing guard."

Sand Dune, Florida

The towns of Sand Dune and Coral Cove both had high school football stadiums that sat over thirty thousand fans; each stadium also had a glassed-in VIP seating section constructed by donations from wealthy citizens. In this section, which was at the top of the west side of both stadiums, stretching between the forty-yard lines, the VIPs from the game's host town provided the opposing town's VIPs with all the food and drink they could consume. Social custom allowed voracious rooting for your own team, but required a show of sportsmanship toward the other team's supporters. That meant no fisticuffs or throwing of food or beverages in the VIP section.

Bull and Lisa had arrived twenty minutes before kickoff and gone straight to the VIP section. Bull had dived into the bourbon and food, making large bets on the game's outcome with the sheriff and city officials of Sand Dune. Lisa was quieter. She stayed in her seat, sipped white wine, and fended off the many attempts to proposition her.

Coral Cove ran the opening kickoff back ninety-five yards for a touchdown. "It's going to be a rout," Bull cheered. "We're going to run these old boys right out of this football stadium!"

"Don't get so excited," Lisa warned. "There's a long way to go."

For most of the game, Bull and his fellow citizens of Coral Cove were able to crow. Their team dominated Sand Dune. The tide turned in the fourth quarter: Sand Dune came roaring back from a sixteen-point deficit. As time ran out, an unheralded sophomore booted a forty-eight-yard field goal, handing Coral Cove a one-point defeat. The Sand Dune VIP rooters went wild, while the Coral Cove VIPs were obliged to sit and take it.

If Coral Cove had won, Bull would've vacated the section immediately to join the celebration of his townsfolk down in the parking lot. Since his team had lost, he was forced to stay and congratulate the Sand Dune VIPs. The loss was so bitter, he consumed more than his normal share of bourbon during the congratulations.

"Stop drinking so much, Daddy," Lisa warned. "You're getting drunk, and we still have to drive home."

"It's a damn sour pill to swallow," Bull said. "We had that game in our pocket!"

"Put on a brave face. You can't let these damn Sand Dune folks know how much it hurts."

"I'll stop drinking," Bull promised. "We'll leave soon."

It was eleven p.m., nearly an hour after the game, before they could finally break away. Prior to leaving, Bull made a telephone call to headquarters.

"That's strange," Bull said to Lisa, who was standing by his side. "There's no answer. Ed's supposed to be answering the phones."

"Maybe he went to the bathroom," Lisa said. "There isn't anyone else to answer the phone if he steps away for a moment."

"It's possible," Bull admitted, then laughed. "Ed's only relief tonight is when he relieves himself."

"That's sick," Lisa giggled. "The loss is affecting your mind."

"Let's go," Bull said. "I hate this town. I'll call Ed from a roadside telephone."

Langley, Virginia

Dino Manetti walked into Steve Boswell's office.

"Have you and Grimes come up with anything?" Boswell asked.

"No," Manetti admitted. "We can't break the UQBC transmissions, nor can we pinpoint them. How about you?"

"I've spoken with every covert military unit command in that area. All of them deny that any of their units are using satellite B-21 for unauthorized UQBC transmissions."

"Well, Grimes had another thought," Manetti said.

"Yeah?"

"He says Kirk's Armory in Fort Benning was broken into last night."

"How the hell does he know that?" Boswell exploded. "That is highly classified!"

"I don't know. He didn't tell me, and I doubt he'd tell you."

"You're probably right," Boswell admitted. "Okay, let's suppose he is right about Kirk's Armory; what is he getting at?"

"He wonders if UQBC gear was stolen. If it was, maybe the thieves are using it."

Boswell sat stunned.

"Get out of here," he said suddenly. "And forget you ever heard anything about Kirk's Armory."

Manetti had a sly smile on his face as he walked out. Once the door closed, Boswell took a black book from a locked desk drawer, searched for a number, then dialed the phone.

"This is Langley. Patch me through to General Downs. And use the scrambler."

Sand Dune, Florida

Bull halted his car a short distance from the stadium to make a second call, but there was still no answer. A tinge of worry surfaced.

Fort Benning, Georgia

FBI agent Pat Holden was watching an Atlanta Hawks basketball game on the TV in his motel room when the phone rang.

"This is Ty Burns. A car is on the way to pick you up."

"Has something else happened?" Holden asked.

"No, but I just received a telephone call from General Downs. It looks like some of the equipment from Kirk's Armory is being used tonight."

"Where?"

"I don't know!"

"Huh? What does that mean?"

"I'll explain when you arrive."

Coral Cove, Florida

Bull Hewitt didn't bother to stop at another phone; he waited until he was within radio range to call Ed Throne at headquarters. There was no answer.

"This is Bull. Anyone near headquarters?"

Ned Ames, one of Bull's deputies, replied. "I'm almost back to town, Sheriff. I'll check headquarters."

"Roger. I'm at least a half hour away stuck in traffic. Find out what's going on."

Four minutes later, Ames reported on the radio. "Sheriff, everyone's unconscious except Ed. I think he's dead."

Hewitt was frightened now. "What do you mean, everyone's unconscious? Who's there besides Ed?"

Ames rattled off the names of the deputies who had stopped in at headquarters to listen to the game.

"Deputies Pond and Blount aren't there?" Bull asked.

"No."

"Deputy Pond! Deputy Blount! Respond," Bull broadcast. When he received no response, he panicked. "All deputies listening, respond!"

Four deputies gave their names; Bull ordered them to the Cardona estate.

"Ned, call all deputies into headquarters," Bull

ordered. "This is an emergency. Next to the radio there's a list of agencies to notify in the event of trouble at Cardona's. On the wall next to the radio there's a red button. Push the button and start telephoning the numbers on the list!"

"Sheriff, the button is ripped from the wall and its components are in pieces and I don't see any list."

Lisa saw Bull's face go white. She reached across and grabbed his hand. "Are you all right, Daddy?"

Her touch brought him back to reality. He gave her a weak smile. "Thanks, girl. I'm fine."

Bull turned on his cruiser's siren and flashing lights, and pulled into the right lane of the two-lane, traffic-filled road.

"As soon as someone arrives at Cardona's, I want a report!" he ordered as he kept his eye out for oncoming cars.

In a matter of minutes, his nightmare worsened.

"Sheriff, there isn't any sign of life here," a deputy reported. "The gates are closed, but I can see bodies lying on the ground. What should I do?"

"Stay where you are," Bull ordered. "Ned, telephone the Florida attorney general's office, the FBI, and anyone else you can think of. Tell them we've got a disaster here."

Chapter Six

Fort Benning, Georgia

Holden had been ushered into Burns's office upon his arrival; behind closed doors Burns had informed him of the unauthorized UQBC satellite transmissions.

"I still am confused," Holden had said when Burns had finished explaining about UQBC. "You've had the same training? You are adept at using this coded clicking?"

"Correct."

"And the CIA has managed to slow these UQBC transmissions down to the point where the clicks are clear?"

"Not quite. The CIA is only intercepting the burst of clicks which a transceiver is bouncing off their satellite to a receiver. That burst is indecipherable."

"I'm still not clear."

"I'll lead you through it step by step. Before a mission, the unit leader decides the UQBC's code-chip setting, and then he decides the frequencies to be used. There are literally millions of possible combinations available to the team leader. Only his unit has the correct settings. So a soldier in that unit uses his mouth clicker to set his message, the code-chip scrambles it, and the message is sent out by the transceiver in a fantastically short burst of electronic blips or clicks. This is what we call the UQBC."

"I see," Holden said. "And only a UQBC receiver whose code-chip is set to the same parameters will translate it back into the clicking code you're conversant with."

"You've got it. I could go get another UQBC unit from Kirk Armory, but it wouldn't decipher their message since it doesn't have the correct code-chip setting. And methodically going through each possible combination of settings would take years. The possibilities are astronomical."

"If these UQBC units are worn by military covert specialists who might be killed on a mission, don't they ever fall into enemy hands?"

"Standing orders are to retrieve all Kirk Armory equipment from the dead, but that isn't always possible," Burns admitted. "In a case where any equipment of the type stored in Kirk Armory can't be retrieved, the Six, or unit leader, and the Two, his second-in-command, have the obligation to destroy it. I can't go into how this is accomplished, but let me assure you that the enemy has never captured any Kirk Armory equipment intact."

Holden perked up. "Can we destroy the stolen equipment to prevent its use?"

"No. We run into the same problem as we do with understanding the UQBC transmissions. We don't know the destruct codes. Only the unit's Six and Two can trigger the equipment destruct."

After their conversation, Holden had been asked to wait in the anteroom while the Green Beret colonel spoke on his office phone to secret people. Burns had stepped outside only once since; thirty minutes ago, he had told Holden that the entire United States civilian and military covert community were frantically trying to discover where the stolen equipment from the Kirk Armory was being used.

"So far, we've been unsuccessful," Burns had said before retreating back behind his office's closed door.

Holden was sipping strong coffee to keep awake when, shortly after midnight, the door to Burns's office opened and Burns waved him inside.

"FBI headquarters in Washington is calling for you."

Holden threw the empty paper coffee cup in the trash basket and hurried inside the office.

"Holden," he said into the phone.

"You're needed in Coral Cove, Florida," the FBI duty officer said. "The details are sketchy, but the local police have called us about a mass murder on United States government property. They say that an important political refugee has also been murdered."

"Who?"

"Luis Cardona."

"Cardona? You mean the former dictator of San Tomas?" Holden asked.

"That's him. Colonel Burns has been ordered to

90

make a helicopter available to fly you to Coral Cove."

The duty officer hung up. Holden had barely replaced the receiver when the phone rang. Burns picked it up, identified himself, and listened without saying another word.

"Order a chopper ready now," Burns said to his aide when he hung up. "C'mon, Holden. I'm going with you."

The colonel raced outside with Holden on his heels. They jumped into a staff car and roared off. The colonel concentrated on his driving, rebuffing all of Holden's inquiries. The car pulled up to a helicopter pad where a chopper was ready to go. The two hustled inside, and the helicopter took off immediately.

"What's going on, Colonel?" Holden asked over the clatter of the chopper's rotary blades.

"You'd better start calling me Ty. It looks like we're going to be spending a lot of time together," Burns said.

"Okay, Ty. Why are you coming along?"

"It looks like Coral Cove is where the UQBC transmissions were coming from. My phone caller said that the Kirk Armory's weapons were used in an attack on Luis Cardona's estate and an attack on the camp of his private army. I was told to accompany you to Coral Cove and help you."

Both men remained silent for the remainder of the flight.

Coral Cove, Florida

A Sycamore County police cruiser was waiting for them when they landed on the sheriff's helipad.

"I'm Deputy Ned Ames," the driver said. "I've been assigned to escort you."

Ames drove them to a military camp about fifteen miles from the town.

"This camp is on U.S. property," Ames said. "Any crimes committed on it fall under the FBI's jurisdiction."

Their car was waved to a halt at the state police roadblock at the camp's gate. Behind the roadblock, the camp's grounds and buildings were brightly lit.

A man in plainclothes motioned them out of the car. "I'm Lieutenant Brown of the Florida State Criminal Investigation Division. I'm your liaison."

Holden and Burns identified themselves. "Did your people turn on the lights?" Burns asked.

"The lights were blazing when the first policemen arrived," Brown said as he led Holden and Burns into the camp.

"How many dead?" Holden asked, motioning toward the blanket-covered bodies lying on the ground.

"Ten outside," Brown answered. "But the real horror is inside."

Brown led them through the door of one of the barracks; he stepped to one side to allow them a full view. Holden nearly gagged at the sight of the many oddly contorted bodies draped over the bunks and chairs. Burns didn't even twitch a facial muscle. "Poison gas killed these men," he said.

"How do you know?" a shaky Holden asked.

"I know," Burns said, then asked Brown, "How many dead?"

"We've counted one hundred ninety inside the buildings. Ten more were found outside," Brown answered. "Two hundred killed in all."

Holden bent down to study one of the contorted corpses. "Not a mark on it. Are all of them like this?"

"All the ones inside," Brown confirmed. "But not outside. One had his throat slashed. We haven't determined what caused the deaths of the other nine."

Brown led them back outside; he randomly chose one of the corpses and pulled back the blanket, revealing a young Hispanic man. Holden bent down and examined the corpse.

"This is baffling," he said after four minutes of intense study. "I can't find any obvious wounds."

"Open his shirt and look at the heart area," Burns suggested.

Holden undid the shirt buttons and studied the bare skin.

"You mean this?" Holden asked, pointing at a small drop of dried blood on the breast. "This couldn't be what killed him. This is no more than pinprick."

Instead of answering, Burns spoke to Brown. "Ask your people to reexamine any body found outside. They'll find similar wounds."

Brown ordered a subordinate to have the bodies reexamined. While Brown was distracted, Burns whispered to Holden, "I'll explain when we're alone. Brown doesn't have a high enough security clearance; he can't be told about the weapons that caused these wounds."

"Okay."

"I'll show you the rest of the camp," Brown said after dealing with the subordinate.

"Pat will go with you," Burns said quickly. "I'd like to check out a few things by myself."

Burns strolled away, leaving behind a baffled

Holden. Brown gave Holden the grand tour of the camp, ending up at a quonset hut.

"This was the command center," Brown said. "It has a direct link with Luis Cardona's estate."

"Why is this camp connected with Luis Cardona?"

"It houses his army," Brown answered. "It's no secret in the Florida Panhandle that this camp was established by our government to train Cardona's troops for a future invasion of San Tomas."

"So, more than likely, Cardona's political enemies are behind these murders."

Brown shrugged.

"Let's look at Cardona's estate," Holden said.

"That's a problem," Brown said. "Technically, it isn't your jurisdiction."

"I was told the local police requested FBI involvement."

"Sheriff Hewitt did, but he may have been premature," Brown said. "It hasn't been determined if any federal crime has been committed there, and the Florida assistant attorney general George Atheas, who is on the scene, revoked Sheriff Hewitt's request for FBI assistance."

"I'll speak to Atheas."

"Okay," Brown said reluctantly. "But George Atheas is not an easy man to deal with."

Brown used his police radio to call his counterpart at the Cardona estate. After ten minutes of back-and-forth conversation, Brown turned to Holden.

"Atheas has given permission for you to view the site, but only as an observer. You have no official capacity there."

"Okay."

"You'll be going alone. I have to stay here."

Burns wandered up just as Holden was entering Ames's police cruiser. The colonel climbed inside.

"Do you have anything to say about the murders in this camp?" Holden asked.

"Yes," Burns said, looking Holden in the eye. "They were done very professionally and efficiently."

"Jesus, you're a cold-blooded bastard."

Burns looked out the window. Holden sat quietly; before attending law school and joining the FBI, he'd served three years as an Air Force lieutenant. The Vietnam War was going strong, but he had spent his tour of duty in Seattle. He'd thought of Vietnam many times, but had never pictured it anywhere near as gruesome as what he had observed in the camp.

The cruiser was halted at the gates of Cardona's estate. A uniformed Florida highway patrolman met them and guided them inside. Although darkness concealed most of the grounds, three bodies and two dogs' carcasses could be observed on the ground.

"It looks just like Nam," Burns said matter-of-factly. He glanced at Holden. "This will be worse than the camp."

Ignoring the patrolman's objections, Burns wandered off into the grounds. The patrolman was unsure whether or not to go after Burns. Before he could make his decision, George Atheas came down the driveway.

"I know about the scene at the camp. There was a slaughter here, too," Atheas said. "I've just received word from Tallahassee that the FBI has been given jurisdiction. I'm to work with you."

"Fine," Holden said.

"There are several other government agencies already on the premises."

"What? Which ones?"

"Alcohol, Tobacco and Firearms and the Drug Enforcement Agency. There are also military and a couple of men who haven't bothered to identify themselves, but they act like they're CIA."

"CIA? Why would anyone from that agency be here?"

Atheas looked at Holden quizzically. "The CIA was backing Cardona's attempt to retake San Tomas. Unfortunately, someone has killed Cardona, his three sons, his administration's ministers, and his military generals. No one remains alive to lead any attempt to overthrow San Tomas's Communist government. These murders will no doubt make the CIA, not to mention the President of the United States, furious."

Since taking office three years ago, President John Mason and his administration had been committed to removing the Communists from San Tomas. Major battles had been fought with Congress over financial appropriations for this effort. President Mason had spoken numerous times on national TV proclaiming his backing of Cardona and Cardona's patriotic army.

"Cardona's murder will have huge political ramifications," Atheas said.

"We'll probably be hearing from the White House soon."

"It's too early for the president to be awake." Atheas grinned. It was a standard joke that President Mason slept through anything. "And his people wouldn't wake him up. He needs his rest. But when he does wake up, he'll be demanding answers! He'll exert all the pressure he has at his command, and that's only more than anyone else has in the entire world."

"So I guess we'd better solve this," Holden said.

Atheas led Holden toward the house. It was four a.m.; the grounds were still pitch-black.

"We've counted forty-nine bodies on the grounds and in the command center. Seven more are dead on the yacht, and six servants were slain in the kitchen."

Atheas guided Holden through the glass doors into Cardona's study. Out of the blackness, Burns appeared. Grandly Atheas gestured. "Meet the liberating forces of San Tomas."

There were twelve bodies in the room; all twelve had suffered multiple wounds, which had caused them to bleed profusely. One had been shot so many times that it had been literally torn to pieces. Pointing to it, Atheas said, "That was Luis Cardona."

"Mother of God," Holden exclaimed. "There isn't much left of him."

"Whoever broke in here certainly didn't like him very much," Atheas remarked. "I've never seen wounds like these before. I've asked the other investigators, and they're just as dumbfounded. Have you any ideas?"

"Not a clue," Holden said, glancing at Burns. "I saw this type of wound for the first time at the camp. I don't know what kind of weapon was used."

"That's interesting," Atheas said. "The same weapons were used in both places."

"Not quite. At the camp, nine bodies have solitary wounds in them which appear similar to these. But there weren't any multiple wounds."

"There are bodies with only a single wound here as well," Atheas said. "Perhaps the weapon has an automatic and a single-shot selector mode."

"You're probably right," Holden said. "My gut feeling is the same people were involved in both attacks."

One of Atheas's people called him away. Holden looked for Burns, but the colonel had vanished again. Holden roamed around looking for Burns, stopping occasionally to speak to other investigators.

At sunrise, Holden was standing on the front lawn; dawn's pinkish light revealed the corpses of men and the carcasses of dogs lying in the plush foliage and on the manicured lawn.

"Only the devil himself could have done this," Holden said to nobody in particular.

Tyler Burns had first donned his country's uniform at eighteen when he entered West Point, from which he had graduated twenty-eight years ago at age twenty-two. He'd seen action in Vietnam and had practiced his craft elsewhere in Southeast Asia, South and Central America, and Africa. He'd even run a few missions into East Germany and the Soviet Union. The CIA wanted him to work for it, but he refused to retire from the Army. He was a soldier first; maybe when he was old and gray, he'd consider joining the Company. His sole gripe with the Army was that he hadn't been promoted to general; he should've received his general's star years ago, but regular Army officers didn't look kindly on promoting practitioners of his type of warfare.

Burns might be in charge of a training brigade, but he was one of the finest field men wearing the green beret; he still went on covert operations, and had been decorated for his actions on missions.

His experienced eye told him the whole story of the attack on the camp and the estate. First, the attacking force had used the stolen weapons and equipment from the Kirk's Armory. And second, the attacking force had been totally professional; he admired their efficiency and planning.

In the dark, it had been impossible to tell how many men had participated in the attack on the camp. It would be necessary for him to return in full daylight to get a better feel for it, but his bet was that no more than five attackers were involved; that estimate was based on the pattern of the corpses lying outside the camp's buildings. It was a given that the attackers were expert riflemen; the absolute accuracy of the shots confirmed that. The knifing had been equally as quick and efficient. The entrance wounds clearly indicated that a Snick had been used. Burns was one of the few men who knew how the weapon had received its nickname: A sharpshooter testing the new experimental weapon had proclaimed, "You can't even hear the snick of a bolt when it's fired." The name had stuck.

The machine pistol version of the Snick, called the Spitter, had been used on Cardona and the men in his study. Officially, neither weapon existed: They were manufactured in a top-secret factory owned and controlled by the United States Armed Services Combined Covert Warfare Group, and were used solely on missions by elite covert units attached to that Group. When not in use, the weapons were stored in Kirk's Armory.

Snuff, the gas used by the attackers, was also a product of the top-secret factory. Burns had spotted the shattered Snuff capsules in the ventilation systems of the three buildings he'd checked. As far as he could determine, the attacking force had killed two hundred men at the camp without suffering any casualties of their own.

As impressive as that was, the attack on the Cardona estate was even more incredible. The estate was nearly as well equipped with security devices as Kirk's Armory, plus it was heavily defended. Yet the attackers had infiltrated undetected and managed to slaughter the defenders. This indicated that the attackers were among the elite of the elite.

Unfortunately, it was impossible for them to cover their tracks as they had when they'd sacked Kirk's Armory. It was one thing to infiltrate an objective like the armory and escape undetected, but an attack with the intent to kill required different tactics. In the light of the rising sun, Burns found the two wall sections where the intruders had penetrated the estate's defenses. He deduced that attackers had come over the wall while being protected by snipers using Snicks; the first intruders had then climbed trees inside the estate and provided cover with their Snicks while the other invaders scaled the wall. A surveillance camera was standing open on an eight-foot pole near one of the invasion routes; Burns made a mental note to have an electronics expert check the camera.

On the beach, he discovered the scuff marks of a diver who had come ashore near the wharf. From the positions of the guards' corpses, he was certain there had been a second diver firing a Seasnick from shallow water. Good military strategy would've required that these divers provide protection while others cleared the yacht of any potential problems. It was obvious that a Snuff gas grenade had been used in the yacht's galley.

An examination of the ventilation system to the

blockhouse housing the guards' sleeping area and the command center revealed the telltale sign of Snuff capsules.

The attack's coordination and planning was impressive. Not only were the attackers well trained, the leader exhibited superior military tactics. Burns estimated that no more than ten men took part in the two-pronged attack from land and sea. He wondered if another, separate unit had attacked the camp, but rejected the idea. The same men had to be involved in both actions; they were part of a trained military covert warfare team.

Burns had made several additional discoveries on the estate. A large quantity of cocaine had been stored in a concrete bunker one hundred meters to the west of the house, but it would be impossible for anyone to ever put this powder up their nose. Small incendiary charges had been detonated in the stacked cocaine packages, blowing them open and setting them aflame. At the same time, explosive containers holding an extremely corrosive acid called Ruin, which had been stolen from Kirk's Armory, had been detonated, dissolving the cocaine into a smoking, foaming mess. The DEA was on the scene, but couldn't safely enter the bunker.

A second bunker nearby contained a large cache of weapons. Ruin capsules and incendiary charges had been used to render the weaponry and ammunition useless. The Alcohol, Tobacco and Firearms people were picking delicately through the debris; the protective suits they wore indicated that they had discovered that Ruin was equally as destructive on human skin as it was on metal.

A military intelligence officer recognized Burns and confided that the attackers had emptied a vault buried under a storeroom off the house's library.

"What was in there?" Burns asked.

"Don't know for sure," the officer said. "But Cardona was rumored to keep extensive records and cash on the premises."

Burns wandered down to the estate's gate and engaged Deputy Ned Ames in conversation; Ames told him what had happened to the deputies on duty outside the estate and in town.

"How about a ride into town?" Burns asked. "I'd like to speak to those deputies."

At the sheriff's office, Burns found what he thought he would find: Snooze had been used on the local law.

"Did the deputy who was killed have respiratory problems?" Burns asked.

"Yeah, he had asthma," Ames answered.

Burns spoke with Blount and Pond, the two deputies who had been subdued in their car outside Cardona's estate. The last thing Blount remembered was Pond exiting the vehicle. At least, Pond had seen his attacker and was able to describe what he was wearing: it was the standard garb for an attacking force of covert soldiers.

"I can't describe him," Pond said. "He had a hood over his head."

After leaving the sheriff's office, Burns made a quick check of the building roof across the street and found the spot where an attacker had kept watch on the police.

Finally, Burns went to a public phone in a gas station; he telephoned General Downs in Washington, D.C., and gave a short report.

"The attackers were my brothers in arms."

Bull Hewitt was feeling excluded from the investigation. It was his county, but the state and federal boys had shoved him aside. Coral Cove's ten-man detective division was participating in the investigation, but it was under the supervision of George Atheas and his unit.

Bull had spent a miserable night. State and federal investigators had poured into Coral Cove; they hadn't bothered to make even a courtesy call on Bull. Finally, Bull had gone to Cardona's estate to observe the mayhem for himself, but he had quickly departed the estate after investigators began asking him questions about Cardona.

Saturday morning had been hell. He'd had to explain to several federal agencies why his police force had been undermanned last night. The questioners were amused to hear that the reason was a high school football game, laughing at Bull for leaving the town unprotected for such a trivial affair.

Worst of all, he had to inform Amy Throne of her husband's death. Amy had broken down; she and Ed had been married for over twenty-five years.

The press began descending at dawn. The massacre at the Cardona estate was world news, and every major news organization wanted to interview the sheriff. Each and every interview contained the same question: "Where were you when the killing was going on?"

The reporters were as amused as the federal authorities by his answer. Their reports made him out as a buffoon who was more interested in football than crime.

The one point in Bull's favor so far was that no one had discovered that Bull was being paid to ignore Cardona's drug operation.

At lunchtime, George Atheas, Holden, and the heads of the other investigative bodies gathered in a conference room at the Coral Cove sheriff's headquarters. Bull Hewitt attended on sufferance only because he had offered the use of the room and made sure it was stocked with food and drink.

The meeting wasn't productive. There weren't any outstanding leads. The only thing accomplished was the election of George Atheas as the sole press spokesman. This pleased everyone: The federal investigators wouldn't have to deal with the press, and Atheas would gain exposure for his future political ambitions.

The only other decision was that there would be a meeting of all investigative agencies on Monday in Tallahassee.

Chapter Seven

Washington, D.C.

An emergency luncheon meeting was held on Saturday in the expensive Georgetown townhouse of presidential aide Dan Fogarty. Six men had been ordered to attend, one representative each from the State Department, Defense Department, Joint Chiefs of Staff, Defense Intelligence Agency, and FBI, and two from the CIA. They were met at the door by armed, stone-faced Marines who escorted them downstairs into the soundproof basement meeting room. There, an amply supplied buffet table was placed against one wall; the officials were told to help themselves and sit down at a table in the center of the room. Coffee and water jugs were on the table; no other liquid refreshments were available.

After the last official had arrived, the basement

door was locked; on the house's main floor, armed Marines took up positions to insure the meeting's privacy. The basement door would not be opened again until Dan Fogarty gave his approval.

As soon as the last official had filled his plate and sat down at the table, Fogarty addressed the group. "Everyone here will consider this meeting confidential. There is a crisis, and the White House is extremely concerned. You all probably know the two men to my left, but let me introduce them anyway. This is General George Downs, the head of the U.S. Armed Services Combined Covert Warfare Group." Downs, sitting directly to Fogarty's left, nodded.

"Next to him is the CIA's Special Projects Director Barry Brennan. He is the CIA's liaison with General Downs's command." Brennan nodded to the men at the table.

"General Downs and Barry Brennan are going to brief you on a serious situation which has arisen. General Downs."

Downs spoke from his seat. "Dan Fogarty says that each of you are trusted confidants of the President, and that you have been privy to the information about the burglary of Kirk's Armory at Fort Benning on Thursday night. Are you all clear about the significance of the burglary to national security?"

The six men at the table assured Downs that they had been fully briefed about all ramifications of the burglary.

"You have also been briefed on last night's murders of Luis Cardona and his associates?"

The group nodded affirmative again.

"The two events are connected," Downs said. "Colonel Tyler Burns, the head of the Covert Warfare Special Training Brigade at Fort Benning, reports that the weapons and equipment stolen from Kirk's Armory were used against Luis Cardona and his forces."

Barry Brennan started passing briefing papers to each man.

"I'll give you a moment to read the brief that Barry is passing out," Downs said. "In it is Colonel Burns's theorized scenario of the attack. Colonel Burns is drawing on his professional experience and his on-scene observations for this scenario. However, he stresses that this is only an educated guess, since he doesn't know how some of the estate's security measures were nullified by the attackers."

The officials shuffled through Burns's report. The FBI's assistant director, Maynard Humphrey, said angrily, "Why hasn't this information been shared with Pat Holden, the FBI agent on the scene? I spoke with him prior to this meeting, and he said Colonel Burns had refused to share information with him!"

"Colonel Burns acted under my orders," Downs said. "Mr. Fogarty had called this meeting, and Burns was ordered to give me a report first so that I could brief you."

"Well, Burns has carried out your orders," Humphrey said. "I expect him to brief Pat Holden now."

Downs glanced at Fogarty before answering. The President's aide nodded his approval. Downs said, "It will be done the moment this meeting ends, Mr. Humphrey."

"One more thing, Maynard," Fogarty added. "On Cardona's estate, there was a bunker filled with weapons and ammunition, and also a bunker filled with cocaine. Under no circumstances will those bunkers become public knowledge. The President has specifically ordered that!" Fogarty paused in order to give his statement full impact. Then he continued, "Those bunkers fall under national security rules, and are not part of any investigation. That will be made clear to all of your people."

"The President was onto the FBI Director early this morning about the drugs and the weapons," Humphrey said. "Pat Holden has been informed that they are not the FBI's concern."

"Now that that's settled, can we get back to business?" said Dante Funicula of the Defense Intelligence Agency. "What worries me about both the armory break-in and the attack on Cardona's camp is that our most advanced electronic security measures were penetrated so easily."

Speaking over the instant protests of Fogarty and several other men present, Funicula continued, "I fully understand that the President is outraged by Cardona's assassination and that Cardona's death deals a severe blow to the President's foreign policy in Central America. I know that the President called this meeting because of Cardona's assassination. We can address that in a minute. But I think that we should consider the impact of someone managing to penetrate Kirk's Armory at Fort Benning, which was protected by the United States's most advanced security devices, and which was considered impregnable. I don't believe that any of the political people have grasped the significance of that."

"Which is?" Fogarty asked impatiently.

"Only that none of our top security military and civilian facilities are safe anymore," Funicula replied.

"We haven't forgotten it, Mr. Funicula," General

Downs said. "The briefing papers address it. Colonel Burns's and Special Agent Holden's conclusions are that the perpetrators left a message meant to assure us that our security wasn't a worry."

"I've read their conclusions, and I'm not convinced," Funicula said. "How do they conclude that the thieves were Americans? How do they come to the conclusion that the thieves were trying to tell us not to worry about future break-ins? Just because the thieves left behind this so-called operational signature? Ridiculous!"

"If I may say something," Barry Brennan broke in. "I agree with Colonel Burns's conclusions. The perpetrators are Americans. They either now are, or have been members of the U.S. Armed Services Combined Covert Warfare Group."

Steven Harris, the CIA Director's special assistant, immediately backed Brennan. "The CIA has run an intensive intelligence check during the past thirty-six hours. We are totally and unequivocally positive that no foreign country has infiltrated any special warfare troops into the U.S.

"Furthermore, we are also totally and unequivocally positive that no foreign power currently has the capability to break into our security facilities. They don't have the knowledge or expertise to bypass the United States's electronic security devices.

"We are convinced that Americans did carry out both the break-in at Kirk's Armory and the attack on Cardona. What we don't know is why they did it. Nor do we know if they were paid to do it by some foreign power."

"All right, that's enough," Fogarty ordered. "Mr. Brennan and General Downs are excused. Thank you very much for coming."

"General Downs! Make sure you order Colonel

Burns to brief Pat Holden," the FBI's Humphrey said as Downs and Brennan climbed the staircase.

"Yes, sir! Immediately," Downs answered.

Fogarty took a radio from his pocket and spoke into it, the basement door was opened, and the two men were released. The door slammed shut behind them.

"President Mason is furious over Cardona's assassination," Fogarty said to the remaining men at the table. "Right now, he doesn't give a damn about any future security breaches. That's a separate problem.

"The President is convinced that Cardona was murdered by the Communists, or at least, the Communists hired his murderers. The President wants the murderers caught, and he wants them caught quickly! The President intends to place them on trial before the world.

"The President orders each of your departments to use every resource to accomplish this goal. We will meet here at noon on Monday to discuss your progress. I'll issue any further instructions from the President at that time."

Arlington, Virginia

The representatives of the Joint Chiefs, the Defense Department, the Defense Intelligence Agency, and the CIA returned to the Pentagon and conducted a second short meeting with General Downs and Barry Brennan.

The DIA's Dante Funicula issued the group's orders to Downs and Brennan. "Assemble a team and capture the attackers. This team is to remain completely independent from the FBI, and from any other agency not represented in this room. Once the team has accomplished its mission, it is to keep the attackers incommunicado. Do you both understand?"

"Yes, sir," Brennan and Downs said in unison.

"After we interrogate them and find out how they avoided Kirk's Armory's security measures, and why they killed Cardona, the attackers will be executed," Funicula said emphatically. "There will be no public trial. The intelligence and military community of the United States can't afford a public trial."

"Capturing these men won't be easy. In fact, it will be damn near impossible," Downs said to the group. His words would prove prophetic in the coming months.

Miami, Florida

Ernesto Guavaro of the Presidential Guard of San Tomas, the missing fiftieth guard from Cardona's estate, was sleeping in a Miami safe house after reporting to his true superiors in Havana: Guavaro was actually a major in the Cuban intelligence service.

Cuba had been Cardona's partner in the drug business; Cardona's death was a potentially fatal economic blow to the island. Cuba needed hard cash to pay for imported goods. Cardona's death destroyed the drug operation, which in turn ended the flow of American dollars into the island.

Even more serious as far as the Cuban dictator, Fidel Castro, was concerned, Cardona's death prevented Castro from attaining his greatest desire in life: to make drug addicts of as many Americans as possible. For the past nine years, Castro had committed most of his island's meager resources to attaining that goal.

Guavaro had been assigned to keep an eye on Cardona. Guavaro had successfully infiltrated Luis Cardona's inner circle, and had become the dictator's trusted confidant and bodyguard. Luis Cardona would not make a move unless Guavaro was beside him; Guavaro may not have been visible, but he was always present during Luis Cardona's most confidential meetings. The result was that everything Cardona ever said was passed on to Guavaro's Cuban superiors, and ultimately to the Russians.

On Friday night, Guavaro had been in his normal spot, a concealed closet cut into one of the study's walls. Guavaro's job had been to shoot anyone who threatened El Presidente's life during the confidential meeting; not even Luis Cardona's sons knew that Guavaro was in the wall with a loaded automatic weapon constantly pointed at the group. Guavaro had been intently listening to the meeting when the intruders crashed through the doors. Out of pure instinct, he had nearly fired on the first ones to enter the room. His better judgment had prevailed at the last second. If it hadn't, he'd be dead now. The intruders had been professionals; he could never have killed them all before they killed him.

He had remained hidden and studied the killers. They were carrying strange weapons. Their heads were covered by tight-fitting hoods with only eye, nose, and mouth slits. Goggles were pushed up on their heads, and small compact masks hung at their necks. He had never seen this equipment before, nor had he seen such weapons, whose total silence had unnerved Guavaro.

He had been unable to identify any of the intruders. Only one had stood out from the rest, because he had been the tallest and largest. Through the hood's mouth slit, Guavaro could see the man's black skin. Guavaro had studied the masks of the other six men: five had been white and one other black.

The intruders' claim about Cardona torturing and murdering two of their friends was of no concern to Guavaro. Over his nine years of service, he had witnessed Cardona torture and murder many people. The leader's statement about executing Cardona to satisfy honor meant nothing to Guavaro.

Long after the intruders had vacated the room, Guavaro had stayed crouched in the concealed closet. Thirty minutes after the attack, he had heard the sound of vehicle engines in the driveway. He still stayed in place even after the sounds had subsided in the distance; a half hour later, he had exited using extreme caution.

Outside the house, Guavaro ignored the dead bodies. Constantly scanning for the intruders, he furtively crept down to the beach. From there, he simply swam out and around the estate's wall. His departure set off alarms in the command center, but there wasn't anyone alive to hear them.

He continued swimming until he was a hundred yards past the estate's wall. At that point, he swam to the beach, and trotted the remaining two miles to his beach house. Never entering the house proper, he went straight to his garage, started his Ford, and drove nine hours straight to Miami.

He had made his report to Havana upon his arrival at the safe house. Havana had ordered him to stay there and await further instructions.

Coral Cove, Florida

At 11:50 p.m., a physically and mentally exhausted Pat Holden finally climbed into the bed in his motel room. He fell immediately to sleep.

In the late afternoon, the FBI's Director had personally telephoned to inform him of the President's interest in this case. The Director had informed Holden that the drug and weapons caches were off-limits; the FBI was only concerned with the murders and any charges revolving around them. He had also ordered Holden to work with the military and the CIA.

"But, Director, by law the CIA cannot operate within United States boundaries," Holden had protested.

"I know it. And I know that working with the CIA pisses you off, Pat," the Director had said. "It pisses me off, too. But the President has ordered it, and he has waived the ban against the CIA operating inside the country for this case. So we'll have to do it. Is that jake with you?"

"Yes," Holden had said reluctantly.

"Good. Now go see Colonel Burns. He's received orders to brief you."

Tyler Burns had been waiting for Holden.

"I'm sorry I couldn't say anything earlier, but I was under orders from Washington," Burns had explained. "The weapons stolen from Kirk's Armory were used in the attacks."

The colonel explained his theory of the attacks on the camp and Cardona's estate, as well as what had happened in town. Burns's voice rang with pride as he described his scenarios. Burns labeled the death of Ed Throne as purely accidental: The deputy was unlucky to have had respiratory problems; the attacking team didn't mean to harm him or any other Americans. Burns made it clear that he considered the invaders brother professionals who had thoughtfully planned their attacks, and systematically eliminated all obstacles.

"I warned you that these were dangerous motherfuckers," Burns had said. "Now you see how dangerous. They killed nearly three hundred of their enemy without suffering a single casualty."

After briefing Holden, Burns had departed for Washington to join General Downs's team. Burns's parting promise had been that he would keep Holden informed, but Holden didn't believe him, since Burns hadn't mentioned the one connection between Coral Cove and Fort Benning: The county sheriff, Bull Hewitt, and the Kirk's Armory sentry, Bo Hewitt, were father and son.

Holden believed that to be the key to solving the case. He intended to follow it up as soon as the meticulous process of gathering physical evidence from Coral Cove was concluded.

Chapter Eight

Every TV network had run prime-time specials on Saturday night dealing with the murders of Luis Cardona, his sons, staff, and soldiers; on Sunday, the nation's newspapers ran whole sections on the murders and the political ramifications, and the TV talk shows were devoted entirely to the subject. America's print and TV political analysts were unanimous in predicting the total collapse of President Mason's Central American policy. The analysts also predicted that San Tomas would become a threat to the tranquillity of Central and South America now that the ruling Communist government no longer had to protect itself against an invasion.

President Mason was furious. He issued a statement through his press secretary: "The assassination of the legitimate leader of San Tomas, Luis Cardona, will not go unpunished. The United

States considers it an act of war, since the assassination took place within our borders as the result of an obvious foreign military operation. The United States is currently evaluating its options. The use of military force against the perpetrators of this heinous crime has not been ruled out."

The reaction was immediate in San Tomas: The premier officially denied that his country had anything to do with the Cardona assassination. No one believed his denials.

In the early afternoon, CNN reported that the United States military's Rapid Deployment Forces had gone on alert, and ships carrying the Fourth Marine Division were moving into the Caribbean. The world's media began to gear up for covering a war.

By mid-afternoon Sunday, CNN began reporting that large sums of cash were being left in boxes on the doorsteps of charitable organizations stretching from Miami to New York. CNN reported that the boxes contained millions of dollars in cash, and each box had the same message written on a sheet of paper pasted to the outside:

This cash was taken from Luis Cardona's vault. It is a portion of the profits from Cardona's illegal drug and weapons smuggling operations. Cardona's illegal activities were sanctioned and protected by individuals and organizations within the United States government. Blinded by their zeal to have the Communist government ousted from San Tomas, officials of the Mason administration, the CIA, and the military helped Cardona poison the American people with cocaine. Please put this money to use in helping the unfortunate.

This written statement diverted the media from the impending war and sent it sniffing around Cardona and his organization. The media's scrutiny alarmed powerful figures in the government, who counseled President Mason to attack San Tomas immediately. However, before Mason could act, his whole administration was rocked by the appearance of documentation that verified the allegations of misconduct on the cash boxes. The documentation proved that members of the CIA, the military establishment, the DEA, and the White House staff knew about, and condoned, Cardona's drug operations within the U.S.

On Sunday afternoon, a large black man distributed packages of documents to all major news organizations with offices in the National Press Building in Washington, D.C. At the same time, another black man was delivering similar packages to TV and radio news bureaus in the nation's capital.

The package labels stated that the documents had come from Cardona's personal files housed in his private vault on his Coral Cove estate. Each package contained information about Cardona's political, military, and drug dealings. Cardona had meticulously recorded all his meetings and transactions; the names of important American military, clandestine, and political leaders were prominently mentioned in the documents.

Most news organizations attempted to check the information in the packages before going public, but one network TV news executive decided to scoop his fellows. His network extended its Sunday night news to an hour and concentrated on revelations based on its share of the documents.

The revelations sent the nation into an uproar as it became obvious that factions within the American government and military had supported Cardona's drug operation. The outrage of the American people forced the cancellation of any possible invasion of San Tomas, forcing President Mason, his administration, the military, and various government agencies to frantically attempt to protect themselves.

On Monday morning, the situation worsened. Triggered by the TV network's premature release of information, the nation's newspapers ran their documents, proving that elements of the American government not only had condoned Cardona's running drugs into the U.S., but had helped him obtain the product. Furthermore, the documents proved that military, diplomatic, and political leaders had intervened in previous drug investigations of Cardona, quashing the investigations and protecting him from prosecution; their reasons for doing so were that the drug earnings were allegedly slated for financing the overthrow of the Communist government of San Tomas.

However, Cardona's records showed that barely a trickle of his drug profits was used to finance his resistance army; most of the money went to line the pockets of the Cardona family and its cronies.

Other published documents revealed that Cardona and Fidel Castro were business partners. Nearly four billion dollars had gone to the Cuban dictator over the last nine years; he had used portions of this money to finance Cuban military operations in Africa, Asia, and Central and South America. The drug loot had also been used to keep the island's Communist government floating in hard currency, which allowed it to purchase goods on the world market.

Washington, D.C.

By Monday morning, the United States was mired in a government scandal that made Watergate look like a schoolboy prank. Many of the country's most powerful men and women were trying to disassociate themselves from Luis Cardona and President John Mason.

Instead of remorse, the guilty all had one thing in common: they craved revenge on the individuals who had attacked Cardona's estate and subsequently released Cardona's secret documents.

The Monday meeting at Dan Fogarty's Georgetown townhouse was canceled. But leaders of the military and intelligence communities held a meeting in an obscure farmhouse in western Maryland.

After two hours of angry accusations, they settled on a course of action. Dante Funicula of the Defense Intelligence Agency was chosen as their spokesman.

On Monday night, Funicula met with General George Downs and Barry Brennan of the CIA in a Virginia safe house. He issued them their orders. "Track down and terminate Cardona's assassins. We want them, and anyone who hired them, dead!"

Havana, Cuba

The collapse of the Cardona drug operations infuriated Fidel Castro, who issued an order to his intelligence service. "Find and kill the men who killed Luis Cardona."

An Execution of Honor

Moscow, Russia

The Russians approved Castro's order, and commanded all of its allies to cooperate. The Communists and the capitalists had finally discovered a mutual objective: termination of Cardona's killers.

Grand Cayman Island

On Monday, a sailboat unobtrusively arrived at Grand Cayman. Its lone sailor docked, and then went to a bank and deposited ten million dollars in cash in seven separate accounts he had established two weeks earlier. At his request, the bank then electronically transferred the money to seven different banks in other areas of the world. The sailor thanked the bank, and went to the hotel suite he had been holding for the last two weeks.

The sailor used a lap computer and the room's phone to electronically transfer the money once again to new locations. The sailor also tapped into Juan Cardona's bank accounts around the world, transferring their funds through various established accounts.

The financial manipulations were repeated numerous times during the next three days until the cash was safely nestled at its final destination. By then, it was completely untraceable.

To further insure that all records of the money had disappeared into the ether, the sailor worked his magic on the banking records: the transactions were electronically wiped from all banks in the complicated money chain. The procedure wasn't difficult for the sailor; after all, he was an electronics wizard.

Thomas L. Muldoon

On Thursday, he sailed the boat back to the island of Jamaica where it had been stolen a week ago. Off the island's shore, the electronics expert arranged four plastic explosive charges around the boat's hull, set the detonator timer, and dove overboard; he confidently swam the mile to shore, ignoring the explosion behind him. Back on Jamaica, he resumed residence in the remote bungalow he'd rented for the month. Next week he'd fly home and rave to friends about his island vacation.

Chapter Nine

The scandal raised by the Cardona documents caused a political upheaval. Under pressure from the American people, Congress began the process of impeaching President John Mason.

However, the voters were so angry that they swept Mason out of office themselves in the November 1988 election. Prior to the release of the Cardona documents, polls had shown that Mason would garner seventy-five percent of the votes; after the documents became public, Mason's popularity descended faster than an elevator with severed cables: he received only six percent of the votes. It was the worst defeat ever suffered by a sitting American president.

Lawrence Sanderson became President-elect.

At his inauguration in January 1989, President Sanderson promised to give America a bright new outlook.

In private meetings, Sanderson and his supporters forged an agreement with the leaders of the opposition party: Sanderson would bury the Cardona scandal in return for the opposition's support in legislative matters.

By February, less than a month into his term of office, Sanderson quietly ordered the FBI to switch its investigators from the Cardona case to other investigations.

FBI headquarters issued Pat Holden an order: pursue all new cases with full vigor; the investigations of the break-in at Kirk's Armory and the murders of Cardona and his people were low priority. In case new evidence did surface, Holden retained nominal responsibility for Kirk's Armory and Cardona, but he was not to actively investigate either case.

Colonel Tyler Burns became a brigadier general in February 1989 and was reassigned to Washington as General George Downs's second-in-command.

While on the surface official Washington had forgotten Cardona, the incident wasn't forgiven by a hard-core group inside the U.S. intelligence agencies and military. Cardona's killers were placed on a permanent sanctions list: The moment any of them were identified, they were to be terminated.

After digesting the information of Cardona's murder, Fidel Castro had ordered Cuban intelligence to find the killers and "Terminate them on sight."

Major Ernesto Guavaro made a clandestine trip to Coral Cove in the first week of November 1988. His goal was to squeeze information from Bull Hewitt. But Hewitt wasn't in the mainstream of either the FBI's or the state's investigation; he had little information to impart.

The only significant fact Hewitt revealed to Guavaro was about the break-in at Kirk's Armory. The Russian KGB and Cuban intelligence services had been aware of Kirk's Armory; they knew it sheltered futuristic weapons and equipment, which was protected by the United States's most advanced security devices. The Communists had always viewed Kirk's Armory, and any other American installation having identical security, as impregnable. The knowledge that someone had successfully bypassed the security devices to penetrate Kirk's Armory heightened the Russians' desire to find the killers. The Russians saw this as an opportunity to make all American installations vulnerable, and they wanted the person who had accomplished the break-in.

The Russians exerted pressure on the Cubans, who changed their termination directive to read, "Capture the electronics specialist! Terminate all others involved with Cardona's death."

Despite the intensity of the search, no new clues had turned up by March 1989. The Communist nations rechanneled their resources to other tasks. By mutual agreement of Moscow and Havana, the task of pursuing the killers was left to Major Ernesto Guavaro.

Bull Hewitt's career as sheriff ended in December 1988. Florida Assistant Attorney General George Atheas's investigation unearthed evidence of Juan Cardona's illegal payments to Bull Hewitt for turning a blind eye to the dictator's drug operation. Once this evidence was made public, the Sycamore County voters, already angered by Bull's failure to prevent the Cardona massacre, petitioned the Florida governor to remove Hewitt from office. The governor obliged in December.

Bull spent 1989 trying to stay out of prison. The strain of fighting the charges against him began to tell; by December 1989, Bull was a shell of his former self.

Bo Hewitt escaped court-martial, but was reduced in rank and transferred out of the First Guard Company in the last week of October 1988. His new assignment was to an infantry platoon stationed in the Philippines. He spent 1989 trekking through jungles and being shot at by Communist guerrillas.

Master Sergeant Lyle Blackman was reassigned from the First Guard Company to supervise Fort Benning's garbage pickup.

Book III

1990

Chapter Ten

Cancun, Mexico

William Means glanced at the weather page of the local English-language newspaper; it stated that the high temperature in Washington on Friday had been thirty-three degrees. Means chuckled at the thought of his former colleagues in the CIA huddled in their thick overcoats while he sat at a table in an open-air restaurant, enjoying a February Saturday in the warm sun of the Yucatan Peninsula.

His former colleagues wouldn't recognize him now. He wore a red muscle T-shirt, white swimsuit, and sandals; his brown hair, which had been worn in a short brush cut, was bleached by the sun and nearly surfer long. Means looked as if he'd spent his life tanning on the beach rather than hiding in alleys and cutting his way through jungles.

Means had enjoyed twenty-two years with the

CIA, but now he never gave it a second thought. Twelve months ago, he had stood in front of a Congressional committee in a closed hearing and taken the rap for allowing Luis Cardona to run drugs into the U.S. He had lied blatantly, swearing that he alone was responsible, and that his CIA superiors knew nothing about Cardona's drug empire. The Congressional committee had voted to have him dishonorably discharged from the CIA with forfeiture of all retirement benefits. Means had received no other punishment for his admission of guilt.

Of course, Means didn't care. To insure his shouldering the blame, his CIA superiors had paid him five million dollars out of a Company slush fund, and guaranteed him an income of one million dollars a year for the rest of his life.

With his new wealth, Means had purchased a beach villa and retired to a life of luxury. In the last year, he'd become a playboy, preying on the female tourists who came to enjoy Cancun's sand and sea.

Means put the newspaper aside and stared appreciatively at the scantily clad women strolling down the main street. Picking up his margarita, he savored the last swallow. The waiter hurried over, asking if he wanted a refill. He declined, and paid his tab.

It was cocktail hour in the resort city. It was time to swing over to the beach for a drink at the pool bar of one of the many major hotels. Now was when those bars were swarming with horny tourist women looking for a man for the night.

Means strolled down the main street, heading away from the town center toward the garage he owned at the edge of town. The garage was a safe place to park his Porsche when he visited town; the first time he had driven into town from his beach villa, he had parked the Porsche on a side street, only to return in two hours to find the car stripped. The chief of police had shrugged, saying, "If you park a car of that value on a city street, you run the chance of it being stolen or stripped. It will happen again unless you purchase a garage."

As he neared the street where his garage was located, a stunning blonde wearing a white thong bikini and a sheer green cover walked toward him.

"Hello," he said, stopping in the center of the sidewalk.

Her blue eyes flickered at him. "Please move aside," she said in Southern-accented English.

Her voice was so enchanting that he moved without thinking. He turned to watch her tight buns undulate under the cover-up's sheer material.

Means realized that he wasn't the only one watching her; she was the focus of every male on the street. The reactions of the women were amusing; wives and girlfriends elbowed their men in anger while flashing disapproving looks at the blonde, who kept on walking toward the city's center.

Means considered walking after her to make another pickup attempt, but decided it would be fruitless. "Besides, there's dozens of women like her on the beach," he muttered to himself. "Time to go get one to cozy up to tonight."

He walked the remaining five or six steps and turned the corner onto the side street. He walked past a man standing in the shadow of a doorway. After Means had passed, the man stepped from the doorway and followed him down the empty street. Means was aware of his presence, but he wasn't concerned; the man was probably just walking down the street, and if by bad luck he was a mugger, Means could easily handle him. Means had been one of the CIA's most dangerous agents and wasn't frightened of anything or anyone.

Means slowed, but the man didn't overtake him; he remained five paces behind the former CIA agent. At the garage entrance, Means lost his temper and turned to confront the man.

"Hey, buddy. You have a problem?"

The man remained silent. Means stared at him, thinking he looked vaguely familiar. He was very fit, had light hair and piercing blue eyes.

"Do I know you?" Means asked.

"Sure," the man answered. "And you also know my friend behind you. Incidentally, he has you covered, so don't try anything stupid."

"Hello, Mr. Means," came a voice from inside the garage. "It's been a long time."

Means glanced over his shoulder. Inside the open door to the garage stood a second man; his right hand was in shadow, so Means couldn't tell what make of gun he was holding, but he definitely had a weapon in his hand.

"Please step inside," the second man said politely.

"Who are you two?"

"Step inside!" the second man repeated a little more vehemently.

Means obeyed the order. He wasn't panicked; he'd been in worse situations. He had hidden several weapons in the garage and inside the Porsche; also, he was deadly with his bare hands. Means considered the two men young and inexperienced; he intended teach them that it had been a mistake to mess with him.

The trailing man closed the garage door.

Figuring the garage's gloom would allow slight moves to go unnoticed, Means edged toward the gun he had hidden in a can on the shelf of the nearest wall.

"It's not there," the man in front of him with the gun said matter-of-factly. "Nor are any of the other weapons you had stashed. We've removed them all."

Ignoring the man with the gun, Means wheeled angrily on the one who had followed him down the street.

"Who the fuck are you?"

"I'm your executioner," the man said. From beneath his shirt he pulled out a Marine K-Bar knife. "I'm here to carry out your sentence. You've been convicted of the murders of Captain Daniel Paige and Master Sergeant Melvin Snipe."

"Paige and Snipe!" Means said in astonishment. "I never killed anybody with those names."

"Think back to the jungles of San Tomas," the man said, the K-Bar in his right hand held low. The knife weaved in a lazy pattern, but the point remained aimed at Means's thorax. "Think back to the time you stood by and allowed Luis Cardona to torture two Marines."

Means face blanched, and he whispered, "Now I remember."

"Mel was dead when we arrived," the man with the pistol said. "But Danny lived long enough to tell us that Cardona was responsible and that you hadn't stopped him."

"I remember you now. You two were on Paige's team!" Means's confidence evaporated as he realized that he wasn't dealing with inexperienced men after all. "You were both Marine Force Recon!"

"That's correct," the man with the gun said. "And now it's time for you to pay for the deaths of our buddies."

"Did you kill Cardona?" Means asked, trying to buy time so that he could think of a way out.

"Our Force Recon team executed Cardona," said the man with the gun. He had been called Two on the night of the attack.

"Our honor required it," said the man with the K-Bar. He had been called Six, and was the team leader. "With your execution, our honor will be fully satisfied."

"Why now?" Means asked. Desperately he looked around for a weapon. "Why did you wait four years?"

"Cardona had to die first," Six said, moving forward. "Afterwards, you were the subject of a Congressional hearing and it was too dangerous to execute you. Then you disappeared. We searched for you, but it took time. Finally we discovered you were living here."

Thinking he had distracted Six, Means lashed out with a karate kick aimed at Six's right elbow. Six easily avoided it; he whirled under Means's kick and slashed his stomach.

Six pulled back out of reach. A shocked Means looked down. His intestines were bulging out, his stomach had been sliced open to the backbone. He tried to hold his body together; blood poured from the wound over his hands and gushed to the ground.

"That was stupid," Six said. "I'm here to execute you, not torture you.

Means raised his eyes in time to see the K-Bar slicing toward his throat.

Langley, Virginia

It took nine days for the notice of Means's death to reach the CIA. For six days his body remained undiscovered in Cancun; only the stink of death finally brought the police to the garage. It took another three days for the deceased's name to meander its way through the U.S. consulate in Cancun to the State Department in Washington, D.C. The State Department was more efficient; it noted the flag on the name William Means in its computer and immediately notified Langley.

The notice of death hit Caroline Jordan's desk on a Monday morning. It was her job to keep track of former employees of the CIA. She brought William Means's file up on her computer. A note on his file indicated that any information pertaining to this agent was to be sent on the fast track to Hank Latham, the CIA's Deputy Director of Operations.

Latham read the notice and called Barry Brennan to his office.

"Means has been murdered in Cancun," Latham said peremptorily. He handed Brennan the file.

"Sounds like it was done by a professional," Brennan observed after he finished reading.

"Goddamn it, Barry! Of course it was done by a professional. Means was too good to be butchered that way by an amateur."

"So what do you want me to do?"

"I want you to investigate Means's death. Find out who killed him."

"Why me? You have dozens of field agents better suited for this job."

"Because you're the Special Projects Director,

and you were involved in the Cardona affair."

Brennan stared incredulously at Latham. "You think this is connected to Cardona?"

"Yes. Means was our liaison with Cardona. His murder strikes me as having been carried out with the same military efficiency as Cardona's."

"We've never actually tied any military men to the Cardona killings."

"I know you haven't," Latham said impatiently. "But we both know that it was a military operation, and you are our connection with the military's Special Forces. Reopen the investigation."

"Does that mean bring in the Covert Warfare people and the FBI?"

Latham stood up from his desk and walked to a huge globe standing on a pedestal in the corner. He spun the globe while he thought. Abruptly, he slammed his hand down and stopped the spinning globe.

"Speak to Downs and Burns, but avoid the FBI for now."

Fort Belvoir, Virginia

On Tuesday afternoon, Barry Brennan met with General George Downs and General Tyler Burns in Downs's office. Brennan told them about the murder of William Means.

"I've been ordered to find his killer. Hank Latham thinks it is someone who was involved with Cardona's death."

"Ty will work with you," General Downs said. He dismissed them from his office.

The two men moved to Burns's spartan office. Behind the desk, a large picture window overlooked the Potomac River.

136

"Latham's worried," Brennan said. "I'm not sure why, but I think he's frightened."

"Why?"

"He was Means's superior on the San Tomas operation. Means's death had him shook. I think he believes everyone involved with Cardona may be a target."

"Could he be right?"

"I honestly don't know," Brennan said. "But if he is, I'd be on the list. I supplied Cardona with covert military teams. They helped him train his men, and they also fought the Communist rebels directly."

Burns stared at Brennan.

"You knew that," Brennan said defensively. "It was my job."

"I wasn't condemning you," Burns said. "I was just wondering if anyone else connected with Cardona has died during the last year."

"We'd better find out."

"Right," Burns said. "And if we draw a blank, we'll know that the killers only had a grudge against Means and Cardona. Maybe that will provide us with the clues we need to track them down."

Chapter Eleven

Luanda, Angola

It was a steamy January night. General Gabriel Sanchez-Marquez, commander of the forty thousand Cuban troops masquerading as advisers, was sitting in his office at his headquarters contemplating his future. Fidel's foreign policy was disintegrating. Angola was the last bastion of concentrated Cuban forces; Cuban soldiers either had withdrawn or were in the process of withdrawing from the rest of Africa. Sanchez-Marquez had been informed by friends in Havana that the Cubans would be withdrawing from Angola shortly, which would make him a general without a command.

Money was the problem. The Russians had ceased paying the Cubans to supply troops to sympathetic Communist governments in Africa, and Fidel's own money pipeline, a drug-smuggling operation, had collapsed two years ago with the death of Luis Cardona. The loss of drug money had made things difficult at home; Cuba could no longer afford to finance any excursions into the Dark Continent.

As it was, Sanchez-Marquez had troops stationed throughout Angola who were feeling the lack of equipment, ammunition, and supplies. Military operations against the anti-Communist rebels had been curtailed; those rebels were becoming increasingly bold, attacking outlying posts.

The phone on the desk rang.

"This is Minister Kwala, General. I've organized an impromptu party. I thought you might like to attend."

Kwala was the Minister of the Treasury, and a close friend of the Cuban general. The two men shared a similar taste: nubile young women.

"I'd love it. I will be there in fifteen minutes."

"Fine. There is a delectable young thing who awaits your company."

Sanchez-Marquez called for his staff car and left his headquarters for Kwala's home. His voracious sexual appetite saved his life.

Twenty minutes after Sanchez-Marquez's departure, a commando raid was launched against his headquarters. Over the years, the headquarters' defense force had become lax; the rebels now swept through them as if they were schoolchildren instead of veteran warriors.

The attackers overran the headquarters compound, killing most of the defenders and all of Sanchez-Marquez's staff. While nearly every Cuban in the headquarters was killed, the rebels' losses were minimal.

The few surviving Cubans insisted that the Angolan rebel attack on the compound had been led by a foreigner, whom they described as a huge black man with ferocious fighting ability. This black man was videotaped by a hidden security camera in Sanchez-Marquez's office.

The black man, about six-foot-four and around 225 pounds, charged into the general's office. He moved to the center of the room, looked around, then turned and ran back out the door. In the process, he stared directly into the hidden camera, which was separate from the normal security system. It was a good thing: the rebels destroyed the security system videotaping facility but missed this hidden camera.

The office videotape was carried back to Havana by the armed guards who escorted the prisoner, General Gabriel Sanchez-Marquez.

Havana, Cuba

General Sanchez-Marquez died before a firing squad.

The Luanda videotape made the rounds of military analysts. In March, it went finally to Guillermo Zagoza, a Cuban Intelligence Service analyst.

Zagoza was a friend of Ernesto Guavaro. They had attended school together, and had joined the Intelligence Service at the same time. Zagoza was more cerebral, Guavaro more physical; Zagoza became an analyst, Guavaro a field agent. From the start, Guavaro had been a supernova in the Cuban Intelligence Service, while Zagoza had toiled brilliantly but unspectacularly behind the scenes. Zagoza had never envied Guavaro; they remained friends.

Now, due to his failure in the Cardona affair,

Zagoza's friend Guavaro's star was tarnished. Castro demanded retribution—not for Cardona's death, but for the blow his killers had struck against Fidel's plans and Cuba's economic security. Guavaro had failed to find the killers, and Castro's wrath was falling on him. The failure wouldn't be tolerated much longer; Guavaro's head was on the chopping block, and the axe was on the downward swing.

Only two nights ago, Zagoza and Guavaro had shared two bottles of rum at a local bar. For at least the fiftieth time in the last two years, a drunken Guavaro had related the tale of his witnessing Cardona's death.

"I can't understand why they haven't surfaced," an anguished Guavaro had said.

"The Russians and the Americans are just as baffled," Zagoza had said in an attempt to comfort his friend. "They haven't uncovered the reasons for Cardona's murder, nor have they identified any possible suspects. No terrorist or political group has claimed responsibility for the killings."

"Fidel doesn't hold the Russians or Americans responsible," Guavaro had said. "He holds me responsible. His aides call me every day and ask if I have made any progress. They threaten me when I say I haven't."

Guavaro was as frustrated as he was frightened. He had heard the killers tell Cardona that he was being executed for the murder of their two friends. They had said that their honor demanded Cardona's execution, but that phrase hadn't narrowed the field for Guavaro; Cardona had tortured and murdered thousands.

Guavaro had ended the night by collapsing on

the street in front of the bar. Zagoza had taken his friend home and put him to bed.

Zagoza keyed the Luanda videotape and pressed the play button. The sight of the black man entering the office immediately jarred Zagoza's memory: Guavaro was searching for just such an individual.

Zagoza telephoned Guavaro. "Ernesto, I have something that will make you very happy."

"Not even the finest whore in Havana could make me happy," Guavaro said. "I am in a hole up to the top of my head, and Fidel is shoveling in dirt."

"If I'm right," Zagoza said, "Fidel will pull you out of the hole and brush the dirt off himself. I think I've found your large black man."

"What!" Guavaro exclaimed. "How? Where?"

"Hurry over here. I have a videotape for you to view."

Guavaro arrived within fifteen minutes. He studied the tape intently.

"What do you think?" Zagoza asked.

"Let me see it again, please."

Zagoza ran the tape three more times. Guavaro's eyes remained riveted on the TV screen. He studied the way the man moved; how he cocked his head as he checked the room; and the way he held his weapon.

"Enough!" Guavaro said finally.

Zagoza turned on the lights. Guavaro was grinning from ear to ear.

"Thank you, my friend," he said. "You will receive a bottle of French champagne."

"Then he is the one?"

"He is the one. I will need photos made of his face."

"Easily done. How soon do you want them?"

"It isn't when I want them that is important, it is when Fidel will want them," Guavaro said. "And he wanted them months ago."

While Zagoza went to make photos from the videotaped image, Guavaro telephoned Castro's office.

"I have news," he told Castro's chief aide. "I've found one of the killers."

"Have you identified him?"

"Not yet, but I'm having photos made now."

"Fax one to this office and telephone the moment you have an identification."

When Zagoza returned with the photos, one was immediately faxed to the Cuban leader's office. The others were circulated within the Intelligence Service and Cuban Military Intelligence. Two hours later, the black man remained anonymous: his face wasn't in any records.

Guavaro relayed this to his superior, who issued an order. "Fax the photo to Moscow. The KGB keeps superior records."

Moscow, Russia

It took the KGB six hours, but it identified the man in the photo. Before the information was sent to the Cubans, an aide brought the file to General Sergei Demetrov, chairman of the KGB.

"Sir, the Cubans have sent us a photo for identification. They say it is a photo of one of the men who killed Luis Cardona," Lieutenant Georgi Krunshykin said, handing over the file.

"So they finally found one of them," Demetrov said. "And he presumably is one of the men who broke into Kirk's Armory?"

"Yes, sir. His name is Theben Stone. He lives in

Paris and occasionally works as a mercenary. Our records indicate he has run operations for the Americans, Germans, French, and British in Africa, the Middle East, and Southeast Asia."

Krunshykin stood silently while his superior read the file.

"This file is incomplete," General Demetrov said. "It only goes back four years."

"As far as we know, he didn't exist before that," Krunshykin answered. "Stone appeared in Paris four years ago and proclaimed himself a mercenary for hire to Western intelligence services. His life since then is well documented, but it is a mystery before that time."

"I don't like mysteries, Lieutenant."

The aide knew better than to comment.

"I want it solved. Put a team on it," the general ordered. "Dismissed, Lieutenant."

"Yes, sir." Krunshykin left the office.

The general sat thinking. The fact that Stone was involved with Kirk's Armory made him too important for the Cubans to handle alone. He made a decision: the KGB would take part in any action against Stone.

Havana, Cuba

The communication from Moscow identifying the black man as Theben Stone sent Guavaro scurrying. He was ordered to assemble a surveillance team, take it to Paris, and keep watch of Stone until the other six attackers were identified. Once that was accomplished, Guavaro was to capture Stone and his six comrades and bring them back to Havana. Castro wanted to be present at their execution.

Before Guavaro could depart for Paris, his superior called him into his office.

"Major, the KGB will be joining your surveillance."

"*Mierdo*," Guavaro said. "The KGB will demand control."

"Most certainly," his superior said. "And you will follow their orders."

Coral Cove, Florida

In the first week of March, Bull Hewitt suffered a fatal heart attack. His funeral was held on the second Monday of the month; it was a sparsely attended affair, insulting for a native son of his stature. Despite his football heroics and long stint as county sheriff, people only remembered him for accepting bribes from a drug kingpin.

While short on mourners, Bull's funeral was extremely well attended by representatives from law enforcement organizations. They brought cameras, and extensively photographed the mourners.

Bo Hewitt watched silently as his father's body was lowered into the ground. On the last day of 1989, Bo had been granted an early discharge from the Army. He had returned to town, and since January 5, 1990, he had been a deputy in the Sycamore county sheriff's department. His intention was to become sheriff one day; when he did, he would avenge himself on those who had abandoned his old man.

Bo no longer resembled the football player he had once been. He was a considerably leaner and meaner man; a tour of duty with the infantry in the Philippines had stripped him of his bulk and shifted his natural aggressiveness into a snarling nastiness. After being transferred from Fort Benning, Bo had spent a year training in the jungles, slogging through knee-deep mud, being drenched by tropical rainstorms, snapped at by poisonous snakes, and threatened by dangerous natives. It had made him smarter; he still enjoyed hurting people, but had developed sense enough to avoid being caught doing it.

Next to Bo at the graveside stood Bull's daughter, Lisa. Standing beside her was her husband, Terry Malloy. The two had been married the previous June in a lively ceremony in Tallahassee, which had been followed by a raucous post-nuptial celebration hosted by Malloy's friends. Their honeymoon had been in Paris, and they acted as if they were still on it; they were wildly and happily in love with each other.

The Malloys still resided in Tallahassee, where Lisa was finishing her degree at Florida State University. Terry had quit school but was very successful in the stock market. As a result of Terry's investments, the Malloys lived a life of wealth.

Terry's best friend, and the best man at his wedding, Joe Craig, stood across the grave from Malloy. Next to him were Roberto Gonzalez and Cecil Jones, two other close friends of Malloy's.

Fort Belvoir, Virginia

A copy of the funeral videotape was delivered to General Tyler Burns. The videotape disturbed Burns; there was something vaguely familiar about two of the men attending the funeral, but he couldn't place them. Finally, Burns assumed he'd seen them during his reconnaissance of Coral Cove after Cardona's assassination. Dismissing the videotape as unimportant, he ordered it stored with the rest of the Cardona file.

Atlanta, Georgia

Another copy of the videotape, this one accompanied by still photos, quickly reached Patrick Holden. It disturbed him as much as it had Burns; like Burns, he couldn't say why.

Holden carefully studied the videotape. Bo's presence reminded him of his intention to probe the Hewitt family, seeking a link between the robbery at Kirk's Armory and Cardona's murder. It also renewed his anger at Tyler Burns, who had never acknowledged the Hewitt connection nor delivered the list of electronics and infiltration experts who had trained at Kirk's Armory.

The more Holden studied the videotape, the more he was fascinated by the four men with Lisa Hewitt. Like Tyler Burns, Holden thought they looked familiar. He was certain that he didn't know the four men, but the manner in which they carried themselves reminded him of something.

Three days later, after numerous viewings of the videotape, it dawned on him why they seemed familiar.

"These four guys resemble each other in their physical movements, facial expressions, and general posture," he said in astonishment. "And they all also resemble Tyler Burns!"

Holden's interest quickened. The more he studied the four men, the more he was certain he was correct.

"These men were once soldiers like Burns," he exclaimed. The men's names were on an accompanying identification sheet. He called one of the

147

FBI agents who worked for him. "I want a background check run on these four names. I especially want their military files."

Atlanta, Georgia

Patrick Holden's assumption that the four men at Bull Hewitt's funeral had served in the military was confirmed quickly: They had been Marines. But acquiring their military service records wasn't so easy. It wasn't until the last week of March before the records arrived from the U.S. Military Depository in Saint Louis, Missouri.

The four men's service records indicated that they had held different jobs in the military. Roberto Gonzalez had been a cook, Cecil Jones a motor pool mechanic, Terry Malloy a clerk, and Joe Craig had worked in blueprint duplication.

"Something's not kosher," Holden muttered to himself.

He retrieved the videotape and watched it again, paying particular attention to the way the four men moved. Finally he said, "There's no way these guys worked in offices!"

He took out their files again. It took only a minute of study to realize that all four men had served at the same locations around the world, and during the same periods of time. And all four had resigned from the Marines in 1987 after serving at least nine years in the Marine Corps.

Holden scanned the files again, making notes as he did.

Terry Malloy, was thirty-one now. He'd quit the Marine Corps at twenty-eight, after serving nine years. His last rank was staff sergeant. Malloy had been born and raised in Fresno, California.

Cecil Jones was a twenty-nine-year-old black man from Rocky Mount, North Carolina. He was a sergeant when he left the Marines. He'd served for nine years, joining the corps when he was seventeen.

Roberto Gonzalez was thirty. He had joined at seventeen as well, and served ten years, attaining the rank of sergeant. He was a Cuban-American from Hialeah, Florida.

Joe Craig at thirty-two was the old man of the group. He'd served eleven years after joining at eighteen. He had been a gunnery sergeant. Craig was from Mascoutah, Illinois.

Holden put the service records aside and stared at his notes. Why had they all decided to leave at approximately the same time after serving for so long? Why had they all chosen to live and attend college in Tallahassee?

Holden's intuition told him he was on to something. The most suspicious fact about the four was their connection to Lisa Hewitt, who was now Malloy's wife.

It was time to take a trip to Tallahassee.

Fort Belvoir, Virginia

General George Downs was notified of the FBI's request for the service records of Joe Craig, Terry Malloy, Roberto Gonzalez, and Cecil Jones. It was standard procedure; Military Records were under orders to notify Downs's office anytime there was a request for the records of a member or former member of the Combined Covert Warfare Group. The request for the four service records had been initiated by Patrick Holden.

"Do you know why Pat Holden requested the

files of four of our boys?" Downs asked Tyler Burns.

"No."

"Well, you'd better find out!" Downs ordered.

Burns asked for copies of the service records which had been sent to Holden. These were the sanitized service record books; the actual service record books of members or former members of the U.S. Armed Services Combined Covert Warfare Group were not given to outside agencies.

Burns opened one of the four record books and stared at a photograph of Roberto Gonzalez.

"Oh, shit!"

He buzzed his aide. "Bring me the videotape of Bull Hewitt's funeral."

The aide appeared quickly. Burns threaded the videotape in the VCR and turned it on. There was Roberto Gonzalez standing at the grave. Burns flicked open the service record books of the other three men, and checked their photographs; they were also on the videotape.

The photographs triggered a hidden memory; he knew why the men had looked familiar when he had initially viewed the videotape: Gonzalez and Jones had trained under him when he'd been in charge of the Special Warfare Desert Training Center outside San Antonio, Texas.

He telephoned General Downs. "I need the genuine record books of four of our former members."

"Bring the request to my office and I'll clear it."

Even with Downs's clearance, it took an additional three days before the genuine service record books appeared. When they were in his hands, Burns read all four. When he was finished, he telephoned Barry Brennan.

"Barry, meet me in General Downs's office in a hour."

"What's up?"

"Trouble. Big trouble."

Burns was waiting for Brennan outside Downs's office. He quickly briefed the CIA operative. Together they entered the general's office.

"These four were involved in killing Cardona. All four were Marine Force Recon!" Burns stated, handing the service records to Downs.

"Former Force Recon Marines. They certainly are capable of carrying out the Cardona attacks," Downs said. He began to read the record books.

"I never even thought of Force Recon when we were looking for possible suspects," Brennan said. "There's so few of them that I've hardly ever worked with them in my career."

Widespread publicity has made the Army's Green Berets and the Navy's Seals household names, but very few Americans are aware of Force Recon, the Marine Corps' elite special forces. Its members endure a combination of the Green Berets and Seals training.

Downs dropped the files on his desk. "These four served in San Tomas. They fought in the delaying action that allowed Luis Cardona and his sons to escape the country."

"That means they were part of a Force Recon team," Burns said. "That's nine Marines. That is the top limit of my projection of how many men attacked Cardona's estate. I've already instituted a computer check to uncover the names of the others in their Force Recon team."

"Good thinking," Downs said.

"We've solved the identification problem, but it still doesn't tell us why these men killed Cardona," Brennan said.

"We'll ask them when we take them," Downs said.

"We'd better get there first," Burns said. "Remember, it was Patrick Holden who made the connection. Of course, he doesn't know who they really are, since he received their sanitized service records, but he'll still be heading for Tallahassee pretty quickly."

"Then let's get moving," Downs ordered. "Tyler, you head the team. Don't attempt to capture these men, it's too big a risk. Kill them!"

"Kill them?" Burns protested. "Sir, I respectfully request that you reconsider that order."

"General Burns, you are to bring these four back in body bags," Downs said sternly.

Chapter Twelve

Theben Stone sat at an outside table in a cafe on the Boulevard St. Germain, not far from the University of Paris. The temperature had been abnormally mild for the last day of March; on this late Tuesday afternoon, men and women were wearing only sweaters or light jackets to ward off the chill.

The bold Parisian women stared openly at Stone as they walked on the sidewalk in front of his table. They found him irresistible; his ebony face was strikingly handsome; his six-foot-four-inch, 227-pound body was sculpted muscle.

Stone was admiring the passing women as much as they were admiring him, but he carefully avoided looking into their eyes. French women weren't shy; any hint of encouragement on his part and one would join him at his table without a second's hesitation. Normally he wouldn't have been averse to that happening: indulging himself with Parisian women was one of life's greatest pleasures. However, he had a date tonight with Chantelle, one of the city's most elegant fashion models. He intended to take her to dinner in a restaurant in Les Halles, maybe go to a jazz club afterwards, then return to his lavish apartment overlooking the Seine on the Quai d'Orsay, and make love.

He took a small sip from his glass of red bordeaux and sighed contentedly. Life was good.

The thirty-three-year-old Stone had moved to Paris four years ago to take up the life of a painter. His fluent French had allowed him to slide smoothly into the life of the city. He had become a popular man, making friends easily. His Parisian friends described Stone as an intelligent, sensitive man, an artist with an athlete's body and pacifist's soul.

They were totally wrong: Ben Stone was one of the most dangerous men alive.

Before moving to Paris, he had spent eleven years in the Marine Corps; for eight of those years he had been a Force Recon Marine, serving as part of a nine-man team that specialized in fighting behind enemy lines.

He had spent those eight years as a Force Recon with the same eight men, growing closer to them than he was to his own family. They had been his family, and he had been theirs; the nine of them couldn't have been more attached to each other if they had all popped out of the same womb at the same time. Each member of his Force Recon team would have voluntarily given up his life if it would have saved another member's life. It had been true when they were Marines, and it was just as true now when they were civilians.

Only seven of the team survived. Two had been murdered in the jungles of San Tomas, Central America. Mel Snipes and Danny Paige were buried side by side in a small Maryland cemetery on the banks of the Potomac River; seven empty grave sites flanked them. Life or death made no difference, Mel and Danny remained part of the team; the surviving seven visited frequently, and fresh flowers were placed on their graves daily by a florist who received a weekly payment for doing the job.

Five of the seven survivors lived in the United States, one in England. However, they spent as much time together as possible. It was fairly common for one or more of the team to suddenly show up in Paris; it wasn't unusual for Stone to visit one of them on the spur of the moment. The last time all seven had been together had been at Terry Malloy's wedding to Lisa Hewitt last June in Tallahassee, Florida. Malloy had been the first, and still the sole, team member to marry.

After the wedding, Stone and his five other unmarried teammates had spent a week together partying in Tallahassee before he returned to Paris. Terry and his new bride had honeymooned for two weeks in the south of France; on their return home, Terry and Lisa had stopped in Paris to spend time with Stone. The three of them had painted the town red until the newlyweds had returned to the States four days later.

During their years on active military duty, team members had not only spent their working days together, they had also shared their weekends and vacations. Seven years ago, the team had been given a week's R&R after a grueling and dangerous mission in Lebanon. They had chosen to spend it together in Paris since all nine spoke fluent French; one of the requirements of Force Recon was that a Marine speak a foreign language, and each member of Stone's team spoke at least one other language besides French. The week in Paris had been one of the greatest in Stone's life; the city had enchanted him.

During the remainder of his years in the Marine Corps, Stone hadn't returned to Paris, but the city had remained in his heart and mind. When he had resigned from the Corps four years ago, it had been the only place he wanted to live.

Unfortunately, most of his teammates lived far from Paris. That was a detriment because they weren't there to apply the brakes to Stone's one overwhelming fault: he craved the excitement and danger of his previous life. Of the seven survivors, Stone was the only one who still played the game.

In his most recent relapse, he had signed a six-month contract with the CIA to train anti-Communist rebels in Angola. While there, he had planned and led a daring attack on the Cuban Army's headquarters in Luanda. The mission had been successful although the primary target, the Cuban commanding general, survived the attack.

The CIA had been pleased with Stone, and had asked him to take another assignment in Mozambique. He had agreed, but said he wanted to spend a few months in Paris before beginning the assignment. Stone had returned to Paris from Angola last week.

As always, his teammates had been worried about him. There were messages demanding that he contact them upon his return. He had done so, and one of them, David Bowles, had flown over from London.

"Ben, we think you're a damn fool," Bowles had said, noting a new scar on Stone's right arm.

"But you still love me," Stone had answered.

"Yes. But it's damn hard." Bowles had broken out a bottle of Cristal champagne.

"Is that to celebrate my safe return?"

"No, we'll celebrate that later. This is to drink to Danny and Mel."

Stone had immediately understood the significance of Bowles's words. "The CIA agent William Means has been executed!"

"In Cancun, Mexico," Bowles explained. "Terry, Joe, and Lisa went down there—"

"Lisa?" Stone interrupted.

"She insisted on it. Since she married Terry she considers herself part of our team."

"Terry is a lucky man," Stone said.

"I'll drink to that. May the rest of us be so lucky."

The two friends had finished the champagne while Bowles told Stone the tale of Means's execution. Afterwards, they had gone out on the town. The next six days had been spent drinking and partying.

It had only ended two hours ago when Bowles had left for the airport to catch a return flight to London. After his teammate departed, Stone had become depressed. In an attempt to lift his spirits, he had taken a walk, stopping to have a drink at this cafe.

The scene on the sidewalk had cheered him up. He ordered another red wine. The waiter returned quickly, placing the glass of wine on the table. As the waiter stepped away, Stone noticed a man staring at him from an adjoining table. Quickly the man glanced away.

Usually, Stone would've ignored the man's attentions. Parisian women weren't the only ones who found Stone attractive. Paris's gay men were constantly trying to catch his eye and gauge his interest. However, this man didn't act as if he were gay; in fact, he didn't act or look as if this were his normal environment. His facial bone structure looked Slavic, his skin was coarse and dirty, and his black suit was badly cut, cheap, and worn, in sharp contrast with the cafe's other male clientele who were well groomed and well dressed.

Stone thought that the man might be part of a surveillance team. It wasn't uncommon for him to be watched by members of the intelligence community; his reputation as a mercenary was spreading, and prospective employers liked to study him before offering employment. In fact, Dave and he had been followed all week by a surveillance team that obviously consisted of trained professionals. The watchers had attempted to remain incognito, but Dave and Ben were also professionals, and had noticed the tails as soon as they had attached themselves. Since they had made no overt moves, he and Dave had ignored them, believing them to be harmless.

However, this man was different from the ones who had been trailing him for the past week. He was harder and had a deadly look about him. Stone's combat instincts kicked in, and his readiness level stepped up a notch.

Surreptitiously Stone studied the area around the cafe. Through the slowly moving traffic, he picked out two men watching him from a table in a cafe across the street. Feigning nonchalance,

Stone continued his sweep. He was being watched by a man who leaned against the wall to the cafe's left while pretending to read a newspaper; a second was smoking a cigarette on the sidewalk to the right of the cafe. Stone knew there would be more men lurking unobserved.

The obvious attention of the two at the cafe across the street worried him: They were too easy to spot. It meant that they weren't part of a surveillance team, they were part of a liquidation team.

And he was their target.

Ernesto Guavaro and his four Cubans had trailed Stone for the past week, observing his revelries with David Bowles. The discreet but thorough surveillance had been maintained with the help of a ten-man KGB team under the direction of Colonel Aleksander Markov.

"This is too easy. Professionals should be suspicious of us by now," Guavaro had told Markov on the second day of the surveillance. "They must know we are here."

"I'm sure they do," Markov had answered. "They just don't care. They are two friends who are glad to see each other. They wish to drink, enjoy life, and make love to women. It is their only concern. These two Americans are acting the way I would. I understand them because it is a very Russian thing to do. Comrades are comrades. Don't you Cubans act like this?"

"No," Guavaro had lied, remembering a time in Cuba when men acted in exactly the same manner.

"I pity you then," Markov had said.

Markov's attitude irritated Guavaro. Ever since Gorbachev had ended the Cold War in 1989, the

Thomas L. Muldoon

Russians had identified more with their American enemies than with their Cuban allies. Russia and Cuba were drifting apart as the island's economy became a bigger burden on the Soviets.

For the rest of the week, the combined Russian and Cuban group kept a tight surveillance on the pair. Meanwhile, a KGB research team unsuccessfully attempted to uncover facts about their lives. When the results of the research team were presented to Markov, he angrily remarked, "Who are these fellows? Were they just born four years ago?"

"It seems so, comrade," the leader of the KGB searcher team reported. "It is a complete mystery to us. We can't find any records on them."

"They must have come from somewhere! Guavaro, you're sure Stone is the man you saw in Cardona's study?"

"Positive, Colonel Markov. There's no mistake about that. Bowles could be one of the others. Two of the attackers were about his height and weight."

In keeping with the termination directive issued by his superiors, Markov had ordered a Czechoslovakian "wet" team brought into Paris. Considering the shambles that the former Eastern Bloc was in, it was quite an accomplishment in itself. Publicly, Czechoslovakia was in the process of becoming democratic; privately, old-line Communists were still in control of much of the state's apparatus. However, their hold was tenuous, and they didn't like to risk their assets outside their own country. Markov had appealed to KGB headquarters; Moscow Center, as KGB agents referred to it, pressured the Czechs into supplying the "wet" team.

It wasn't that Markov or Guavaro couldn't have terminated Stone; neither were virgins in the field of murder. They just didn't want to be bogged down by the act. Their goal was to root out Stone's henchmen, and to capture the electronics expert. Stone was obviously not an electronics expert, but Bowles possibly could be.

When Bowles had left for the airport, Guavaro, Markov, and their teams had followed, hoping that if Bowles wasn't the electronics expert, he would at least lead them to someone else.

Before leaving, Markov had issued an order to the leader of the seven-man Czech "wet" team: "Terminate the black man."

It didn't come as a surprise to Stone's teammates that he would draw some country's attention sooner or later. They knew he was their weak link, the one who inevitably would cause their downfall. Yet they refused to censure him for continuing to work with the CIA and other free-world intelligence services. In their eyes, Stone was entitled to live any way he chose; they had all sworn the same oath and taken the same risks, and they would always stand together.

After they had been evacuated from San Tomas, carrying what remained of Danny Paige and Mel Snipes, the seven of them had made official complaints against Cardona. The Pentagon and CIA had rejected those complaints, refusing to take any action against Cardona. Their official complaints had been destroyed, and they had been ordered to forget what had happened in San Tomas.

They couldn't stomach those orders; it was strictly against their code of honor and duty. All seven immediately resigned from the Marine Corps.

The seven of them swore a solemn oath to avenge Danny and Mel. When they swore it, they did so with their eyes open, knowing that they were sealing their own fate. When it came time to execute Cardona for Danny's and Mel's murders, they expected to suffer the consequences: Some, or all, of them would die; the survivors would be hunted, and eventually tracked down, by the authorities.

It had taken more than a year of planning. The operation had been carried out with greater success than expected: They hadn't suffered any casualties. It was inconsequential to them that, to execute Cardona, they had to kill nearly four hundred of his soldiers, security guards, and associates; those deaths were necessary acts of war. However, they did regret the death of Deputy Throne: he was a civilian who had nothing to do with Cardona.

The attack had taken place sixteen months earlier, but they knew it hadn't been forgotten and that they were being hunted. They knew they were living on borrowed time. It was a tribute to the tactical genius of their leader, Joe Craig, and the brilliance of their electronics expert, Ted Billings, that they had survived the attack and remained undetected for so long.

The unexpected sixteen-month grace period had allowed Joe Craig to form contingency plans that would guarantee their disappearance when Ben Stone's obsession inevitably caused their discovery. There were new identities waiting for them now, plus, courtesy of Juan Cardona, an abundance of cash to finance their new lives. Ted Billings had successfully dispersed the money taken from Cardona's vault into seven untraceable bank accounts, five million dollars for each team member; under Joe's direction, Ted had used the remaining millions of dollars to purchase houses in various locations around the world to use as safe houses.

They were stocked with weapons, automobiles, and other necessary equipment.

David Bowles was a round-faced, green-eyed, thirty-one-year-old Texan whose sandy hair was receding. His vast charm, gregarious manner, and ready wit made him a popular man wherever he went. He was also a very tough man; the six-foot, 185-pound Bowles had served ten years in the Marine Corps, eight in Force Recon, and attained the rank of staff sergeant.

Bowles was a budding novelist who lived in London. He was also the only one of Ben Stone's Force Recon teammates to live outside the United States. Stone's teammates had been concerned about the big man. Joe Craig, the team's leader, had asked Bowles to check in on Stone after he returned from Africa.

Bowles would have flown over to Paris anyway within a week or so, but the request from Craig had sent him there immediately. If there was one person Bowles looked up to in this world, it was Joe Craig. In fact, the whole team felt that way about Craig: He was the rock their team had been built on.

As usual, Bowles's visit to Stone had turned into a six-day party. On the first day, Bowles noticed that a surveillance team had latched on to the pair of them. Stone had assured him it wasn't anything remarkable, claiming he was often under surveillance by friendlies. Since the watchers hadn't done anything but watch for six days, Bowles had accepted Stone's assessment.

However, Bowles's view had changed as soon as his taxi pulled away from Stone's apartment and the surveillance team followed him.

"Damn it," he had muttered aloud in English, causing the French taxi driver to inquire if there was a problem.

There certainly was, but Bowles couldn't tell the taxi driver about it. "No," he said in French to the driver. "I'm just sorry I have to leave Paris."

The driver accepted that and turned his attention to the road. In the backseat, Bowles considered the situation. It was obvious that the team's grace period had ended. A foreign intelligence agency must have identified Stone as one of Cardona's executioners. That intelligence agency had attached a surveillance team to Stone, and Bowles's visit had identified him as one of Stone's associates. Now the surveillance team was watching him, waiting for him to lead it to more of Cardona's executioners.

The entire surveillance team appeared to be following him, which meant it no longer cared about Ben Stone, which meant Ben was in great danger. Someone must have been left behind to eliminate Ben.

Bowles fought down an urge to return to Stone's aid. Joe Craig had foreseen this exact scenario, and had forbidden Bowles to deviate from set procedure.

"Ben's on his own for now," Bowles muttered to himself.

Bowles paid the taxi fare at the entrance to British Airways at De Gaulle Airport. Inside, he used a public phone to telephone Stone's apartment, hoping to catch Ben at home. After six rings, an answering machine picked up. Bowles didn't leave a message. He hoped that Ben had realized the surveillance team had deserted him, and that he was in danger. Like Bowles, Stone had a procedure to follow which Joe Craig had designed to cover this situation.

Bowles's orders were specific: He was to warn the rest of his teammates. Unfortunately, the French phone system was still primitive in many ways. Ted Billings had been unable to establish an untraceable communications system that would work from a French public telephone; he had set up such a system, but only in the team's safe houses scattered in various areas of France. Bowles couldn't go to one of those safe houses with a surveillance team sticking to his backside.

Bowles boarded his plane to London. He had to remain calm until he returned to London. A system existed there that had been specifically designed for him by Ted Billings.

Two of the watchers boarded behind him. From his first-class seat, he watched them out of the corner of his eye as they passed, heading for their seats in the rear. One was unquestionably Cuban; the other was presumably Russian, since a pack of Russian cigarettes was sticking out of a shirt pocket. Bowles's anxiety level increased.

He waved away the stewardess's offer of champagne and asked for tomato juice. Sipping his juice, he planned his next move.

Stone figured that he had only minutes before the professional killers would make their move. He took a long look at the beautiful women strolling down the tree-lined street. Regret welled up inside him. He was going to miss Paris.

It suddenly occurred to him that Bowles was also in danger. The killers now watching him must have been left behind by the surveillance unit that had trailed them all week. His first thought was to go to David's aid. He dismissed it quickly. David was a professional; he would spot the tails, analyze the situation, and react appropriately. David would obey Joe Craig's orders, just as Stone must obey the ones Craig had issued to him.

Craig had planned for the team being discovered. He had designed meticulous plans of escape covering all possible contingencies. Stone had several routes he could follow, but first he must extricate himself from his current entrapment.

He casually ordered a third glass of wine. When it was delivered, he asked the waiter for the location of the toilet.

"In the back of the cafe, monsieur," the waiter said.

Stone slid his chair back and stood up. His table was at the sidewalk's edge, so he had to walk through the other tables to reach the cafe door. As he navigated the narrow space between tables, he passed directly behind the chair of the man in the bad suit.

The killer saw Stone coming and turned his head away, pretending to watch a woman walking on the sidewalk. In doing this, bad suit exposed the back of his neck to Stone.

Stone stumbled slightly, putting his left hand out to steady himself against the back of bad suit's chair. Out of Stone's left sleeve snapped a five-inch, icepick-bladed combat knife. Stone drove it expertly into bad suit's spinal column. Stone quickly withdrew the knife. Bad suit's head slumped, and blood trickled down his shirt collar.

Stone continued walking toward the door, expecting to hear a call of alarm behind him, but none of the cafe's patrons had noticed bad suit's death.

Stone safely entered the cafe. Apparently, none of the killers on the street had noticed bad suit's demise either. The interior was poorly lit. It took a second or two for his eyes to adjust to the dim light.

With sight came the knowledge that he had made a potentially fatal mistake. Bad suit wasn't the only killer in the cafe; another was lounging at the bar just inside the door. The man was staring at Stone, his hand gripping a pistol under his voluminous cloth jacket.

Stone still had the combat knife cupped in his left hand. The man spotted it and drew his pistol. Before the pistol cleared the man's jacket, Stone threw the combat knife underhanded. The deadly blade flew unerringly into the man's right eye. The man released his pistol and brought both hands to his face. Blood poured through his fingers, and his dead body fell off the bar stool.

The busboy walked in from the kitchen carrying a tray of glasses just as the body hit the floor. He dropped the tray in horror. The crash of breaking glass galvanized Stone. He bolted past the busboy and entered the kitchen. An old woman was standing there.

"Door!" Stone demanded.

She pointed toward the rear of the kitchen. Stone raced by her and out the back door. It led into a narrow alley. To his left was the Boulevard St. Germain; Stone turned right, but the alley ended in a locked steel door leading to another building. He yanked at the door. It wouldn't budge.

Stone rolled up his right pants leg and removed the Spitter from its leg holster. He said a short prayer of thanks to Joe Craig; normally, Stone went unarmed around Paris. Craig had changed that after Stone had returned from Angola. David Bowles had delivered Craig's new order: Stone was to carry weapons at all times. Bowles had explained that Craig had become concerned about Stone's high visibility, and that Stone was isolated in Paris without another team member nearby to help in an emergency. Stone had scoffed at Craig's apprehensions, telling Bowles that Craig was becoming a worrywart, but he had started carrying weapons. Everyone on the team followed Joe's orders without deviation.

Craig had drummed into each team member that a Spitter could only be used if absolutely necessary. The use of a Spitter would bring American intelligence agencies running. The CIA and Military Intelligence would know the Spitter came from the break-in at Kirk's Armory. Whoever used the Spitter would be identified as a former Force Recon Marine. The logical next step would be to identify the other members of his team. Within a day, the whole team would be fugitives.

Stone didn't see any way of escaping without using his Spitter. He just hoped David Bowles had sounded the alarm to the rest of the team.

Holding the Spitter at the ready, Stone stepped cautiously out of the alley.

London, England

Changing time zones in his flight across the English Channel, David Bowles arrived at London's Heathrow airport at four-thirty p.m., exactly the same time as his departure from Paris. Since he possessed an Alien Resident stamp, he breezed through passport control in Terminal Four, losing his two watchers, who remained bogged down at the entry point. It wasn't really important; the watchers would surely have additional manpower waiting outside.

Like every member of his team, Bowles was a consummate professional who had gone through arduous training to become Force Recon. He'd been through Army jump school, Army Ranger school, and Army Special Forces school; he'd trained at the Navy Seals school and had undertaken many hours of training at other clandestine speciality schools.

He didn't panic. This wasn't the first time he'd been followed, although it was the first time his team hadn't been close enough to provide support. He calmly collected his bag from the luggage carousel and walked out of the customs area.

In the open air, he took stock of his surroundings as he casually headed for the taxi stand. Two men standing by the road were clearly watching him. He hesitated, allowing other passengers to take the first couple of waiting taxis. He climbed into the sixth taxi in line.

"Where to, mate?" the driver of the distinctively shaped London cab asked.

"Harrod's."

The huge department store wasn't his final destination. Bowles owned an expensive flat in Mayfair near Hyde Park, which he wouldn't go near until he had shaken his tails.

"As fast as possible, please."

"Certainly, mate," the driver said. "But traffic is heavy at this time of day."

Bowles was counting on heavy traffic. The taxicab couldn't outrun any of his watchers' cars. London cabs were reliable, and had a great turning radius in the city's narrow streets, but they were very slow, especially on the high-speed motorway from Heathrow to London. But the heavy traffic crush was sure to catch the cars of some of his watchers, which would give him a few less people to deal with when he made his move.

The two watchers from the plane came hurrying out of the terminal doors as his cab pulled away. Bowles looked out the cab's rear window. A green British Ford had pulled to the curb to pick up the two men. On the cab's tail was a white Taurus; three cars back was a blue Volkswagen. Sitting in the passenger's seat of each car was one of the watchers who had been waiting outside the terminal. Bowles knew that there was at least one watcher's car ahead of his cab, and probably several more behind. He had faith that not many of them would be close enough for him to worry about by the time his cab reached Harrod's.

The traffic became heavier as the cab approached central London. It appeared to Bowles that only two of the trackers' cars were still with his cab.

It was also becoming darker as his cab inched toward Harrod's. He made a decision: He wrote his address on a slip of paper and took one hundred pounds from his wallet. He passed the money and paper to the driver.

"I'm jumping off at the next tube station," Bowles said. "Take my bag to that address and give it to my doorman. Keep the change for your trouble."

"Thanks, mate. There's an Underground station on the Green Line straight ahead."

In front of Harrod's, Bowles jumped out and joined the pedestrians on the sidewalk. The British might have a reputation for being quiet and reserved, but it wasn't true; Bowles knew that the first rule of living in London was to never stand in the way of an Englishman who was rushing to a pub or to his home after work. Bowles had violated that rule; he had barely made the sidewalk before he was brushed aside by a man with a briefcase. Swung partially around by the bump, Bowles saw the green Ford pull to the curb and disgorge the two watchers from the plane. The white Taurus was there as well; one man came out of that car.

Bowles tried to blend in with the throng. The congestion became heavier at the entrance to Knightsbridge Underground Station. Advancing with the crush of the crowd, he went through the ticket machines and down the people-glutted escalator.

Luck was with him. A Green Line train pulled into the platform as he hit the bottom of the steep escalator. He rushed for it, as did every other person in the station. He had to fight his way into a car. Once aboard, he looked back. His followers were pushing their way toward the subway train. Two of them made the train before the doors closed; only one made it into his car.

The train hummed through the tunnel. Bowles didn't exit until it reached the Green Park station. As soon as it stopped, he rushed through the door and became part of the human stream heading for the up escalator. Both of his followers exited the train, but the surge of the departing subway riders kept them from closing in on Bowles. At the escalator's top, Bowles was thirty feet ahead of the first watcher, who was hopelessly trapped on the escalator.

Bowles briskly walked out to Piccadilly Street, quickly rounded the corner, and reentered the Underground through the Stratton Street entrance.

He sped through the ticket machines and pushed his way onto the down escalator, glancing back for his pursuers. There were none; he'd lost them outside.

He rode the first train that came into the station, getting off at Covent Garden. To make sure he had shaken his pursuers, he ducked in and out of pubs, doubled back on his trail, and finally studied the crowd from the doorway of an Indian restaurant for several minutes.

Satisfied that he had evaded his tails, he went to a public telephone box and dialed a London number. A machine answered.

"You have reached the offices of the Evacuation Service. Leave a message." The message was Ted Billings's little joke.

Bowles removed from his pocket a gold cigarette lighter with a Marine Corps globe-and-anchor decoration on its side. The lighter was a miniature transmitter; the decoration was the transmitter's key. He placed the lighter against the phone's mouthpiece and pressed the globe decoration three times, stopped, then pressed it twice more. It sent an electronic code to the answering machine.

Bowles put the phone to his ear and waited while the answering machine dialed a second telephone. When it answered, he repeated the process of sending a code with the lighter. It dialed another machine. After the fifth machine had answered, Bowles tapped a more complicated code with the lighter. It dialed a new number.

In the United States, Ted Billings answered the phone. It was after six in London, one p.m. Ted's time.

"It's Dave. We're blown. Evacuate immediately!"

"What's your situation?" Billings asked.

"I'm clear, but Ben is in trouble."

"Right. I'll pass that on to Joe."

"I'll wait for Ben at his first safe house."

"Maybe I should fly over there after I've warned the guys," Billings said. "You two might need help."

"No! We'll be all right. Besides, Joe's escape plan for us doesn't include you."

"You two stay safe."

"No problem," Bowles said. "Semper Fi, buddy."

After Billings hung up, Bowles redialed the first London number. When the machine answered, he tapped out a destruct code on the lighter's key. He hung up and walked away from the public phone. The first machine's phone recorder was automatically issuing instructions to all the other answering machines along the line; the machines would wait three minutes before self-destructing, melting all equipment and destroying the telephonic connections. Since the telephone company wasn't aware of any of the phones' existence, there would be no trail for anyone to follow. Ted Billings had used his electronic magic to insure it.

Bowles rushed toward Charing Cross train station to begin his elaborate escape plan. He wasn't heading for his London apartment; he would never approach it again. He was heading for his hideaway apartment in Brighton where he had stashed clothes and documents. After collecting his new identity papers, he'd cross the channel and make his way to Milan, Italy, where he was scheduled to hook up with Ben Stone. From there, the pair would journey to the States and rejoin the rest of their team.

Thomas L. Muldoon

Boston, Massachusetts

Ted Billings's first inclination to jump on an airplane and help Dave and Ben escape Europe had been anticipated by Joe Craig; Joe had issued him strict orders forbidding it.

Billings obeyed orders, especially Joe's orders. It had been driven into him in the Corps along with ideas of honor and duty. The team had all laughed at the Marine Corps's bullshit, but underneath it all, each of them fervently believed the Corps's credos.

"We are Marines," Captain Dan Paige had often said to his team. "On top of that, we are Force Recon Marines. We are the elite of the elite! We protect and avenge our own. We never abandon them."

Joe had echoed that sentiment after Danny and Mel were tortured and murdered, "No one else cares, so we have tried Cardona and found him guilty. His sentence is death. He will be executed by us. Our honor demands it."

Billings had joined the team as a brown bar, a second lieutenant who had just graduated from Massachusetts Institute of Technology. In a typical Marine Corps foul-up, instead of being assigned a job that best utilized his genius in electronics and computers, he'd been assigned as an infantry officer after completing Officer Candidate School and the Basic School at Quantico, Virginia.

In a strange twist of fate, it had turned out to be exactly the right move for him. He loved the infantry. He had volunteered for all the difficult combat training schools, finally qualifying for Marine Force

Recon. The day he had joined the team, he felt completely at home.

Despite being an officer, he'd readily followed Joe Craig's suggestions. Even Danny Paige, who held the rank of captain, had listened to Joe. Craig was a born Marine, the finest on the team, which meant the finest in the Marine Corps. Danny Paige frequently urged Craig to apply for Officer's Candidate School, feeling that if Craig was an officer, the Marine Corps would benefit more from his outstanding leadership, tactical planning, and coolness in combat. Craig refused, stating he wasn't officer material. Danny Paige wasn't fooled, nor were the rest of Craig's teammates; they all understood the real reason behind Joe's refusal: he didn't want to leave the team.

No one on their team would accept any promotion that would separate them from the others. They were a perfectly trained and harmonious group of men; something special: the best in the Marine Corps, which meant the best in the U.S. armed forces, which ultimately meant the best in the world.

After Paige's and Snipes's murders, Billings, then twenty-nine, had resigned from the Corps like the rest of his teammates. He had returned to graduate school at Massachusetts Institute of Technology, where he completed his doctorate in record time. During graduate school, he'd started his own business, marketing his computer and electronic inventions to the Defense Department and commercial firms. He retained his more exotic inventions for his own and his teammates' uses.

Billings had kept himself in tiptop shape. Joe Craig had demanded that they all keep in combat physical condition. At six feet and 186 pounds, he could run all day and fight with the best of them. His curly brown hair and blue eyes attracted scores of women, but he remained unattached, knowing the day would come when he would have to run and hide. It was too bad, really; he was quite attached to a girl from his hometown of Seabrook, New Hampshire.

Billings unscrewed the bottom of his telephone and attached a cigar-shaped electronic device to the wires inside. He tapped in a telephone number using the buttons on its face, and hit the device's control button, which automatically dialed the number he had entered while preventing any telephone company computer from registering the call. In Tallahassee, a phone rang and Roberto Gonzalez answered.

"Berto, it's Ted. Is Joe there?"

"No, he's playing basketball with Cece." Gonzalez was referring to Cecil Jones. "But he has his beeper with him."

"Beep him. When he telephones you, tell him the shit has hit the fan in Europe. Ben and David are up to their ears in it. David has just passed the word for us to evack."

"Goddamn! Do they need help?"

"David says no, but he'd say that anyway. Joe's plan won't let us help them, in any event."

"Shit, Ted, you know Joe will want to go. We'll have to chain him down to prevent him."

"I know, but just remind him that he's the man. He can't go get himself killed and leave us leaderless."

"I'll try, compadre. You out now?"

"Within an hour. I'll see you sometime this afternoon."

"Right, amigo," Gonzalez said. "Semper Fi."

Billings hung up. He looked around at the computers, large screen TV, stereo, and other furniture in his study. It didn't matter that he was leaving it all behind; if the truth be known, he had been bored silly for the past year.

He took one final scan to make sure he hadn't left behind any weapons or sensitive electronic devices, such as the machine he'd used on the telephone. Satisfied, he walked out of his home forever. His escape plan had been worked out a year ago, and everything he would need in the future had been stashed at his first hideaway.

France

Ben Stone came out of the alley. Waiting for him were two of the killers, each facing in opposite directions.

"Here he is," the one facing him yelled loudly in a language which Stone recognized as Czech.

Before the Czech could bring his machine pistol to bear, and before the other Czech could turn around, Stone hosed them with his Spitter. Fired from a distance of less than three feet, the weapon's projectiles shredded the two Czechs.

Stone ran down the sidewalk away from the cafe. Twenty feet in front of him, a parked car's door opened, and a third Czech stepped out. Crouching behind the open door, the Czech opened up with an Uzi. Stone dove between two parked cars. As he was in the air, one of the Czech's bullets smacked into his leg.

The wound didn't slow Stone down. He barely hit the ground between the two cars before he popped up, and fired his Spitter on full automatic at the Czech shielded by the car door. A Spitter's ammunition was potent, but it wasn't armor-piercing. The Czech would have remained perfectly safe if he had stayed shielded behind the car's metal door. Stupidly, the Czech stood up to fire through the open window of the already opened door: his head popped like a melon as the Spitter's slugs hit it.

Stone glanced down at his leg; he was bleeding heavily, but there wasn't time to stem the flow. Slugs started smacking into the vehicles around him. Crouching low, he stepped completely into the traffic-congested Boulevard St. Germain and started running down the street toward the traffic light.

The two remaining Czechs, who had been sitting in the cafe across the street, indiscriminately fired at him with their automatic weapons. The bullets missed Stone but struck innocent pedestrians as well as occupants of the cars halted in traffic.

Bullets were buzzing around Stone when he reached the stoplight. He opened the door of the first car in line, a Fiat, and pulled the driver from behind the wheel.

"Pardon," he said in French. "But this is an emergency. Lie flat on the street so you won't be hit by a bullet."

The driver did what he was told. Stone jumped behind the Fiat's wheel and roared away. The Czechs continued firing at the Fiat's rear.

"Shit," Stone muttered. "These two fuckers are insane. They're mowing down everything in sight."

Once he was out of range, he made a right turn and slowed down. It would take ten or fifteen minutes for the police to sort out the confusion behind him. He would have that grace period before they started looking for the Fiat. In the meantime, he stopped at all traffic lights and stop signs. He didn't want to draw the attention of the police by committing a traffic violation.

He drove across the Seine on the Pont de Sully and parked the Fiat near the Bastille. There was a package lying on the backseat. Stone grabbed it and ripped it open. Inside was a sheer black women's slip.

"A present for your lover," Stone said with a laugh. "It won't look as good on me, but I'll wear it anyway."

He rolled up his pants and wrapped his leg with the black slip, tugging it tight enough to stop his bleeding. Then he abandoned the Fiat.

Stone limped down several streets until he discovered a Peugeot that looked as if it had been parked for more than a day. Breaking into it was simple. He hot-wired the Peugeot and drove away. While he was moving, he turned on the car's radio; a newsman was speaking about the gunfight on the Boulevard St. Germain. The newsman said there were many deaths and injuries.

"Every damn gendarme in France will be looking for me now," Stone muttered as he drove along within the speed limit. "And a black man my size isn't going to go unnoticed for long."

He figured it wouldn't be long before the police blocked all avenues of escape from Paris. He had to get into the countryside before that happened. Unfortunately, his safe house within the city limits was on the opposite side of town from where he was. There wasn't enough time to get to it, which meant he had to abandon the documents and equipment necessary for him to get into Italy and ultimately out of Europe.

Fortunately, Joe Craig had taken into account

that a hasty evacuation of Paris might be necessary, and had developed a backup plan for Stone's escape.

Stone drove out of Paris. On the city's limits, he took the motorway toward Reims. In that city was another safe house which contained the necessary documents for his alternate escape route. The first step on that route was to reach Reims without being arrested. Luckily, it was now dark, making it difficult for any policeman in a car to determine the skin color of any driver on the motorway. He was taking a chance driving the stolen Peugeot; the owner might discover it missing and inform the police. But he had no other choice.

He felt blood dripping down his leg again, but he ignored it. The wound wasn't serious; the Czech's round had passed cleanly through Stone's leg without doing any damage to major muscles, arteries, or bones.

The one problem that really bothered him was how to reach David Bowles and alert him that the backup plan was in effect. The original plan called for Stone and Bowles to use forged military identification and forged orders, which would allow them to fly out of Milan with American soldiers who were being routinely rotated back to the States. That was out of the question now as far as Stone was concerned; the documents necessary to bypass the airport's civilian control areas were in his safe house in Paris. Bowles could still use the escape route through Milan, but David would never abandon him.

That left only the alternate plan. The first step of that plan called for him to reach Reims safely.

Chapter Thirteen

London, England

After losing Bowles on the crowded Piccadilly Street outside Green Park Underground Station, Guavaro had blown up at Markov.

"I told you it was too easy," Guavaro had said to the Russian. "Bowles is a professional. He knew we were following him."

The Russian had glared at him and said, "I'll find the bastard!"

Still angry, the two had returned to the Underground and taken a train to Kensington. The Russians had a safe house in that area. Inside the Victorian townhouse, they were informed of Stone's escape and the uproar in Paris.

"Fucking Czechs," Markov roared. "They can't do anything right."

Markov telephoned his superior in Moscow. It

was a mistake, Markov ended up frying on the grill.

"Let me explain the facts of life to you, Markov," his KGB superior had said. "We are unhappy with you. The high command and the politicians are anxious over the shootout in the Paris street. They are afraid that our country will be connected to it. At the moment, we are trying to lull the world with our new spirit of glasnost. We do not want the world to think that Russia is governed by a pack of mad dogs. Do you understand what that means?"

"Yes, sir," Markov stammered. "You want more discreetness."

"What we want is that electronics expert," Markov's KGB boss said. "Capture him quickly and do not cause us any further embarrassments. You know the price of failure."

Markov turned white with terror. However, Guavaro wasn't gloating; he was just hanging up on a conversation with his own superior.

"Fidel is tiring of your failures," Guavaro's superior warned. "I don't believe I need to explain what that means."

Georgia

At two p.m. on Tuesday, eight p.m. in Europe, Joe Craig, Roberto Gonzalez, Cecil Jones, and the Malloys were just entering Georgia on Route 319, a two-lane, tree-lined road connecting Tallahassee, Florida, with Thomasville, Georgia. Lisa and Terry, who was driving, were alone in their white Porsche following Craig's blue Volvo. Gonzalez was driving the Volvo, Jones sat next to him; Craig was in the rear, studying papers he had taken from a briefcase.

Terry Malloy drove silently, occasionally taking

quick glances at his wife. He was concerned about her, wondering if she would be able to cope with the rigors of running and hiding from the world's major intelligence services.

Malloy was a California farm boy who had found his purpose in life in the Marine Corps. He'd even loved boot camp at Parris Island, where he had befriended Joe Craig, an Illinois farm boy. They became inseparable.

Malloy had turned out to be an exemplary recruit; the only one better was Craig. Joe had finished first in the recruit class, Malloy second. Their goal was to become Force Recon; after boot camp, they volunteered for every training camp necessary to attain that goal. In every training unit, Craig placed number one with Malloy a close second. This would have caused jealousy and hatred in most men, but it hadn't in Malloy or Craig; neither ever considered or acted as if they were in competition, instead they cooperated with each other at every opportunity.

Terry Malloy was a handsome man with blond hair and blue eyes, Craig was an average looking man with blue eyes and brown hair. Both stood five feet, eleven inches tall and were in superb physical condition.

From the moment they met, Malloy knew he'd always be Pancho to Craig's Cisco. Craig was a leader, a man others followed. Malloy didn't denigrate his own leadership ability; he just knew that Joe Craig was someone special. For the first time in his life, Malloy had found someone he admired.

By the time they had qualified as Force Recon Marines, the two had been bonded as brothers. Astonishingly, the Marine Corps recognized what it had in Malloy and Craig and assigned them to the same Force Recon unit.

Craig had the same remarkable effect on his new teammates. The nine-man team had evolved into a close-knit family, sharing the same code of ethics and the same goals. The nine men had developed an intimate feeling for each other; they ate together, went to war together, and played together. It molded them into the finest Force Recon team in the Marine Corps.

In many ways, the nine teammates had an idyllic existence, even though the team's assignments were often bloody and dangerous. They truly loved each other, and believed they would stay together forever.

Luis Cardona had shattered that dream, and the U.S. Armed Services Combined Covert Warfare Group had destroyed the surviving team members' spirit. The U.S. military's and government's refusal to prosecute Cardona for killing American servicemen made each team member question their military careers. Each went through a period of inner turmoil: Were they risking their lives for a government that didn't care about them? Were they serving under military superiors who didn't value their lives? Was a foreign dictator more important to U.S. military and government leaders than a murdered Marine?

If it hadn't been for Joe Craig, the finest Force Recon team in the Marines would have died a disillusioned death. Joe brought them out of their blue funk.

"If they won't punish Cardona, then we will," Craig had said. Simple words, but they had brought the team back together.

Joe had developed a plan to avenge Mel and

Danny. It would take years to implement, but in the end, Cardona would be executed, his drug and gun-running operations ruined, and it would ruin the people in the U.S. government and military who had protected Cardona and condoned his illegal activities. Participation was strictly voluntary, and any of them who chose to participate could expect to end up being killed or being a fugitive. To a man, the seven remaining team members had voted to avenge Mel and Danny, and to hell with the consequences.

The first part of the plan had been to resign from the Marine Corps, which each of them had done when their enlistment had ended. As civilians, they began preparations to attack Cardona in his Coral Cove estate. Long months of intelligence work and planning had preceded the attack.

During the planning period, Craig discovered that the sheriff of Coral Cove had a daughter attending Florida State University in Tallahassee, where all but Ben Stone and Ted Billings had taken up residence. Craig made a cold-blooded decision to use the young girl; Malloy, who was the handsomest man in the unit, was assigned to develop a relationship with her. Craig's reasoning was that nobody would question Lisa Hewitt bringing her boyfriend and his friends to Coral Cove, which would enable the team to move freely around their objective.

Malloy had approached the job with enthusiasm after his first look at Lisa walking across campus; he never foresaw that the prey would entrap the hunter. After only a few dates, Malloy fell in love with Lisa.

Oddly, Craig wasn't upset; he seemed to have anticipated Malloy's attachment to Lisa. Before

Malloy had come to grips with his emerging feelings, Joe had walked up to him one day, wrapped his arms around him, and said, "I'm happy for you, buddy. It's about time you fell in love. Lisa is terrific. You'll both be very happy."

Craig had never insulted him by asking if he wanted to pull out of the operation. Craig knew that Malloy's feelings for Lisa wouldn't interfere with his commitment to Cardona's execution of Cardona for the murders of Snipes and Paige.

A month after the successful attack on Cardona's estate, David Bowles had moved to London. At his going-away party, Dave had said to Terry, "I'll be back for the wedding."

"What wedding?" Terry had asked.

Dave made a gesture toward Craig, who had answered for all of them. "Quit fucking around. Marry the girl."

A month later during the Christmas holiday, Terry had taken Lisa to Key West. On the balcony of their room at the Marriot, Terry had professed his love for her.

"I love you, too," she said, kissing him.

"You might not after I finish telling you this story," Terry had said.

He had confessed his involvement with the attack on Cardona's estate. He had told her about Cardona murdering Danny Paige and Mel Snipes, and the team's need to execute Cardona for their deaths.

"Did you use me?" she had asked.

"Yes," he had admitted, conceding that she had been his, and his friends', excuse for spending time in Coral Cove while they planned the attack on Cardona's estate.

"It hurt to use you," he had said. "I fell in love

with you very quickly, which wasn't part of the plan. But I couldn't stop; I had an obligation to my teammates. I couldn't ignore that obligation."

Lisa had been upset. She had cried and accused Terry and his friends of being murderers. Strangely, her accusation wasn't based on Cardona's execution nor the deaths of nearly four hundred men during the attack. Being Southern, Lisa had understood the team's sense of honor and its desire to revenge the deaths of Mel and Danny. But she did condemn him and the others for the death of Ed Throne, a man she had known all of her life.

Terry accepted the blame without telling her that Roberto Gonzalez was the man whose assignment was to knock out the police station, and who had set off the gas that killed Throne.

"It was an unforeseeable accident," he had explained. "We didn't intend for him to die."

"I need to think," she had said. "Leave me alone for a day."

He had checked into another room, and sat biting his fingernails while she thought about what had happened. It had taken thirty-nine hours, but finally Lisa had decided to forgive him—and the rest of the team. Of course, it hadn't hurt Terry's cause that Lisa loved him more than life itself.

They had married in June 1989 and were ecstatically happy.

Lisa had become a de facto part of the team. When they had discovered William Means's location, and he was going to accompany Joe to execute the former CIA agent, Lisa had insisted on taking part in the execution. Lisa had strolled down the street wearing a thong bikini, distracting

Means long enough for Joe Craig to slip into the doorway behind the former CIA agent.

The two cars neared Atlanta, where the group had purchased an expensive townhouse under an assumed name.

"What next?" Lisa asked when she saw the city's skyline.

"We follow the escape plan. We're blown now," Terry admitted. "We'll never live anywhere under our own names again."

She turned pale as she realized the full implications.

"I'm a liability to you and the rest of the guys," she suddenly said.

"You're not a liability to me. You're an asset. My life isn't complete without you."

"I love you, Terry. I won't let you or any of the guys be captured because of me."

"You won't. Joe's escape plans have included you from the day he realized I loved you. Besides, we put it to a vote more than a year ago, and all agreed that you were one of us."

Tears ran down her face. She unbuckled her seat belt, leaned over, and kissed her husband. "I love you and I love them too. But if it becomes too big of a risk, I want you to leave me behind."

"None of us will agree to that. You're going with me, and that's it. Each of the guys will tell you the same thing. You know they will."

Lisa had accepted these men as family; she was closer to them than she was to her own brother. They reciprocated those feelings. She knew Terry was telling the truth.

"Okay, darling. I don't want us to separate anyway." Lisa removed his hand from the gear shift, kissed it, and held it with a contented smile on her face.

The two cars reached Atlanta just before six p.m. Terry followed Craig into a high-crime section of south Atlanta. Joe stopped, and motioned Terry to park the Porsche at the curb.

"Roll down your window, honey," Terry said. "And say goodbye to the Porsche."

Terry turned off the car but left the keys in the ignition.

"It will be stolen within minutes," he said. "It will disappear forever, leaving no clue that we were here."

They piled into the backseat of the Volvo. She was wedged snugly between her husband and Joe Craig. For the first time, she realized her husband was armed: his concealed weapon pressed against her side. She shifted away from it only to discover that Joe was also carrying a weapon under his shirt.

"Sorry about this, Lisa," Craig said.

"It's all right. I knew this might happen when I married Terry."

"Never thought we'd have a BAM on the team," Cecil Jones quipped from the front seat. "Not that Lisa fills any description of any BAM I've ever seen."

The men laughed. Lisa nudged her husband. "What's a BAM?"

"It's a woman Marine," Terry explained. "BAM means 'broad-assed Marine.' "

"That sounds like an insult," she said. "I'm going to have to teach you guys to appreciate women more. I won't have any male chauvinists around me."

"You can't teach us to appreciate women more

than we do," Jones said. "We've appreciated them all over the world!"

Lisa blushed, and the men laughed again. Gonzalez pulled the Volvo over to the curb.

"The townhouse is two blocks away," Joe said. "We don't want anyone to see us pull up there in this car. We'll walk from here. Berto, get out with us. Cece will get rid of the Volvo."

Cecil Jones slipped behind the wheel when they all had exited.

"Where's he taking it?" Lisa asked.

"To join the Porsche," her husband answered.

The four of them walked two blocks to an exclusive complex of attached townhouses. Suspicious of their approach by foot, the gate guard stopped them and demanded to know why they wished to enter. Craig had anticipated such a response, and had called ahead to authorize their entry.

"Mr. Sealey left our names. We are using his townhouse for a few days," Craig said. "I'm Bill Hatfield."

The guard checked his roster, found Hatfield's name, and waved them through.

"By the way, Mr. Boise will be along shortly. He's with us," Craig said. Boise was Cecil Jones's alias.

The townhouse was a spacious three-bedroom, two-bath with an attached garage at the rear. Craig handed the key to Terry, who unlocked the door. Lisa started forward, but Terry held her back while Gonzalez and Craig slipped inside with drawn Spitters.

"Let them check it first," Terry said.

A few minutes later, Gonzalez returned to the door. "All clear. Joe says to do what you gotta do, then meet him in the kitchen for a meeting."

Lisa yawned.

"Do you want to lie down?" Terry asked quickly.

"No! I'm part of the team. I take part in all meetings. Nothing is kept secret from me."

"She's right," Gonzalez agreed. "Go to the bathroom and then come to the kitchen."

When Terry and Lisa entered the kitchen, Gonzalez had cold meats, salads, and bread spread on the counter. "The kitchen is stocked with food and drink," Gonzalez said. "Joe called ahead and had it delivered. We'll eat during the planning session."

"Where's Joe?" Terry asked.

"Checking for messages."

Craig was in the study, which was furnished like an office. On a table next to the desk sat an ordinary-looking telephone answering machine. The red light was blinking regularly.

Instead of simply rewinding, Craig reached around the back of the machine to depress a button disguised as a screw, turning off the destruct function, which would melt the tape and machine if an unauthorized person tried to remove or rewind the tape.

Once the destruct was disconnected, Craig pushed various screws around the machine's exterior, turning off the automatic erase function. Once that was done, he pushed the regular rewind button. After the tape had rewound, he had to go through another sequence of screw pushes that permitted the messages to play ungarbled.

The machine was another of Ted Billings's ingenious inventions. It was attached to a phone that wasn't registered with any phone company. To make this phone ring, callers had to use an elaborate code system that funneled calls through other untraceable, unregistered telephones.

Craig finally cleared the machine of all booby

traps and listened to a series of messages.

His face was grim when he returned to the living room. Before he could say anything, Cecil Jones walked in the front door with Ted Billings in tow.

"Look who I found on the street," Jones said. Everyone greeted Billings warmly.

"Too many for the kitchen, let's go in the living room," Craig said. The six of them went into the living room, bringing their drinks and food plates.

"I've got bad news," Craig said once they were all seated. "David and Ben are in trouble. Every police force in Europe is looking for Ben after a gunfight in Paris. The Communists are looking for both of them."

Craig briefed them on Stone's problems in Paris, and Bowles's evasion of a surveillance team in London.

"So to sum up, Ben had to vacate Paris immediately. He didn't have time to visit his city safe house. He had to leave behind his documentation for his first escape option through Milan. Plus, he's been wounded in the leg. David is in better shape. He has all his documentation papers and could still escape through Milan."

"But he won't," Cecil Jones said matter-of-factly.

"No, he won't," Craig answered. "David won't abandon Ben."

"What are we going to do?" Malloy asked.

"You, Lisa, Cece, and Ted aren't going to do anything," Craig said. "Berto and I are going to Europe to help them."

This was a major deviation from their plans. Originally, the group was to drive to Atlanta, which was a hub airport for many major airlines, and board different planes using false names. They would randomly city-hop around the country, choosing flights on the spur of the moment and paying cash for their tickets. This would make it impossible for anyone to trace them. Ultimately, they would end up on the West Coast, where new identities had been established for them by Ted Billings and Joe Craig.

"No way," Jones and Billings shouted at the same time. Terry was also shouting his disapproval. Lisa sat quietly while Billings, Jones, and Malloy protested that they were going along.

"Knock it off," Craig ordered. "We're not all going. Terry, you have to take care of Lisa."

Malloy started to protest.

"Don't give me any bullshit," Craig said. "Lisa is your main concern. Besides, we need you to prepare our new homes."

"Okay," Terry said sheepishly.

"Cece, you have to go with Terry and Lisa," Craig said.

"Shit, Joe," Jones said.

"Cece, you understand our problem here," Craig said, cutting Jones off. "Remember, we had to leave you and Ben behind in Germany when the team ran the Moscow operation. Black faces aren't as uncommon in France as they are in Russia, but they do stick out. We'll have enough problems blending Ben into the scenery. Besides, Ted needs your help. Okay?"

Jones thought about it for a second, then reluctantly agreed. He had joined the Marine Corps to study electronics, and he'd been the team's official electronic surveillance specialist, although that position had disappeared once Ted Billings's talents had become apparent. Instead, Jones had filled other needs competently and courageously, backing up Billings whenever necessary.

"Before you get to me, I'm telling you I'm going," Ted Billings announced. "Cece knows enough about electronics to handle the next phase. You're going to need my talent to get in and out of Europe safely."

Craig thought about it for a second, and adjusted his plan; his ability to make such spot adjustments was what made him a tactical genius.

"You're right. We are going to need you. You go."

Billings smiled his thanks.

"I want you to use your magic to get us to Europe before the FBI starts watching airports. It's only a matter of time before the CIA and the FBI connect Ben to us. Get Cece, Terry, and Lisa tickets for their first flight as well."

Billings went to the study to do his tasks. Craig turned to Gonzalez.

"Berto, send David and Ben a message saying we're coming. I want them in the Baden-Baden apartment. David will have to get Ben across the German border."

Billings used electronic banking to pay for the airline tickets, drawing funds from discretionary accounts kept under assumed names. On all future flights, the Malloys and Jones would pay cash for their tickets. Billings used legitimate stock to print airline tickets on the computer printer in the study.

He gave Lisa, Terry, and Cecil the tickets for their first flight. "This way you can go straight to the gate without stopping at the terminal counter," he said.

Ten minutes later, Jones and the two Malloys left by taxi for the Atlanta airport.

By eight p.m., Billings, Craig, and Gonzalez were on a Delta flight to Frankfurt, Germany. Their passports and credit cards had false names, but were perfectly legitimate thanks to Billings.

Before leaving, they had signed the townhouse's deed and donated it to the Archdiocese of Atlanta. All the electronics equipment had been destroyed, and the telephone line disconnected. A cleanup crew had been hired; that evening, all traces of the team's occupancy would be wiped from the townhouse.

Reims, France

Bowles's escape from England had been carried out without a hitch. After visiting his Brighton safe house, he'd taken a train to Manchester. From there, he had boarded a flight to Luxembourg. In Luxembourg City there was a safe house with an attached garage housing a BMW.

Along his route, Bowles had periodically checked predesignated message centers. They had all been clear until he reached Luxembourg; there he'd received Ben Stone's panicky message.

Bowles's schedule had called for him to drive the BMW over the German border to the city of Dusseldorf; from there, he had been scheduled to catch an airplane to Munich, and then a second plane for Italy. After receiving Stone's message, he had abandoned his schedule and driven into France.

He had reached Reims shortly before midnight. After accessing Stone's condition and the situation, Bowles had used his electronic scrambler to call through to the Atlanta townhouse. The team hadn't arrived yet, so he left a message that the original escape plan was unworkable.

An hour later, Roberto Gonzalez had telephoned. "We're coming to help you."

"It's too dangerous, Berto," Bowles protested. "I'll get Ben out."

"Joe says we do it. That ends the discussion. He wants you and Ben in Baden-Baden."

"We'll be there."

Actually, Bowles was relieved that he was getting help. He would need it to get a wounded Stone out of Europe. Ben had shrugged off his leg wound as a mere scratch, but he was limping badly and had lost quite a lot of blood. Ben wasn't physically capable of moving quickly or for an extended period.

Getting to Baden-Baden normally wouldn't have been too difficult; guards usually waved cars across the border between Germany and France. However, there was a nationwide alert for Ben; French border guards would be stopping any black men attempting to go through border crossings. If Ben hadn't been wounded, the two of them could have crossed the border in a remote area on foot. Since that was impossible, it left only one alternative.

"Well, old buddy," Bowles said. "It looks like you're in for a rough night."

"Oh, shit, David. Don't tell me I have to ride in the trunk."

"You've done it before. Remember Beirut?" After a successful mission to terminate two of the men who had planned the bombing of the Marine garrison in Beirut, Stone and Gonzalez had been hunted by Shiite Moslems. Stone was too physically conspicuous to ride inside their Fiat; he had been forced to curl up in the narrow trunk of the tiny car while Gonzalez drove it out of the city.

"Yeah." Stone shuddered. "I still have nightmares about it."

"The BMW's trunk is much larger than the Fiat's. Besides, we'll put in some padding."

"I still don't like it. There were no roadblocks in Beirut. There's sure to be one on the French-German border. I could be trapped in the trunk without any way to help in a fight."

"We're not going to fight our way through. They're looking for you, not me. There are 'dipple' license plates on the BMW, and I'll flash the guards a diplomatic passport. The border guards won't even slow us down."

"Damn, I still don't like it," Stone said reluctantly. "But I suppose it's our only choice."

They had left Reims an hour later. Two hours later, at four a.m., they had smoothly passed through the hastily erected border roadblock in Strasbourg. One look at the BMW's diplomatic plates and the guards had waved them around the waiting traffic. Five miles inside Germany, Bowles had stopped the car and opened the trunk.

"I'm growing too old for this," Stone said as he stiffly climbed out.

"Let's hope we both continue to age," Bowles answered.

"Amen to that, brother," Stone said fervently.

Chapter Fourteen

London, England

The threats of punishment by their superiors had forged Guavaro and Markov into a cohesive team. During the night, they caught only brief snatches of sleep while they desperately tried to reacquire Bowles and Stone. They activated hundreds of agents, sending them to airports, railway stations, and shipping ports throughout Western Europe; they imported additional agents from Russia, the former Iron Curtain countries, and the former East Germany to join the search. All their efforts failed: by noon Wednesday London time, six a.m. in Atlanta, Bowles and Stone were still at large.

Atlanta, Georgia

At seven-thirty a.m. on Wednesday morning, Patrick Holden exited I-85 at the Atlanta airport. CNN Radio News was carrying an in depth report about yesterday's shootout in Paris. According to CNN, the French were attributing the event to a battle between terrorist organizations.

CNN reported: "Two members of one of the terrorist groups indiscriminately fired automatic weapons on a crowded Paris street in an attempt to kill a terrorist from another organization. Five terrorists were killed. Thirty French citizens were killed or wounded. French authorities vow vengeance. Police are currently rounding up anyone with known terrorist affiliations."

"Typically French," Holden muttered. "They make excuses for terrorists who attack Israelis or Americans, but their attitude changes if the same terrorists touch a Frenchman."

CNN's report continued: "One of the terrorists was a large black man, who escaped in a stolen car. The car was later found abandoned near the Bastille. The terrorist is believed to have escaped Paris. There is a continent-wide alert out for him."

Holden turned off the radio as his car approached the executive jet waiting to transport him and his team of agents to Tallahassee.

Tallahassee, Florida

Holden's jet landed at nine a.m. Waiting for it were representatives of the Leon County Sheriff's Office and the Tallahassee Police Department.

"I'm Captain Gill," the TPD representative said.

"I'm afraid the people you are after have fled."

"Damn it, someone must have tipped them," Holden said.

"It wasn't anyone local. Our help was requested only a couple of hours ago," an offended Gill said. "Neighbors said they left yesterday."

"I wasn't accusing you," Holden apologized. "Let's take a look at their homes."

Holden rode in Gill's cruiser. They had to cross the city to get to Killearn, an area of large expensive houses. The Malloys lived in a two-story house with a lake behind it.

"Neighbors saw the Malloys yesterday morning," Gill said. "But no one has seen them since then."

Police cars surrounded the house. A policeman accompanied by a lithe brunette approached Gill and Holden.

"This is Mrs. Joyce," the policeman said. "She lives next door."

"I'm Lisa's best friend," the woman said.

"Did you see them leave?" Holden asked.

"No," she answered. "But I peeked in the garage window just now. They must have used Terry's Porsche. Lisa's Mercedes is still there."

Holden asked Gill to put out an APB on the Porsche. The TPD officer went to his car and put out an APB.

"Do the others live near here?" Holden asked Gill when he returned.

"About five miles away."

They climbed back into the cruiser and drove on a series of roads under the canopy of tree branches. Finally they approached a large brick house in the woods off Buck Lake Road. The house sat in a grove of trees; a pool was in the back yard. The nearest neighbor was a half-mile away. The three-car garage was windowless; it was impossible to tell if any cars were missing.

"Gonzalez, Craig, and Jones shared this house," Gill said.

"We're going to need search warrants," Holden said.

Four cars full of men arrived in Killearn an hour later. Seeing the police and FBI agents standing outside the Malloys' home, the four cars drove past without stopping. Inside the cars were General Tyler Burns and ten Green Berets in civilian clothes.

Burns found a public phone in a shopping center off Kerry Forest Road on the edge of Killearn. His men stood casually by on the sidewalk, preventing anyone from approaching, while Burns attached a portable scrambler to the phone. When it was set, he called Fort Belvoir for further orders.

"General Downs, please. It's General Burns."

Burns knew Downs would answer on a phone with a scrambler, so he activated his portable unit. Burns was forced to wait five minutes before Downs came on the line.

"What's wrong, Ty?"

"The FBI is here. What do you want me to do?"

"Wait one," Downs ordered.

There were three minutes of silence before Downs returned. "Patrick Holden is in charge. Approach him and tell him whatever you feel is necessary. It's imperative that we find those Marines fast, and the FBI provides our best chance for accomplishing that task."

"Why?" Burns asked. "What's wrong?"

"All hell is breaking loose up here."

"What's changed since I spoke with you last night?"

"Didn't you hear about the shootout in Paris?"

"You mean the terrorist attack?" Burns asked.

"That wasn't any terrorist attack, although the French haven't figured that out yet. It was a Czech liquidation team after an American mercenary employed by the CIA. The guy's name is Theben Stone, and he just did a job for the agency in Angola."

"What's that got to do with us?"

"Everything! Stone is a former Force Recon Marine. He managed to kill five Czechs before escaping. The remaining two Czechs fired down a public street with automatic weapons, trying to stop him. They killed thirteen civilians and wounded seventeen others."

"Good for Stone and bad for the French," Burns said. "Maybe it will teach them not to let those people operate in their country."

The American military hated the French for their official policy of allowing terrorists to move freely through their country in exchange for terrorism not being aimed at French citizens or French interests. The military also detested France for its refusal to allow American fighter planes to fly over its territory during the attack on Libya several years ago.

"Normally, I'd say the same thing," Downs admitted. "Not this time, however."

"Why? I don't see any significance for us."

"Stone used a Spitter."

The significance hit Burns. "I understand. It was one of the Spitters stolen from Kirk's Armory and used in the attack against Cardona. It makes sense. Stone was Force Recon. He must be connected to the former Marine Force Recons here."

"One of their nine-man Force Recon team. Two

of the team were killed in San Tomas."

"So that's the connection with Cardona. How did the two die?"

"In action in the jungle," Downs lied.

Burns realized from the tone of Downs's voice that his superior was lying. A long-forgotten bit of gossip fluttered through Burns's mind about Americans being killed by Cardona's forces. He couldn't remember the details exactly; he'd have to think further about it.

"If four of the remaining seven were in Tallahassee and one in France," Burns said, "where are the other two?"

"David Bowles lives in London and Dr. Ted Billings in Boston. Both are missing, according to the people we've sent to their homes."

"Is Billings a medical doctor?"

"No, a Ph.D. You can guess his speciality."

"Electronics?"

"Correct, and he's been through the training center at Fort Benning."

"Why didn't we pick that up?" Burns asked.

"Somehow the Marine Corps failed to take account of his background and didn't classify him as an electronics specialist. His Military Occupational Speciality listed him as Force Recon. His electronics background wasn't mentioned in his records, he wasn't even the team's electronics specialist. Cecil Jones held that designation. Jones's name came up in the search for electronics specialists who had gone through training at Kirk's Armory. Jones was quickly eliminated as a possibility because he just didn't have the know-how to break into Kirk's Armory."

"But Billings does?"

"Obviously, and we want him very badly," Downs

said. "Since the attempt on Stone's life, the CIA and military intelligence have been working frantically to discover why the Czechs were after him. What they have learned is disturbing."

"What have they learned?"

"Castro had issued a termination order for everyone taking part in the Cardona killing," Downs said. "The Russians modified Castro's order to exclude the electronics expert, who they want as much as we do. A week or so ago, the Communists identified Stone as one of Cardona's killers. They have had Stone under surveillance since then in the hope he would lead them to the electronics expert, or to other members of his team who might lead them to the electronics expert."

"Apparently he has," Burns said. "Otherwise why would Stone's death have been sanctioned?"

"That's what we believe. We can only hope that they don't already have Billings."

"What do you want me to do, sir?"

"Contact Holden and get any information you can from him. Use your best judgment on what to tell him."

"Yes, sir."

"And, Ty, we are modifying your orders. Capture Ted Billings. Kill the other six. If you can't capture Billings, make sure you kill him, too. We can't let the Russians have him. Do you understand?"

Yes, sir, but I don't like it one bit!"

Langley, Virginia

Downs hadn't spoken to Burns from his Fort Belvoir office; he was actually in an office at CIA headquarters.

"Do you think Burns will carry out his orders?"

the CIA director Joseph Standish asked. He was a Boston Brahmin, a direct descendant of Miles Standish; he had neither a sense of humor nor an ounce of compassion for anyone below his social standing. Standish was a political appointee, a former ambassador to Great Britain who had served as the chairman of President Sanderson's election organization.

"I don't know. If he discovers the real reason those ex-Marines went after Cardona, he might decide they had justification and refuse to terminate them."

Donald Collins and Henry Latham, the two other CIA executives in the office, exchanged worried glances. They were career CIA operatives who had been elevated to their deputy director positions by President Sanderson. Their predecessors had been tarnished by the Cardona scandal; the two former deputy directors had officially resigned but actually had been forced out when Sanderson had taken office.

Collins was the CIA's Deputy Director of Intelligence, known as the DDI, Latham was the Deputy Director of Operations, the DDO. Latham and Collins had been vital cogs in the CIA's San Tomas strategy; they had aided Cardona with his drug and weapons smuggling. Their involvement had been buried, protected by the deal made with William Means for him to take the fall before Congress.

"We can't have Burns ignoring his orders! These men must be terminated," Latham insisted. He had an additional incentive for wanting the Marines dead: he had been William Means's superior and had helped cover up Cardona's murder of the two Marines. He had realized this morning that Means had been executed for the murder of those two

Marines, and feared that he too might be targeted for execution. As soon as he understood the connection, he had assigned himself protection; he didn't intend to take a step outside Langley's gates unaccompanied by CIA bodyguards.

"They must die, General," Standish agreed. His loyalty was to President Sanderson. Standish knew the President didn't want the Cardona can of worms to resurface. "If their reason for killing Cardona became public knowledge, it would cause a national and international uproar. The President would be furious."

"Not as furious as every active-duty Marine and former Marine," Collins said. "Who knows what they would do if it became known the U.S. government didn't prosecute Cardona for butchering two of their brethren? I've worked with Marines; they believe that Semper Fidelis crap."

"The Marine Corps would demand a reopening of the Cardona investigation, and former Marines who are now civilians would drum up public support for it," Latham agreed. "They would want the blood of anyone involved with the cover-up. I wouldn't sleep at night if any Force Recon Marines decided I was responsible for hiding Cardona's murders. It wouldn't be just the seven men we are now hunting that we'd have to worry about, it would be damn near every man who had ever served with, or is currently serving with, Force Recon. They would consider our deaths executions demanded by their honor."

"Which is exactly what Ty Burns would conclude was the seven former Force Recon Marines' motivation for killing Cardona. He would consider that reason righteous, and refuse to carry out his orders to terminate them," Downs said. "That's why we must speed things up. We have to find and kill these seven men quickly. I mean all seven of them must die. We can't even capture Billings, the electronics specialist. If any of these men are captured alive and talk, we'll have a disaster on our hands.

"Not only Burns, but no other soldier, sailor, airman, or Marine in combined Covert Warfare operations would ever trust the CIA, the U.S. government, or me again. Even the troops in regular military units would raise hell if it became public knowledge that two Marines were slaughtered by a foreign dictator and the hierarchy of the military, government, and intelligence agencies did nothing about it.

"It would be chaos. Soldiers follow orders because they know that their country and their superiors care about them. Destroy that belief—and the knowledge of what happened with Cardona *would* destroy it—and the United States no longer has an effective military!"

"And the CIA and other intelligence agencies would also be destroyed," Collins said. "No American would have any faith in an agency that allows the deaths of two Marines to go unpunished because it needed the dictator who had murdered them. We've just put the Company back together; we can't allow it to be torn apart again!"

"From strictly an intelligence point of view, there is an additional problem with Billings," Latham added. "If any foreign country gets its hands on him, our national security is totally compromised."

Standish summed it up. "We all agree, those seven Marines must be terminated. How do we accomplish it?"

"Right now, all seven are fugitives," Collins said. "We don't have a clue to where five of them are at this moment, but we do know that David Bowles and Theben Stone are trapped in Europe. They haven't had time to escape.

"The French have identified Stone as the black man they are searching for. Since he resides in Paris and hires out as a mercenary, French Sûreté had a file on him. The Sûreté gave his file photo to the French police, which has had it distributed throughout Europe. Every country in Europe's intelligence agency and police force are looking for him. The French have closed down their borders, and say they are positive Stone is still in France."

"But the French are unaware of Bowles," Latham added.

"He will go to Stone's aid," General Downs said. He handed Latham Bowles's and Stone's service record books. "They'll escape France. Probably already have."

Latham began to read one of the service record books as Standish said skeptically, "Aren't you crediting them a little too much, General?"

"Sir, these men are Force Recon Marines," Collins said to back up Downs. "They are capable of anything. I can't stress that enough."

Latham's whistle drew the other three's attention.

"These guys are really something." Latham tapped Bowles's and Stone's record books. "Both are fluent in French and Arabic. In addition, Bowles speaks German and Russian and Stone speaks Spanish. Both have extensive field experience. These two are extremely dangerous."

"So are their teammates. All of them are deadly," Downs said. "They certainly are armed with Snicks, Spitters, and other bits of exotic weaponry. And they are all well trained. Mr. Standish, ordinary police won't catch any of them unless they make a mistake. These men don't make mistakes!"

"Wrong, General," Collins said. "Stone has already made a very serious one. If he had stayed incognito instead of operating as a mercenary, we'd still be wondering who killed Cardona. Stone is the weak link on that team."

"Donald's right," Latham agreed. "Stone has already made one stupid mistake. There is a good chance he'll make others. When he does, he'll bring down the rest of his team."

"Maybe you're right," Downs admitted.

"What are we going to do?" Standish asked.

"I have Barry Brennan waiting outside," Latham said. "He's worked for years with the type of men we're searching for. I'm going to bring him in here. Let's hear his suggestions."

Latham pushed the intercom button and ordered Brennan into the room.

"That's the situation to this moment, Barry," Latham said after he had briefed the agent. "We don't believe the Russians or Cubans have identified the rest of Stone's and Bowles's team, but it won't take them much longer. The FBI have put out an alert for their arrests, and Communist agents inside the U.S. will learn the details. We'll have Communist hit teams knee deep in this country."

"The Communists won't have to come to the States," Barry Brennan said. The others looked at him intently.

"These men were part of a very tight-knit Force Recon team," Brennan explained. "You don't think they'll allow Bowles and Stone to sweat it out over there alone?"

"Shit!" General Downs said. "Of course not! They'll go to help."

"Right, and we'll have them all trapped in Europe," Brennan concluded. "That's where we should focus our efforts."

"Brennan, get over there immediately," Standish ordered. "Track down those men!"

Tallahassee, Florida

Tyler Burns was waiting when Patrick Holden returned to the three bachelors' home with a search warrant.

"What are you doing here?" Holden asked coldly. He hadn't forgotten that Burns had withheld vital information about Bo and Bull Hewitt. "This is an FBI operation, not a military one. Get out of here."

Burns misunderstood the cause of Holden's anger. "I know it's an FBI operation. I'm not here to interfere."

"The hell with you. If you hadn't withheld information sixteen months ago, we might have questioned these men then."

"What are you talking about?" a bewildered Burns asked. "I had no knowledge of these people."

"But you did know that the sheriff of Sycamore Country's son was on guard duty at Kirk's Armory the night it was robbed. I'm referring to Bull Hewitt's son, Bo, who we found trussed up. Just to refresh your memory, Sycamore County is where Coral Cove is located. It's where Cardona lived and was murdered. You didn't bother to say anything about the connection between the guard and the sheriff."

"Bull Hewitt's son was one of the guards?" a shocked Burns asked. "I honestly didn't know that."

Burns became aware that TV and print journalists had arrived on the scene and were drifting toward him and Holden, drawn by their loud voices. "Pat, could we move somewhere a little more private?"

Holden noticed the journalists. "My car," he said, walking toward a rented Ford. The day was hot and muggy; both men were sweating when they slid inside the car. Holden started the engine and turned the air-conditioning to high.

"How could you not know that Hewitt's son was on guard duty?" Holden demanded.

"The guard unit wasn't under my command," Burns said. "And no one informed me of the sentries' names."

Holden stared at Burns, assessing the honesty of that statement.

"Okay. I'll buy that explanation. Why are you here now?"

"Your interest in these men's service records was brought to my attention. I decided to look at them, too. Copies were brought to me, but I recognized them as having been sanitized. I asked for their genuine service records."

"Genuine service records," Holden interrupted. "What do you mean?"

"These men were Marine Force Recon. Their genuine service records are kept sealed, and sanitized ones are substituted for viewing by unauthorized personnel. Once I saw their genuine records, I knew you had hit paydirt. I came here looking for them."

"What's Marine Force Recon? I've never heard of it."

"It's the Marine Corps's version of the Army's Green Berets and the Navy's Seals," Burns said.

211

"Are Force Recon Marines capable of carrying out the attack on Cardona?"

"Easily. And without a doubt, these four did it," Burns said. "But they weren't alone, they had help from three other Force Recon Marines."

"Seven of them! It seems impossible that seven men could carry out that attack." Holden said.

"I assure you the seven of them did it."

Once again Holden heard the ring of pride in Burns's speech, which had so infuriated him in Coral Cove.

"Why are you proud of them? They're just murderers!"

"I can't help being proud of their professionalism. As a military operation, it was executed superbly. It proves these men were superbly trained," Burns said. "Besides, I don't think of them as murderers. I have a strong suspicion they had an excellent reason for killing Cardona."

"Why in God's name do you think that?"

"It's just a theory. I'll tell you when I've confirmed it," Burns said. "But it's beside the point, I'm as committed to catching them as you are."

"I don't know why, but I believe you," Holden said. "I'll expect you to tell me their motive the moment you know it."

Holden's cellular phone rang. He picked it up, said a few words, then listened.

"Yes, sir," he said before switching it off. "That was my boss," Holden said to Burns. "I've been ordered to work with you."

"You won't be sorry. I'll cooperate fully with you," Burns said.

"I'm telling you right now, I won't allow these people to go free," Holden warned. "Don't try to hinder their arrest."

"I won't," Burns lied. There wasn't any need for Holden to know about the termination orders.

"Tell me about these men," Holden said.

Burns briefed him on the four who lived in Tallahassee as well as the other three men. He briefed Holden on the situation in Paris, filling him in on the Russians' and Cubans' desire to capture Ted Billings and kill the other six.

"So Paris wasn't a terrorist action, but an attempt to kill Theben Stone?"

"That's correct."

"We'll look into that after we search this house," Holden said.

The two left the car and walked up a stone path to the front door, where a specialist was attempting to open the lock.

"Can't do it, Mr. Holden," the specialist said. "It's some type of electronic locking system. I tried shutting off the power. It appears to be self-contained."

"Knock down the door—" Holden started to order.

"Don't!" Burns quickly cut him off. "It's booby-trapped."

"Why would they leave booby traps? You said in Coral Cove that these men didn't want to kill Americans. Why would that change now? They were obviously expecting us; that's why they ran before we got here."

"They definitely weren't expecting us! They evacuated yesterday."

"So?"

"Either Theben Stone or David Bowles warned them about the Cubans and Russians. That's who they were expecting to show up looking for them."

Burns's statement stopped Holden. Until then, he had been sure that someone had tipped the men off about the FBI's interest in them.

"Jesus! Radio our people at the Malloys' house not to break in," he ordered a nearby FBI agent.

"How do we check?" Holden asked Burns.

"They left a signature for us at Kirk's Armory. Let's see if they left one for us here."

Burns studied the front of the house. Seemingly out of place was a lone cactus among the green boxwood shrubbery. Burns bent over and examined the cactus, finally reaching down and scratching away the dirt at its base. He came up with a key.

"The house is booby-trapped all right, but they left a key. Tell your men at the other house to look for another cactus. That's where they'll find the house key."

Burns turned his key in the door lock, opening the house.

"That should have deactivated all the other booby traps, but have your men be extremely careful. You better get a bomb expert in here as well. Do the same with the other house."

Holden ordered it done, and his team scattered warily through the house.

"They won't find any clues to where they've gone, I can assure you," Burns said. "Let's check the garage."

The opened garage revealed a Porsche and a Jaguar.

"Which car is missing?" Holden asked a nearby agent.

The agent checked a list. "Joe Craig's Volvo."

A policeman chimed in, "One of the women reporters told me that she dated Craig."

"Let's speak to her," Holden said.

A lovely redheaded woman was brought through

the police lines. She identified herself as Julie Williams.

"Yes, Joe and I dated," she confirmed. She wouldn't reveal any intimate details of their relationship. She claimed she had no idea where Craig had gone.

"He did drive a Volvo," she said. "He claimed it might not be the world's fastest car, but it was the safest."

Holden thanked Julie Williams. He refused to answer any of her questions about the FBI's interest in Craig, and had her escorted back behind the police lines.

After she left, Burns said, "In his choice of car, Craig may have unwittingly given us an idea of how he thinks. It may help us later."

"Do you really think we'll have that much trouble capturing them?"

"Pat, we haven't got a hope in hell of capturing them unless something goes wrong somewhere. They had this all carefully planned. It was how they were trained. They'll have a number of fall-back positions and identities already intact . . ."

Burns suddenly stopped short. A look of revelation lit his face. "Let's get out of here. There's nothing here to find. Put someone else in charge."

"Why? Where are we going," Holden sputtered.

"We're going to Paris."

"Why?"

"Something *has* gone wrong," Burns said. "They have two of their team on the run in Europe. If the French reports are correct, one of them is wounded. Even if their escape plan calls for Bowles and Stone to make their way back on their own, at least a couple of the men from here will try to help them. After all, they're former Marines, and Marines never abandon their buddies. There is no question about it, this is our break. If Bowles and Stone get out of Europe, we'll never have another shot at finding any of them."

Chapter Fifteen

London, England

Just after one p.m. on Wednesday, Colonel Aleksander Markov received a telephone call from the KGB's resident agent at the London embassy.

"Moscow sent a package to you in the diplomatic pouch. An agent will bring it to you as soon as possible."

A half hour later, a package containing photos and records was delivered to the safe house. A persevering clerk in KGB headquarters in Moscow had hand-checked the massive archives, attempting to find David Bowles among the thousands of photos taken of unidentified Americans in San Tomas and surrounding countries during Luis Cardona's regime. The clerk had struck paydirt: Bowles had turned up in two photos; in one he was with Theben Stone and two other men; in the other he was with three different men. The accompanying fact sheets stated the men were unidentified military advisers.

"Take a look at these photos," Markov said to Guavaro. "Do you recognize any of them?"

Guavaro studied the two photos. He picked one of them up and pointed to a man who stood with his left arm around Bowles.

"His name is Daniel Paige. He was a captain in the United States Marines."

"Marine Force Recon, you mean," Markov said. "That's why Bowles's and Stone's pasts are a blank. They were Force Recon."

"Cardona murdered Paige and a Marine sergeant named Melvin Snipes," Guavaro said. "I counted seven men in Cardona's study. Adding Snipes and Paige, that makes nine. That's a Force Recon team."

"So these men killed Cardona to avenge their comrades' murders!" Markov said, admiration in his voice. "And they did it on their own. They even went against their own government. These men are even more formidable than I imagined."

"We'll handle them," Guavaro said confidently.

At five p.m., Havana informed Guavaro that Cuban agents in Miami had reported that fugitive warrants had been issued by the FBI for Billings, Jones, Gonzalez, Craig, the Malloys, Stone, and Bowles. A Cuban deep-cover agent within the CIA had confirmed that the FBI had linked these fugitives with Cardona's murder.

"Our agent in the CIA says that these men are former Force Recon Marines," Guavaro told Markov. "He identifies Ted Billings as the electronics expert who cracked Kirk's Armory. Our agent says the CIA believes that Bowles and Stone have been joined in Europe by a few of the others."

"That makes sense," Markov replied.

"We must find these men before the CIA does!"

"We'll find them first."

"How?" Guavaro asked. "Europe is a big place."

"Stone is the key. A black like him will stand out in most European countries. For him to blend in, he must be in a country where black American soldiers are common," Markov reasoned.

Markov went to the map of Europe on the wall. He pointed to Germany.

"This is where he is! And that's where we're going!"

Germany

Joe Craig had ordered Bowles and Stone into Germany for exactly the reason Markov had deduced: the huge black man was less conspicuous in a country crawling with black American soldiers. Craig hadn't underestimated his opponents' collective intelligence: Germany was the obvious choice for Stone to go to ground, and it was where the opposition would concentrate its search. Craig hoped to have Stone and Bowles back in the United States before that search could collect any dividends.

Craig, Billings, and Gonzalez reached Frankfurt at eleven a.m. local time. They passed smoothly through German customs and immigration; their American passports weren't even stamped by officials.

The three took separate cabs to the Frankfurt Hauptbahnhof. In the bustling central railroad station, they boarded the first train south to the historic city of Heidelberg.

Thomas L. Muldoon

At the Heidelberg railroad station, they were just three more Americans—nobody special in this city with a major concentration of American troops. Still being cautious, they each took their own taxi to a residential suburb ten miles from the main U.S. Army base. Their cabs deposited them in different locations within the suburb; they walked the remainder of the way to a safe house that had been purchased and maintained with money taken from Cardona's estate. It was an enormous, three-story stone house across the street from a large park bordering on the Neckar River.

Craig arrived first and waited outside. When Billings appeared, Craig crossed the street, opened the iron gate in the eight-foot-high stone wall that surrounded the house, and walked the one hundred feet down the flagstone path to the front door. The grass and shrubbery on both sides of the path had been carefully manicured—a lawn service kept good care of the house's grounds. Billings slipped inside the gate behind him as Craig used his key to open the heavy wooden front door.

Once inside, he removed his Spitter from its leg holster and stepped to the left of the door. Billings came inside, took out his Spitter, and moved to the right. Rapidly they checked the bottom floor for intruders.

"Nothing," Billings reported at the back door.

"Wait here for Berto," Craig ordered. "I'll check the rest of the house."

Craig went up the stairs. Methodically he checked the second and third floors, pausing only briefly to glance out a third-floor window at the famous Heidelberg Castle, two miles to the west on the opposite side of the river.

When he returned downstairs, Gonzalez was waiting with Billings in the kitchen.

"The two cars are okay," Gonzalez reported. On the side of the house was an attached garage whose doors opened out into a back alley. In it were a German Ford and an American Chevrolet.

"You prepare the house," Craig said to Gonzalez and Billings. "I'll go get David and Ben."

Craig took the blue German Ford from the garage and drove forty-five minutes south on the autobahn to Baden-Baden. He wasted no time in sightseeing. He pulled up in front of the apartment house where Stone and Bowles were hiding, picked them up, and drove directly back to Heidelberg.

After everyone had greeted each other, Craig held a meeting in the kitchen while they ate roasted chicken and potato salad that Billings had purchased at a local grocery store.

"We'll spend the night here. Since only Ted and I speak German, I don't want any of the rest of you to step outside the house. If anyone comes to the door, either Ted or I will handle it. Is that understood?"

Gonzalez, Stone, and Bowles nodded.

"Ted. Are we being hunted?" Craig asked.

"I've tapped into the CIA transmissions between Frankfurt and Langley. They're definitely looking for us," Billings said. It had taken him only minutes to penetrate the CIA's supposedly impenetrable security net. It had been easy: Billings's electronics company had designed many of the electronic and computer security measures the CIA used. "Langley has issued termination orders for all of you. Me it wants alive!"

"It figures," Craig said. "We're an embarrassment who could dredge up matters best kept buried. You they want for your electronic knowledge. Do they know how many of us are here?"

"No. But they know some of us came to help David and Ben. As of three p.m. our time, nine a.m. in Langley, the CIA hasn't even pinned our location down to Germany. They have a Europe-wide alert out for us."

"I overestimated the bozos," Craig said. "It's obvious we'd want Ben in a country where there were plenty of American military. I'll bet the Russians have figured it out already."

Gonzalez, Bowles, and Stone finished eating.

"You three sleep," Craig ordered. "Ted and I will take first watch."

After the others had left the kitchen, Billings asked, "What are we going to do about Ben?"

"Berto says Ben's wound isn't bad, but he lost a lot of blood," Craig answered. In addition to being a fully trained Force Recon Marine, Gonzalez had been the team's corpsman—in Army lingo, the medic. "The leg wound is healing, but Ben is going to be slowed awhile. Berto recommends that Ben rest for at least a day."

"Does that change your plans?"

"Yes, I'd intended for us to be back in the States tomorrow night. Now we can't leave here until Friday. By that time, Germany will be flooded with people searching for us."

"How are we going to get out of here with so many people concentrating their search in this country?"

"We're going to use your magic, Ted, and make the whole team disappear," Craig said.

For the next ten minutes, Craig explained his plan in detail to Billings.

"It's brilliant," Billings said when Craig finished.

"I'd better get working on the requirements."

Billings went to the special workroom built behind a closet on the house's second floor. Craig wandered into the living room where Gonzalez was staring at the news on TV.

"Berto, you're supposed to be sleeping. Are David and Ben asleep?"

"Yep. David fell asleep instantly. I had to give Ben a sleeping pill."

"Why are you watching the news when you can't understand a word of German?"

"If I see anything that might pertain to us, I'd call you or Ted to translate."

"Don't worry about it now, I'll watch the late news," Craig said. "Since you're awake and Ted is in his workroom, you guard the house. I'm going to make sure our secondary cars are all right."

Craig always had a backup escape plan to use if his first choice was compromised. In case the house was discovered and the two cars in the garage were rendered unusable, there were two additional cars in two separate leased garages a half mile away. Every member of the team knew where the garages were, and the best route to reach them.

Craig went up to the third floor and opened a closet in the main bedroom; inside were stored German-style clothing in his sizes. Craig chose blue wool pants, white shirt, black shoes, and a blue woolen jacket.

Walking down the street, he passed for any other good burgher out for an evening stroll. Several times he muttered a pleasant "Guten Abend" to other strollers; his German accent was good enough to fool the natives.

In an hour, he'd completed his meticulous check of the emergency cars and the surrounding neighborhood. Before he returned to the house, he stopped at a grocery store to buy food and beer. He strolled home carrying two plastic sacks of groceries as if he had lived in Heidelberg all his life.

Washington, D.C.

During Holden and Burns's flight by executive jet from Tallahassee to Washington, Patrick Holden spoke by telephone with FBI Assistant Director Maynard Humphrey.

"Colonel Burns believes the men we are hunting are in Europe."

"Then you'll go to Europe," Humphrey said. "I'll make the arrangements."

Their jet landed at Bolling Air Force Base in southeast D.C. at four p.m. A helicopter was waiting to ferry Holden and Burns to nearby Andrews Air Force Base, where Humphrey's influence had secured them one of the small executive jets detailed to the President of the United States. Barry Brennan was waiting when their helicopter landed.

"What are you doing here?" Holden asked.

"I've been assigned to coordinate the CIA's network of agents," Brennan said. "We'll aid you in your search and provide any backup you need. Your headquarters will confirm it. Humphrey wants you to telephone him."

Holden headed for the hangar office to use the telephone. When Holden was inside the office, Brennan said to Burns, "Twenty Green Berets are en route to Frankfurt on a CIA chartered jet. You are in charge of them. Your new orders are to kill all the Force Recon Marines."

"I'm not taking that order from you," Burns said.

"I didn't expect you to. Call General Downs. He's expecting you."

Burns went to a phone in a different office from Holden's. He returned to Brennan in a matter of minutes; Holden was still talking to his headquarters.

"Downs issued me my orders," Burns said unhappily. "He told me you were in charge of the sanction." In CIA lingo that meant that Brennan was heading the assassination team.

Before the conversation could go any further, Holden returned.

"We're set. Let's get aboard."

They boarded the executive jet, but it didn't take off until six p.m., Eastern Daylight Time, midnight in Germany. They would be flying to Rhein-Main Air Force Base in Germany; it was the United States's military airport coinciding with the German civilian airport, Frankfurt International.

After the plane had taken off, Burns, Holden, and Brennan brainstormed about the fugitives' options and came to some decisions. Holden spoke with the United States's legal attaché, an FBI agent, at the American embassy in Bonn. The attaché, John Dockery, promised to meet their plane when it arrived in Frankfurt on Thursday at nine a.m.

"I'll have to bring a German liaison," Dockery said.

"Can we skip involving the Germans?" Holden asked.

"No," Dockery answered.

"Well, we'll just have to deal with it," Holden said.

When Holden told Brennan and Burns, they both objected.

"Dockery says it can't be helped. The Germans must be involved," Holden explained.

Brennan and Burns couldn't complain further without raising Holden's suspicions.

"The Germans won't be any more of a problem than Holden," Burns said when Holden was out of earshot. "He'll try to prevent us from carrying out our orders."

Brennan's reply chilled Burns. "Holden is expendable if he gets in the way."

Frankfurt, Germany

Guavaro and Markov arrived at nine p.m. on Wednesday night. They were picked up at the airport and driven to a Russian safe house in Sachsenhausen, one of Frankfurt's neighborhoods. Under orders from Moscow, agents from Russia and former Communist countries were pouring into Germany to aid in the search for the hiding Marines.

Markov took charge of the search when he stepped into the Sachsenhausen command center. Guavaro stared at the large map of Germany affixed to the wall.

"Where is the most likely location for them to hide?" Guavaro asked. He was totally ignorant about Germany.

"Southern or central Germany," Markov answered. "Most of the American bases are located in those areas. The British military controls the north, so American blacks stick out there. I think we can eliminate southeastern Germany and concentrate our forces in the southwestern section of the country."

"Why the southwestern area?"

"It's the only safe spot for them. I don't see them going to Munich, Nuremberg, or one of the big American areas to our east. Those areas are too near to the former East Germany."

"The Americans will reason similarly," Guavaro said.

"But they are handicapped. They have to be careful. They can't offend the Germans. We don't give a damn about the Germans. We've already lost this country. We can do whatever is necessary."

An agent handed Markov two messages.

"The French killed the two remaining Czechs from the 'wet' team in a gun battle near Reims," Markov said after reading the first.

"The French are scouring the Reims area for Stone," he said after he read the second message. "They found the stolen Peugeot abandoned in a garage. Several people witnessed a black BMW with German diplomatic license plates leave the area. The checkpoint at Strasbourg reported this BMW passed into Germany at four a.m. this morning."

"So our fugitives are in Germany," Guavaro said. "You were right!"

"They couldn't have gone far," Markov said. "We will concentrate our search from Frankfurt to Freiburg in southwestern Germany. There are large concentrations of Americans in that area. They must be hiding there."

"I suggest we take this opportunity to sleep," Guavaro said.

"You're right, my Cuban comrade. We will need our rest, because tomorrow we will hunt down the Americans and kill them."

227

Heidelberg, Germany

Joe Craig and Berto Gonzalez were huddled in front of the living room TV watching the news.

"Shit," Craig suddenly exclaimed. He waved off Gonzalez's demand for an interpretation. Craig intently listened to the news report.

"Well, that's blown it wide open," he muttered after the report ended.

"What's going on, Joe?"

"Bad luck. You can never foresee that in planning any operation. Two of the Czechs who tried to murder Ben were caught and killed in a gunfight near Reims, so the French police concentrated their search in the city. They found Ben's car, and witnesses described seeing David's BMW, including the diplomatic plates. Strasbourg reported David's car passing through this morning. The German newsman says the search for Ben and his unknown accomplice is now centered in southwestern Germany. That's where we're sitting right now."

"What are we going to do?"

"Nothing for the moment," Craig said. "If we panic, we're sure to get caught. You go get some sleep. I'll take the watch. I have some thinking to do."

After Gonzalez had gone upstairs, Craig wandered into the room where Billings was working. He told Billings the bad news.

"Are you going to change your plan?" Billings asked.

Craig's plan was to use military transportation to fly to the U.S. The team would use forged credentials stating they were members of the Combined

Covert Warfare Group to commandeer a whole airplane or, at least, seats in a scheduled transport. This was a common procedure for covert warfare specialists, and they had done it a hundred times when they were on active duty. No one ever questioned a man with credentials from the Combined Covert Warfare Group as long as the man followed proper procedures. Billings would insert the correct authorizations in the air base computer. The base's commanding officer would be notified that a team from the Combined Covert Warfare Group was arriving and would be requiring immediate transportation to the U.S. Billings would give the operation a name, and stamp it top secret; the base commander would readily provide an aircraft and would never acknowledge that a team had passed through his base.

Base commanders were used to having their bases invaded by special warfare teams from the U.S. Armed Services Combined Covert Warfare Group. U.S. military base commanders around the world were under orders to supply transportation and other amenities to the Covert Warfare Group.

"I don't see any need for changes," Craig answered. "We can't move any sooner than Friday because of Ben's condition. We will continue on schedule. Hasty decisions lead to mistakes. Mistakes get people killed. I don't want any of our people killed because I made a hasty decision. Just determine all possibilities for Friday."

"Don't worry, I already have several. You get us to one of those bases, and I'll make sure we get a plane."

Billings looked at Craig. "You look a little weird. Are you sick?"

"No," Craig answered. "I have the eerie feeling I

always get just before going into combat. I think we'll be going to war soon."

"So what's the problem?" Billings said. "We've done it before against big odds. The team has full confidence in you, Joe."

"What the hell," Craig laughed. "A few good men should be able to take on the rest of the world. Isn't that what we were taught in boot camp?"

"Fucking A! Semper Fi, Joe."

"Right on, Ted. As we leathernecks like to say, 'Gung Ho!' "

The two buddies laughed and went quietly back to work.

Torrance, California

The Malloys and Cecil Jones had adopted new identities and were settling into new homes: the Malloys were now the Jordans; Cecil Jones was Cecil Meeker. Their new houses were in middle-class neighborhoods in different sections of Torrance, California. In two other middle-class neighborhoods, there were two additional houses that Jones and Terry Malloy had to prepare for occupation by the other members of the team.

Ted Billings and Joe Craig had purchased the four homes more than a year ago; they had created a new identity for each team member, an identity so elaborate that it would pass even the most intensive scrutiny. Lisa and Terry greeted their neighbors, explaining they had moved to California from Missouri. At his home, Jones told people he was from New York.

Jones went straight to work installing the electronic phone and security devices in all four houses. Until the communication equipment was up and working, Jones and Malloy remained out of touch with the team in Europe.

Coral Cove, Florida

Deputy Sheriff Bo Hewitt was on the midnight to eight a.m. shift from Wednesday through Sunday; on those five nights, he ate dinner at nine p.m., watched a little TV, and then reported to work. It was a boring existence.

On this Wednesday, he was microwaving his dinner when someone knocked on the door of the house he'd inherited from his father. Bo retrieved his service revolver from the holster hanging on the coat rack and flicked on the porch light. Through the spyhole in the front door, he could see a well-dressed man standing on the porch. Bo opened the door, keeping his right hand with the revolver hidden behind his right leg.

"Yeah?" he said.

The man removed a wallet from a coat pocket and displayed it to Bo. There was a badge and an identification card inside.

"I'm Special Agent Bob Dunphy. I'm with the FBI. May I speak to you for a minute, Mr. Hewitt?"

"Sure, come on in," a bewildered Hewitt said. He slid the revolver back into the holster hanging on the coat rack. "What can I do for you?"

The FBI agent stepped into the living room.

"Have you heard from your sister today?"

"Lisa? She's in Tallahassee."

"No, she isn't. She's a federal fugitive."

"You must have mistaken her for someone else. My sister has never done anything wrong in her whole life."

"Unfortunately for her, she married Terry Malloy. He's the one we're actually looking for. Him and his friends. They're prime suspects in the Cardona murders."

Bo was shaken. It all came rushing in on him. Malloy and his friends had frequently invited him to party with them in Tallahassee while he was in the Army. They'd been interested in his Army job as a guard at Fort Benning. He'd escorted Joe Craig and Ted Billings around the base several times. He'd even supplied them with answers about the security of the armory he watched.

"Did they break into the Fort Benning armory, too?" he asked.

"Yes," Dunphy said. "I'd like to ask you some questions about that as well."

Dunphy asked questions about Fort Benning; Hewitt supplied carefully sanitized answers. Bo didn't want to become an accessory to the crime.

"Do you know if these men were ever on Cardona's estate?"

"I don't know," Hewitt admitted. "They were frequently in Coral Cove with Lisa, but I don't know where they went while they were here."

Twenty minutes later, the FBI agent was satisfied.

"Remember, you're a lawman now," Dunphy warned Bo. "If you hear from your sister, it's your duty to call us."

"Don't worry. If I hear from my sister, I'll make sure justice is done," Hewitt answered.

He closed the door behind the FBI agent and leaned against it, thinking of how Malloy and his friends had contributed to his father's and his own disgrace. Hatred surged inside him.

"I'll kill those bastards myself," he said out loud.

Chapter Sixteen

Heidelberg, Germany

It was a typical German spring day: cold and drizzly. Ted Billings and Joe Craig left the safe house at seven-thirty on Thursday morning, driving the second car in the house's garage: a green American Chevrolet bearing U.S. Armed Forces license plates. The pair were dressed as U.S. Army officers; Billings was a full colonel, Craig wore a major's bronze oak leaves. Their American Chevrolet didn't stand out on the roads of southwest Germany; a great many American cars were evident in the morning traffic. Heidelberg had a U.S. Army base, and numerous other Army and Air Force bases existed to the north and west of the historic city.

Billings had worked through the night to find American airfields with available aircraft capable of fulfilling Craig's escape criteria. This morning, Billings and Craig intended to personally reconnoiter each air base; once they were north of Heidelberg, and away from the saturation of U.S. Army bases, they intended to make a quick change from their Army uniforms into the U.S. Air Force uniforms in the trunk of the Chevrolet. In doing so, neither would be promoted: their Air Force uniforms would have the same rank as their Army uniforms. They each carried identification cards and papers for whatever uniform they wore.

Gonzalez, Stone, and Bowles remained behind in the Heidelberg house. Gonzalez and Bowles had spent the night sharing guard duty and were groggy from lack of sleep. "You guys catch some Z's," Stone said to them after Craig and Billings departed. "I'll keep watch. I'm wide awake."

Frankfurt, Germany

The executive jet landed at Rhein-Main Air Force Base on the dot of nine a.m. on Thursday; the jet had barely rolled to a stop before a movable stairway was shoved against the plane. A man, bundled up against the chill and huddled under an open umbrella, climbed the stairs and entered the open door.

"Good to see you, Pat," said John Dockery, the FBI's legal attaché at the American embassy in Bonn.

"You too, John," Holden answered. "This is Barry Brennan of the CIA and General Ty Burns."

Dockery shook hands with the pair.

"Afraid I only brought one spare," Dockery said, holding out an unfurled umbrella. "We'll have to share."

Sharing an umbrella, Holden and Dockery descended the stairs; Burns and Brennan followed behind with the second umbrella. At the bottom of the stairs, a man in a raincoat and hat waited.

"This is my German counterpart, Klaus Braunfeld," Dockery said. "The German Federal Police have set up a command post downtown. We're to use Klaus's office."

After they had settled in the Mercedes limousine, Holden asked, "Anything new?"

"You know about Reims and the BMW with diplomatic plates passing through Strasbourg?" Dockery asked.

"Yes."

"Klaus's people located the BMW this morning in Baden-Baden. It was parked in an apartment building's garage."

"We were extremely lucky," Braunfeld said, his English carrying only a trace of an accent. "One of the building's occupants became curious about the BMW when he noticed that its license plates had been removed and it was parked in a slot of an apartment which he thought was unoccupied. He called the local police, and they identified the car."

"I take it our quarry had split?" Brennan asked.

"Yes, but not unnoticed. Another curious neighbor saw a blue Ford pull up in front of the building late yesterday afternoon. The neighbor didn't see the driver, but she did see the two men who came out of the building and jumped inside."

Dockery took over from Braunfeld. "The neighbor described the men. One was a large black man with a severe limp. The other was a sandy-haired, balding man."

"Bowles and Stone," Burns exclaimed.

"Klaus and I went down there early this morning. We showed the witness photos of Bowles and

Stone, and she confirmed they were the men she saw. Then we checked the previously unoccupied apartment; it showed signs of having been recently occupied. The apartment is legally owned by a Bernhardt Stein."

"By the way," Braunfeld added, "Stein translates as stone in English."

"Stein is a ghost," Dockery said. "The German computers are filled with authentic records for the man; unfortunately, he doesn't seem to actually exist."

"The bureaucrats are fuming," Braunfeld said. "They can't understand how their computers were invaded and their records falsified."

"This isn't unexpected," Burns said. "Our fugitives are very experienced and intelligent. They are experts at evasion tactics. They will have purchased residences and registered automobiles in many different countries in Europe. Those purchases will be duly recorded in government computers."

"They'll have proper credentials to match each residence and car," Brennan said. "If necessary, they can change identities a dozen times. Their credentials will pass even the most detailed inspection."

"Exactly how do they do this?" Braunfeld asked.

"And why doesn't any agency have their fingerprints on record?" Dockery added. "Klaus's people found two separate sets of fingerprints inside the apartment. We ran them through German police records and Interpol. They weren't on record. I had the prints run through FBI headquarters and they weren't recorded there either. I thought these men were former American Marines?"

Burns and Brennan stood silently. Holden answered. "I guess you haven't been informed of their background."

"Actually, I have," Braunfeld said. "But I didn't mention it to John since I wasn't sure if he had clearance."

"What clearance?" Dockery demanded.

Rapidly Holden filled Dockery in on Bowles's and Stone's background.

"Shit!" Dockery complained. "Someone should have told me. What if I had come up against them without knowing how deadly they were?"

"I had nothing to do with it, John. You'll have to complain to Washington," Holden said. "Have you got anything else on Stone and Bowles?"

Dockery was fuming; to give him time to regain his composure, Klaus Braunfeld took over.

"The neighbor tried to see the license plate of the blue Ford but could only see part of it. We ran the partial license plate number through a computer to derive a list of possibilities. As you can imagine, the list was quite lengthy. When we eliminated all but the blue Fords, the computer narrowed it down to approximately two thousand possibilities. Police are checking the addresses. However, it will take a while."

"Any description of the driver?" Brennan inquired.

"No," Braunfeld answered.

"What are your thoughts on the driver, Ty?" Holden asked.

"I would eliminate Terry Malloy. He'd stay behind in the States with his wife," Burns said. "Tactically, I'd eliminate Cecil Jones as well. He's black, and they already have enough trouble with Stone's black skin. My guess is we have either Craig, Gonzalez, or Billings here. Maybe two or more of them."

"We have photos of all of them," Holden said. "Let's have the German police put out a bulletin for all five."

Brennan and Burns were uneasy. Brennan said, "Isn't it better we keep the possible presence of Craig, Gonzalez, and Billings quiet?"

"No," Holden said firmly. "I want them captured quickly!"

Having finally regained control of himself, Dockery jumped in. "You aren't the only ones who want them. Tell them, Klaus."

"The Russians want them," Klaus said. "And they have a good shot at getting them. Despite the certainty of unification, Russia hasn't lessened its presence in East Germany. Not to mention the many agents it has in my country."

"Not to mention the availability of the Stasi, East Germany's state police," Dockery added.

"Yes, the Stasi agents will also be utilized," Braunfeld admitted. "And it gets worse. Despite the much-publicized breakdowns of the Communist governments in the Eastern bloc, their infrastructures are still intact and subject to Russia's will. German intelligence has informed my department of an influx of agents into Germany from the former Soviet bloc. According to our intelligence units, the Russians are conducting an intensive search for the same five men as you. And they are concentrating their efforts in the southwestern area of Germany."

"How did they pick this area?" Burns demanded.

"Some smart one probably deduced it originally," Braunfeld explained. "And if he needed any proof to back up his deduction, the curious neighbor in Baden-Baden gave it to him. After she spoke to us, she called the press. Stories of Stone being in Germany were in this morning's newspapers and on radio and TV news broadcasts. And the existence of two men helping him was included in the stories."

"It's imperative that we find these men first," Brennan said forcefully. "Billings can't be captured by Russians!"

"What about Billings's partners?" Holden asked.

"We have to take care of them, too," Brennan answered enigmatically.

Heidelberg, Germany

Two hours after Billings's and Craig's departure, Stone grew bored with sitting downstairs. There was nothing for him to do, and watching TV didn't help since he couldn't speak the language. In the field, Stone was the perfect Marine, able to sit or stand immobile for hours while on guard. But for some inexplicable reason he didn't consider his present situation as guard duty.

After ten minutes of restlessly prowling the bottom floor of the house, he climbed the stairs to see if either of his two buddies were awake. They weren't; they were sleeping soundly in two of the second-floor bedrooms; he tried not to wake them as he returned downstairs.

The drizzle had increased to a steady rain. Stone went to a front window and looked outside; the rain was pelting against the glass, blurring his vision. The street outside the gate was empty, the foul weather keeping the suburb's residents inside their houses.

He made a decision: it was the perfect opportunity to go outside and test his injured leg. Stone decided that the safe house was in an isolated suburb which the enemy was unlikely to have under surveillance. The minimal risk of his being seen was negated completely by the rainy weather. The rain would provide him with perfect cover.

He was conscious of being the target of an intensive hunt by the police, intelligence agencies, and military of countries from several continents, but, like many men who risk bullets and bombs for a living, he considered himself invulnerable. That unshakable belief was his one blind spot; it had lost him Paris, and was about to have even more disastrous results.

The house was a fortress: It was guarded by sophisticated alarm systems and had booby traps and explosives strategically placed around it. It took Stone five minutes to deactivate all the security alarms and defensive systems.

It was nine thirty-five when he stepped outside into the rain wearing a gray raincoat and a slouch hat pulled down over his head. He walked briskly down the path to the gate, opened it, and crossed the empty street into the park.

Stone had a momentary pang of guilt for disobeying Joe Craig's order not to step outside the house, but he shrugged it off. No one would ever know he had been outside; he intended to be outside the house for only a short period, just long enough to work the kinks out of his injured leg.

Frankfurt, Germany

The discovery of the fugitives' BMW in Baden-Baden had prompted Colonel Markov to shift his forces, saturating southwestern Germany; he deduced that the Marines had gone to ground in the Heidelberg or Stuttgart areas, both of which had huge concentration of Americans. The coverage in the Heidelberg area was especially intensified; agents were stationed on nearly every block of the city and its suburbs. It was only by pure chance that Craig and Billings hadn't been spotted when they drove away from the house this morning; Stone wasn't so lucky.

The telephone rang in the Russians' Sachsenhausen headquarters at nine-forty, not five minutes after Stone had stepped into the street outside the Heidelberg house.

"The big black one just walked out of a house and crossed the street into the park," an agent reported, explaining where he was located.

"We have them," an excited Markov exclaimed after hanging up on the agent. "Stone has just been observed in Heidelberg. I told you, Guavaro. The man makes mistakes. He's their Achilles heel."

"What is your plan?" Guavaro asked.

"I've ordered my people to back off and watch him. Under no circumstances are they to allow Stone to spot them. There will be no mistake like the one in Paris. No action will be taken until I arrive and take charge personally."

"Isn't Heidelberg far from here? Won't it take us a long time to get there?"

"It's less than a hundred miles. We'll be in Heidelberg in under an hour. There aren't any speed limits on German autobahns. We can drive as fast as we want. Let's go."

Heidelberg, Germany

Stone returned to the house in good spirits after his walk. His leg was a bit weak, but he could function; he wouldn't be a physical burden to his teammates. Carefully he shook out his raincoat and hat over the kitchen sink and put them in a closet. Then he reconnected the security devices.

He was still bored. He turned on the radio in the living room, searched for the Armed Forces Network's English broadcast. He found the correct station, listened for a second, then quickly shut it off.

"My damn luck," he said aloud. "Only shitkicker music being broadcast."

With time on his hands, Stone decided to clean his weapons, the task of last resort for every idle soldier in the history of the world. He and his four buddies were all carrying Spitters, which were great for covert warfare operations, but Stone still preferred a weapon that made a loud bang when it was fired. The safe house had a fully stocked arsenal of standard military weapons in the basement. Its automatic and semiautomatic weapons hadn't been used or cleaned in the past year.

Twenty minutes later, Gonzalez strolled downstairs to find Stone surrounded by weapons and cleaning materials. "You look happy, bro."

"Shit, yeah, Berto. Snicks and Spitters are fine, but Marines should use weapons that go bang."

"Know what you mean. Move over and let me have a whiff of that gun oil." Gonzalez grabbed an oily rag, a case of cleaning equipment, and a can of gun oil.

"Do you still dream of invading Cuba, Berto?" Stone asked as he jammed a cleaning rod down the barrel of an M-16.

Gonzalez had originally joined the Marines at the urging of his Cuban-born father, who had wanted him to learn how to fight. His father hoped Berto would use his Marine training to help Cuban

242

freedom fighters invade the island and overthrow Castro.

"Only if I do it alongside you and the rest of the team. Otherwise I couldn't give a good crap about Cuba."

"Your daddy pissed about that?"

"Yeah, he's very big on overthrowing Castro and moving back to Cuba. He can't forgive me for saying I'm not Cuban and I don't want to live in Cuba."

In Gonzalez's Hialeah, Florida, neighborhood, Spanish was the only language spoken by the old people. People like his father were actually Cubans occupying America. They didn't want to learn English, nor did they want to interact with the Anglos and blacks who lived in surrounding neighborhoods. Gonzalez thought they were all crazy; his best friends were four Anglos and two blacks. He would die for them, and they would die for him. As far as he was concerned, it couldn't get any better.

"I'm a true-blooded American," Gonzalez declared. "My father can't understand that."

"Do you wish we were still in the Corps?" Stone asked, changing the subject.

"Hell, yes," Gonzalez said. "I loved the Corps! I loved Force Recon!"

"Me too," Stone said. "I miss it."

The two former Marines sat silently. The subject made all of them maudlin; none had wished to leave the Corps.

"We had to do it," Gonzalez said after a moment or two. "We were honor-bound to execute Cardona for Danny's and Mel's murders."

He changed the subject. "I'll be damn glad to get out of here and back to the good old U.S.A."

"Yeah," Stone said, shaking his melancholy. "California living is going to be mighty fine."

"You ain't gonna miss war no more?"

"To tell you the truth, I will miss it. But Joe is going to force me to put my gun aside. Beat my sword into a plowshare, as the preachers say."

"You'll try to use that plowshare on every woman you meet."

"It's a tough chore," Stone said solemnly. "But someone has to do it."

The two comrades laughed.

"What the hell's going on down here?" Bowles said groggily as he came down the stairs. "Can't you let a man sleep?"

"The author is finally awake," Gonzalez kidded.

"What is this? A gun sale?" Bowles said, staring at the weapons littering the room.

"Just doing a little spring cleaning," Stone said. "I do hate a dirty weapon."

"Give me a rag," Bowles said. "I hate it as much as you two do."

Contentedly, the three buddies cleaned the weapons and chatted about their future life in California.

Frankfurt, Germany

Shortly after noon, a message for Barry Brennan was delivered to the German Federal Police headquarters. Brennan read it, then said to Holden, "Ty and I have to attend a meeting."

"Okay, I'll keep watch. Stay in touch."

On the way downstairs, Burns asked, "What's up?"

"Don't know," Brennan answered. "The CIA station chief for Germany wants us."

A vehicle was waiting outside. Burns and Brennan entered, and the car pulled away. The car took them to the Kaserne, a military base in the heart of Frankfurt. An Army helicopter, its blades whirling, was waiting for them.

"Get on the chopper, please," the driver said from the front seat.

"Where is it taking us?" Burns asked.

"Don't know," the driver mumbled.

They stepped out of the car; a soldier waved them toward the helicopter. Inside the door, a large man wearing sunglasses sat in one of the seats.

"That's George Tanner," Brennan said to Burns. "He's a Company diver." Diver was a CIA term for a specialist in "wet work."

Brennan and Burns stepped inside. Brennan shook hands with Tanner and introduced him to Burns as the helicopter took off.

Above the thrumming of the chopper's blades, Tanner said, "We're going to Heidelberg. We've intercepted a message from the Russians. They're bringing their forces in concentration to Heidelberg. We believe they've found your fugitives."

"Shit," Brennan exclaimed. "Have we found them ourselves yet?"

"No," Tanner said. "General Burns, your Green Berets are en route. Your combat gear and uniform will be waiting for you when we land."

"Thanks," Burns said.

"Mr. Brennan, the other members of the Diver Team are en route as well," Tanner said.

"Fine," Brennan said. "Do the German Federal Police know about this?"

"No, but German Intelligence does. For the moment, they're withholding it from the police and allowing us to handle it. I don't know how long the moratorium will last."

"Holden is going to go berserk when he finds out," Burns said.

"We couldn't tell him," Brennan answered. "What would we do about him when he tried to prevent us from carrying out our assignment?"

"I suppose you're right," Burns said reluctantly.

The remainder of the flight was made in silence. In twenty minutes, the helicopter landed on the Army base in Heidelberg. Two trucks loaded with Green Berets were waiting. Burns was handed his gear by a sergeant; he climbed into the back of the first truck to get dressed.

Tanner and Brennan stood outside.

"Where are our people?" Brennan demanded. Tanner used a radio he'd kept concealed during the helicopter ride.

"Outside the gate waiting for us. The Russians seem to be concentrating on a neighborhood about ten miles from here. It should take us fifteen minutes to reach it."

A fully combat-ready Burns jumped down from the first truck's rear.

"You two climb into the second truck's cab," he said to Tanner and Brennan. Accompanied by a Green Beret captain, Burns boarded the cab of the first truck. The trucks raced away from the helicopter pad.

Heidelberg, Germany

Gonzalez had just stepped out of the second-floor bathroom when the alarm went off with a teeth-clenching buzz. He sprinted to a back window and looked out.

"Intruders in the rear," he yelled downstairs. "Blow the motherfuckers away!"

On the first floor, Stone and Bowles scrambled for the weapons they had just cleaned. Stone went to a front window; Bowles raced to the rear.

Bowles took a quick peek out the kitchen window. Five men were over the wall already, and several others were on top.

"Fire in the hole," he shouted, pressing a button recessed into the kitchen window's sill.

The button detonated a set of claymore mines, cleverly disguised as part of the house's outside decorations. The roar of the four mines filled the air; thousands of deadly pellets shredded the men in the yard and on the rear wall. The wall was shattered in two places by the force of the pellets.

"We have hostiles all over the fucking front!" Stone fired his M-16, killing two and sending the rest scrambling behind the inadequate cover of leafless shrubbery.

"More in the alley," Gonzalez yelled. From his observation point on the second floor, he could see armed men slowly creeping down the sides of the alley behind the house's rear stone wall. Gonzalez began firing his M-16; his first blast hit three men, but the rest moved against the wall and out of his sight. Despite the futility of hitting anyone, he kept firing into the alley to retard the attackers' movements.

Bowles deserted the kitchen to go into the living room for the M-60 machine gun he had cleaned earlier. He returned with it to the kitchen and set it up on a table by the second kitchen window. Bowles closed the window's curtains, concealing the M-60 from outside observers. Bowles placed his M-16 and four grenades on the counter, and checked the detonators to the three other sets of claymore mines that were mounted on the back of the house.

"Berto! I have the rear," Bowles yelled. "Help in front!"

Gonzalez abandoned his perch at the second-floor rear window and ran to the front of the house. He looked out the window, spotted the crouched attackers, and opened fire. With Gonzalez's firepower added to Stone's, the first wave was decimated.

The two ceased fire when movement stopped in the front yard.

"Ain't this fun!" Gonzalez's laugh carried down the stairs.

"That it is," Stone laughed back.

Guavaro and Markov were in the park across the street, sufficiently distant from the house not to come under direct fire. Over a hundred men were at Markov's disposal. His plan had been to quickly overrun the house with sheer numbers, capture Billings, and kill the others before the German authorities or the American Army could react to the gunfire.

Markov had assigned a crack thirty-man KGB unit to assault the rear of the house, holding the remainder of his seventy-odd men in front. That force was made up largely of agents from the former East Germany and several other former Soviet bloc nations.

In front, the initial assault had consisted of fifteen men, with the remainder held in reserve. The fifteen had been in the front garden when the sudden explosions had boomed from the rear. Immediately, withering automatic rifle fire had opened up from the first floor, joined in a minute or so by fire from the second floor. The fifteen men had been cut to pieces; dead and wounded bodies littered the manicured front lawn.

Incredibly, the house's defenders had beaten off the initial assault.

"What are we going to do, comrade?" Guavaro roared. "All this noise will bring the police and the Americans quickly."

"We'll have to rush them. We can't afford a prolonged firefight. We'll just have to overwhelm them with numbers."

Markov spoke quickly into the radio. "Rush them now. I don't care about casualties. Do it!"

The respite ended; a barrage of automatic rifle fire commenced from the street and park, driving both Stone and Gonzalez away from the windows. As Stone pulled away from the window, he saw the second wave starting to climb over the wall into the front garden.

"There's a damn army out there," Stone roared. "We won't be able to hold them off for very long."

Gonzalez charged downstairs. "We must get down into the basement. Don't forget to set the claymores to remote triggering."

Bowles set the remote firing device on the unused three sets of claymores in the house's rear; Stone did the same for the yet-to-be-used four sets in front.

"Ready," Bowles said.

"Ready here," echoed Stone.

"Let's go," ordered Gonzalez from the basement door.

Bowles and Stone charged for the door as the men in the front garden opened fire. A solid hail of bullets hit the front windows, shattering them. Slugs pounded into the inside walls and ricocheted wildly. In the rear, the KGB team's survivors climbed the wall and fired into the house's rear windows.

Stone safely reached the door, descending to the second step of the stairs leading to the basement. Before Bowles could reach the door, a ricocheting bullet fired from the rear hit him, sending him spinning directly into the bullets streaming through a front window. His body was literally torn apart by multiple hits.

Stone crouched down and peeked around the door's corner at floor level. He saw Bowles lying on the floor.

"David!"

Disregarding his own safety, Stone scrambled to Bowles and pulled his body back to the door. Inside the basement stairway, he checked Bowles for a pulse. There wasn't any.

"Oh, shit, David. I'll make the bastards pay," he whispered fiercely. He removed the remote control to the rear defenses from Bowles's shirt pocket and added it to the one for the front defenses that he was carrying.

"Berto," he shouted downstairs, "David's bought the farm."

"Get the hell down here," Gonzalez ordered. "We'll mourn David later."

Carrying the two remote detonators, Stone went down into the basement.

"Blow them all now," Gonzalez ordered. "Give the bastards the whole shebang!"

Stone pushed all seven buttons at the same time. The twelve remaining claymore mines in the rear, and the sixteen set in front, detonated. Their backblasts shook the stone house, and their pellets knocked down the front and rear stone walls, killing every living thing in front of the walls, wounding or killing many of the attackers behind the walls.

All firing ceased; there was an eerie silence.

"Let's vamoose," Gonzalez said. He opened a trapdoor cut into the basement floor. A rope ladder led down into the old sewer system running below the house. Gonzalez and Stone climbed down. At the bottom, Gonzalez pressed a button on the wall which automatically closed the trapdoor. The trapdoor wasn't extraordinarily well camouflaged in the basement floor, but it would take any intruders several minutes to find it; by then, Gonzalez and Stone would be gone.

The sewer was six feet high and five feet wide. It had small walkways on the sides; noxious water flowed down the middle. The sewer ran for nearly five hundred meters before a more modern pipe took over its duties. At its end, a second trapdoor exited into the common basement of a group of connected houses on a side street.

Before racing down the sewer, Gonzalez pressed an electronic detonator: it destroyed the room containing Ted Billings's electronic devices. He pressed a second detonator: it destroyed all of the Kirk's Armory equipment and weapons that had been left in the house.

Markov stared in disbelief at the decimation of his troops. The Russian was no stranger to violence, but he wasn't a soldier; killing to him was the silent use of a knife or a muffled gun. The ear-shattering firefight and subsequent claymore detonations, which brought death so quickly to so many, were completely foreign to him. In less than four minutes, ninety percent of his force was rendered inactive.

A loud explosion sounded inside the house; it was followed by a series of muffled explosions.

"What—?" he started to ask, but the agent with the radio, who was standing next to him, interrupted.

"American troops are coming. We must leave now!"

Markov regained a semblance of his composure. "Everybody out! Take the wounded if you can."

Markov led five Russians toward the cars they had parked five hundred meters away on a side street. Guavaro and his four Cubans hustled after the retreating Russians. Markov and his group turned the corner on the side street, coming face to face with Stone and Gonzalez who were just exiting the basement door of a house fifty feet down the sidewalk.

"There they are!" Markov screamed, and dove behind a car.

Gonzalez and Stone carefully scanned the street for hostiles before leaving the building.

"Be alert," Gonzalez warned. "Those motherfuckers could be anywhere."

They stepped into the street, their weapons cocked and ready. The six Russians suddenly rounded the corner.

"Ben! Unfriendlies!" Gonzalez opened up with his M-16, knocking down three Russians before he dove for cover behind a parked car.

Stone didn't dive for cover; he courageously charged the enemy with his M-16 blazing. He killed four Cubans and two Russians before his weapon clicked on empty.

"Drop back, Ben," Gonzalez yelled. "I'll cover you."

Gonzalez fired several bursts, but Stone didn't retreat. He ejected the empty magazine from his M-16, and was snapping a fresh one into the chamber when Markov stepped out from behind a car and pointed his H&K 9 MM pistol at Stone's forehead.

"Die, you bastard," Markov said in Russian, and pulled the trigger, killing Stone instantly.

At the sight of Stone's body dropping, Gonzalez came out from behind the car and charged, firing his M-16 on automatic. Markov's body flew backward from the force of the bullets that hit him. Gonzalez fired until his M-16 was empty.

At the sound of the M-16's bolt slapping open, Guavaro, who had never turned the corner of the building, stepped out with his H&K ready. He calmly shot Gonzalez twice, once in the chest and once in the stomach; Gonzalez's body went sprawling on the sidewalk.

Cautiously, Guavaro approached Gonzalez, who was lying on his back, muttering incoherently in Spanish.

"You are Mexican?" Guavaro asked in Spanish.

Although dying, Gonzalez recognized Guavaro's accent.

"I'm an American, you fucking Cuban Commie prick," Gonzalez said proudly. "I'm a Cuban-American!" He mustered his remaining strength, lifted his head, and spit in Guavaro's face.

Guavaro reacted instantly, firing two rounds into Gonzalez's head. Guavaro looked around; bodies were scattered all over the sidewalk. He didn't check any of his comrades for life signs; instead, he ran down the street until he reached Markov's automobile.

"Where is the colonel?" the Russian driver asked.

"Dead! And we will be too if we don't get out of here."

The driver started the car and pulled away from the curb.

"Not toward the park," Guavaro ordered. "Go the other way."

The driver made a series of short turns in the street and drove away from the park. In a few minutes, they were clear of the area.

Guavaro had no intention of traveling very far with the Russian. Guavaro was a hunted man, and he could hide better if he was on his own. The first thing he had to do was get out of Germany and into France, a country where he could speak the language.

"To the French border," he ordered, cutting the Russian's protest short.

Chapter Seventeen

Heidelberg, Germany

The trucks carrying General Burns's forces had just cleared the base's gate when an explosion boomed in the distance; it was followed quickly by the sharp cracks of gunfire.

"Let's go," Burns ordered the driver. "Forget the traffic laws!"

As the truck raced toward the house, Burns leaned out the open window listening to the battle. There was a deep, echoing boom ahead. Burns, an experienced combat veteran, accurately assessed it as a rapid series of explosions rather than a single massive one.

"Claymores," he said to the captain riding with him. "Go faster, driver!"

The vehicle came under fire as it crossed a bridge over the Neckar and entered a large park bordering the residential area. The driver slammed on the truck's brakes and jumped out; Burns vaulted out his side and hit the deck as the windshield shattered from the impact of several bullets. The Green Beret captain's body slumped out the open door, a gaping wound in his forehead. The ten Green Berets jumped out of the truck's rear and took defensive positions; the second truck stopped, and its contingent of Green Berets followed suit.

Burns assessed the situation. As far he could tell, his forces were under fire from only three or four of the enemy. He issued orders: Green Berets assaulted the snipers and suppressed their fire.

During the Green Berets' brief fight, there had been no further gunfire around the house. Burns led his men across the park toward the house. Suddenly the sound of automatic weapon fire rang out from a different section of the park. As abruptly as it had erupted, it ended.

"Over there, General," a Green Beret said. "It's coming from a street down the block."

"Follow me," Burns said. Ten Green Berets trotted behind him. His force was still more than a hundred yards from the street when two single pistol shots rang out.

"Double time," he ordered. The Green Berets ran toward the side street. Before they could reached it, four police cars with klaxons howling blocked their way.

Frankfurt, Germany

The command center in Federal Police Headquarters stilled as people listened to the excited voice of a police radio operator report on the violence in Heidelberg. Dockery translated for Holden: "There have been several explosions and concentrated gunfire in a wealthy residential area of Heidelberg. According to that radio operator, American troops are moving to the location."

The report ended, and the room's decibel level went through the ceiling as the top officials hustled toward a table on the opposite side of the room.

"Do we know where General Burns is?" Holden asked suspiciously.

"No," Dockery replied. "He never returned from his meeting."

"Ask Klaus if he knows where Burns and Brennan went!"

Braunfeld had joined the top officials; they were looking at a map spread on a table. Dockery crossed the room and tapped Braunfeld on the shoulder. The German turned, an angry expression on his face. Holden couldn't hear what Braunfeld said to Dockery, but he knew it wasn't pleasant.

Dockery's facial muscles were doing an angry jitterbug when he returned to Holden. "The Germans are royally pissed off. I've known Klaus Braunfeld for three years. We are good friends, but just now he almost bit my head off."

"What exactly is happening?"

"Apparently, it's similar to what happened at Cardona's estate. There are dead bodies everywhere," Dockery said.

Holden began to ask another question, but held it when he saw Braunfeld stalking across the room. "Come with me!" Braunfeld ordered. "A helicopter is waiting to take us to Heidelberg."

"Why do we need to go?" Dockery asked.

"Just come now!" Braunfeld marched off down

the corridor; Dockery and Holden hurried after him.

"Jesus, Pat. I hope Brennan and Burns aren't involved," Dockery whispered to Holden just before they climbed aboard the helicopter.

"I hope so too," Holden said. "But I wouldn't make book on it."

Craig and Billings, dressed in Air Force blue, had spent the morning at the American Air Force base at Kaiserslautern. After deciding that Kaiserslautern wouldn't satisfy their needs, they had headed for Rhein-Main Air Force Base. On the outskirts of Frankfurt, the report of the Heidelberg violence flashed across the radio. Craig turned the volume up.

"We have just received a report from Heidelberg that explosions and gunfire have occurred in a quiet residential area," the German announcer stated. "Police are responding. We have no further details at this time."

"Our guys!" Billings said.

"Pull over there," Craig ordered, pointing to a telephone call box on a street corner. "Check it out!"

Billings haphazardly double-parked and rushed to the box carrying his electronic telephone device. Sitting in the car twenty-five feet away, Craig could see the frustration on Billings's face. His stomach turned sour; he left the car and walked over to the call box.

"Bad?"

Billings nodded. "Very bad. The lines are dead. I tried the house's regular phone first. An automatic message came on and said the phone was out of order. Next I used the electronic device to ring the telephone in the house's electronics room. The result was negative."

Craig put his hand on his friend's shoulder and asked, "Did you receive a kickback signal?"

"Yes, the destruct mechanism was triggered."

Both men looked down at the ground: triggering the electronic room's destruct mechanism meant the team had run into serious trouble.

Billings looked hopefully at Craig. "Okay, we know they had to abandon the house. But they still might have escaped."

"If any of them did, we'll know soon enough. They'll follow procedure and send us a message."

"Should we head for the next safe house?"

"No, it's in Munich. That's too far," Craig said. "If we aren't the subjects of a manhunt already, we soon will be. We have to go to ground. The best place to hide is under their noses. We'll use our identification papers and fake orders to check into the Rhein-Main transient officers' quarters."

The radio continued to update the situation in Heidelberg. Just before Craig and Billings entered the front gates of Rhein-Main Air Force Base, the newsman announced, "We now have a reporter on the scene. We go to him live."

A different voice came on. "I am on the scene in Heidelberg where a ferocious gunfight took place. Apparently, terrorists attacked an expensive home occupied by American Army officers. The reasons for the attack are unknown as of this moment. Corpses are piled outside the house. Early estimates say more than fifty of the terrorists were killed. Police sources indicate at least one man dead inside the house. There have been no identifications made as yet. We will update you when we have more information."

Billings turned down the radio volume. "One of our guys bought it. Let's hope the other two are all right."

Craig remained mute, thinking about his early life. It had been a constant source of pain and embarrassment; there was nothing worse than living in a small farming community when your parents were divorced. Anytime his mother and father crossed paths, as they did frequently in such a small town, they fought bitterly, not caring where they were or who was watching. Most of the time the fights were verbal, but sometimes his parents would end up striking each other.

They were both alcoholics who cared little for him or for anyone else. Until his grandmother had died when he was eleven, Joe had slept at her house; after that, he had spent nights sleeping at friends' homes. He refused to enter the hovels of either of his parents—not that they ever asked him to come and live with them. Despite his home life, he had persevered, becoming the town's best athlete and student. His classmates had elected him student body president in both his junior and senior years in high school; the senior class had voted him most likely to succeed.

Several small colleges in Illinois offered him athletic scholarships, but, wanting to move far away from his hometown, he had turned them all down and joined the Marines. His plan had been to serve four years in the Marines and then use his accrued G.I. Bill benefits to attend college on the West Coast.

In boot camp he'd met Terry Malloy; a kindred spirit, Terry became his brother. They went through Force Recon training together; they had even been the lucky two Force Recon Marines chosen for special training with Britain's elite Special Air Service.

The Marines made Craig even tougher than he had been. He could endure severe climates and arduous training without complaint; under any conditions, he remained cool, his thought processes clear and precise.

Force Recon gave him the family he never had. Malloy was the first member, his other seven teammates became the rest. He embraced them, he cared for and loved them; they returned his feelings.

Finding the mutilated bodies of Mel Snipes and Danny Paige in the jungle of San Tomas had been a devastating blow to Craig. Two of his family had been murdered; part of him had died with them.

While Billings steered the car through Rhein-Main's front gate, Craig silently mourned: He knew that another of his family was dead, and he suspected that all three were gone.

The world was killing him a piece at a time.

Heidelberg, Germany

It was a minor miracle that nobody was killed when the four police cars blocked Burns's troops. Their occupants came out with guns drawn.

"Hold your fire!" Burns instantly ordered his Green Berets.

The Americans lowered their weapons. The Germans didn't fire, but continued to point their guns at the Americans.

A fifth police car arrived, and a heavy man with a florid face climbed out.

"What are you doing here?" he asked Burns in English. "Why have you fired your weapons in a German town?"

Burns stepped forward and identified himself.

"I don't care who you are," the German said. "I

wish to know why you have fired your weapons!"

Burns tried to explain, but it didn't have any effect. The German took a dim view of Burns's and his Green Berets' involvement in the incident.

At that point, a car carrying a police commander arrived. The commander ordered the police to holster their guns before he stepped up to Burns.

"I'm Commander Dirsche," he said in English. "I'm taking you into my custody. Your men are to put down their arms immediately."

It was an explosive moment. The Green Berets didn't want to disarm.

"Do it," Burns ordered.

The Green Berets placed their weapons on the ground.

"A truck will be here presently to take these men back to the military base," Dirsche said to Burns. "You will come with me."

Burns issued further orders to insure the Green Berets' compliance, then joined Dirsche in his car. The car took them down the street to the front of the house. It was a wild scene: at least thirty ambulances and police cars were parked haphazardly on the street and in the park; bodies and stones from the front wall were scattered in the street, and the grass in the front garden was red from blood.

"Did your men do this?" Dirsche asked after they left his car.

"No, we had nothing to do with it."

Before Dirsche could ask any more questions, Barry Brennan walked up accompanied by another German.

"Commander Dirsche, Ich bin Helmut Schreiber." He showed Dirsche a leather wallet containing his identification and led the police commander away.

"Schreiber is a German Intelligence officer," Brennan explained. "He's been placed in charge."

"Where are Tanner and the rest of the divers?"

"Disappeared into the mist," Brennan said. "They were never here, if you get my drift."

Schreiber returned alone. He addressed them in English. "You two may remain, but you are to stay with me. You are to do and say nothing. Is that understood?"

Both Americans agreed to the terms.

"What happened here? My government reluctantly agreed to allow your forces to handle this situation. However, you didn't tell us there would be a war. My superiors aren't happy."

"We didn't foresee this," Brennan said.

"As you Americans say: bullshit. You knew these men were former Force Recon Marines who weren't likely to surrender quietly. You also knew that the Russians wanted them dead. How could you not foresee what would happen if these two opposing forces clashed?"

Schreiber stalked away, heading for the house.

"We're in deep shit," Brennan whispered as they slowly followed Schreiber. "The President isn't going to like this at all. He'll come down on Standish for involving the CIA. I imagine your boss, General Downs, will hear a few harsh words as well."

Burns shrugged. "I have no control over what happens back in the States, and neither of us could have prevented this from happening."

"Our bosses will still hold us accountable."

"Probably, so let's go see exactly what we are accountable for."

He followed Schreiber into the house. Burns hoped the former Marines had escaped. His sympathy was with them; the whole world was against them, yet they valiantly kept fighting.

He'd be damned if he wasn't becoming their biggest fan.

The rain stopped and the sky cleared just as the Federal Police helicopter circled the Heidelberg house. On the ground below, crowds of reporters and the curious were being restrained by police blockades.

"They definitely fought a battle," Dockery said, looking down at the corpses lying in front and back of the house. "I hope those aren't American bodies."

Braunfeld frowned deeply. "Land in the park," he ordered the helicopter's pilot.

When the chopper was on the ground, Braunfeld led Holden and Dockery across the street, through the barricades, and into the house. Burns, Brennan, and Helmut Schreiber were in the living room.

"Herr Schreiber, *wir mussen sprechen,*" Braunfeld said. The two Germans walked out of the room.

"Are those dead American soldiers on the ground outside?" Holden angrily asked Burns after the Germans had departed.

"Calm down, Pat," Burns said. "We had absolutely nothing to do with this."

"They are Russian agents," Brennan volunteered.

"So the people we have been searching for were in this house and the Russians found them first?" Dockery asked.

"Yes," Brennan said.

"The Russians paid an enormous price for their ingenuity," Burns added.

As he had several times in the past, Holden detected a sense of pride in Burns's statement. Holden let it pass for now. He asked, "Did our fugitives escape?"

Motioning for Holden to follow, Burns walked into the hall where there was a body with a sheet over it. The general reached down, pulled back the sheet, and revealed a bullet-ridden corpse.

"David Bowles didn't make it," Burns said with a hint of sadness in his voice.

"What about the others?"

"Don't know," Burns muttered.

The two Germans reappeared; the Americans fell silent.

"Please come with us," Schreiber ordered stiffly.

The group walked out the back door. Bodies were scattered everywhere.

"How did they kill so many?" Dockery asked Burns. The two Germans glanced inquisitively at the general.

"Very cleverly. It looks like they had claymore mines sprinkled around the grounds in the front and the back of the house. The mines were probably disguised as house decorations. If you look up at the wall, you'll see where the backblasts blew holes in the stone. I noticed the same thing on the front of the house. Claymores are deadly. They throw out hundreds of ball bearings when detonated. The claymores were positioned to fire downward, sweeping the areas in front and back of the house."

"Where would they get the claymores?" Holden asked.

"It wouldn't be a problem," Burns said. "These people could bypass security devices protecting armories. They probably just stole the claymores. They weren't the only weapons they had; there was an armory in the basement. I noticed an M-60 machine gun mounted at the kitchen window. Bowles's body had an M-16 next to it."

"There must have been wounded," Holden said. "Not every attacker could have been killed."

"There were wounded," Schreiber said. "We've found many wounded men in the near vicinity who were trying to escape, but they were too seriously injured to travel far. Our roadblocks have captured a few less seriously wounded."

"There probably weren't many lightly wounded," Burns said. "It's clear the invading force tried to overwhelm this position, and most of them were killed or badly wounded trying to do it."

"Bowles died defending the house," Holden said. "Where are the others?"

"They've flown the coop. I know you don't like to hear this, Pat, but the men inside this house were professionals. They are the best of their breed. They wouldn't be caught unprepared. You can rest assured they had a safe route out of the house in case of trouble."

Klaus Braunfeld returned from conferring with a police officer by the back gate. "You're correct, General. It exits to a side street about five hundred meters away."

"How do you know that?" Holden asked.

"Because the local police have found more bodies there," Braunfeld said.

"What!" Burns was shaken.

"Let's take a look," Schreiber said.

They marched down the back alley to a pleasant, tree-lined street. To their left, they could see the main street and the park.

"This must be a nice place to live under normal circumstances," Dockery commented.

"It is," Braunfeld said. "Many of Heidelberg's high-ranking officials live here. That's why this incident will cause so much trouble."

They headed down the street toward the park and main street. Near the corner, they came across more bodies covered by white sheets. Helmut Schreiber went to talk to a uniformed policeman.

"It looks like two groups unexpectedly ran into each other," Burns said as he scanned the scene.

"The local police suspect that an old sewer runs between the house and this street," Klaus Braunfeld said. "They're searching for the entrance now."

Schreiber returned. "There are twelve bodies," he said. "One of them is a black man. Please take a look."

The group walked up and looked at the corpses under the sheets.

"This is Roberto Gonzalez," Holden said.

"And this is Theben Stone," Burns said, looking down at the black man's corpse.

The men checked all of the other bodies.

"No more of our fugitives," Holden said.

"No, the rest were attackers," Burns said. He studied the scene. "It looks as if the attackers walked around the corner, discovered Stone and Gonzalez, and a firefight erupted. Stone must have charged the group on the corner, emptying his M-16 into them. See the expended magazine?" Burns pointed to it on the ground next to Stone. "The fresh magazine is next to it. Before Stone could reload, he was gunned down."

Burns walked over to Gonzalez's body and crouched down to study it.

"Gonzalez didn't die in the firefight, he was executed," he said angrily. "Gonzalez is out of ammo.

He must have been trying to reload when he was shot. But he was wounded, not killed. Someone walked up and finished him off by putting two rounds into his head."

Strangely, Holden felt angry. "Executed! What bastard would do that?"

"A Russian or Cuban, that's who," Brennan said.

The group turned to look at the CIA agent; he was bent over another corpse.

"This is a Cuban assassin named Sanchez."

Brennan pointed to the body next to Sanchez's. "And here we have the body of Colonel Aleksander Markov. He's one of the KGB's top men."

"A Russian!" Schreiber roared. "The fucking Russians have dared to commit such an atrocity on German soil!"

Braunfeld was equally furious. "Germany is no longer divided. We can take action against the Russians. We will not idly sit by and allow them to invade Germany again. The fucking Russians will pay for this!"

Burns's face was a maelstrom of emotion. "You're certainly right," he said fiercely. "Someone definitely will pay for this."

Frankfurt, Germany

After Craig and Billings had checked into the Rhein-Main transient officers quarters, Billings had gone to Base Operations to check scheduled flights out of Germany.

Billings returned at four; Craig was sitting on his bed with his head in his hands, listening to the radio. "What has happened, Joe?"

Craig raised his head; tears were rolling down his cheeks.

"They're all dead. It just came over the radio. Three Americans died in the attack."

"All three dead! Could the report be wrong?"

"I don't think so. I've checked the emergency message center. It's blank. Besides, Ben was definitely identified by the authorities. His body was found in the street with that of another American. Police say a third American died in the house. They didn't name Berto or David, but we know it's them."

Billings sat on the bed; he put his arm around Craig's shoulders. "It's not your fault, Joe. We all knew this could happen."

"If I had been there, I might have been able to save them."

"I don't want to hear any of that shit, Joe. Berto, David, and Ben were professionals. They knew what to do. You wouldn't have made any difference. And you know it!"

"Yeah, I know it. But that doesn't make it any easier."

"Shape up!" Billings said sharply. "Berto, Ben, and David knew the risks and accepted them. The team will never forget the three of them. But remember what you drummed into us: The dead are dead; forget them until there's time to mourn."

"Ted, for an overeducated fucker, you're a real hardass." Craig sat up with a lopsided grin on his tear-streaked face. "I taught you too damn well."

Billings shrugged. "Now, how are we going to get out of here?"

Gathering himself together, Craig thought for a minute. "What did Base Ops have available in the way of flights?"

"Nothing to the U.S. of A. until tomorrow."

"Forget that. We need to get out now."

"Well, there's a seven p.m. hop to Rota, Spain, a six p.m. to England, and a flight in an hour to Athens." These were all Military Air Transport System flights carrying supplies, equipment, or troops.

"Do we have the proper credentials to make the Athens hop?"

"No problem," Billings said. "But why Athens? It's a long way from home."

"The flight is immediate and we'll be on the airplane for less than two hours. Hopefully, we'll be in Greece before anyone realizes we've left Germany. It's easy to slip in and out of Greece. We can use our old contacts to help us travel through the Mideast into Asia. From there, we'll enter the States from the Pacific side. Nobody will expect us to travel that way. It will take a few days, but it'll be safer."

"I like it," Billings said. "We have safe houses in several countries along that route. I'll be able to monitor the CIA's, FBI's, and military's moves from the safe houses' computers. Each house has the equipment necessary for us to forge new documents. We can change identities a dozen times if needed."

"Terry and Cece will be worrying about us," Craig said. "But we don't have time to make contact with them now. Will your miracle telephone device work in Athens?"

"It will work anywhere," Billings said in an offended tone. "As long as Terry's secure phone is operational, we can speak to him from the middle of the Saudi desert and nobody will be able to track the call."

"Fine. Let's get out of here," Craig said. "Germany has lost its appeal. Too many good men die here."

Chapter Eighteen

Bonn, Germany

West Germany didn't wait until morning to express its outrage over the Heidelberg attack.

On Thursday at eleven p.m., five p.m. in Washington, the West German Chancellor filed an official protest with the United States, demanding an apology and threatening to rescind the treaties that allowed the U.S. military to have bases on German soil.

The Soviet Union not only received the demand for an apology, it received a stiff penalty: West Germany severed diplomatic relations pending a summit conference to discuss appropriate reparations. Severing diplomatic relations halted the negotiations on unifying East and West Germany; the Soviet Union had been on the verge of agreeing to the reunification in exchange for massive financial, technical, and industrial aid from West Germany.

The West German government also ordered its police and intelligence agencies to arrest any known or suspected Soviet agents; in addition, West Germany sealed its eastern border, refusing entry to Russians and citizens from former Soviet bloc countries.

Washington, D.C.

At eight p.m., Joseph Standish, the CIA director, arrived at the White House. He was immediately ushered into the Oval Office.

"What the hell is going on with your people in West Germany?" President Sanderson demanded as soon as Standish stepped into the room.

Like a schoolboy called on the principal's carpet, Standish stood before the Chief Executive's desk and briefed him on the Cardona affair.

"What has this to do with Heidelberg?" asked Sanderson in the middle of Standish's recitation.

"The men inside the house were former Marines who have been identified as three of Cardona's murderers. The Russians tried to kill them."

"And the CIA involvement?"

Standish lied: "We were trying to apprehend them and the four other ex-Marines involved in Cardona's murder."

"Fuck that, Standish." The President used a rare vulgarity. "The CIA is to cease chasing these men. Law enforcement is the business of the FBI. Do I make myself clear?"

"Yes, sir."

Langley, Virginia

Standish had hidden his fury while in the President's presence; the President had humbled and humiliated him, forcing him to bite his tongue and take it.

"That bastard has lost touch with reality," Standish said out loud when he was back in his car. He waited until he had left the White House grounds before using his car telephone to call his DDO, Henry Latham, and arrange an emergency meeting for eleven p.m. By the time he reached Langley, he'd regained his composure.

General George Downs, Henry Latham, and the DDI, Donald Collins, were waiting for Standish in his office. Before addressing them, he poured himself a large Scotch from the wall bar.

He took a sip, then said peremptorily, "The President has ordered us to stay away from the ex-Marines."

"Jesus," Collins exclaimed. "We can't do that."

"We must," Standish replied. "And we will!"

"Joseph! Those ex-Marines will destroy us if they are captured!" Latham said emphatically.

"Don't you think I know that?" Standish replied.

"You have a plan, don't you?" Latham said.

"Yes. I've thought the problem through thoroughly during the drive back from the White House. Our agency is officially out of it. Henry, you're to call off our diver team as well as any of our other assets assigned to the case."

"That doesn't seem like much of a plan, Joseph," Latham said.

"The President said that the ex-Marines aren't our concern anymore, but he never mentioned that they weren't the military's concern. After all, they are former members of the U.S. Armed Services Combined Covert Warfare Group who have turned rogue. As rogues, they remain General Downs's problem. The President didn't ban George and his Covert Warfare troops from the hunt."

Standish's statement brought smiles to Latham's and Collins's faces. Downs wasn't as ecstatic. "Wait a minute, Joseph. You're placing me out on a limb."

"But not on the very end of the limb where it's sure to break off. That's where you'll be if any of the ex-Marines talk publicly," Collins reminded him. "If it becomes public knowledge that you sat back and did nothing even though you knew Cardona had tortured and murdered two American Marines, what do you think will happen to you?"

"The CIA ordered me to do nothing!"

"C'mon, George. We may have nominally been your superiors in San Tomas, but you could have blown the whistle on Cardona if you wanted to. You were perfectly willing to bury the whole affair, and so were the top military brass in the Pentagon. A Communist government in San Tomas didn't sit any better with the Pentagon than it did with the CIA or the White House. All of us agreed that Cardona was the only man who had any chance of overthrowing the Communist regime."

"Covert Warfare didn't have anything to do with Cardona's drug operation," Downs said. "That was the CIA."

"And we paid for our folly. The CIA director was removed—"

"And William Means was bribed to take the fall so the rest of you could escape," Downs interrupted. "Are you asking me to serve as the sacrificial lamb this time?"

"Not quite, George," Standish said soothingly. "All I want is for Covert Warfare to terminate these men. The CIA will quietly provide whatever information and support it can to help."

"What are you offering me?"

"You're about to retire from the Army anyway. Complete this task and retire immediately. We have a very good job waiting for you with the agency," Standish said. "Even if the President finds out that the Covert Warfare Group terminated these men, there won't be any repercussions to you. You'll be safely tucked away here in Langley."

"Your second-in-command Burns can take the fall," Collins said. "He's eager to catch those ex-Marines anyway. Just give him the responsibility while you quietly begin filling out your retirement paperwork."

Downs thought about the offer, weighing the pros and cons. "All right," he said finally. "I'll assign complete control to Burns. When he terminates the ex-Marines, I'll retire from the Army and come over here."

Moscow, Russia

The Kremlin had been notified of West Germany severing diplomatic ties at one a.m., Moscow time, on Friday. Government leaders were awakened by subordinates and told of the action. Through the early morning hours, these leaders began arriving at the Kremlin for private discussions with President Mikhail Gorbachev.

Sergei Demetrov, chairman of the KGB for the past twenty years, arrived at seven a.m. He was met by four armed security men—always a bad sign in the Soviet Union—and escorted to the cabinet room. As part of Russia's democratization, the KGB had officially lost its former status; in reality, it was as powerful as ever. The power of the Communist leadership had also officially died with democratization; its demise was a myth as well.

Around a long table sat the most powerful men in Russia; Gorbachev sat at one end. The seventy-year-old Demetrov was directed to the empty chair at the other end.

"Why did you approve Markov's attack without discussing it with us first?" Gorbachev asked Demetrov the moment he was seated.

"The KGB doesn't need prior approval for any action," Demetrov protested.

"Markov staged a battle on German soil!"

"His orders were to capture the electronics expert and kill the others. He had them surrounded in Heidelberg, and I felt it was in our best interests—"

"Our best interests!" Gorbachev interrupted. "Is it in our best interests to have the West Germans cut off diplomatic relations with us just as they were about to agree to our every demand in return for us allowing the reunification of Germany? Is it in our best interests for the world to believe we are still a violent nation that doesn't respect any other nation's sovereignty?"

"Markov's attack was necessary to achieve the goal of capturing the electronics expert," Demetrov said stubbornly. "I approved his plan."

"Are you happy with the result of your decision?" Gorbachev exploded. "Markov and an elite thirty-man KGB team killed. Another twenty Russians dead. Not to mention our allies' casualties. We had less people killed and wounded in most of the battles in Afghanistan!"

"But—"

"Keep your mouth shut!" Gorbachev screamed. "Didn't you consider the consequences of our forces starting a pitched battle in the heart of a West German city?"

"Aleksander Markov recommended the attack. He was an experienced and reliable officer," Demetrov said. "I trusted his judgment. His father fought with me in the Great Patriotic War."

"You old fool," Gorbachev raged. "Markov is dead and so is his father. And soon you will join them."

Gorbachev pushed a button under the table. The doors opened and guards rushed in. Pointing at Demetrov, Gorbachev ordered, "Take this idiot away and lock him up! Don't be gentle doing it."

Demetrov was dragged screaming from the room. Gorbachev addressed one of his aides. "Get Petroski."

The aide rushed out. In a moment, he returned with Igor Petroski, a hard-looking man in his fifties.

"Petroski, you are the new head of the KGB," Gorbachev said. "Before you take your seat, you are to order the withdrawal of all KGB personnel from the hunt for the Americans."

"Immediately, sir." Petroski scribbled an order on a pad. He walked back to the door and opened it. "Korkov!"

An aide standing outside came to attention. Petroski handed Korkov the written order. Petroski turned and faced the table. "Any other orders?"

"One more," Gorbachev said. "No further cooperation will be given to the Cubans in this matter.

That means by us or any of our former satellites! The Cubans are on their own."

"Yes, sir." Petroski scribbled a second order and handed it to Korkov. "Have these orders carried out instantly."

Petroski closed the door; Gorbachev waved him to a seat at the table and said, "Now let us try and figure a way to extricate ourselves from the mess Markov and Demetrov have caused in Germany."

Frankfurt, Germany

It was after eleven on Thursday night when Burns, Brennan, and Holden checked into the Intercontinental Hotel. The exhausted trio had gone straight to their rooms after agreeing to meet for breakfast at nine a.m. in the hotel's main restaurant.

Ty Burns was prematurely awakened by a knock on his door at six a.m.

"Yes?" Burns said to the Army captain in full uniform standing in the hall.

"Sorry to wake you, sir," the captain said, "but I have orders for you from General Downs."

"Come in."

The man stepped inside and handed Burns a briefcase.

"You're to read the contents now," the captain said. "I'm to take the briefcase with me when I leave."

"Do you know what's inside?"

"No, sir. I have no authorization to know. General Downs ordered me to bring the briefcase to you and then bring it back to Fort Belvoir."

"Bring it to me?" Burns said in surprise.

"Yes, sir. I just arrived from the States, and the plane is waiting to take me back."

"All right. Do you want to go downstairs and have coffee while I read this?"

"No, sir. My orders are to stay with the briefcase at all times."

Burns became suspicious. "And I'm not to copy any of the papers in the briefcase?"

"No, sir."

Burns understood Downs's intention: sending written orders under this scenario gave the Covert Warfare Group's leader complete deniability. The captain hadn't seen the written orders in the briefcase; he would return with them to Fort Belvoir, where Downs would destroy them, leaving no official record of any orders having ever been issued to Burns. If there was a screwup, Burns would take the heat.

Burns sat in a cushioned chair by the window. "Take a seat, Captain." The captain pulled the desk's chair in front of the door.

A half hour later, the captain was gone and Burns was wondering where the hidden hook was in Downs's orders: essentially, all the general had done was put the chase and termination totally under Burns's control, making it unnecessary for Burns to file written reports to Fort Belvoir.

Since he was awake, Burns began his normal morning routine: he performed a half hour of calisthenics in his room and took a five-mile run along the banks of the Main River. By eight-ten, he had finished his exercise, showered, and dressed. At eight-fifteen, he was reading Friday's *Stars & Stripes* newspaper when the phone rang.

"Ty, it's Barry. Afraid I'm not going to make breakfast. I have orders to return to the States."

"Why? What's happened?"

"I can't discuss it on the telephone. But I have a few minutes before the car arrives to take me to the airport. Why don't you come down to my room? It's room four-twelve."

"I'll be right there," Burns said. After disconnecting from Brennan, Burns rang Holden's room.

"Pat, this is Ty. Are you dressed?"

"I've been awake for an hour," Holden answered. "I was just about to call and see if you wanted to go downstairs early."

"Meet me outside room four-twelve instead. Brennan's being pulled out and he wants to speak to me. You'd better come along."

"I'll meet you there," the FBI man answered.

Rather than wait for an elevator, Burns walked down the two floors to Brennan's room. Holden was there waiting for him. Burns knocked on the door, and Brennan immediately opened it; the CIA agent frowned when he saw Holden. "Why did you bring him?"

"I thought it was necessary," Burns replied. "There's been enough deception in this affair."

Brennan hesitated for a second, then nodded approval. "I guess you're right. Come on in."

Inside the room, Brennan held his fingers to his lips; he went to the TV, turning the volume up loud; then he flicked on an ultrasonic anti-bugging device on his bed stand.

"Every Communist agent in the world knows the Intercontinental is the residence of choice for visiting American military and civilian officials," Brennan explained. "There are more listening devices aimed at this hotel than you can shake a stick at."

"What's going on? Why are you being pulled out?" Burns asked.

"The President has ordered the CIA out of the hunt for the ex-Marines," Brennan answered, looking askance at Holden.

"Go ahead," Burns said. "Pat understands that he has to keep his mouth shut about anything he hears in here."

"Do you?" Brennan asked Holden directly.

"I do and I will."

"Okay." Brennan turned to Burns. "I wanted to give you a warning. You're being set up by my bosses at the CIA and by General Downs."

"What do you mean?" Burns said sharply.

"Your orders haven't changed, have they?"

It was Burns's turn to glance at Holden.

"Nothing I hear goes any further," Holden swore.

"Even if you don't like what you hear?" Burns asked.

"Even if I don't like it," Holden responded.

Burns said to Brennan: "No, my orders haven't changed. In fact, they have been strengthened. I have been given total responsibility for the operation. General Downs doesn't even want reports from me; he just wants results."

"So the ex-Marines are to be terminated still," Brennan stated, rather than asked. Holden sat up straight and stared at Burns.

"That's correct," Burns replied. He waved down Holden's protest. "We'll discuss it later, Pat. Barry has to leave, and I suspect he has more to tell us."

"That's right," Brennan said. "As I said before, you're being set up, Ty. Downs is ready to retire from the military the moment you terminate the ex-Marines. He will move to the Company, and you will be in command of the Covert Warfare Group."

"So? How am I being set up?"

"The President ordered the CIA out of the hunt, but he forgot to order the military out of it. If there's another Heidelberg fiasco, it will be you who is held accountable since you have full control. After the operation is finished, Downs will be gone and you will be on the hot seat at Covert Warfare; you'll catch any political fallout for the operation."

"Did the President approve the termination order on the Marines?" Burns asked.

"No, he was never asked."

Burns sat quietly, thinking about it for a moment before replying: "I see. Thanks for the warning, Barry."

"You owe me one," Brennan said.

"One more thing," Burns said. "If the President didn't issue the termination order, who did?"

"The top brass at the CIA and the Pentagon."

"Why are they are so hot for these Marines to die?" Burns asked. "And why did the Marines kill Cardona?"

Both Burns and Holden gazed intently at the CIA agent.

"Warning you is one thing, Ty. Giving you classified information is another."

Burns took a step toward Brennan.

"Barry, we've been friends for a long time, but I swear I'll kick the living shit out of you if you don't tell me the reason everyone wants my boys dead!"

Brennan fell into a fighting posture, staring at the Green Beret; Burns promptly adopted a fighting stance of his own. Brennan was no coward; he was highly trained in hand-to-hand combat, but he knew Burns was his master. The two men glared at each other, ready to do battle. Suddenly Brennan relaxed. "All right, Ty. I guess you deserve to know."

Burns settled into the nearest chair. "I'm listening."

"You already know the seven Marines were all members of the same Force Recon team. It was a superb team, maybe the finest special forces team ever assembled by any country. It was so good that Langley wanted the Covert Warfare Group permanently assigned to the CIA. Downs would have done it except for his fear of the Marine Corps Commandant's reaction. You know that Marines take care of Marines, and the Commandant would never have allowed these nine Marines to become full-time spooks. Hell, the Commandant hated having this team under Covert Warfare Group's control. The Marine Corps knew what it had in this nine-man Force Recon team and had its own uses for them. But, under the Covert Warfare Group's charter, the Commandant had to allow General Downs's primary control of not just this one but all Force Recon teams. So General Downs had to tread carefully: He couldn't assign the team permanently to the CIA, but he did assign it to us as often as possible. Anyway, Downs gave the team to us for use in San Tomas."

"And something serious happened there?" Burns asked.

"Yes, something serious happened," Brennan admitted. "As I've already said, this was a superb Force Recon team. Each of its members was multilingual, highly intelligent, extremely tough, doggedly loyal, unwaveringly dedicated, and thoroughly trained.

"Unfortunately, the team was too good. It discovered that Cardona was smuggling drugs into the United States and that Fidel Castro was his partner. Naturally, this infuriated all nine Marines. They saw it as their duty to destroy Cardona's drug operation."

"Didn't they report it to their superiors?" Burns asked.

"Of course. Captain Daniel Paige, the team's leader, reported it and requested his team be pulled out of San Tomas."

"Why wasn't that honored?" Holden asked.

Brennan looked at him as if he were an idiot. Burns came to the FBI agent's rescue. "Simple, Pat. Paige and his team were working for the CIA in San Tomas. The CIA already knew about Cardona's drug involvement."

"Right on the nose," Brennan said. "Paige's request caused ripples all the way to Langley. The orders came straight from the Director's office back down to William Means, the agent in charge of the San Tomas operation: 'Straighten these Marines out and tell them to keep their mouths shut.'

"By this time, San Tomas was falling apart. The Communists had pushed Luis Cardona and his forces out of the capital and into the jungle. Paige's Force Recon team was fighting in the jungle to slow the Communist advance. When Means received his orders from Langley, he in turn ordered Captain Paige to report to him immediately at Luis Cardona's jungle headquarters. A helicopter picked up Paige and delivered him to the headquarters. Paige brought Gunnery Sergeant Melvin Snipes with him."

"Paige thought he was about to receive extraction orders," Burns surmised. "That's why he brought his top sergeant along."

"I suppose so. Anyway, the moment the chopper hit the ground, Luis Cardona took them both prisoner. He put ropes around their feet and suspended them from a tree branch. For the next four days, Cardona tortured Paige and Snipes unmercifully."

"What!" Burns stood up angrily. "And what the fuck did Means do?"

"He stood by and watched."

This time it was Holden who erupted. "Watched? Why?"

"Because the two Marines weren't important to United States interests, it was Cardona who was important. The President, Congress, the Pentagon, and the CIA were backing him in a fight against Communism."

Holden was stunned by Brennan's explanation; Burns was seething.

"Means is a dead man. I swear I'll find him and make him pay."

"You're too late," Brennan said. "Means was knifed to death earlier this year."

"By one of Paige's and Snipes's teammates, I bet," Burns said.

"Means's killer remains unknown, but I'd say you'd be making a sound wager."

"Go on," Burns said. "Tell us the rest of the San Tomas story."

Brennan detailed Cardona's tortures of Snipes and Paige. Holden was made physically ill by the description and suddenly bolted for the bathroom. Burns was feeling very queasy himself, but he managed to control his jumpy stomach. Nothing more was said until Holden returned to his seat. He made no excuses for his reaction; he just motioned for Brennan to continue the story.

"As I said earlier, these Force Recon Marines were tough. Despite Cardona's mutilation and torture, they both survived for four days. One of them died just as the CIA's helicopters arrived to evacuate Cardona, his family, and his top people. The other Marine was near death, so Cardona left him to suffer, believing he would die within minutes.

"It was a mistake. Somehow he survived until his seven teammates arrived hours later. He told them the whole story before he finally expired. They went berserk, but there wasn't anything they could do to Cardona, who was on his way to Florida."

"This strikes a bell. I remember hearing some scuttlebutt about this, but I discounted it. It was just too unbelievable." Burns's face reflected his anger and agony. "I figured if it was true, we would punish anyone who killed and tortured American soldiers."

"You were wrong," Brennan said. "The seven remaining Force Recon Marines followed official procedure to report Cardona's murder of their buddies, first going through their CIA controls, and when that didn't work, through military channels. After they learned that their written reports had been destroyed and that no action was being taken against Cardona, they raised holy hell. They threatened to go out of channels and report the atrocity directly to the Commandant of the Marine Corps. General Downs called them to Fort Belvoir and reprimanded them; he reminded them that they had been on a covert operation in San Tomas and that their secrecy oaths bound them to complete silence about such operations. He threatened them with military prison if they continued to make an issue of Cardona. Downs's threats were backed up by the others present at the meeting: two Army generals from the Pentagon, representatives from the CIA and the Defense Intelligence Agency, and an aide of President Mason."

"To the seven Marines, it must have seemed like everyone in the line of command was against them," Burns said. "I understand now why they resigned from the Marines and went after Cardona."

"Their motive for murdering Cardona was revenge," Holden said.

"You have it totally wrong, Pat," Burns said. "What they did wasn't out of revenge and it wasn't murder." He cut Holden's protest short. "I know you believe it was murder, but Barry and I know better."

"You see, Pat, the Marines' motive wasn't revenge," Brennan said. "In the Marines' eyes, it was simple justice. Cardona received a just punishment for what he did to Paige and Snipes."

"Cardona deserved punishment, but I don't agree that what they did was right," Holden quickly exclaimed.

"Pat," Brennan said in exasperation. "Try to see it from their perspective. They had tried to do it the right way. They wanted Cardona brought before American justice, but the system totally failed them. Cardona was free, and nobody intended to make him accountable for Snipes's and Paige's murders."

"Cardona remaining unpunished was a stain on their honor as Marines and men," Burns interjected. "You see, the nine of them lived by a code of honor that bound them to each other. They had undergone the toughest training in the world; training that was specifically designed to instill in them this code of honor. Remember the Marine Corps credo: Semper Fidelis, Always Faithful. And the fact that these nine men were Force Recon, Marines who relied totally on their teammates for survival, reinforced the Semper Fidelis creed even more. These nine Marines were tight! They were brothers! They were family! Then Cardona slaughters two of their family and their superiors order them to forget about it.

"Impossible! They were psychologically incapable of forgetting it. It was naive of General Downs to order them to do it and expect that order to be carried out; he should have foreseen that they wouldn't allow Cardona to walk away scot-free."

"It was inevitable that they would go after Cardona and execute him for murdering their two buddies. It's exactly what Ty would have done," Brennan said. "In fact, it's exactly what I would've done."

Holden sat transfixed. It was a viewpoint he hadn't considered. His own military experience in the Air Force hadn't demanded such life-and-death closeness, although he had observed it in fighter pilots who flew in the same squadrons. Air Force fighter pilots probably would have felt the same way as these seven Marines; warriors didn't stand by and allow their brothers to be murdered.

"I concede your point," Holden said. "But I'm still sworn to bring them to justice. In a trial, their psychological state would be a mitigating circumstance taken into consideration by a jury. The jury might even acquit because of it."

"Of course they would acquit," Brennan stated flatly. "Every ordinary American and every American soldier would rally behind these Marines. That's exactly why they will never live long enough to be brought to trial."

"I don't follow," Holden said.

"He means that if the Marines go to trial and tell their story publicly, it would destroy this country's military," Burns said. "How could an American soldier be expected to obey an order if he believed his life was superfluous to the person who originated that order? The reason American soldiers accept their orders is their belief that they are fighting for their country and that their superiors value their lives. A soldier expects his superiors to care about him as a human being; to do everything possible to protect him and keep him safe, not just throw his life away meaninglessly. The American soldier is not a disposable commodity!

"Yet the soldiers in the American military forces would consider that Daniel Paige and Melvin Snipes weren't human beings to their superiors. Their murders were tacitly approved by some of this country's top military and civilian leaders. Those leaders didn't seek punishment for Cardona like every American soldier, or citizen, would expect; instead, they protected Cardona and tried to cover up Snipes's and Paige's murders. If these Marines ever publicly tell their tale, no American soldier would ever follow orders again; they simply would not trust their superiors."

"And no right-thinking American citizen would ever trust their government again," Brennan said. "One of the greatest things about our country is that Americans see each individual as important; a citizen's life is not to be forfeited for political expediency. The country would be outraged if it ever hears what happened to Paige and Snipes.

"Besides, the investigation conducted after the appearance of Cardona's papers didn't touch most of the top people who knew about or were involved with his drug operation."

"And it certainly didn't uncover any of the military or civilian leaders who buried Cardona's murder of Daniel Paige and Melvin Snipes," Burns chipped in. "They still hold their military and civilian posts. They definitely don't want the Marines to go public."

Brennan's phone rang; he answered it. "My ride is here. I have to go."

Burns and Holden rode down in the elevator with the CIA agent. In the lobby, the three men shook hands; Brennan went out the door to his waiting car, Burns and Holden went into the restaurant. Both of them had lost their appetite and only ordered coffee. Silently they sipped it while keeping their own counsel.

Finally Holden broke the silence. "I don't much like my job right now, but I'm still going to track these men down and arrest them."

"I know how you feel," Burns said. "I've been in this man's Army a mite too long. Maybe it's time to retire."

"Does that mean you're dropping out?"

"No, it doesn't," Burns said emphatically. "I'm here for the duration. If I quit, someone else will be assigned to do my job."

"I'm not going to sit idly by and allow you to kill these men," Holden said just as emphatically.

"I have no intention of killing them, Pat. I'm staying to insure that they remain alive. And that you do, too."

"I'm in danger?"

"You are," Burns said. "But don't let it concern you. I'm the guardian angel who's going to make sure you and those boys live a long life."

At eleven o'clock, Ty Burns and Pat Holden walked into Klaus Braunfeld's office in the Federal Police headquarters. John Dockery and Helmut Schreiber were already there, sitting at a small conference table, sipping coffee, and chatting with Braunfeld. Burns and Holden poured themselves coffee from the urn on a cart against the wall and joined the other three at the table.

"I'll give you a quick wrap-up of what we have learned from the house in Heidelberg," Braunfeld said. "Theben Stone, David Bowles, and Roberto Gonzalez were the dead Americans. Of course you knew that already. Our forensic people went over the house with a fine-tooth comb. Among other things, they came up with nine separate sets of fingerprints. Four sets were those of people who maintained the house, three were those of the dead Americans, and the other two sets were not on record with us or Interpol."

"They aren't on record in Washington either," Dockery said.

"Joe Craig and Ted Billings," Burns said. "It has to be their prints."

"That's our best guess. At least, we're sure of Craig. We showed his photo to neighbors and to clerks in the neighborhood stores. Several people identified him, although none of them realized he was an American. He chatted with a clerk in the grocery store where he bought food and the clerk swears Craig was a native German," Braunfeld said.

"His file says he's fluent in German," Burns said. "So is Billings."

"Makes it more difficult to find them," Helmut Schreiber said as he wrote on his note pad.

"Yes, it does," Braunfeld agreed, making a note of his own. "At any rate, we know Craig and Billings were absent at the time of the attack. A neighbor walking her dog reported seeing a green American Chevrolet leaving the house at seven-thirty in the morning. Two men dressed in American Army uniforms were in the car, and the car had United States Armed Forces plates on it."

"Was the blue German Ford from Baden-Baden in the house's garage?" Holden asked.

"It was," Braunfeld said. "It had legitimate German license plates and registration, although the owner doesn't seem to exist. The Chevrolet's license and registration are also legitimate; John says the United States Army has a record of a green Chevrolet registered to a Colonel Samuel Bell who lives at the Heidelberg house. Of course, he doesn't exist either."

"Let me make a slight correction. Colonel Bell isn't a living person," John Dockery said. "However, he does exist in the military computers, or at least he has a very well established identity in the computers. The military's computer shows that Bell has been issued all the proper and legitimate licenses and credentials issued to all American military personnel in Germany."

"Clever," Holden said. "All our fugitives must have legitimate documents and identifications."

"All three of the dead men did," Braunfeld said.

"Did you find anything else in the house?" Burns's voice carried a tinge of concern.

"Sadly, we didn't find much. Some type of incendiary and corrosive device had totally destroyed one of the rooms. Everything in it had been turned to useless slag. There were also small piles of melted metal throughout the house and in the basement armory. Do you know what they could have been?"

"Not a clue," Burns said. He was relieved that the Marines had taken the time to destroy the weapons and gear from Kirk's Armory. "Although the destroyed room probably housed their communication and computer equipment."

"The destruction was remarkably effective," Braunfeld admitted. "Our experts couldn't identify anything within the room."

"The dead men were carrying M-16's. We have managed to trace their serial numbers," Dockery said. "According to Army records, these M-16's are safely stored in an armory in Mainz. The base computer indicates that they are still in their original shipping crates. The Army is conducting a physical inventory now. It's only partially completed, but the Army has discovered that other weapons are missing."

"Those weapons will spread around Europe in other safe houses," Burns said.

"Eventually, we'll find all of their safe houses in Germany," Dockery said. "Our military and the German government are running computer checks to match up German and American car registrations at the same addresses. When we have the results, we'll have the safe houses."

"No, we won't," Schreiber said. Everyone focused their attention on him. "Just because there are cars registered to the Heidelberg house in both the American Army's computer and the German national computer, don't be fooled into thinking this will be duplicated at the other safe houses. These men are too intelligent to make that kind of simple mistake."

"We'll see, Helmut," Braunfeld said. "Meanwhile, every policeman in West Germany is searching for the green Chevrolet."

"And the American military police are searching

at every American Army and Air Force base for the car," Dockery said.

"I have something vital to report," Schreiber said. "My unit has been interrogating the wounded from Heidelberg. A few have talked freely, giving up entire Communist spy networks within West Germany and other European countries. Of particular interest is the information supplied by one of the wounded Russians, who says the assault team's second-in-command was a Cuban major by the name of Ernesto Guavaro. We had a photo of him in our records."

Schreiber passed the photograph around. "According to the wounded Russian, Guavaro's orders are to exterminate the men who killed Luis Cardona. Castro has personally assigned him to this task."

"Did Guavaro die in Heidelberg?" Burns asked.

"No, he escaped," Schreiber answered. "He's probably out of Europe by now."

Atlantic Ocean

Ernesto Guavaro was 30,000 feet above the Atlantic on an Iberia Airlines flight heading for Miami.

After the botched attack, Guavaro had forced Markov's Russian driver to take him to Saarbrucken near the French border. In an empty parking garage, Guavaro had slit the driver's throat and left him in the car.

Guavaro had strolled down the street to the train station, purchased a ticket to Paris with cash, and boarded the train that arrived ten minutes later. He had safely crossed the German border while sipping wine at a table in the dining car.

Guavaro hadn't lingered in Paris; after his arrival

at the city's main train station, he had taken a taxi straight to DeGaulle Airport and boarded the first available flight to Madrid.

In Madrid, he had spent a restless night in a hotel near the airport. At eight o'clock on Friday morning, he had boarded the plane to Miami.

Frankfurt, Germany

At four p.m., Burns and Holden met again with Dockery and Braunfeld in the German's office; Helmut Schreiber wasn't present at this meeting. Dockery had some important information to relay. "We found the green Chevrolet. It was parked at the Rhein-Main air base."

"Any trace of Craig and Billings?" Holden asked.

"No, but we did discover that a Colonel O'Neil, answering Billings's description, and a Major Hawke, answering Craig's description, checked into the base transient officers' quarters yesterday."

"Are they there now?" Holden asked.

"They have disappeared. They didn't check out of the transient officers' quarters, and their uniforms are in the closets in their assigned rooms. Yet no one has physically seen them since four-thirty or so yesterday afternoon."

"Did any flights leave Rhein-Main last night?" Burns inquired.

"Three. One to Rota, Spain, another to England, and the third to Greece. None of the flight manifests listed an O'Neil or a Hawke."

"They were on board one of the three flights," Burns stated. "They just changed their identities again."

"They must have gone to England or Spain. It's the shortest route back to the U.S.," Holden said.

"Let's start searching for them in those two places."

"It's useless, Pat, they're long gone," Burns said. He paused to consider his options. "Remember in Tallahassee I told you it was significant that they took Craig's Volvo rather than the two faster, gaudier cars in the garage?"

"So?" Holden asked curiously.

"It's an indication that Craig was the leader there and that he's the leader now, even though Billings carried more rank in the Marines. Craig's service record book stated he had turned down Officer Candidate School a number of times. His record book carried several commendations and personal letters from his commanding officer, Daniel Paige, touting Craig's superior tactical and leadership ability. Craig, not Billings, lived in Tallahassee, which was close to Cardona in Coral Cove. Craig's the leader, all right."

"Okay, so Craig's the leader," Holden said. "I still don't see what you're implying."

"I'm starting to get a feel for how Craig thinks. He drives a Volvo, a safe, sturdy car; to me that means Craig doesn't take unnecessary chances. He knows the whole world is searching for Billings and him. He'll want to make sure Billings and he are clear so that they don't lead us to Malloy, Malloy's wife, and Cecil Jones. So speed won't be his priority; safety will."

Burns snapped his fingers. "He'll have taken the plane to Greece."

"That's in the opposite direction from the States," Dockery protested.

"I see where Ty's going," Holden said. "Craig's taking the long way back to the States. Billings and he will enter the country through the West Coast."

"Right!" Burns said. "Our chances are nil of

catching them until they try to enter the States. Craig's team ran many operations in the Middle East and Asia. He'll have contacts there willing to help, and there will be safe houses waiting for them. Billings will use his electronic genius to check our pursuit; if we are anywhere near them, Billings will pick it up. Unless they make a mistake, they'll go undetected. I wouldn't want to bet my life on Craig making a mistake."

"Aren't you putting a little too much faith in him, General?" Dockery sneered. "After all, he made a mistake and his hideout was discovered in Heidelberg."

"No, he didn't make that mistake, he doesn't make mistakes," Burns said. "His planning of the Cardona operation was so perfect that he didn't lose a man. His escape was planned so perfectly that we were so baffled, we didn't even know who had attacked Cardona. We still wouldn't know if Theben Stone hadn't made the stupid mistake of calling attention to himself in Paris. And Stone made another mistake in Heidelberg when he took a morning walk on the public streets. You can bet Craig didn't authorize that walk.

"Now Stone's dead, and he was the team's one Achilles heel. The rest of his team obviously follow Craig's orders to a tee. No, Craig won't make any mistakes, and he won't allow his people to make any more."

"What do you think we should do?" Holden asked.

"You and I will head for California immediately. We'll set up shop and try to catch them as they enter the States."

"How much time do we have?"

"Craig will take his time but he won't dawdle forever. He doesn't want his other people to be exposed for too long without him around to provide leadership. My guess is at least five days, but no more than a week, before they get back to the States."

"What if he isn't heading for the States?" Dockery asked.

"I can field this one, Ty," Holden said. "I'm starting to get the same feeling about Craig as you.

"John, Craig's people are in the States. Lisa Malloy is the key. Craig wouldn't endanger her by subjecting her to life in a foreign country. Her comfort and her ability to fit into a foreign environment will be Craig's prime consideration. The men could probably fit in anywhere because of their training, but Craig will make concessions for Lisa's welfare."

"Sounds like you're starting to admire the lad as much as I do," Burns commented.

"Perhaps," Holden admitted. "But I still intend to arrest him. Let's go to California."

Miami, Florida

When he landed, Guavaro found a new ten-man assassination team waiting for him.

"Major Guavaro, here are your orders," said the intelligence officer who had brought the team from Cuba. Guavaro was handed a hand-written order from Castro: "Kill Terry Malloy, Ted Billings, Cecil Jones, and Joe Craig. Do not fail me or you will pay with your life."

Chapter Nineteen

Los Angeles, California

Tyler Burns's and Patrick Holden's executive jet landed at Los Angeles International Airport on Saturday at eight a.m. The duo were heavily jet-lagged; they had flown from Frankfurt, stopping only for a few hours in Washington for service to their jet. During the stopover, they had curled up on couches in a hangar office and tried unsuccessfully to sleep.

The FBI's L.A. office had a car waiting.

"I'm to take you to Santa Monica," the driver said. "The sixth floor of a federal office building is being prepared to serve as your headquarters. Washington has sent the fugitives' photos and other relevant information there."

"Call ahead and have the staff assembled for a

meeting," Holden said. The driver used a cellular phone to make the call.

Over forty men and women were waiting when Holden and Burns stepped off the elevator on the sixth floor. The two men walked into the center of the group.

"We'll make introductions later," Holden said. "It is imperative that we get our network up and working immediately. We expect the two fugitives Joe Craig and Ted Billings to make an attempt to enter the United States sometime between Sunday and Thursday. We don't know where exactly, only that it will be somewhere on the West Coast. I want maximum coverage of all possible entry points into the western United States in place by tonight. Do we have a coordinator from the Coast Guard here?"

A brown-haired woman in civilian clothes raised her hand. "Here, Mr. Holden. I'm Lieutenant Sorrento."

"Fine. I want the Coast Guard to board all ships coming in from Asia starting this afternoon. Is there a coordinator for Immigration & Naturalization?"

A man stepped forward; Holden issued him instructions. Holden called out other agencies; when their representatives stepped forward, he issued them orders.

"If we remain vigilant, I'm confident we will apprehend the fugitives," Holden said at the meeting's conclusion.

An agent led Holden down a corridor to a large corner office. "You're sharing this office with General Burns," the agent said. The office had two desks, two computers, three fax machines, five telephones, and various other gadgets.

Burns, who had stopped to make a phone call,

arrived a few minutes later. He closed the door and said, "This is a waste of manpower."

"How do you draw that conclusion?"

"Pat," Burns said in exasperation. "I have tremendous respect for you, but you still haven't come to terms with who we are dealing with here. Ted Billings and Joe Craig have been trained to infiltrate hostile countries that have the manpower to close a border down tighter than we can. Those countries have never succeeded in keeping Billings and Craig from moving in and out them. They'll go through your setup like shit through a goose."

"You said we had a chance to stop them here!" Holden said angrily.

"There's always a chance, it just isn't a very good one."

"Are you suggesting that we simply abandon this operation?"

"No, we'd catch all kinds of hell if we did. We have to go through the motions at least."

"Do you have something more productive in mind?" Holden asked.

"Not really," Burns admitted. "Just a hunch that something unforeseen is about to occur which will temporarily make these boys visible to us."

"Why do you think so?"

"Well, I've been doing a lot of thinking about Joe Craig. His thinking in the past was brilliant and unorthodox, but he didn't have one factor to deal with like he does now. And that factor places limits on him."

"Lisa Malloy," Holden said.

"Right. He is undoubtedly concerned about her well-being. Caring for another's well-being is an admirable quality in a human being, but it can be disastrous for a leader. If we find Lisa, Craig and the other boys might surrender rather than place her life in jeopardy."

The operation was up and humming by Saturday night. No one was slipping into the West Coast of the United States. On Saturday night, Holden and Burns slept in the beds provided for them in a room connecting to their office.

On Sunday morning, over breakfast of coffee and doughnuts at their desks, Holden said, "I've thought about our conversation yesterday, and my intuition tells me that the greater Los Angeles area is the optimum spot for our fugitives to go to ground. Lisa Malloy would feel comfortable here: she wouldn't have to acclimatize to another country. L.A. is large and ethnically diverse; the men would have blended in perfectly. They could disappear here, and we'd never find them as long as they had proper documentation."

"That's no problem," Burns said. "Ted Billings could handle that easily."

"Exactly," Holden said. "I have this overwhelming feeling that the Malloys and Cecil Jones are not too many miles distant from us right now. And I believe Billings and Craig are headed here, too."

"Pat, you amaze me. I think you've hit it right on the nose."

The pair conferred further, deciding to circulate photographs of Billings, Craig, the Malloys, and Jones to all local police forces in Southern California. Holden's request for more agents was approved by Washington; he intended to flood the Los Angeles area with FBI agents, hoping one of them would spot the fugitives.

Vancouver, Canada

On Sunday morning, Craig and Billings woke up in a safe house that Billings had set up in Vancouver the previous year.

Patrick Holden and Tyler Burns had convinced themselves that they were beginning to "think like Joe Craig." They were incorrect. Yes, Craig did have concerns for Lisa Malloy, but other than that, Holden and Burns were miles away from matching the tactical mind of the former Force Recon Marine. Craig was an unorthodox thinker who had the rare ability to recognize an opportunity when it arose and instantly adapt his plans to take full advantage of it; it was one of the keys to his tremendous leadership and tactical planning genius.

Billings and Craig had arrived in Athens on Thursday night, ditched their military uniforms and identities, and exchanged them for civilian clothes and identities. They had assumed Irish nationality, using passports legally obtained from the island nation. Years ago, while they were still in the Marine Corps, Billings had read about Ireland's offer to reclaim people of Irish descent; all one had to do to claim Irish citizenship was produce a birth certificate proving that one parent or grandparent had been born in Ireland. With citizenship came an Irish passport. At the time, Billings had seen the offer as a chance to test his skills. Using false names and inventing family histories, he had manufactured the necessary documentation for every member of the team, including Stone, Jones, and Gonzalez. Joe Craig had seen the possibilities even back then; he had kept the Irish passports and identity documents locked up in a safety deposit box. The team had used them regularly while in the Corps. Joe had summed up their feelings: "The Corps can keep track of us if we use our authentic passports. That makes me nervous. Sometimes I like to disappear."

In Athens, Craig's original plan to circumnavigate the globe and enter the West Coast of the United States died a premature death: an airport departure board was the basis for a new plan.

"Change of plans, Ted," he had said. "We're flying Aer Lingus to Shannon."

Billings was accustomed to Craig's sudden switches; he didn't even blink when Craig went to the Aer Lingus counter and paid cash for two coach-class tickets to Ireland. They arrived in Shannon late Friday night, slept at an airport hotel, and flew out Saturday morning on an Air Canada flight to Toronto.

They showed their Irish passports to Immigration and were granted entry into the country. They stayed in Toronto only long enough to call Torrance from an airport phone; Ted Billings had attached his special device to the telephone to insure there was no record of the call.

Terry answered the phone in Torrance. "I'm relieved to hear from you. We've been worried ever since we heard about Ben, Berto, and David."

"We're fine," Craig said. "We expect to arrive sometime Monday night. I want you ready to move if necessary. Torrance might not be as safe as I first thought. I've had time to think and I've been rehashing my recent decisions. I've realized that I've been so worried about Lisa's welfare that I've become predictable."

"I told you not to worry about Lisa," Malloy protested. "She can adapt."

"She'll have to. From now on, she isn't going to be a factor in my planning."

After the call ended, they had taken the first flight to Vancouver. They might have driven across the border into the United States upon arrival, but Craig decided against it at the last second.

"Let's play it safe and make sure we're in the clear. We'll spend the night in the safe house, and you can tap into various U.S. security and police agency systems."

Saturday night, Billings had used the equipment in the safe house.

"The FBI has the West Coast sewn up tight," he had said to Craig. "It's a good thing your instinct was to stop at the safe house. If we had just driven to a normal border crossing, we would be dead or arrested by now."

"So we can't get in the easy way?" Craig asked.

"No. We could hike in, though."

Craig considered it: crossing the border in a rugged, mountainous area would be easy for the two former Force Recon Marines. "No," he said finally. "It isn't worth the time or effort. I have a better idea."

On Sunday afternoon, using different names, they flew from Vancouver back to Toronto. In Toronto, they resumed their Irish identities and purchased tickets on United to Chicago. In Chicago, they became Americans again; using new identities, they purchased tickets on a late Sunday flight from O'Hare Airport to Phoenix, Arizona.

They spent Sunday night in a Scottsdale safe house, a condo purchased with Cardona money; in the condo's garage was a Buick which would carry them to Los Angeles on Monday.

Thomas L. Muldoon

Torrance, California

On Joe Craig's orders, Terry Malloy and Cecil Jones spent Sunday afternoon dismantling and destroying the security and communications systems Cecil Jones had just installed yesterday in the team's other three houses.

Lisa Malloy was left alone to stand sentinel on the communications center in the fourth house, the one she and Terry would have shared. The communications and security systems in this house wouldn't be dismantled until Ted and Joe arrived.

Leaving Lisa alone was a mistake: She had nothing to do but dwell on what had happened in the last few days. The violent deaths of Bowles, Stone, and Gonzalez had dispelled her romantic notion that being a fugitive was similar to playing hide-and-seek.

When the news of their friends' deaths flashed across the TV screen, both she and Terry had crumpled into crying jags. Cecil Jones had been inconsolable, moving to a corner and banging his fist against the wall while bawling uncontrollably, he and Roberto Gonzalez had been nearly inseparable. She felt the first doubt about her ability to cope when the two men, who had acted as if they were in the middle of a breakdown, quickly regained their composure. In her husband's poker face, she didn't see her lover; she saw a man who routinely walked with death.

For two days, Cecil and Terry had refused to discuss their dead friends; nor would they admit their concern for Craig and Billings. On Saturday morning, she hadn't been able to stand it any longer.

"I'm worried about Ted and Joe," she said. "Why haven't we heard from them?"

"They are all right," Terry said. "Joe will get them out safely."

Despite his words, Terry's eyes had reflected his concern. Joe's telephone call later in the day released Terry's tension.

"We have to prepare to move again," Terry had said when he hung up.

Cecil had nodded as if he had read great significance into Craig's order. "Finally!"

"Yes, finally," Terry had repeated.

"What's going on?" she asked. "What are you two sharing that you aren't telling me?"

Cecil looked at Terry, then mumbled something about having a chore in the kitchen. After he had left the room, she said, "Tell me, Terry!"

"Joe's finally thinking straight again," Terry said reluctantly. "Up until now, he's been too worried about your comfort and state of mind. He was becoming predictable. That's all changed. He's become the old Joe again; his first concern is the team's safety."

"And he wants us to move because he feels we'll be safer somewhere else?"

"Yes, but the next place may not be as hospitable. Are you sure you still want to come along?"

"I love you, and you're not going anywhere without me," she had assured him. "I'm a member of this team, too."

I'm glad you feel that way." He took her in his arms and kissed her. "My life wouldn't be complete without you."

They had spent Saturday night making love. It had been a wonderful night, but there was something frenetic about it, as if they both knew it might be their last lovemaking together. They hadn't spoken between bouts of lovemaking but had remained silent, thinking their own thoughts. She didn't know where his thoughts had run; hers had been plagued with doubts about the future.

On this lonely Sunday afternoon, her fears were running riot. Her confidence was eroding. She was beginning to understand what a life on the run would be like. She hadn't taken it seriously; in her heart, she'd imagined that some day she would go home again. The reality of never returning to Coral Cove was weighing on her mind.

Impulsively she left the communications room and went into the kitchen; she picked up the telephone which was legally registered to the house.

"If I'm going to disappear," she said aloud, "I'm not doing it without saying farewell.

Coral Cove, Florida

The phone was ringing when Bo Hewitt came inside after his afternoon run. He hurried to answer it, hoping it wasn't the sheriff ordering him to report for duty early.

"Hello, Bo. It's Lisa."

"Lisa! Where are you?" The sound of her voice shocked him; he hadn't realized how much he missed her.

"I can't tell you, Bo. I just called to hear your voice."

"I've missed you, Lisa. When are you going to come home?" Bo reached over and flicked on a newly installed device that the telephone company had provided to police officers.

"I'm afraid I'm never coming home." Bo could

hear her crying. "I'm never going to see you again!"

"Listen to me, Lisa. Come home now. Terry is a wanted man. Everyone in the world is hunting for him and his friends. Three of them were killed in Germany the other day. If you're with them when the police find them, you could get hurt."

"I'm sorry, Bo. I can't abandon Terry. I love him too much."

"Don't you love me? You're abandoning me!"

"I do love you, Bo,' she sobbed. "I just wish Daddy were alive so I could talk to him. I just don't know what to do."

"Tell me where you are and I'll come to get you."

"I can't, Bo. I must go now. It was wonderful hearing your voice. Just remember I love you. If I can, I'll call you again sometime in the future."

"Lisa. . . . Lisa!" Bo shouted into the buzz of the dead telephone line. He slammed the phone down in fury and looked at the device. On its slot it displayed in digital numbers 310-383-5278; it was the number of the telephone Lisa had used to call him.

Being Sunday, it was the final day of his five-day work week. After tonight's shift, he had two days off, which he had planned to spend lounging on the beach. Lisa's call had changed his plans.

Bo showered and dressed for work. He was going in early so that he could use the police system to track down the location of Lisa's telephone. Once he found it, he'd telephone Delta Airlines and make a reservation for the first flight out of Tallahassee on Monday morning. He would fly to wherever Lisa was and drag her home. If Terry Malloy or any of his friends tried to prevent him from bringing Lisa home, Bo was prepared to deal violently with them.

Thomas L. Muldoon

Miami, Florida

Ernesto Guavaro was sipping strong Cuban coffee, contemplating a bleak future, when he received a phone call from an agent he had placed in Coral Cove. The agent was monitoring a bugging device on Bo Hewitt's telephone.

"The girl just telephoned," the agent said. "She talked to her brother for two or three minutes."

"Did she say where she was?" Guavaro asked hopefully.

"No. But after she hung up, Hewitt went in to work early. He must have traced her call somehow; the deputy on our payroll reported that Hewitt was attempting to match an address and a telephone number. Afterwards, Hewitt made a reservation on Delta Airlines for a flight from Tallahassee to Atlanta to Los Angeles tomorrow."

"Good job," Guavaro said. "I want you to take the same plane as Hewitt. I will meet your plane in Los Angeles."

"I will make my reservation now," the agent said. "See you in L.A."

His conversation finished, Guavaro gathered his ten-man "wet team" and headed for the airport to catch a red-eye to Los Angeles. Tomorrow, Hewitt would lead Guavaro to the quarry.

"By tomorrow night," Guavaro whispered, "Fidel will be toasting me as a hero of Cuba."

Torrance, California

Terry and Cecil returned at dinnertime; by then, Lisa had regained her composure. She didn't mention her call to Coral Cove. Unsophisticated about

310

electronic eavesdropping, she didn't realize her telephone call could be traced.

Cecil had brought his meager traveling gear along; tonight he'd sleep in one of the two extra bedrooms. It was an indication that the men expected to vacate the house as soon as Craig and Billings arrived.

"You have to get ready," Terry said.

He led her upstairs. Inside their bedroom, she hugged Terry tightly.

"I'm frightened," she said.

"Don't be. I'll take care of you."

He stroked her hair, trying to soothe her. The heat had risen in both of them and they made love.

When they returned downstairs an hour later, Jones was cleaning a strange-looking weapon on the living room coffee table. Lisa walked over and picked up a similar weapon. "What is this?"

"It's called a Spitter," Terry explained. Seeing Lisa's worried look, Terry added, "We just want them working properly. We don't expect to actually need them."

Lisa didn't believe him. A chill ran down her spine; she had a premonition of future violence.

"I'm part of the team now," Lisa said. "Show me how to use and clean it. There may come a time when I may have to use one of these Spitters."

Cecil and Terry exchanged smiles. Cecil handed Lisa the third Spitter; Terry flipped her a silicone-doused rag.

"Welcome to boot camp, Private Lisa," Cecil quipped. "The first thing a Marine learns is your weapon is your friend. Take care of it and it will take care of you."

"If this was boot camp in Parris Island and I was the drill instructor, I'd have to make a new recruit

311

like you sleep with your weapon," Terry said.

"Well, I guess you're lucky this isn't Parris Island," Lisa said sweetly. "Because in this boot camp, the drill instructor gets to sleep with the new recruit."

Chapter Twenty

Coral Cove, Florida

At eight a.m. on Monday, the end of his work shift, Bo Hewitt parked his squad car in front of the station. Inside the station, he found his watch commander in the coffee room.

"I'll be out of town for the next two days," he told his commander. "I've got a little honey lined up and I'm taking her to a cabin in Alabama."

"As long as you're back for your next shift in two days, I couldn't give a fuck," the watch commander said. He didn't like Bo very much; as far as the watch commander was concerned, Bo couldn't have filled one leg of his daddy Bull's trousers.

Bo stopped at his home to change clothes and to grab the overnight bag he'd packed the day before; then he drove to Tallahassee to catch his plane. At the Tallahassee Airport, he ignored the curbside baggage handlers and carried his bag to the airline's desk, where he showed his police identification and notified the clerk that there was a pistol in his bag. Bo signed the necessary form allowing him to transport his weapon in his baggage.

Worn out from his late shift, Hewitt settled wearily into his seat for the short hop between Tallahassee and Atlanta; he never noticed the Cuban agent who sat in the row behind him. During the thirty-minute layover, he ate breakfast in one of the quick-food spots in the airport's concourse. The Cuban agent sat across the concourse in one of the waiting areas and watched Hewitt eat.

When the Los Angeles flight was ready for boarding, Bo walked to the head of the line at the gate, flashed his police shield to the attendant, and was the first passenger to board the airplane. At his coach seat by the window, he accepted the stewardess's offer of a pillow, bunched it up between the seat and the bulkhead, and fell instantly asleep. Guavaro's agent kept watch from a seat three rows back.

Los Angeles, California

Hewitt slept the whole flight, not waking until the plane's tires hit the runway at Los Angeles International Airport just before two p.m. When Bo cleared the airplane's gangway, Guavaro's man was ten feet behind him; the Cuban agent maintained that distance all the way to baggage claim.

The baggage delivery was slow, causing Hewitt to fret. He was concerned that some baggage handler might steal his pistol. Guavaro's agent watched Hewitt impatiently pace back and forth at the baggage carousel. When he spotted two men from the

Cuban wet team walk into the baggage area, Guavaro's agent nodded his head toward Hewitt. Once the two agents indicated they had Hewitt in sight, Guavaro's agent left the baggage area and returned to the airline terminal to catch a return flight to Miami.

It took twenty minutes, but Hewitt's bag finally appeared on the carousel. He resisted the impulse to check if his weapon was inside; instead, he left the baggage area, returned to the terminal, and entered a men's room. Inside a cubicle, he opened his bag; his Glock 17 automatic pistol was still there. Leaving the pistol in his bag, he went to the Avis counter and filled out the forms to rent a car.

"I'm not familiar with the Los Angeles area. Could you give me directions to Torrance?" he asked the counter woman.

"Certainly." She handed him a map and pointed to Torrance. "It's not too far south of the airport."

"Don't you have a more detailed map? I'm looking for 125th Terrace."

"Sorry, you'll have to ask directions when you get to Torrance."

Hewitt went outside to the rental agency's bus stop. The inner traffic ring was jammed with cars and buses; it took ten minutes before an Avis shuttle bus came along.

The two Cubans had trailed him from the baggage area. Once they had confirmed that Hewitt was actually waiting at the Avis bus stop, one of the Cubans ran to an illegally parked white Ford with two men in it and jumped in the backseat. The Ford pulled away from the curb and headed for the Avis parking lot outside the terminal grounds. The other Cuban waited until Hewitt boarded the Avis bus before returning to the terminal to question the woman behind the Avis counter.

"A man named Hewitt was just here," the Cuban agent said, slipping a hundred-dollar bill across the counter. "Where was he going?"

The counter woman palmed the bill. "He asked directions to Torrance. He said he was going to 125th Terrace."

The Cuban hurried back outside to a blue Ford. Two other Cubans were in front; Ernesto Guavaro was sitting alone in the rear seat. Behind Guavaro's car was a green Ford carrying four other members of the wet team. The agent slipped into the rear seat next to Guavaro and reported Hewitt's destination.

"We'll pick him up outside the Avis lot," Guavaro said to the driver.

The blue Ford pulled away from the Delta terminal with the green Ford close behind. Guavaro issued his orders over a hand-size radio to the occupants of the other two cars.

"Stay close to Hewitt's car. There will be a lot of traffic on the freeway, and we don't want to lose him. I'll go ahead and wait at the freeway exit the clerk advised him to take. From there, we'll be more discreet. I don't want him tipped to our presence. I want him to lead us to the girl and her friends."

The FBI was monitoring all flight arrivals into Los Angeles. Hewitt's presence on a flight from Atlanta was red-flagged by the FBI's computer, which had been programmed to search airline rosters for anyone with the same name as any of the fugitives and anyone who had a similar name with only a few letters changed. It was an extreme long shot, one that Ty Burns had said was totally useless.

"If you think someone as intelligent and experienced as Ted Billings would only change a few letters and fly under some name like Tod Bolling, you're hallucinating," Burns had scoffed to Holden.

"I'm under no delusions that it will bear fruit," Holden answered. "But it's standard operating procedure in an FBI manhunt."

In this case it paid off. Bill Donovan, a bright young FBI agent who had taken the time to study the fugitives' dossiers, was alerted by the computer's red flag that noted the name of Beauregard Hewitt on a Delta flight from Atlanta. Donovan made a phone call before he took his information down the corridor to Holden's and Burns's office.

"Mr. Holden, Lisa Malloy's brother just deplaned in Los Angeles."

"What the hell is he doing here?" Holden said in surprise.

"Maybe this is the break we were discussing earlier," Burns said. "Maybe his sister called him to come and get her."

"Do we have a tap on Hewitt's telephone in Coral Cove?" Holden asked Donovan.

"No, sir."

"Call the Sycamore County Sheriff's Department. Find out if anyone knows why Hewitt is in Los Angeles."

"I already have," Donovan said. "No one at the sheriff's office knew he was coming here. The duty officer said Hewitt finished his shift this morning and isn't scheduled for duty again until Wednesday at midnight. While I was on the phone, the duty officer called Hewitt's watch commander. He said Hewitt told him he was going to Alabama with a woman and would be unreachable for the next two days."

"So he lied." Holden paused to gather his thoughts. He addressed Donovan: "Here's what I want you to do. Get into the Pacific Bell computers and run a search of the long-distance records. See if there was a telephone call from the greater Los Angeles area to Hewitt's Coral Cove telephone number in the last two days."

"That search will take a while," Donovan said.

"And it may be fruitless," Burns chimed in. "Remember, these people have access to electronic equipment that completely bypasses any telephone records."

"Both of you have a point, but I still want to make a computer search," Holden said.

"I'll start right on it," Donovan said.

"On your way down the hall, tell Jim Stacy I want him."

Donovan left; a minute later, Jim Stacy came to the door. "You want me?"

"Yes. Take two agents and go to the Delta terminal at the airport. Take a photo of Bo Hewitt with you. He's Lisa Malloy's brother. Show it around and see what you can find out. And check all of the car rental agencies. Maybe he rented a car and told the clerk where he was going."

"Okay." Stacy left.

Turning back to Burns, Holden said, "I have a feeling Hewitt knows where Lisa is."

"Maybe," Burns said.

"When we find them, you and I will check it out alone."

"That won't be standard FBI procedure."

"I learned from Heidelberg," Holden said defensively. "If we charge ahead full force, we'll spook them and there will be bodies everywhere."

"You don't kid me, Pat. You don't want these boys hurt any more than I do."

"Okay, I don't want them hurt. Do you think they'll give themselves up to us?"

"Who knows?" Burns answered. "All we can do is provide them with that option."

"Could they know that the CIA and the Covert Warfare Group have them on the termination list?"

"What planet have you been living on for the last week?" Burns said sarcastically. "Have you forgotten that Billings can tap into our national security net?"

"So they know."

"Of course they know," Burns said. "And that makes them even more dangerous than before."

Torrance, California

Hewitt pulled his car to the curb in front of a modest two-story brown wooden house. The curtains were drawn; he couldn't see any sign of life.

Before putting his overnight bag in the car's trunk, he had removed the Glock 17 and stuck it into his belt. He pulled it out, careful to keep it below window level. He ejected the magazine, checked the load, reinserted the full magazine, and cocked the pistol. Stepping from the car, he concealed the cocked pistol under the map he had obtained at the airport, and carried it up the walk to the door. Hewitt rang the doorbell.

"Bo, what are you doing here?" a surprised Terry Malloy asked when he answered the door.

"I want to see my sister," Bo said. He pointed the Glock 17 at Malloy. "Step back inside."

"Sure, Bo. take it easy."

Malloy walked backward into the living room

with Hewitt following him. When the door slammed behind him, Hewitt looked over his shoulder.

Cecil Jones, a cold expression on his face, pointed a Spitter at Bo. "Drop your gun!" Jones said.

Flustered, Hewitt turned back to Malloy.

"He means right now, Bo." Malloy was also pointing a Spitter.

Hewitt dropped the Glock 17. Jones stepped forward and kicked it to one side.

"Come forward," Malloy ordered. He took two steps backward and Hewitt followed him. "Halt there."

Never taking his Spitter off Hewitt, Jones bent over and picked up the Glock 17 with his left hand. He stuck the weapon in his belt.

"Why are you here, Bo?" Malloy asked. "And how did you find us?"

"I told you I'm here to see Lisa," Hewitt said. "She telephoned me yesterday."

"She never mentioned it," a surprised Malloy said.

"She's too afraid of you to say anything. Where is she?"

A perplexed Malloy lowered his weapon and nodded for Cecil Jones to do the same. He said, "Did she tell you where we were? Have you told the authorities?"

"I haven't told anyone," Hewitt answered. "I'm only interested in taking my sister home where she'll be safe. The rest of you can go to hell, for all I care."

"You haven't answered my question, Bo. Did Lisa tell you where we were? Did she ask you to come here?"

"No, she didn't ask me to come here. She called to tell me goodbye," Hewitt admitted. "I have a tracer device attached to my phone. It gave me the number of the telephone she called from, and I found the phone was registered to this address."

"Did you tell anyone at all you were coming here?"

"No! Now, where is Lisa?"

"She'll be back in about a half hour. She went to have her hair cut. She insists on being the most beautiful fugitive on the FBI's most wanted list," Terry laughed.

"As if she had any competition," Jones said with a grin.

The two friends laughed together while Hewitt stood bewildered.

"Loosen up, Bo," Malloy said finally. "We're not going to hurt you. If she wants to go with you, I won't stop her. Do you want a beer?"

"Okay," Hewitt grunted. He sat down on the living room sofa.

"I'll be right back with a cold one." Malloy motioned Jones to join him in the kitchen.

"Cece, slip out the back door and take a look-see. Make sure Bo's not lying about being alone."

Chapter Twenty-one

Torrance, California

Never approaching close enough to be noticed, Ernesto Guavaro's forces had easily kept track of Bo Hewitt while he was on the freeway. The Cubans' three Fords had closed on Hewitt's after he exited the freeway and moved onto city streets.

The white Ford was directly behind Hewitt's car when he turned off Mission and onto 125th Terrace. The white Ford didn't turn the corner after Hewitt; it pulled to the curb on Mission, allowing the two other Fords to pass: both cars made the turn and followed Hewitt down 125th Terrace.

When Hewitt parked in front of a brown two-story house, the two Fords drove past him, continuing down the street and turning the corner onto Viejo. Both cars made a U-turn and pulled to the curb.

"Colonel Guavaro, there was no car in the driveway next to the brown house and there were several newspapers on the lawn," the agent in the front passenger seat said. "The owners must be away."

"So?" Guavaro asked impatiently.

"There was also a high hedge. Any car parked in that driveway would be screened from the brown house."

Guavaro calculated the odds. After a few seconds, he issued an order by radio to the green Ford. "Return down the street and park in the driveway next to the brown house."

The green Ford immediately complied. Guavaro removed a pair of binoculars from the case and studied the brown house. He watched as Bo Hewitt walked up to the front door, losing sight only momentarily when the green Ford blocked his view as it pulled into the next-door-neighbor's driveway.

When his view was clear again, he caught a quick glimpse of Terry Malloy at the door.

"Our quarry is in the brown house," he said into his radio. "Remain in place until I have formulated a plan."

The street was deserted at this time of day in this double-wage-earner neighborhood: Residents were at work and children at school. This wouldn't be the case much longer; it was three-thirty, and schools would let out any minute. Soon it would be impossible to approach the house without being observed by the neighborhood children. If Guavaro was to avoid having any witnesses, he would have to make his move quickly.

His options were limited. One was to rush the house with his ten men, but he rejected that instantly. He didn't want his men slaughtered; he suspected this house had similar defenses to the one in Heidelberg.

While he was groping for a suitable strategy, the driver of the green Ford reported over the radio, "Colonel, a black man has just come out into the back yard."

"Get down on the car floor!" Guavaro ordered. "Don't let him see you!"

Guavaro checked the brown house through the binoculars. A black man appeared from behind the high hedge and walked into view.

"Cecil Jones," Guavaro said out loud.

As Jones walked slowly toward the street, a glimmer of an idea struck Guavaro: if Jones was outside reconnoitering, the house's alarm system must be turned off.

"Car two," he radioed to the three men in the white Ford parked on Mission. "Drive around to the parallel street behind the house and see if it is possible to climb over the back fence without anyone seeing you. If it is, move into position to attack the rear of the house."

Cecil Jones studied the deserted street; his combat sense told him something was out of tune. Experience in Beirut and other foreign cities had taught him that an empty street didn't mean that danger wasn't lurking close.

He slid his hand under his loose shirt and gripped his holstered Spitter. Cautiously he turned right and walked down the sidewalk toward the end of the block.

When Jones's hand moved under his shirt, Guavaro knew that something had triggered the former Marine's suspicion. Jones was headed down the sidewalk toward the driveway where the green Ford was parked.

"Car three, he's coming toward you," Guavaro warned over the radio. "If he comes up the driveway to your car, kill him! Make sure you use silenced guns. After you kill him, quickly drag his body out of view."

Cecil Jones was tense. His combat sense was churning, telling him that danger lurked ahead of him in the street. He stopped by the hedge separating his house from the next and considered returning to warn Terry. Finally he decided he didn't have sufficient information to sound a warning; he moved slowly forward again.

"We are in position," Guavaro's radio squawked. Two of the men from the white Ford had climbed the house's back fence.

"One of you stay at the back door, the other move up on the side of the house away from the hedge and cover the front door," he ordered.

Lisa Malloy's car turned onto 125th Terrace. She had the air-conditioner running and was singing along to a rock & roll song on the radio.

Cecil Jones was inching up the sidewalk, his eyes flickering in every direction. In the next driveway he spotted an Avis sticker on the rear bumper of a green Ford. Jones knew instantly that a rental car shouldn't be parked there.

"He's spotted you," Guavaro shouted into the radio. "Take him out!"

The four Cubans barreled out of the green Ford. Jones dodged behind a tree and hosed the two nearest Cubans with his Spitter, killing them instantly.

The other two took refuge behind their car and snapped off a couple of silenced rounds, missing Jones by a wide margin. Jones fired the Spitter again; its light projectiles ricocheted harmlessly off the car's metal, but they made the Cubans duck down, giving Jones the opportunity to run for the house.

He had taken only one step when Lisa's car pulled into the driveway behind him. He stopped moving and shouted, "Lisa! Pull out and drive away!"

The two Cubans took advantage of Jones's hesitation: They came out from behind their Ford and set themselves in a two-handed firing stance. Jones caught sight of them out of the side of his eye. Desperately he spun around and fired. Rounds from Jones's Spitter killed one of the Cubans, but the other fired two lethal shots into Jones's chest and head. The surviving Cuban took no chances; he ran up to Jones's prone body and fired again into his head.

Guavaro had been held spellbound by the action, but he recovered when he saw Jones drop. "Grab the girl!" Guavaro ordered over the radio to the Cuban covering the front door.

Lisa had watched in horror as Cecil Jones died on the sidewalk. The sight of the Cuban applying the coup de grace to Jones unfroze Lisa. She opened her car door, intending to run for the house. Her left leg hadn't even cleared the door's sill when a rough hand reached inside and grabbed her by the hair. She was savagely yanked out of the car and thrown down on the driveway. A gun barrel was jammed against her head, and a heavily accented voice ordered, "Don't move, woman, or you die!"

"Quick! Drive up to the house," Guavaro ordered the driver of his car. It took only a few seconds for his blue Ford to reach the front of the brown house.

"Get the bodies out of the street," he ordered the driver and two agents in his car. They jumped out to help the Cuban from the green Ford haul Jones's corpse off the street. His body was thrown into the green Ford's trunk; the bodies of the three dead Cubans were stuffed in the green Ford's backseat.

Terry Malloy heard a car pull into the driveway. "Here's Lisa now," he said to Bo. Both men looked expectantly toward the front door.

A moment later, a second car halted in front of the house. Terry vaulted out of his chair and rushed to the window. There was a white Ford parked at the curb; four Hispanic-looking men were picking up Cecil Jones's bloody body; another man had Lisa spread-eagled on the driveway and was pointing a pistol at her head.

"You dirty bastard!" Malloy whipped out his Spitter and aimed it at a bewildered Bo. "You brought others along with you. I'm going to kill you!"

"I didn't bring anyone!" a frightened Bo screamed. Hewitt had always considered himself tough, but now he was looking into Malloy's merciless face and knew he was about to die. Hewitt lost control of his bladder. The wet stain that spread on his trousers saved his life.

"Just stand still, Bo," Terry said in disgust. "If you move, I swear I'll kill you."

Malloy glanced out the window. Two men were

walking toward the door. One of them was holding a pistol to Lisa's blond head. The other man knocked loudly on the door.

Malloy slid from the window to the side of the door. "What do you want?"

"Malloy, Jones is dead," a voice said. "If you don't open this door right now and allow us to come inside, I'll kill your beautiful wife as well."

Malloy opened the door.

Los Angeles, California

Jim Stacy reported back to Holden at four p.m. "Bo Hewitt rented a car from Avis. He asked directions to 125th Terrace in Torrance."

"Thanks, Jim," Holden said. "Send Donovan in here."

"Narrow your Pacific Bell search down to the Torrance area," Holden ordered Donovan. "Someone in that area made a telephone call to Bo Hewitt in Coral Cove. I want to know where it was made from."

"Yes, sir," Donovan said. "Narrowing the search to Torrance should bring us quick results."

Donovan went to complete his task; Holden and Burns continued to sift through field reports.

Ten minutes later, Jim Stacy returned to Holden's office holding a fax. "The bodies of the three former Marines killed in Heidelberg have been claimed. Gonzalez, Bowles, and Stone are being airlifted back to the States tomorrow morning."

"Did their families claim their bodies?" Holden asked.

"No, sir," Stacy said. "The bodies were claimed by a law firm in Washington, D.C. An agent from headquarters has spoken to the firm. The firm's head lawyer produced wills which specified that the law firm is responsible for the burial of Stone, Bowles, and Gonzalez. It seems that all nine Marines from the Force Recon team drew up wills with this firm eight years ago."

"That's not unusual," Burns said. "The nine Marines thought they might die in combat, so they each made a will."

"All nine wills have an identical clause," Stacy said. "It specified that each of the nine Marines was to be buried in a small cemetery located on the Maryland bank of the Potomac River."

"As tight as they were in life, I suppose they thought it fitting that they should be buried together," Burns said.

"That's what the lawyer said," Stacy agreed. "But the really odd thing was their desire to be buried in that exact spot. Eight years ago, they purchased twenty acres of undeveloped land along the river and convinced the state of Maryland to designate five of the twenty acres as a cemetery. The remaining fifteen acres were to be granted park status."

"Ted Billings had something to do with that," Holden said.

"Who ever did what, that land will always remain a park and cemetery. There's a perpetual trust that will guarantee it. The trust is extremely well financed; there will always be money to take care of the park and cemetery," Stacy said.

"Another curious point is that the five-acre cemetery is strictly reserved for the Force Recon team, their families, and their descendants. No one else can ever be buried there."

"I bet there are only two graves there now," Burns said.

"Daniel Paige and Melvin Snipes," Holden said.

"How did you know?" Stacy asked.

"Never mind," Holden said. "Anything else?"

"The three men who died in Germany will be buried there next Friday. They will have a Marine honor guard."

"Why did they establish their cemetery at that spot?" Holden asked.

"The lawyer said it was a significant spot to them," Stacy said.

"What's the significance?" Holden asked.

"The view," Stacy answered. "The cemetery is directly across the Potomac River from Quantico Marine Corps Base in Virginia. Apparently, the two existing graves and the seven designated future graves have a fine view of Quantico."

"I've walked along the Virginia side of the river many times," Holden said. "Quantico is where the FBI Academy is located."

"It's also the location of something else," Burns said. "It's the site of Force Recon's most difficult training school. Every candidate striving to become Force Recon must survive that school. It is the final, and most difficult, hurdle a Marine must survive to qualify for the golden wings of Force Recon. Those golden wings are pinned on the new Force Recon Marine at Quantico."

"That's what the lawyer said made this land significant," Stacy said. "The graves are directly across the Potomac from the parade ground where their golden wings were pinned on their chests."

Torrance, California

Guavaro had taken possession of the house. He kept five men inside with him; the other two were in separate cars parked on Mission and Viejo. Their job was to monitor traffic turning onto 125th Terrace, serving as an early warning system against anyone who might approach the house.

The three prisoners had been stripped naked and tied to chairs in the basement. Before confining him to the chair, Guavaro had forced Malloy to turn on the house's alarm system. Malloy had balked at first, but his defiance quickly melted when Guavaro had threatened to kill Lisa. Terry had docilely turned on the system.

After positioning three of his men throughout the house, Guavaro came down the stairs into the basement carrying the strange weapon that had been taken from Malloy. The two men watching the trio looked guilty; one was nervously wiping his lips, and the other had a sheen of sweat on his face. It took only a second for Guavaro to realize what was stirring them up. He walked over to the bound trio and stopped in front of Lisa.

"You have a marvelous body," he said. He glanced over his shoulder at the other two Cubans. "She looks like she might be fun in bed. What do you think, amigos?"

Both men answered affirmatively. Their eyes were already playing out fantasies.

"Perhaps we'll have time to enjoy her later." He cupped one of Lisa's ample breasts. "I'll have to make time."

Terry Malloy remained impassive while Guavaro fondled Lisa; his Marine Force Recon training had taught him how to react if he was captured: Be silent, don't antagonize anyone, and don't let the bastards know your weakness.

Bo didn't have the same training as Terry to fall back on. "You son of a bitch! You'd better leave my sister alone!"

Guavaro dropped Lisa's breast and moved over in front of Bo.

"What will you do if I don't? Kill me?" Guavaro taunted. "You're hardly in a position to do that. In fact, I would categorize you the same way I did your father, Bull: You're a gasbag who has no bite to back up his threats."

"You didn't know my father if you think that."

"On the contrary, I knew Bull quite well," Guavaro said. "I was the one who delivered your father his payoff money from Luis Cardona. After Cardona's death, your father continued to give me information. Bull Hewitt was a slime! He was a man for sale!"

"You're lying! My father was a great—" Bo started to shout.

Guavaro cut him short with a backhand across the mouth. "Enough of this. Keep your mouth shut. I have very little time to play games."

Guavaro focused his attention on Lisa and Terry. "Where are Ted Billings and Joe Craig?"

The Malloys remained silent.

Guavaro studied the husband and wife. He needed leverage to make them talk. He gave Bo Hewitt a calculating look: Bo was expendable.

He refocused on the Malloys. "I'm warning you, I want an answer! Where are your two friends?"

Neither of the Malloys said anything. Terry's face remained impassive, Lisa screwed hers up into a defiant mask.

"So you don't want to cooperate," Guavaro said. "I can make you cooperate."

He moved in on Lisa and began running the Spitter over her naked body, sticking the muzzle into her belly button and her vagina. Lisa shuddered, Terry didn't react, and Bo started screaming obscenities.

"You are well trained," Guavaro said to Terry Malloy. He addressed Lisa and Bo. "I won't get any information from this man, it would be useless to try. He'll sacrifice all of your lives to protect his comrades."

Guavaro placed the Spitter under Lisa's chin and lifted her head. "But you'll tell me, little darling, won't you?"

He dropped her head and turned to the screaming Bo Hewitt. "I'm tired of you!"

Guavaro pointed the Spitter and pulled the trigger. The weapon emitted no sounds, but pinpricks of blood blossomed all over Bo Hewitt's body. Guavaro continued to fire; Hewitt's body vibrated from the multiple impacts. Bo was long dead before the Spitter ran out of ammunition.

Lisa was screaming, but Guavaro ignored her. "Ah, yes," he said, looking at the Spitter he was holding. "The nasty little weapon that you used in Coral Cove. It's most effective."

Guavaro slapped the hysterical Lisa across the face and jammed the Spitter against Malloy's chest. "You have exactly two seconds to tell me the whereabouts of Craig and Billings," he snarled at Lisa. "If you don't, I'll pull the trigger and your husband will die. Then my men and I will rape you repeatedly while we wait for the other two. But you can save us all that unpleasantness by simply telling us where they are."

"Don't say anything, Lisa," Terry managed to get out before Guavaro jammed the Spitter into his mouth, breaking several teeth. Blood began to flow down Malloy's chin.

"Your time is up, Mrs. Malloy. Say goodbye to your husband."

Fear plain on her face, Lisa screamed, "No! Don't kill him! Joe and Ted will arrive tonight! They're driving in from Arizona!"

Chapter Twenty-two

Los Angeles, California

With the search area narrowed, Pacific Bell's computer rapidly turned up a long-distance call made from Torrance to Bo Hewitt's Coral Cove home.

"The telephone is registered to 651 125th Terrace," Bill Donovan said. He produced a map of Torrance and pointed to a street. "Here it is. Between Mission and Viejo."

"General Burns and I will check it out," Holden said to Donovan. "You take charge while I'm out of the office. Keep monitoring our network for any sign of Ted Billings and Joe Craig."

"Don't you think you should take along backup?" Donovan suggested.

"No. We're only going to take a peek at the house, we're not going to knock on the door," Holden said. "No action will be considered until we have Craig's and Billings's whereabouts pinned down."

"I understand," Donovan said.

"If you need me," Holden said, "call my car telephone."

Torrance, California

Rush hour traffic delayed them, and it was after six p.m. when their car finally exited the freeway. They made better time on the city's streets, fifteen minutes later, Holden turned off a large commercial avenue onto Mission and headed for 125th Terrace. Once they were off the commercial street, the area became residential.

"Our fugitives have money?" Holden said. "This doesn't look like their type of neighborhood."

The streets swarmed with children of mixed ethnic backgrounds; men were gathered in driveways drinking beer and chatting. There weren't any women visible; no doubt they were inside cooking dinner.

"It's textbook," Burns declared. "Our soldiers are taught to seek out and blend into this type of neighborhood. It's the kind where people are more concerned with putting bread on the table than asking questions. In fact, this neighborhood is so textbook that I'm amazed Craig actually set up shop here. Lisa Malloy's presence must be completely clouding Craig's thinking. He's fallen back on his training rather than improvising like we've seen him do in the past."

As they cruised down Viejo in their white Chevrolet, Burns's head kept swiveling, studying both sides of the street. Just before the corner of 125th

Terrace, Burns sat upright and looked straight ahead.

"Pat, don't alter your speed," Burns ordered when Holden turned onto 125th Terrace. "And for God's sake, don't look at the house as we pass it!"

Holden complied: He drove down 125th Terrace and turned right on Viejo.

"Keep going," Burns said. "Don't change your speed and don't look back."

The puzzled FBI agent continued driving until he reached a main commercial street.

"There's a Big Boy restaurant. Let's have some coffee," Burns said. "I'll explain inside."

Dutifully, Holden parked the car in the restaurant's lot. The two men entered the building and were promptly seated in a large booth.

"What was that all about?" Holden asked.

"Wait until after we order," Burns said as the waitress appeared at their table. The men ordered coffee and sandwiches, remaining silent while the waitress poured their coffee.

"The house was under surveillance," Burns said after the waitress walked away. "There was a white Ford parked on Viejo with a dark complexioned man sitting behind the wheel. There was another Ford, this one blue, driven by a second dark-complexioned man on Mission. Actually, surveillance isn't the correct word; outpost is a better one."

"What do you mean?"

"The house was occupied. Bo Hewitt's rental car was parked in front and there was a Buick in the driveway. In front of the Buick there was a green Ford. Out of the corner of my eye I glimpsed a man looking out the first-floor picture window."

"So we're too late? Someone arrived before us."

"That's right, and they aren't Americans. My guess is that the Cubans are in control of the house. Bo Hewitt must have led them here."

"Shit!" Holden exclaimed. "How did the Cubans surprise these Force Recon Marines and capture the house?"

"Probably had something to do with Lisa Malloy."

"If there are Cubans inside, they must be led by that Cuban major, Ernesto Guavaro, we were told about in Germany," Holden said. "He has orders to kill our boys!" Burns said, starting out of the booth.

"Sit down, Ty. Guavaro hasn't done it yet or else he wouldn't still be inside. His presence indicates that Craig and Billings haven't arrived," Holden said thoughtfully. "He's waiting for them."

"That has to be the answer," Burns said, settling back down. "He must expect them soon or he wouldn't have his men sitting in cars to give an early warning about anyone approaching the street."

"If Guavaro is expecting Billings and Craig, that means they evaded our blockade and are in the country," Holden said.

"I told you it was a waste of manpower."

"Don't rub it in," Holden pleaded. He asked a more serious question: "Do you think Guavaro has killed everyone else inside the house?"

"Lisa Malloy has to be alive. The Cuban would need her as a pawn to use with Craig and Billings," Burns said. "The odds aren't so good for her husband, brother, or Cecil Jones. If I were the Cuban, I'd kill Malloy and Jones; they are too dangerous to remain alive."

"What are we going to do?" Holden asked. "Should we call in reinforcements?"

Before Burns could answer, a man stepped up to their booth and said in a polite voice, "I wouldn't do that."

Holden and Burns stared up at the man and stiffened. From under the coat draped across his right arm, Joe Craig was pointing a Spitter at them.

Joe Craig and Ted Billings had made the drive from Phoenix to Los Angeles quicker than anticipated; it was four-thirty p.m. when they stopped in Inglewood so that Billings could telephone the Malloys' secure phone in the hidden basement room. It was normal security procedure; neither of them expected anything other than for Terry Malloy to answer the phone.

"The line is dead," Billings said as he climbed back into the car. "Could Terry or Cecil have disconnected it already?"

"No," Craig said. "They have trouble."

Guavaro should have been suspicious of Terry Malloy's passive willingness to activate the house's alarm system. Malloy had not only activated the system, he had dialed a code sequence into it which destroyed the basement's hidden communications center and illuminated ultraviolet lights set under the front and back eaves of the house's roof.

"We'll take a closer look," Craig said. "If the warning lights are on, we'll know the house has been taken."

Fifteen minutes later, they were driving down Viejo.

"Far enough," Craig said.

Billings pulled into a side street; he made a U-turn and parked with the car's hood pointing toward Viejo.

"Our street is three blocks up," Craig said. "We'll make our reconnaissance and meet back here in twenty minutes."

Craig walked down the block toward Mission; Billings walked down Viejo. Twenty minutes later, they were back in their car.

"There's a watcher parked on Mission in a blue Ford," Craig reported. "I bypassed him and went down the parallel street to the rear of the house. The back warning lights are lit."

The warning lights under the eaves had been strategically placed. If you were aware of their presence, if you were wearing the proper eyewear to make their ultraviolet light visible, and if you knew exactly where to stand on the streets parallel to 125th Terrace, you could see the warning lights shining through the trees and other houses. You could check them in perfect safety; no one on a parallel street could be seen from any of the house's windows. An invader could walk around outside the house and never notice that the lights were burning unless he was wearing a special set of glasses to make the ultraviolet light visible.

"There's another watcher on Viejo," Billings said.

"In a white Ford," Craig said. "I saw him on the way back. I avoided passing close to either Ford. I'm sure their drivers didn't spot me. But I did get close enough to see that the drivers were Hispanic, probably Cubans."

"There are more of them inside the house," Billings said. "The front warning lights are on, too."

"Well, we have a definite problem," Craig stated. "In a few hours it will be dark. We'll have to wait until then to do anything about it."

The two had been discussing their options when Burns and Holden had driven past on Viejo. Craig noticed them instantly.

"Two more," he said. "Did you see them?"

"In the white Chevrolet," Billings answered. "I know the man in the passenger seat. His name is Tyler Burns. He's a Green Beret colonel, or at least he was the last time I saw him. Bo pointed him out to me during one of my visits to Fort Benning."

"Interesting. I wonder what he's doing here."

"Their car was headed toward Terry's street," Billings said. "He must be after us."

"Start up," Craig ordered, opening the car door. "I'm going to see if they drive past this street on Mission."

Craig ran down the street behind Burns's car. In a moment, he came running back.

"They just drove past," he said. "They're heading for the main thoroughfare. Whip out on Viejo and beat them to the main thoroughfare. Turn left and we'll come at them from the front."

With a masterful piece of driving, Billings succeeded in making it to the main thoroughfare, and into a convenience store parking lot, before the white Chevrolet turned the corner at Mission. When it did, the Chevrolet stopped in the Big Boy's parking lot directly across from the convenience store.

"What do we do now?" Billings asked as they watched Holden and Burns walk into the restaurant.

"We recruit additional forces," Craig replied. "Pull across the street."

Billings carefully pulled across and parked in the Big Boy's lot. They both exited the car and entered the restaurant.

"Cover me," Craig said to Billings. With his Spitter under a coat, Craig walked directly up to the pair's booth and spoke to them. In a moment, he headed back to the door and motioned for Billings to accompany him outside.

On the sidewalk, Billings asked, "What did you say?"

"I extended an invitation to talk. It looks as if they are accepting," Craig said as Holden and Burns came out the restaurant door. The group moved to Holden's Chevrolet.

"If you don't mind, one of you will sit in the back with me," Craig politely requested. "The other will sit behind the wheel. Ted will sit in the passenger's side."

Burns opened the rear door and slid into the car; Craig came in behind him. Holden sat on the driver's side, Billings on the passenger's side.

"You obviously know who we are," Craig said. "Who are you?"

"I'm General Tyler Burns and this is FBI Special Agent Patrick Holden."

"General Burns, huh? Ted says you're a Green Beret from Fort Benning, so that must mean you are a member of the Combined Covert Warfare Group."

"That's right," Burns admitted. "I'm one of you."

"You're not one of us, you're a general!" Craig said sharply. "We were taught a hard lesson: high-ranking officers couldn't care less about us."

"I had nothing to do with killing your friends in San Tomas."

"You know about it?" Billings exploded.

"Yes—" Burns said.

"Did you do anything about it?" Billings interrupted in a loud voice. "Hell, no, you didn't. Mel and Danny were tortured and murdered, and officers of your rank told us to forget it ever happened."

"I didn't—" Burns tried to say.

Billings talked right over Burns's protests. "General officers and the CIA let Cardona run drugs into the States and poison little kids just so you could achieve some pie-in-the-sky military objective. They said those objectives were more important than Danny's and Mel's lives. Well, Danny and Mel were important to us, and we weren't going to allow anyone to waste them and get away with it!"

"Easy, Billings," Holden said soothingly. "General Burns and I just learned about San Tomas four days ago."

"Even if what you say is true, other military and civilian leaders knew about it a long time ago," an unconvinced Billings replied. "They didn't give a shit."

"Well, I give a shit," Burns unexpectedly shouted. "I intend to get the bastards that covered it up."

"How, General?" Billings said mockingly. "General George Downs must be your boss. When we refused to accept the CIA's code of silence, Downs reminded us of our secrecy oaths and threatened to throw us in a military prison if we didn't obey his order to remain silent. Then he sent our team into Laos on a suicide mission, hoping that the seven of us would die there and solve everyone's problem."

"He tried to kill you?" Burns said in amazement.

"He tried and failed," Craig answered. "Even without Dan Paige and Mel Snipes, we were too good to die in the jungle."

"Thanks to you," Billings said to Craig before addressing Holden and Burns. "Downs inserted us into the mountain region, then cut all radio communications with us. When we arrived at our objective, we discovered it was a trap: The enemy had been tipped that we were coming. We completed the mission anyway, thanks to Joe. Then we walked out of that damn country. By the time we reached safety, Joe had convinced us to keep our mouths shut about San Tomas. Downs was shocked when we showed up in the Bangkok safe house. Since we didn't renew our complaints, Downs believed he had taught us a lesson and we would remain silent forever."

"But he underestimated you," Burns said. "You took care of Cardona yourselves."

Both Craig and Billings smiled slightly, but neither answered Burns.

"Downs is screwing Ty like he did you," Holden said. "Downs is setting Ty up to take the fall over you."

"Big deal. We all have problems," Billings said angrily. "Our friends are dead, and we're being hunted."

"I promise you, I'll find a means of making Downs pay for covering up the deaths of your two friends," Burns shouted at Billings.

"Don't you worry about Downs," Billings shouted back. "He's going to pay—"

"Shut up, Ted," Craig said sharply.

Billings looked at Craig; they remained silent, but communication seemed to flow between the two. Billings gave a wry smile, then leaned back against the window.

Craig turned his attention to Burns. "Calm down, General. For the moment, I'm inclined to accept your word that you weren't in the know about San Tomas. I'm going to provide you with the opportunity to prove you truly are one of us and that you care what happens to us."

"How are you going to do that?" Burns asked curiously.

"I'm going to trust you." Craig inclined his head toward Holden. "And Mr. Holden, too. You both can help to rescue our friends inside the house back there."

"Wait a second! This is an FBI matter now," Holden said. "I have a lot of sympathy for what you've gone through, but it's gone far enough. Now you're going to let me handle it! I'm placing both of you under arrest."

"Under arrest," Billings laughed. "You seem to have a misconception about who are holding the guns."

"Your guns aren't a threat anymore," Holden stated. "I don't believe you'll kill us."

"Put your Spitter away, Ted," Craig ordered. "The man has called our bluff."

"Joe!" Billings protested.

Craig slipped his own weapon under his shirt and repeated, "Put your Spitter away."

This time Billings followed Craig's order.

"That's better," Holden said. "Now we're going to call in my men."

"No, you aren't," Craig stated. "Any action involving the authorities will get our friends killed."

"He's right," Burns declared. "The men inside that house are Cuban agents who will kill their captives at the first sign of police and damn the consequences. You call in your people and you're signing the death warrants of everyone inside the house."

Holden thought about it. The Cubans weren't the same as the desperados he usually dealt with;

the Cubans would kill their hostages without worrying about their own lives.

"What is our alternative?" he asked reluctantly. The other three men in the car visibly relaxed.

"Let me outline the situation," Craig said. "We know the house is occupied by hostiles. We don't know how many. We have two more hostiles sitting in cars on outpost duty. You spotted them or you would've stopped at the house."

"Ty spotted them," Holden admitted. "I never saw them."

"It is irrelevant who spotted them," Craig said. "We're sure that at least one of our friends is alive, because the warning alarm has been tripped."

"What warning alarm?" Burns asked.

"There are several," Billings explained. "The communications room had been destroyed, and the secure telephone line is dead. That's one warning. And the warning lights on the house are burning."

"That means that whoever triggered the alarm thought that he or she would still be alive when we arrived," Craig said.

"How do you figure that?" Holden asked.

"Simple," Craig answered. "If they thought they were going to be killed immediately, they would have triggered the explosive charges which would have destroyed the house. This leads me to believe that Lisa is still alive and the house was taken without a battle, which probably means that more of our friends are alive."

"How do you know there wasn't a battle?" Holden asked.

"For two reasons," Billings explained. "If there was and our side won, our friends would have abandoned the house and left us a message. If there was and our side was in danger of losing, our friends would have retreated to the basement communications room and blown up the house to kill as many of the enemy as possible. That way, Joe and I would have fewer of the enemy to face on our arrival."

"Jesus, that's drastic!" Holden exclaimed.

"Not really. The communications room is in the basement and has been reinforced," Billings said. "It probably would survive the blast."

"Probably?" Holden said. "How reassuring!"

"You can't live forever, Mr. Holden," Billings chuckled. "Wouldn't you blow the house to lessen the odds against the comrades you knew would be coming to your rescue?"

"I don't know," Holden answered truthfully.

"Take it from me," Billings said. "Any of us would. Not blowing the house is significant."

"Ted's correct," Craig said. "My guess is Terry was the one who decided not to blow the house. He was protecting Lisa. The odds are that Cecil is dead, but Terry and Lisa are probably alive. Most likely, the Cubans believe we will bargain for Terry's and Lisa's lives."

"You will bargain, won't you?" Holden asked.

"No," Craig answered.

Holden was shocked; Burns was too, but he covered it up. He asked, "Do you know Bo Hewitt is in there?"

"No, but that explains it," Craig said.

"Explains what?" Burns asked.

"How the house was discovered," Craig said. "I bet Lisa telephoned Bo and he traced the call. He came charging out to help his sister and led everyone else here."

"We found you because a call was made from this

address to Bo Hewitt," Burns confirmed. "The Cubans must have followed Bo."

"Bo has no value, so the Cubans have probably killed him," Billings said.

"To answer your question, Mr. Holden, we won't bargain with them," Craig said. "It's pointless. There's nothing to be gained by it. In the end, they'll just kill everyone anyway."

"Isn't that condemning your people to their deaths?" Holden said.

"On the contrary, it's their only chance," Craig explained. "Terry is a professional. He knows we're not going to bargain, although he probably hasn't told Lisa. He wouldn't bargain if he was sitting out here. Lisa's and Terry's survival hinges on our ability to get inside the house and kill the Cubans before the Cubans can kill their hostages."

"I've already said there will be no more killing," Holden exploded.

"I'm afraid it's the only way," Craig said. "The only way to stop the Cubans is to kill them. Terry knows we will attempt a break-in. He expects it. He'll be waiting for an opportunity to aid us."

Burns said, "At this level, Pat, hostages are always murdered. Remember, the Cubans inside are under direct orders from Fidel Castro to kill these men. The Cubans will carry out their orders even if they must forfeit their own lives."

"It has come down to decision time," Craig said. "Are you in or not?"

Burns said, "Why don't you two step out of the car for a minute? Pat and I have something to discuss."

Guavaro was beginning to feel edgy. He wanted to end this affair and return to Havana where Fidel could lavish honors upon him. Guavaro wondered if the girl was right about Billings and Craig. Where were they?

He thought they had arrived around six o'clock when his man stationed on Viejo had reported two men in a white Chevrolet turning onto this street. Guavaro had stood at the front window and watched the car drive past. It seemed that neither of the men in the car was Craig or Billings, since the car hadn't slowed down, nor had the men exhibited any interest in the house. When the watcher on Mission reported that the car was driving away, Guavaro dismissed it from his mind.

But then things had started to go wrong. A half hour later, he'd been forced to recall his outposts when a police car challenged one of the cars. People had arrived home from work; a nervous neighbor had noticed the watcher's Ford and called the police to investigate. The police had bought the watcher's story that he was waiting for a friend, but Guavaro had been forced to bring the two watchers in, since they had come under police scrutiny. It made him nervous to have all seven of his men inside the house; he didn't like being without advance outposts.

Guavaro went downstairs; the basement reeked of the woman's fear and the pungent smell of a dead body losing its bodily functions. He confronted the two naked hostages. "When are your friends due?"

The man remained impassive. The woman was staring at her brother's bloody corpse, which Guavaro had purposely left by her side.

Guavaro removed his silenced Glock from its shoulder holster and jammed it into the man's face.

The Spitter he'd used on Bo Hewitt was empty, and the Cuban didn't know how to reload it.

"Answer me, woman, or I blow your husband's head off!"

"They should be here anytime," she suddenly screamed. "I don't know when exactly. They're driving in from Arizona. Maybe they weren't leaving there until dark."

Guavaro stared at the woman's nude body, lust rising in him. It would be nice to relax for a half hour or so with this woman. He could see the same lust etched on the face of the guard.

Turning to Malloy, Guavaro said, "Tell me how the security system works."

The man remained silent. Guavaro carefully pointed his pistol at a point on Malloy's right thigh where there were no major arteries. "One more chance to tell me."

Malloy remained impassive; Guavaro pulled the trigger. Malloy's body arched in agony, but he remained silent. The bullet had passed cleanly through his thigh; it was not a life-threatening wound, although blood started to flow copiously. The Cuban moved his gun to the man's left thigh.

"I will slowly blow you to pieces if you don't speak."

"Stop it! Stop it! I'll tell you!" Lisa screamed. "Bandage his leg and I'll tell you."

"Tell me first, then I'll bind his wound."

"The whole house and the back yard are alarmed. When the alarm system is on, no one can enter without us hearing a loud buzzer."

"How do you turn it on and off?"

"There's a switch by the back door. Terry armed it when you ordered him to do it. The switch is up now. Press it down and it shuts the system off. Since the system is armed, all you have to do is push the switch back to the up position to turn the alarm back on again."

Looking over his shoulder at the guard, Guavaro spoke in Spanish, explaining the system. "Test it," he ordered. "Turn it off, and have someone go out in the back yard. Turn it on again and see if the alarm sounds. Make sure you cut it off fast. We don't want the neighbors to notice."

The guard went upstairs. In three minutes, a loud buzz filled the house, then was abruptly cut off. The guard came back down and nodded to Guavaro. "It works."

"Fix my husband's leg," Lisa begged. "Please, I'll do anything."

Guavaro appraised the beautiful blond woman. The alarm system gave him more confidence. Perhaps there was time to have a little relaxation for himself and his men. It would be a shame to kill this beautiful woman without sampling her body first.

"Bandage his wound," he ordered the guard, "And bring me a knife to cut the woman's bonds. We are moving her elsewhere."

Malloy's face remained impassive, but Guavaro noticed a savage glint in his eyes. It made Guavaro shiver: it was as if he'd just looked into his own grave.

Holden's and Burns's conversation was short and to the point. "I don't like this," the FBI agent said. "It goes against all my training."

"It's our only option," Burns said. "If you call in reinforcements, you're condemning the hostages to death. These men have a plan. Let's help them."

"What do you make of Craig?"

"In over thirty years in the military, I've only seen a few like him," Burns said. "He's a natural leader. Men believe in him; his presence inspires confidence. Can't you feel it?"

"There is something magnetic about him," Holden agreed. "All right, let's do it!"

Burns motioned the two men back to the car.

"We will do it your way," Burns said once they were all back in the car. "But the condition is that we help."

"I'm against it," Billings protested.

"We can use them," Craig said, overruling Billings. "The general is a Green Beret and has gone through similar training to ours. Mr. Holden can be placed in a position where he will be useful."

"I want it understood that you two are still under arrest, and when this is over, I'm taking you in," Holden said. "I'll make sure that all the mitigating circumstances surrounding the Cardona incident become known. I don't quite understand why you took it upon yourselves to kill Cardona, but I can see you had provocation."

"We didn't kill him, we executed him for his crimes," Craig explained. "We did it for honor, Mr. Holden. Our honor and the honor of our two friends who Cardona murdered. We are United States Marines! We believe in honor! We were trained to respect honor. Executing Cardona was the only honorable thing we could do."

"Damn straight," Billings added. "We were Marines then, and we are still Marines at heart. Marines don't allow fellow Marines to be killed without retribution. We have a saying in the Marines: our payback is a motherfucker. That's what Cardona learned: fuck with the Marines and we put some serious hurting on you."

"Fucking A," Craig said seriously.

"Do you know the Marine Corps motto, Mr. Holden?" Billings continued. "It's Semper Fidelis. Always Faithful. We believed it then, and we believe it now. The men in that house believe it—that's what's keeping them going. They know we're coming for them."

"Semper Fi, Mr. Holden!" Craig agreed. "Semper Fi! They know we're coming."

Billings's and Craig's outburst raised a glimmer of understanding in Holden: These men were dedicated to their comrades. The Marine Corps motto wasn't just a slogan, it was a way of life for them. Admiration for their spirit flowed through him. He was so overcome by it, he failed to notice that neither Billings nor Craig had agreed to come into custody after the action was finished.

Burns was overcome by Billings's statement; he looked as if he wanted to hug the two former Marines. As a military leader, he had tried to instill such fierce loyalty in his troops. Unfortunately, many soldiers only played lip service to the idea of honor and fidelity. Burns's voice dripped with respect: "What do you want done, Mr. Craig?"

"Call me Joe," Craig said. The four men exchanged first names.

"We are hampered by all the activity on the street. We'll have to wait until it dies down. It's seven now; we should wait until midnight or after. That gives us plenty of time to prepare for the attack on the house."

"What kind of preparation?" Burns asked.

"We need the special equipment and weapons available to Covert Warfare. Only you can acquire it for us, Ty. You can get it either from the Force Recon depot in Camp Pendleton in Oceanside or from the Navy Seal headquarters in San Diego. El Toro Marine airfield isn't too far from Torrance. You can use your credentials to requisition a helicopter, fly to San Diego or Oceanside, and be back in three hours."

"Aren't we all going?" Burns asked.

"It would be better if we weren't seen with you. After all, we are federal fugitives. Pat can remain here with us," Craig said. "Ted can supply you with a list of the equipment we will need as well as our sizes for the combat uniforms. We only need three sets, since Pat doesn't know how to use the equipment."

"Okay, give me the shopping list. I'll bring the gear back," Burns promised. "Then we'll take those Cuban bastards!"

"Fucking A, General," Billings declared. "Semper Fi!"

Chapter Twenty-three

Torrance, California

As darkness descended, Ernesto Guavaro removed Lisa Malloy from the basement. His belief was that to isolate her from her husband would make it easier to control both of them.

"You cause any problem," Guavaro warned Terry Malloy, "and we will kill you and take our pleasures with your wife."

Guavaro ran his hands over Lisa's bound body, exploring all her private places. "So voluptuous," Guavaro moaned theatrically while looking directly at Terry. "It almost makes me want you to cause trouble. She would provide hours of entertainment for my men and me."

He stepped back and waved two of his men forward. "Take her upstairs and strap her to a bed."

The two men rushed forward to Lisa's chair. As

they had been briefed prior to entering the basement, they made lewd remarks in English and extravagantly fondled her body while they released her from the chair.

Lisa was wild with fear. She fought the men as they dragged her toward the stairs. Her frantic eyes sought her husband; he watched impassively, as if she were a stranger. Their eyes locked; it was as if they achieved a telepathic connection between them: *We're part of the team. Joe will free us,* rang loud and clear in her mind.

Her fear dissipated. She flashed Terry a grin before she was dragged out of his sight.

General Tyler Burns returned at eleven p.m. driving a blue van. Inside were the necessary uniforms, communications gear, weapons, and other equipment on Billings's shopping list.

"I ditched your Pontiac," Burns said to Craig and Billings. "I thought a van would be better for carrying and storing our equipment. Also, it gives us a place to change."

"Good thinking," Craig replied. "That's why you're a general."

Burns studied Craig, trying to determine if the remark had been sarcastic. Craig, his face totally expressionless, was checking the equipment. Burns glanced at Billings; there was a hint of a snicker on his face.

"When do we attack?" Holden asked, disrupting Burns's thoughts.

"Sometime after midnight when the neighbors are in bed," Craig answered. "We don't want a nervous neighbor calling the police, complaining about prowlers."

"Don't you have an exact time in mind?" Burns asked.

"Joe will know when the time is right," Billings said. "He has an instinct for when sentinels are being inattentive."

Craig finished his inventory. "Everything we need is here."

"I had to go to San Diego to get it all," Burns said. "The Marine Force Recon depot at Camp Pendleton didn't have all the equipment on your list."

"Figures," Billings said. He looked at Craig; both of them laughed.

"What's so funny?" Holden asked.

"It's an inside joke among Marines," Craig said. "We're only given outdated equipment and weapons the Army and Navy have rejected."

"Damn Navy and Army can't fight worth a lick, but their sailors and soldiers sure look and eat good," Billings said with a sly grin aimed at Burns.

The general stifled his response; he realized the two Marines were baiting him. Disappointed by Burns's reaction, Billings continued: "Can you handle being a grunt, General?"

"In this action, Joe's the general and I'm a private," Burns replied. "I understand that."

"Good," Craig said, ending any further attempts by Billings to provoke Burns. "That's settled. Now here's what we are going to do."

Craig laid out his tactical plan. It seemed flawless. Burns had only two minor questions, which Craig quickly answered. The plan called for Burns, Billings, and Craig to play major roles in the attack; Holden was given a lesser role.

"You don't know how to use the equipment Ty brought back from San Diego," Craig explained. "So you can't participate in the invasion of the house. However, you have an important role. You will remain parked on Viejo in the Chevy and serve as the communications center."

"Who will I be communicating with?" Holden asked.

"Your own forces. The other FBI agents and local police you bring in as backup."

"I thought you didn't want any involvement by the FBI or local police," Burns said in astonishment.

"Not in the actual attack," Craig said. "But it's prudent to have a reserve force in case something goes wrong."

Holden was relieved: he had been about to insist on having FBI reinforcements in the vicinity.

"There's a school two miles from here," Craig said. "It has a large parking lot that can be used as a staging point."

"Sounds fine," Holden agreed.

"You'll have to keep in touch with your forces by public telephone."

"Why?" Holden asked suspiciously. "Why can't I use my radio?"

"The Cubans are bound to have equipment that allows them to monitor FBI or police radio channels. You would just tip them off."

"Is that likely?" Holden asked Burns.

"Sure. It's standard procedure to monitor official police channels while on an operation," Burns answered.

"If they are monitoring radio channels, how are you going to communicate?" Holden asked.

"With these babies." Burns held up an apparatus that looked like thin wires attached to an ear plug. "Special Covert Warfare radios which can't be monitored."

"May I continue?" Craig said to Holden.

"Yes."

"Once we begin moving in on the house, you're not to use your car telephone. There's always a remote chance that the Cubans also have equipment to monitor any calls from cellular or car telephones."

Holden glanced at Burns; he nodded, confirming the possibility.

"Unless you're positive that something has gone wrong or I've informed you the house is secure, you're not to call for the reinforcements on your phone."

"So I'm just to sit in the car and wait?"

"No, you must remain alert! If the Cubans try to escape from the house, it's your job to prevent them from using the cars at the curb or in the driveway."

"Okay." Holden was glad that he had one active role in the attack. "I block them off."

"Right," Craig said. He looked at his watch, then addressed Holden again. "Drive the Chevy up to the main thoroughfare and telephone your headquarters from a public telephone in a gas station or restaurant. I want your men in place by midnight."

"Okay."

Craig said to Burns and Billings, "We'll change in the van and be ready when Pat returns."

"Let's check your proficiency with 'click,'" Craig said when they were in the van. "Click" was the slang term for the clicking code used by Covert Warfare teams.

Burns and Craig put on their headsets. "Go across the street," Craig ordered Burns.

Once the general was in position, Craig clicked, "How do you read?"

The message was sent by Craig's transmitter as an ultra-quick Burst Communication that was received by Burns's radio and slowed to understandable speed. The UQBC wasn't bounced off a satellite, since both men were closer than two miles to each other.

It took five seconds for Burns's reply to click in Craig's ear: "I read you five-by-five."

"Your reply is unacceptably slow," Craig clicked. "Come back to the van."

It took several more seconds before Burns started back across the street; he was red-faced when he stepped back into the van. "I'm a little out of practice," he said sheepishly.

"You'd better improve dramatically before Pat returns," a no-nonsense Craig said. "Your slow responses could get us killed."

"I know."

"We're going to drill for the next hour," Craig said. "You stay with the van. Ted and I will go a block away and communicate with you. You will be designated as the Two, Ted will be the Three, and I'll be the Six. Understand?"

"Yes. Let's get at it."

Billings and Craig left the van and disappeared down the street.

In the CIA radio center in West Virginia, Bill Knack's board lit up. He called Harry Grimes.

"I have UQBC transmissions registering on satellite B-14."

"Where's that located?" Grimes asked.

"Over Southern California."

"Probably the Seals at San Diego," Grimes said,

checking his duty log. "I'll have to call their base. They don't have permission to use the satellite."

Lisa lay naked, spread-eagled on top of a large double bed. Her hands and feet were bound to the posts and a gag was stuffed in her mouth. A thirtyish, balding Cuban was standing by the window; he was supposed to be serving as a sentinel, but his gaze was fastened more on her nude body than the back yard.

Strangely, her situation didn't terrify her. Guavaro had badly miscalculated in isolating her from her husband. It hadn't made her more pliable, it had toughened her into reinforced steel. She was now as brave as any other member of the Force Recon team.

Guavaro should have left her in the basement, strapped helplessly in a chair with her brother's dead body on one side and her wounded husband on the other. Down there she had been frightened witless; alone up here, her mind was crystal clear and prepared for action.

She had feigned fear when Guavaro had come into the room and threatened to rape her. She had feigned fear when the other seven Cubans had come into the room at various times and run their hands over her breasts and vagina while bragging of their sexual potency. She could see that her pretended fear fed the men's lust for her.

"You will all have your turn," Guavaro had promised them. "But first we have our mission to complete."

So far, nobody had actually tried to rape her. However, the seven Cubans, Guavaro included, not standing guard in her room occasionally came to the door and stared at her with unabashed desire.

When one stared at her, she pulled against her ropes in pretended fear while purposely moving her body provocatively. Each man reluctantly went back to his post, even though it was obvious their minds were clouded with lust.

That was exactly her intention: force the Cubans to think about her body. As long as their focus was on her, their full concentration wasn't on the outside of the house. Somewhere out there, Joe Craig and Ted Billings were lurking. Soon they would be coming for her and Terry.

The sliver of a moon darting in and out of the rapidly moving, dirty-brown clouds made the landscape around the Malloy house a constantly changing panorama of blacks and grays. To the watchers inside the house, the whole neighborhood looked like a perpetual-motion shadowland. It couldn't have been better for Craig and his troops if the night had been pitch-black. In this shifting, murky light, the human eye couldn't adjust long enough to interpret what was stationary and what was not; every stone, every leaf, every piece of grass became a moving intruder. The Cuban sentinels raised false alarms numerous times after midnight; it stretched Ernesto Guavaro's patience and brought his wrath down upon the sentinels.

"Make sure the next time," he had ordered at one o'clock on Tuesday morning.

By two o'clock, the sentries had settled down, their thoughts more on Lisa Malloy's naked body than the view outside their windows.

Guavaro was asleep in the upstairs rear guest bedroom. It had been a long, nerve-wracking day, and a few hours of sleep was crucial to restore his body to peak efficiency.

He wasn't worried about the ex-Marines; like most professionals, Guavaro believed that dawn was the time to expect an attack. Until then, he felt secure, especially since the house's alarm system was on and working. Having been witness in Heidelberg to the effectiveness of the former Marines' security system, Guavaro put great faith in it.

In the master bedroom, Lisa lay awake on the bed, thinking about a conversation she'd once had with Joe Craig and Berto Gonzalez. She had asked them what it was like to be in combat. "Aren't you scared? Aren't you afraid you'll be killed?"

"Me, naaaw," Berto replied. "Nothing could kill me. I'm never scared in combat."

Joe had laughed. "Berto never scared? Don't buy his macho bullshit, Lisa. The first time he went into combat and bullets started hitting around him, he wet his pants. I know, I was lying next to him when he did it."

"Is that true?" Lisa asked Berto. "Did you wet your pants?"

"Yes, I did," Berto sheepishly admitted. "I thought I was a coward and all the guys would rib me for it. But Joe set me straight pretty quick."

"What did you say to Berto?" Lisa asked.

"I told him the truth," Joe said. "Everyone is scared about going into combat; only a fool feels no fear. The trick is to control your fear and do your duty. The more experience you have under combat conditions, the better you become at controlling your fear. When you can think clearly and act swiftly even though underneath it all you are scared shitless, then you're truly a brave man, or a brave woman as the case may be."

As she waited to be rescued, she knew that she was thinking clearly and was ready to act swiftly. She was truly one of the team. Her teammates would soon free her. When they did, Ernesto Guavaro was going to find out that Lisa's payback was a motherfucker.

In the basement, Terry Malloy was preparing for action. For hours he had worked tirelessly on his bonds as he had been taught to do in a class on prisoner behavior; he had loosened the ropes enough to free himself whenever he desired.

He wasn't in bad condition, considering his treatment. His thigh wound was painful but not debilitating. His mouth ached as a result of a blow from the ugly, large Cuban who was guarding him; he would need a dentist to repair his teeth, but it wasn't serious enough to worry about.

When the time came, he could function normally. It was difficult sitting here without knowing what was happening to Lisa, but he knew it was necessary to remain calm and not cause a disruption, which would hamper Joe's rescue.

The one thing he did know was that Lisa hadn't been raped yet: The big ugly across from him kept describing in graphic terms what he was going to do to Lisa later. He kept boasting he would make Lisa cry out with pleasure. He mocked Terry, saying Lisa would beg him not to stop once she discovered he was so much more of a man than her husband.

Terry glanced at the large clock mounted on the finished basement wall. It read two-ten.

* * *

Sensing that this was the correct moment, Joe Craig used his tongue to vibrate the wire and click out a message: "Begin the attack!"

Terry Malloy became instantly alert. He knew, he just knew: Joe Craig was on his way into the house. Slowly, with his eye on the ugly guard, Malloy slipped out of his bonds.

Pat Holden sat in his darkened Chevrolet on Viejo with one of the Covert Warfare radios held against his ear and a compact combat radio on the seat beside him. He nervously fingered his car phone. Two miles away, a group of FBI men and a police SWAT team waited in a school parking lot for his call.

Despite having been in many stakeouts, Holden was having difficulty controlling himself. He didn't like waiting at the rear, but he understood that the three military men were better qualified to slip up on the house undetected.

A series of rapid clicks came through the Covert Warfare radio. He couldn't decipher them, but he had been told that the clicks would signal the beginning of the action.

He removed his hand from the phone and put it in on the key in preparation for starting the car. With his other hand, he removed the Covert Warfare radio, placed it on the seat, and picked up the combat radio. He was ready to head for the house and stop any escaping Cubans.

Chapter Twenty-four

Torrance, California

Shrouded in a hooded, mottled black, brown, and gray uniform, Craig crawled across the dry grass in the back yard of the house directly behind the Malloys' house. As soon as the Malloys' garage shielded him from the brown house's second-floor windows, Craig rose and dashed the remaining ten feet to the garage.

The garage's brick wall connected with a six-foot-high wooden fence, forming a barrier between the two properties. Craig edged along the wall until he reached the connection with the wooden fence. At the connecting corner, he counted up five bricks from the ground. Keeping his fingers on the fifth row, Craig moved sideways, counting until he reached the eighth brick.

With his left hand on the brick, he checked his

surroundings. Once he was satisfied that the yard behind him was clear, he leaned his Spitter against the wall, placed his right hand against the brick's upper right corner, his left hand against the lower left corner, and pressed firmly. When he heard a slight popping sound, he released the brick; it slid six inches out from the wall on the four steel rods connected to its back. Set in the concrete behind the brick was a closed electrical switch. Craig flicked open the switch; the house's alarm system was now useless, although anyone checking the control box inside the house would be deceived into believing it was working properly. Craig shoved the brick back into position and examined his handiwork. The brick was flush with the wall again.

"Alarm neutralized," Craig clicked through his radio. "Six going up. Two, move to garage."

Burns began crawling across the yard toward the garage as Craig effortlessly scaled the wall and slid silently over the edge and onto the garage's flat roof, an act that would have normally triggered the house's security alarm. In the shifting light, Craig's uniform rendered him indistinguishable from the tar and debris lying on the roof. Without advancing further, he meticulously scanned the house's windows.

"Six reports one man in second-floor center window. Second in master bedroom window. Third in kitchen," he clicked. "Three, report!"

Ted Billings had taken a half hour to cautiously advance from Viejo to the house's side hedge. Responding to Craig's command, Billings issued his report: "Three reports two guards upstairs, a third on ground floor."

Craig swiftly evaluated the situation: six men observed, one or two probably guarding the hostages. Add a leader. Add two as a precaution. He clicked: "This is Six. Operative enemy number is eleven. Three, confirm!"

"Roger, Six," Billings clicked. "Three confirms eleven the magic number."

"This is Six. Confirm, Two."

"Two confirms eleven," Burns acknowledged. His response had improved with an hour of practice, but his use of "click" still wasn't anywhere near as proficient and effortless as Billings's and Craig's.

"This is Six. Two, move to roof."

Burns scaled the wall and reached the roof. Craig gave Burns a moment to focus on the house before tapping the general lightly on the shoulder and pointing out the two guards in the second-floor windows. Once Burns had confirmed each sighting, he clicked, "Two ready!"

Burns was armed with a silenced Uzi instead of a Snick or Spitter. The futuristic weapons were deadly, but their slugs were too light to penetrate window glass; the Uzi's heavier slug would easily smash the window glass and kill anyone standing behind it. Burns aimed the Uzi at the guard in the closest second-floor window.

"This is Six. Three, report!"

"Three ready!"

"This is Six. Moving now!"

A vigilant Burns remained in position, his Uzi aimed at the Cuban on the second floor. Craig slid slowly forward on the roof until he reached the front of the garage.

"Six going down." Craig oozed over the edge of the roof and dropped lightly to the driveway at the house's only blind spot: the garage's left corner. It was separated from the house's right rear corner by three feet, an area visible only if someone stuck his head out of one of the rear windows or if someone walked into the back yard.

Craig dropped flat on the three-foot-wide paved walkway stretching from the garage to the kitchen. Keeping close against the house's wall, he crawled forward until he reached the kitchen door. At the door, he crouched and raised his Spitter into firing position. When he was set, he took a quick peek through the door's window: The only occupant was standing at the kitchen sink with a drinking glass in his hand. His pistol was lying on the counter beside the sink.

Craig ducked back down and clicked: "Six in position. Report readiness!"

"Two ready."

"Three ready."

"This is Six. Go on my command!" Craig clicked. Burns and Billings prepared for battle.

"Go!"

Burns fired his silenced Uzi, shattering the glass of the upstairs hall window and killing the Cuban looking out of it. Shifting to the master bedroom window, Burns fired a rapid burst into the skull of the Cuban who had his head turned from the window as he stared at Lisa's naked body on the bed.

The din of shattering glass sounded through the house. Guavaro rolled out of bed onto the floor. An instant later, bullets and glass flew into the bedroom as Burns sprayed the second-floor windows with his silenced Uzi.

In front, Billings fired his silenced Uzi, taking out the Cuban silhouetted by the TV in the front room. Quickly, Billings fired a short burst into the front upstairs bedroom where he had observed two guards. From his firing angle by the hedge, he didn't have a chance of actually hitting either of the guards; his hope was that the shattering glass would send both guards to the bedroom floor.

The instant he clicked the "go" order, Craig popped up and smashed the kitchen door's window with the butt of his Spitter. At the sound of breaking glass, the Cuban filling his drinking glass from the water faucet looked over his shoulder; spotting Craig, he dropped the glass and grabbed for his pistol on the counter. He never reached it; Craig reversed his Spitter and fired a three-shot burst through the broken window, hitting the Cuban in the heart.

Craig reached through the hole in the glass and unlocked the kitchen door.

In the basement, Terry Malloy had shed his bonds and was creeping toward the dozing guard he called Big Ugly. The sudden noise of breaking glass upstairs woke Big Ugly; he stared unbelievingly at the naked Malloy standing a few feet in front of him. Big Ugly actually laughed. "What are you going to do, gringo? Whack me with your prick?"

Malloy was too professional to exchange banter with an armed man. He instantaneously launched a karate kick to Big Ugly's right elbow, paralyzing the guard's gun hand and sending his pistol flying. Malloy flowed forward and delivered a sharp punch just above the guard's heart, stunning Big Ugly. Without a break in his motion, Malloy took Big Ugly's head in both hands, twisted it sharply to the right, and snapped Big Ugly's neck. Malloy released Big Ugly's head, and the guard's body slid limply from his chair onto the floor.

Without bothering to clothe himself, Malloy

picked up the guard's silenced Glock and ran upstairs.

Terry Malloy very nearly died when he popped out of the basement door. Joe Craig had his Spitter pointed at the middle of Malloy's bare chest.

"Damn it, Terry," Craig said in a harsh whisper. "You know better than to make unannounced moves during an attack. Another ounce of trigger pressure and you would have bought the farm!"

"Sorry, Joe." Malloy held up his hands in apology, and Craig shifted his Spitter to cover the hall.

"Where are Lisa and Cecil?" Craig whispered, ignoring Malloy's naked state.

"Cecil is dead. Lisa is upstairs."

"How many are in the house?" Craig whispered.

"Eight. I killed one in the basement."

"This is Six," Craig immediately transmitted to Billings and Burns. "Correct number of enemy is eight, not eleven. Repeat, eight. Confirm!"

"Two confirms."

"Three confirms."

"This is Six. I have Terry. Basement secure. Two enemy KIA. Six is now operative number alive on ground floor or above. Confirm!" He didn't ask if they had shot anyone; possibles didn't count, only corpses.

"Two confirms six."

"Three confirms six." Billings clicked an additional warning: "Attack noisier than we thought. Sound of breaking glass loud. Lights are coming on in neighbors' houses. People will be in the street soon."

"Roger, Three. Lift your fire to the second floor," Craig clicked. "Six checking first-floor front."

Craig whispered to Malloy, "Cover the stairs."

Craig expertly checked the ground floor, doing it swiftly without ever endangering himself. He found the dead body in the living room.

"This is Six. One enemy KIA," he clicked. "Operative number now five. All on second floor. Two, confirm!"

"Two confirms five."

"Three, confirm!"

"Three confirms five. More lit houses. Two people in street."

"This is Six. Understood! Three, are you receiving resistance?" Craig moved back to where Malloy was watching the stairs.

"This is Three. No resistance. But now believe one guard only in front bedroom. Second guard no longer visible."

"This is Six. Report, Two! Any resistance?"

"This is Two. No resistance. Have observed no movement since attack began."

"This is Six. Terry and I are going upstairs. Prepare to give twenty seconds of intense covering fire on command!"

"Terry, operative number is five," Craig whispered. "I will go first upstairs."

The two had been together for so long that, even with this minimal amount of information, Terry Malloy understood perfectly what Joe Craig intended. He whispered, "Right."

"This is Six," Craig clicked. "Commence firing now!"

Billings and Burns poured heavy fire into the upstairs windows. In a low crouch, Craig charged up the stairs, keeping close to the left wall. Malloy provided him cover, firing from the bottom, shooting up the right side of the stairs.

Just below the top, Craig halted; a Cuban's body was on the landing in front of him. He grabbed the corpse's shirt and yanked it down the stairs, clearing the top. As he was doing it, he automatically clicked: "This is Six. Operative number is four. Two confirm."

"Two confirms four."

"This is Six. Three, confirm!"

"Three confirms four."

"This is Six. Continue repressive fire until my command!"

As soon as the body bumped on the stairs behind Craig, Malloy ran up the right side until he reached Malloy.

"This is Six. Cease fire!" The sound of impacting bullets halted.

Malloy and Craig exchanged glances; simultaneously they dove into the hallway with their guns extended. Craig landed on top of Guavaro, who had just crawled out of the bedroom. Guavaro squirmed, trying to bring his pistol to bear on Craig. He didn't even slow Craig down: Craig used his left elbow to land a solid blow to the Cuban's jaw, knocking Guavaro out. Without stopping to check the Cuban's condition, Craig rolled off the body to get into position to cover the front of the house.

Malloy ignored the fight behind him and checked his assigned area. Satisfied it was clear, he turned to see how Craig was doing. His friend was rolling off a prone enemy's body when another Cuban appeared from nowhere. Malloy spun swiftly and emptied his weapon into the Cuban who was just bringing his own pistol to bear on Craig. The dead Cuban dropped, and Malloy's pistol clicked empty; he discarded it and claimed the unconscious Guavaro's Glock.

Craig didn't dwell on how close he had come to death; he continued to perform his responsibilities. "This is Six. Move into house. Operative number is two. Confirm, Two!"

"Two confirms operative number two. Moving to house."

"This is Six. Confirm, Three!"

"Three confirms two. Advancing to house."

Before Craig could whisper a command to Terry Malloy, a Cuban came dashing out of the front bedroom. Craig shot him. Automatically, he reported that the operative number was one to Billings and Burns.

"There's one more," he whispered urgently to Malloy.

"In Lisa's bedroom," Malloy answered.

"Let's take him," Craig said.

Both men charged into the master bedroom; diving to opposite sides, they rolled into position to fire. "Body," Malloy said at the sight of the corpse on his side.

"Clear," Malloy said, and then quickly used "click" to inform Billings and Burns that the house was now free of the enemy.

It wasn't until Malloy and Craig regained their feet that they realized Lisa was naked on the bed.

Craig discreetly averted his eyes and said to Malloy, "Free Lisa and both of you get dressed. We must leave quickly. This place will be crawling with cops in a minute."

Craig walked out of the bedroom. Malloy ran to the bed and ripped off Lisa's gag.

"What took you so long?" Lisa said with a smile. "I've been lying here naked waiting for you."

"I was tied up a lot longer than expected in the basement," Malloy laughed as he freed her.

"Lucky for you I'm still in the mood." Lisa kissed him.

Craig stuck his head back in the room. "Will you two please cut the crap? We have to get out of here!"

Laughing, they scrambled off the bed and headed for the closet. Craig stepped back in the hall and removed the miniature combat radio from his belt. "Pat, come into the house. Are the police here?"

"No," Holden answered as he drove toward the house. "Neighbors probably called the police, but they are under orders to stay out of this area."

"Fine, we don't need them here."

"Should I call in my forces? They're still waiting in the staging area."

"Not yet. Wait until you appraise the situation in here."

Billings and Burns came running up the stairs just as Craig finished speaking to Holden. They stopped at the top of the stairs and looked down at Guavaro; he was conscious, but too frightened to move. "Don't hurt me," he begged. "I'm valuable."

Craig stalked angrily over to the Cuban. "You son of a bitch," he growled, aiming his Spitter at the Cuban's face. "You've killed your last American!"

"Wait, I know many secrets!" Guavaro cried out. "I can be an asset to your government."

"No!" Burns shoved Craig's Spitter aside. "Don't kill him. He's worth more alive."

Lisa and Terry came out of the bedroom and stopped behind Craig; Billings stood stock still behind Burns. Holden arrived at that moment and echoed the general's order. "No more killing!"

Craig glared at Burns and Holden; time stood still as everyone remained frozen waiting for his reaction. Craig's blue eyes were icy as he examined each person on the landing. He focused on Billings and snarled, "What the hell do you think you're doing, Ted? Get your ass moving and make sure the house is secure!"

Billings took off downstairs as if he'd been shot from a cannon. Everyone else shifted uncomfortably. Craig stepped up toe-to-toe with Burns and stared into his eyes. Unnoticed, Lisa reached over and took the Glock from her husband's hand.

"Are you giving the orders now, General?" Craig said.

"That's right. I want this man alive. He can provide valuable information which will aid the United States in its fight against Communism in South and Central America."

"You claimed that you were one of us, General, but you're not," Craig said with vehemence. "You aren't any different from your boss General Downs or the top brass in the CIA and the Pentagon. They wanted to use Cardona, you want to use this man. The fact that he was responsible for the death of several of our friends makes no difference at all to you."

Craig shoved Burns out of the way. "Well, you can fucking forget it." He aimed his Spitter at Burns and Holden. "Drop your weapons, and drop them now. Don't make the mistake of thinking I'm kidding."

Neither Holden nor Burns made that mistake; one glance at Craig's face convinced them he was perfectly serious. They dropped their weapons and Terry Malloy scooped them up.

"Stand stock still," Craig said. He aimed his Spitter at Guavaro. Lisa ordered sharply, "No, Joe!"

Craig looked at Lisa.

"No," she repeated. Craig stared at her inquisitively.

Lisa stepped forward, touched Craig's arm, and gazed into his eyes. The other men could see that something passed between them; Craig smiled, eased his grip on the Spitter, and stepped aside. Guavaro breathed an audible sigh of relief.

"Don't think you're getting off, you bastard," Lisa said fiercely. She took a step forward and stood over the prone Cuban. "I owe you some payback for my brother and for Cecil Jones!"

Before Burns or Holden could protest, Lisa shot Guavaro in his right eye; his head bounced once and came to rest with a pool of blood forming beneath it. Undaunted by the empty, bloody eye socket, Lisa fired a second shot into Guavaro's brain.

There was neither satisfaction nor revulsion on her face when she first looked at her husband, then at Craig. She dropped her pistol; and held out her hands; each man took one.

"We're still on our mission," Craig said. He released her hand, picked up the pistol she had dropped, and handed it back to her. "Every team member stays armed until the mission is over."

Through the centuries, innumerable men have died for less of a smile than the one Lisa bestowed on Joe Craig. Her husband wasn't jealous; he beamed proudly at his wife and best friend.

Burns broke their revery. "I guess that was justice. What are you going to do now?"

"We're leaving," said Craig.

"Wait a minute," Holden protested. "You can't

leave, you're all under arrest. You agreed to go into my custody when the attack on the house was finished."

Terry had kept Holden and Burns covered; Lisa swung her pistol up and aimed it at them also.

"I never agreed to any such thing," Craig said. "If you think back, I completely ignored you when you suggested it."

Craig brought his Spitter to bear on the two men and waved the Malloys down the stairs. "We're leaving now."

"I'll stop you," Holden said.

"How? I have your weapon."

"I'll use one of these dead Cubans' guns."

"You called my bluff in the restaurant parking lot. Now I'm calling yours," Craig said. He lowered the Spitter and started down the stairs. "I don't believe you'll shoot us. We're leaving now."

"I mean it," Holden said, searching the hall and finding a discarded weapon.

"Halt!" he cried, pointing the pistol at Craig, who had reached the bottom of the stairs; the Malloys had already disappeared.

Burns shoved Holden's gun aside. "Marine, wait a minute!"

Craig stopped and stared up at Burns. The general said, "Don't worry. The four of you are officially dead as of this moment. No one will be searching for any of you after today."

"Is that the straight poop, General?"

"Right from the horse's ass," Burns said with a smile. "I really am one of you, I just forgot it for a second. Will you forgive me?"

"You do what you've promised and we're square. What about Holden?"

"I'll explain it fully to Pat. He's not a bad guy.

He'll understand. Everything will be all right. I guarantee it."

"I'll hold you to that, General."

"Please contact me in the future. I'll probably have a few jobs that no one can handle except for you and your team."

Craig stared at Burns, then slowly ginned. "I might just do that, General. Green Berets have always needed a few good men to pull them out of the shit when it hit the fan."

Craig snapped to attention and gave Burns a razor-sharp salute. A happy Burns returned it.

"Semper Fi, General!" Craig said before disappearing around the corner.

Chapter Twenty-five

Torrance, California

The moment Joe Craig disappeared from sight, Patrick Holden protested bitterly to Ty Burns. "What the hell do you think you're doing? We can't allow them to go free!"

"We aren't allowing them, they are doing it on their own," Burns patiently answered.

"We can stop them!"

"How? By shooting them?" Burns said. "You don't want to do that, do you?"

Holden stared at the pistol in his hand. "No, I suppose not, but I do intend to call my men to block their escape."

Holden ran down the stairs. Burns followed at a slower pace; at the bottom, he found a fuming Holden standing at the open front door.

"They stole my car! My telephone was in it!"

Holden spied a telephone on a table in the living room: he hustled over to it and picked up the receiver. "It's dead!" He slammed it down.

"There may be another phone in the kitchen," Burns suggested.

Holden brushed past Burns and ran into the kitchen; a phone hung on the wall. He stepped over the body of the dead Cuban and picked it up. "Damn it! This one is dead, too!"

"Want to bet that all of the phones are useless?" Burns said casually.

"Why do you say that?" Holden asked suspiciously.

"I suspect Billings disconnected them," Burns said. "Remember Craig ordering Billings to make sure the house was secure?"

"Yes," a mystified Holden said.

"Craig already knew the house was secure. Malloy told him how many Cubans were inside, and Craig kept a body count as he moved through the house. All the Cubans were accounted for. What Craig actually ordered Billings to do was to make sure we couldn't prevent their escape."

"Shit!" Holden exclaimed. "I wondered why he barked at Billings. It was out of character for Craig."

"He spoke sharply because Billings was mesmerized by the argument over Guavaro. Craig was just reminding him of his duty."

Holden stared down at the dead Cuban for a moment, then gazed at Burns, who was still wearing his hooded, mottled, attack uniform. "I swear, Ty, I'm going to hunt them down."

A look of distress crossed Burns's face. "It would be the worst thing you could do."

"It's my job!"

"Think about it," Burns pleaded. "If you put their

names on the FBI's fugitive list, they'll not only be pursued by every legitimate law enforcement agency in the United States and the rest of the world, they'll also be hunted by the Cubans, the Russians, the CIA, the Pentagon, and numerous other agencies. A lot of people want these three Marines dead!"

"I want them alive."

"If you managed to capture them—a very big 'if,' I may add—none of them would ever live long enough to stand trial. And that includes Lisa."

"I'd make sure they were protected."

"C'mon Pat, you aren't that naive. No matter what you did or where you incarcerated them, someone would find a way to kill all four of them!" Burns exploded. "There are too many people in the military and intelligence communities who could be hurt by a public trial. Top government officials couldn't afford a public trial either; it would only reopen the Cardona investigation, and too many of them barely escaped the first one! Besides, it is essential that the Marines' reasons for executing Cardona remain secret."

"Do you feel the same way?"

"As much as it would pain me, I'd kill them without a moment's hesitation rather than let their testimony destroy the foundation of our country's defense. And make no mistake about it, it would. No common soldier or mid-ranking military officer would ever trust his superiors again if they learned that Cardona's killing of two Marines was covered up by those superiors and Cardona continued to operate with impunity."

"I'll be damned!" Holden said incredulously. "You never intended for me to arrest them!"

"No, I didn't," Burns admitted.

"You lied to them," Holden said in disgust. "You swore you were one of them."

Burns spun on his heel and started toward the living room. Holden stepped over the dead Cuban and followed.

"Admit it, Ty. You lied to them!"

In the living room, Burns faced Holden. "I didn't lie to them, I am one of them. I intend to make Downs and the others involved in the deaths of the two Marines in San Tomas pay for their actions."

"Ty, now you're lying to yourself," Holden said in exasperation. "Why can't you just admit it? You aren't like those Marines."

Burns stood rigidly, his face contorted in anger. "I am exactly like them! It's just that you don't understand any of us. They swore an oath to preserve this country just as I did. You've seen how they value their honor. I value mine the same way! Do you think they would act differently if our roles were reversed?

"Hell, no, they wouldn't! They would kill me if it came down to me or the nation's security. They wouldn't like it any better than I would, but they would do it!"

Holden digested the substance of Burns's tirade. "Maybe you're right," he said finally. "Maybe you and they are alike."

"Damn right we are. And because we are so alike, and I don't want them to die, I gave them an out. Craig recognized it for what it was. Why can't you?"

"You mean we declare them officially dead?"

"Yes!"

"Just how do we get away with such a blatant lie?"

Something in Holden's eyes sent a wave of relief over Burns. "All we have to do is swear that before he died Guavaro confessed to killing Ted Billings,

Joe Craig, Lisa Malloy, and Terry Malloy, and that Guavaro told us their bodies would never be discovered."

"Why should I go along with that?" Holden asked.

"Because you're a good guy and you don't want them to die. Besides, you're sympathetic to them. You believe they had good reason to kill Cardona and they shouldn't be punished for his death."

Unexpectedly, a series of clicks sounded in Burns's ear. He didn't understand the message, since he hadn't been prepared for any communications in "click."

"Just a minute," he said to Holden. "Someone is signaling on my click radio."

Burns used click. "Say again."

An answer came immediately. "This is Six. Three, acknowledge by satellite bounce."

"It's Craig," Burns said aloud to Holden. He used his tongue to flick the switch that made his UQBC bounce off the nearest CIA satellite; then he clicked: "This is Three. Go ahead, Six."

Wheeling, West Virginia

Bill Knack called Harry Grimes on his internal phone. "I have more unauthorized UQBC satellite transmissions in Southern California."

Torrance, California

"This is Six. Has Holden agreed yet?"

"This is Three. Agreed to what?"

"This is Six. To our being dead?"

Burns was amazed. His face must have reflected it, for Holden asked, "What's wrong?"

"Craig wants to know if you've agreed to mark them as officially dead," Burns said aloud.

"How could he possibly know we're arguing about that?" Holden asked. "Does that radio you're using send voice signals? Is he able to overhear our conversation?"

"No, it doesn't send voice and he can't overhear us," Burns said. "And I don't know how the hell he knows we're arguing."

Another message clicked in Burns's ear. "This is Six. What's Holden's answer?"

"He's asking for your answer," Burns said aloud.

Holden shook his head and grinned. "Tell him he's dead. How is it that I'm being questioned from a man in his grave?"

Burns translated Holden's answer into click. The reply made him smile; he said to Holden, "Craig says all true spooks speak click."

"Wise ass!" Holden laughed. "Ask him how we're going to explain all the dead Cubans."

Burns translated faithfully; Craig's reply came instantly. "This is Six. You should find the explanation easy, Three. After all, you're a general. They were killed by the military Covert Warfare team you were leading."

Suspicion began to spread through Burns. "This is Three. Say again."

"This is Six. You led a Covert Warfare team against the house. The neighbors saw us leave. They will tell police. You tell police we were the Covert Warfare team. You sent us away to protect our identities."

"This is Three. You had this planned!"

"This is Six. You're the general; think about it."

Burns's face turned red. He clicked: "You son of a bitch!"

"This is Six. You're on report, Three, for failure to identify yourself before signal and for using profanity. That's incorrect radio procedure. Back to training for you, Three. Unfortunately, Two and Six are unavailable to help you further."

"What the hell is being said?" Holden asked irritably. He knew it was important: Burns's face was changing colors. Burns waved him off and then clicked: "This is Three. The practice was a setup?"

"This is Six. You needed practice, as expected. It was convenient. Think about it."

"This is Three. I don't understand."

"This is Six. You go off for equipment driving our car, return in van."

Burns was shocked. He said aloud, "Shit!"

Wheeling, West Virginia

"None of the Covert Warfare people in Southern California will admit to an unauthorized UQBC satellite transmission," Harry Grimes said to Bill Knack.

"Well, somebody is doing it. Look at my board," Knack said. "It's been registering a series of unauthorized UQBC transmissions for the last two minutes. This isn't normal; this is like a damn telephone conversation!"

Torrance, California

"Goddamn it, tell me what's being said!" Holden demanded.

"In a minute, Pat," Burns said. He clicked: "This is Three. You have been manipulating me."

"This is Six. It was necessary. Think about it—you'll work it out. You are a general. Tell Holden his car is parked four blocks away. Except for the click radio I'm using, all the equipment you borrowed from the Seals is in the trunk. Do you copy?"

"This is Three. I copy. What happens to that radio?"

"This is Six. I'll mail it to you. I wouldn't want to be responsible for misappropriating government property."

"This is Three. What about the government property you misappropriated from Kirk's Armory?"

"This is Six. Kirk's Armory? Never heard of it."

"This is Three. Will you contact me in the future?"

"This is Six. If you carry out your promises, you can expect to have a message from beyond the grave. You won't even need a psychic with a crystal ball. Tell Holden it was nice. Six over and out!"

Wheeling, West Virginia

"The unauthorized UQBC transmissions have been bouncing off the satellite for six minutes now," Bill Knack said.

"None of the Covert Warfare people ever transmit for that long," Harry Grimes said.

"Well, whoever was doing it has either hung up or they're in close enough proximity not to need the satellite any longer," Knack said. "The board is no longer registering any unauthorized UQBC transmissions being bounced off the satellite."

Torrance, California

Burns pulled his hood off and removed the radio beneath it. "They're gone," he said to Holden.

"Will you tell me what was said now?"

Burns explained Craig's suggestion on how to explain the attack on the house. Holden considered it. "Might work."

"It will work," Burns said.

"Craig had this planned all along!" Holden said. "He laid the groundwork for it when he sent you to acquire equipment and weapons—the type of stuff that could only be used by a Covert Warfare team."

"That was his purpose for sending me alone," Burns agreed. "Craig knows the procedure for drawing equipment. He wanted my name on the requisition forms for the equipment and weapons. Plus, he knows that not even a general can just sign out that equipment without a reason. On the requisition forms, I stated that it was for use in a Covert Warfare mission, and that I was alone because my Covert Warfare team was under orders not to be observed by anyone not connected to the mission. That happens often enough for it not to be questioned. As far as the Seal Depot was concerned, there was a Covert Warfare team here."

"Didn't you suspect something was wrong when Craig and Billings refused to accompany you to the weapons depot?"

"Not really," Burns said. "Hell, the truth is I didn't suspect anything at all. Craig's explanation about being a wanted fugitive who shouldn't be seen with me was plausible. Besides, I had my own plan and I didn't want him to come to San Diego with me."

"Your own plan?"

"I intended to manipulate the Marines; I never realized that Craig could manipulate me. Remember, I'm a military officer. A general. Sergeants like Craig don't outthink generals."

"But Craig isn't an ordinary sergeant."

"Talk about a gross understatement," Burns laughed. "Craig isn't ordinary by any definition at all."

"How were you trying to manipulate him?"

"I suspected he wouldn't stand still for being arrested by you, but I had to be prepared to kill them all if he did. Craig was too wary for me to kill easily, so I had to be canny about it. Remember, due to Ted Billings's wizardry, Craig knew about the termination orders out for him and his team. To kill them and preserve this country's military, I had to be prepared to die, too. That's why I substituted the blue van for their car."

Holden understood the significance immediately. "The van's wired with explosives?"

"That's right. If they had agreed to the arrest, I would have insisted that they be transported to jail in the van. I would have blown it up on the way."

"Killing yourself and me too, since I would have been in the van."

"I would have first tried to isolate Craig and his friends in the van by themselves. If that was possible, I would have detonated the van's explosives by remote control. They would have been the only ones killed. If that didn't work, I would have done everything in my power to keep you out of the van. In that scenario, I would have died with them. Unfortunately, if neither of the first scenarios worked, and you insisted on traveling in the van, you would have died with us."

"I was wrong, you are one of them," Holden said. "You would have died to keep your honor intact. And it didn't matter if I went with you."

"It mattered, but I still would have done it."

Holden smiled. "Thank God Craig saw through your plan."

"He indicated that to me in our click conversation, but how did you know?" Burns said in surprise.

"I remember Craig's remarks when you returned with the van. He knew what you had done."

Burns smiled wryly. "I thought he was just being sarcastic, but he was really chiding me for underestimating him. And now that I think of it, while you were away setting up the backup forces, Craig decided my click was too rusty and I needed practice. He and Billings went out in the neighborhood and left me alone in the van. For about an hour, they sent me click messages and I answered. For that hour, they were out of my sight."

"How far away could they have been?"

"There's no telling. The normal range is two miles, but the range is limitless if you bounce the radio signal off a satellite. In the conversation Craig and I just had, he told me to bounce my signal off a satellite, which meant he was more than two miles away and he didn't care that I knew it. However, last night he didn't have me bounce the signal off the satellite, which led me to believe they were both within a two-mile radius of my position."

"I don't understand. How could they fool you?"

"One of them could have remained within the two-mile radius, and every time I made a transmission to the one out of range, the one who could hear my transmission would repeat my message, bouncing his transmission off the satellite. That way the one out of range would know what I transmitted and could answer me by bouncing his return message off the satellite back to me. I wouldn't know he was doing it. There's nothing in the equipment that registers whether an incoming message used a satellite. Of course, the CIA's satellite monitoring station in West Virginia would register the unauthorized satellite use, but I'd have to call them to find out about it."

"Sounds complicated. If you're only hearing clicks, wouldn't it be easier to dupe you by having one of them act as if you were communicating with both of them?"

"Jesus Christ, Pat, I hadn't thought of that. Yes, that's very possible. Billings and Craig were extremely fluent in click; both of them used it as easily as English. Either one of them could have conversed with me and pretended to be both parties. The other one could have gone anywhere and done anything during the hour they were theoretically helping me practice. Of course, the two of them would have been in contact with each other, and they would have had to use a satellite bounce to do it. Their UQBC transmissions would have registered in West Virginia."

"It doesn't really matter how they did it," Holden said. "Under the ruse of practicing with you, either Craig or Billings left the neighborhood."

"It was probably Ted Billings," Burns said glumly. "With his electronics expertise, he could have done anything during that missing hour."

"Now that I think of it, while you were in San Diego acquiring the equipment and weapons, Craig ordered Billings to reconnoiter the area," Holden said. "Craig and I stayed in the car and talked. Billings was gone a very long time."

"So he did something then as well," Burns said. "What could it have been?"

"Who knows? Probably something to do with

their escape. Maybe he rented cars or something."

Holden's words reminded Burns of something Craig had clicked to him.

"They definitely rented at least one car. Craig said your Chevrolet was parked four blocks away and my equipment was in the trunk. They must have had a car waiting at that location. They switched to it and drove away."

"If I hadn't agreed to them being dead, Craig wouldn't have told you about the parked Chevrolet. I'd have put out an all-points-bulletin on it, and all the time they would have been riding in a different car. That Craig is a pisser!"

"He certainly is. He manipulated you as easily as he did me," Burns said.

"What do you mean?"

"He lulled you into passivity by suggesting you bring your own forces in as a backup, but that you keep them two miles away so as not to warn the Cubans. Craig even picked their staging area. From that distance, your forces couldn't prevent the Marines' escape after the action was over. However, the knowledge that the backup was there convinced you that you had control of the situation."

"Did you know what he was doing at the time?" Holden asked.

"I wish I could say I did, but I didn't. I just figured it out a moment ago. It was an element I would never have considered. And Craig made sure I didn't think about it by having me recommend that you keep the backup forces that far away. He asked me to advise you on what kind of equipment the Cubans might be carrying. Remember, I was the one who said they would have monitoring equipment with them."

Holden paused in thought. "Thinking back, your

exact words were: 'It's standard procedure.' "

"That's right. So?"

"Craig put those words in your mouth."

Burns's jaw dropped. "I'll be damned! So he did! The brainy son of a bitch!"

"You admire him, don't you?"

"Yes, I can't help it. I'm still wondering how we took this well-defended house without taking a single casualty. Frankly, I don't think the mission would have been nearly so successful if I had planned and led it."

"I admire him, too," Holden said. "He sure bamboozled us."

Holden suddenly broke out laughing. "I really regret that Craig, Billings, and the Malloys were killed by the Cubans. If they were still alive, it would've been a tremendous challenge to try and catch them."

Six blocks away, Joe Craig took four beers from the refrigerator and walked into the living room. He handed a beer to Lisa, Terry, and Ted before he sat down.

"Everything satisfactory?" Ted Billings asked.

"Yep, we're dead," he answered.

"How sweet death is," Terry said. He kissed Lisa on the cheek.

Lisa ignored her husband and asked worriedly; "Are you sure they were fooled?"

"Don't worry, Lisa," Craig answered. "I bounced my UQBC transmission off the satellite so the CIA's West Virginia listening post would register it. If Burns contacts them, they'll confirm the transmission. But I doubt he will; he believes we're a long way from here."

"How can you be sure of that?" she asked.

393

"Because I set him up to believe it," Craig answered.

She looked bewildered. Her husband explained: "Burns is a general, he's used to conventional thinking. Joe is unconventional, he does the unexpected. If Burns was in charge, he would have had us running for our lives. Joe knows that running is dangerous. It's best to go to ground in a safe place and wait it out."

Ted Billings took over. "This was a safe place that nobody in authority knew about." It was the house that Billings and Craig had intended to occupy in Torrance; the house that had been opened and then shut down again by Cecil Jones and Terry Malloy. "By now, Burns has realized that Joe and I could have been anywhere while we were practicing click with him last night. He'll have convinced himself that one of us left the area to carry out some scheme. He'll never believe that both of us were always very close to him and, in fact, did converse with him in click."

"That opinion will be reinforced by Holden, who will remember that Ted was outside the car for a long time last night," Craig said. "Between the two of them, they'll develop an escape theory that will have us in South America by now."

"But we don't intend to just stay here?" Lisa said in distress.

"Why not? Don't you like it here?" Craig asked.

"It's not that, it's just that I'm part of the team now," Lisa said. "And I'd hate to see the team go into retirement."

Her husband and Billings looked at her in amazement. Joe Craig just smiled. "We're only going to remain here until next week, then we're heading to Montana to fully train you as Force Recon."

Lisa smiled broadly and hugged each of them in turn. When she was finished, she said to Craig, "Thank you."

"No need to thank me," Craig replied. "You're one of the team, and the team must prepare for any future action. After all, I did assure General Burns that although we are officially dead, if our country needs us, we can be resurrected."

JIM DeFELICE
COYOTE BIRD

The president is worried—with good cause. Two of America's spy planes have disappeared. Soon he—and the nation—will face a threat more dangerous than any since the height of the Cold War. A secretly remilitarized Japan is plotting to bring the most powerful country on Earth to its knees, aided by a computer-assisted aircraft with terrifying capabilities. But the U.S. has a weapon of its own in the air—the Coyote, a combat super-plane so advanced its creators believe it's invincible. Air Force top gun Lt. Colonel Tom Wright is prepared to fly the Coyote into battle for his country—and his life—against all that Japan can throw at him. And the result will prove to be the turning point in the war of the skies.

__4831-0 $5.99 US/$6.99 CAN

CHINA
CARD
THOMAS BLOOD

With the Russian economy in a shambles, and the hard-line leaders in power, renegade KGB operatives an ultra-secret document detailing the exact location of over one hundred tactical nuclear weapons secretly placed in the U.S. during the height of the Cold War. Thousands of miles away, in Washington, D. C., a young prostitute is found brutally murdered in a luxury hotel. The only clue—a single cufflink bearing the seal of the President. These seemingly unrelated events will soon reveal a twisting trail of conspiracy and espionage, power-brokers and assassins. It's a trail that leads from mainland China to the seamy underbelly of the Washington power-structure . . . to the Oval Office itself.

__4782-9 $5.99 US/$6.99 CAN

R. KARL LARGENT

RED WIND

When a military jet goes down off the California coast, killing the Secretary of the Air Force, it is a tragedy. When another jet crashes with the Undersecretary of State on board, it becomes cause for investigation. When a member of the State Department is found shot in the back of the head, his top-secret files missing, it becomes a national crisis. The frantic President turns to Commander T. C. Bogner, the only man he can trust to uncover the mole and pull the country back from the brink before the delicate balance of power is blown away in a red wind.

___4361-0 $5.99 US/$6.99 CAN

THE
JAKARTA
PLOT
R. KARL LARGENT

The heads of state of the world's most powerful nations—the United States, Russia, Japan, Great Britain, Germany, and France—are meeting in Jakarta, on the island of Java, to issue a joint declaration to the Chinese government. China must stop its nuclear testing or face the strictest sanctions of the World Economic Council. But a powerful group of Communist terrorists—with the backing of the Chinese government—attack the hotel in which the meeting is taking place and hold the world leaders—including the Vice President of the United States—hostage. The terrorists have an ultimatum: The WEC must abandon its policy of interference in the Third World . . . or one by one the hostages will die.

___4568-0 $5.99 US/$6.99 CAN

Dorchester Publishing Co., Inc.
P.O. Box 6640
Wayne, PA 19087-8640